NO NIGHT IS TOO LONG

BARBARA VINE

HARMONY BOOKS • NEW YORK

To Phyllis Grosskurth

Published by Harmony Books, a division of Crown Publishers, Inc., 201 East 50th Street, New York, New York 10022. Member of the Crown Publishing Group.

Random House, Inc. New York, Toronto, London, Sydney, Auckland

Originally published in Great Britain by Viking/Penguin in 1994.

HARMONY and colophon are trademarks of Crown Publishers, Inc.

Manufactured in the United States of America

Library of Congress Cataloging-in-Publication Data
Vine, Barbara
No night is too long / by Barbara Vine.—1st ed.
I. Title. PR6068.E63N63   1995
823'.914—dc20   94-13064

ISBN 0-517-79964-2

10 9 8 7 6 5 4 3 2 1

First American Edition

T I M

1

Outside a high wind is blowing and making the sea rough. It's a long time since I saw such big waves breaking on this gray pebbly shore. The sea is a pale brown, the color of weak coffee with a little milk in it, a phenomenon caused by sand stirred up into the water. Even on fine summer days the sea is brownish here, seldom blue and clean.

Soon it will be dark and I shall no longer be able to see these colors, such as they are. The dirty coffee brown and the gray. Out there, by night, the sea and the beach become invisible and only the road can be seen, lit by the lamps, the road and the sea wall. Beyond the wall might be a town lying out there or fields, but for the sound of the sea, its withdrawing roar and rattle of stones and the crash it makes as the wave returns and breaks. But for these sounds anything might be spread out beyond the wall, even a dark fjord with an island in its midst, a pair of eagles in the top of a tree, the forked tail of a humpback whale rising out of the waters. Who knows what may be anywhere when you can't see?

I'm writing these things down to get me into the way of writing. To make a start. But I see that all I've done is bring myself back to the stuff of my dreams, those dreams I'm attempting to escape from. All roads, it seems, lead to the island, and as time passes they do so more directly and insistently, not less. I'm writing this down in the hope of blocking those roads, of turning them into cul-de-sacs and signposting them: NO THROUGH WAY.

To block, not to be cured. I'm not so innocent nor so optimistic as to believe that. I'm not innocent at all. It's laughable to use that word about myself. And I don't believe that any therapy, my own or that administered by someone else, can take away this burden, this fearful remorse. I don't believe what someone said, that the writer is the only free man, for once he has set down his pain, his shame, and the sorrow of his heart, he'll be rid of it for ever.

I believe only, or tell myself that I do, that once I see it before me on the page, in black and white as they say, then the dreams will go away. Isn't it inconceivable that when the material of those dreams is laid out in precise lines of print, it will still go on being rendered back to me pictorially by night?

The dreams will go and I shall see the rest in what they call perspective. Why do I keep writing "as they say," "what they call"? It must be because I've been daily farther and farther removed from the world of reality, so that I question all these useful words and handy catchphrases. Because "they" are people alien from myself, happy people who sleep without dreaming and use words without thinking, who have no need to analyze everything they and others do and say.

Yet would I be writing at all but for the letters that have been coming now for the past six months? Letters aren't really what they are. Gratuitous pieces of information. Accounts of historical events. Stories, only they're all true. At least, I think so. Happenings, all with a common theme and, though interesting enough to most people, peculiarly *germane* only to me. Relevant to me alone, and therefore sinister.

Therefore menacing. Such communications don't arrive in a vacuum. They don't happen and then cease to happen without consequence, without sequel. They portend something more, something to follow and perhaps not just printed matter that comes through the post. So better write it down now while I have the chance.

This seems to be the place to insert the first one, the first "castaway" extract. Here it is:

Alexander Selcraig, called Selkirk, a bad-tempered man, while on a voyage to America, quarrelled with his captain, on the grounds of the latter's alleged incompetence. Selkirk believed that the ship on which they sailed was about to sink, due to inefficient maintenance. He asked to be put ashore on the nearest island, confident that others on board would choose to be exiled with him. However, none did and he was marooned alone.

He had been right. The ship sank. But this was of little comfort to Selkirk in his predicament. Five years passed. He read the Bible, grew vegetables, cured goat meat, and listened to the clamorous howling of sea lions. Eventually he was rescued, only to be cast into prison by his Spanish captors. It was another five years before he was returned to his home in Scotland. .

As a man of your education must know, Daniel Defoe based his book Robinson Crusoe *on the events of Selkirk's life. Some have called it the first English novel.*

That was the first one. The envelope bore American stamps and, of course, an American postmark. For obvious reasons I always open such letters quickly. The name and address on the envelope were typed and, oddly for a letter from America, there was no sender's address on the flap, so I opened this one very quickly.

I've grown used to this paper, though at that time I don't think I'd seen it more than once before. On that previous occasion, in the Goncharof Hotel in Juneau, Isabel had a pad of yellow lined paper. When I asked her about it, she said, "What do you mean, what is it? It's a legal pad." So, whoever is sending these things to me writes, or rather types, on yellow legal-pad paper.

There is no central heating in this damp seaside house. I lay a coal fire before I go out in the morning and light it when I come home. I tossed the envelope into the fire without a thought. There was no address on the enclosure and no signature. I read it again and I thought about it and after a while I thought it couldn't be a coincidence, it must be deliberate. Someone knew and had sent me this to show me he knew. Or she knew.

That frightened me. It frightened me more than if the envelope had contained a direct threat. It made me understand that my guilt and my fear were two separate entities. Fear was an added burden. I found I was trembling a little as I sat there by the fire. Who had sent me that précis of Selkirk's experience? Who could know? And how could anyone who knew that also know that I lived here?

The menace hung over me. It was another presence competing with his ghostly presence. My life is a dull one. I go to work and come home again, sometimes calling in at the Mainmast for a single half-pint of Adnam's, the only drink I have these days. I read, I cook myself something. Now that I've begun this memoir, I write. He is there, glimpsed out of the corner of my eye or seen as a shadow falling across the floor. Sometimes, but not as often as I should, I go on the bus to see my mother. He is often with me and since the castaway story on legal-pad paper came, that was with me too.

Of course I wasn't in any doubt about the threat when I got the next one.

Defoe suggested that tales of the island or the longboat are retold and passed on because they offer "light into the nature of man." Do you feel that your experiences have illuminated man's nature for you personally?

Pedro de Serrano, a Spaniard, was sailing in the Pacific in 1540. His ship sank and, the only survivor of the wreck, he swam until he reached an island. There was no fresh water to be found there, no grass, only barren rock.

Serrano lived on small sea creatures and, having cut the throats of turtles, drank their blood to slake his thirst. So he lived for three years until another mariner arrived on the island from another wreck. At first Serrano took this to be the devil, fled from him and could not be convinced that his pursuer was a man and a Christian until he heard him recite the Apostle's Creed.

The two men remained together on the island for a further four years before they were rescued. By that time, their skin burnt dark brown, their hair and beards long and shaggy, they looked so much alike that they were taken for twins by their rescuers, who "with admiration beheld their hairy shapes, not like men but beasts."

Legal-pad paper again. The name and address on the envelope handwritten this time, the postmark San Francisco, one stamp bearing the face of Harry S. Truman, the other of Wendell Willkie. It came two weeks after the first and, for some reason, I didn't throw the envelope away. When a crime one has committed becomes known to someone else, when one is aware that it's no longer a secret, it becomes concrete, it becomes real. It can't have been imagined, it can't be the product of a disturbed mind. There is no longer a chance that a mistake has been made.

I knew what I'd done as soon as I'd done it. I needed no confirmation from others. But now that confirmation had come in this strange oblique way, I didn't so much confront my act as have my act confront me. Like his ghost it stood before me, but unlike him, it was solid, not unsubstantial, not shadowy and half-hidden. It was real, it had really taken place, I had done it, and I knew this as absolute truth because someone else also knew it.

Writing all this down won't stop the letters—there have been three more since the one from San Francisco—but it may help to lay his ghost. The dreams, after all, come only by night, when I'm in bed asleep. His ghost appears to me everywhere and at any time. I saw it a few moments ago, for instance, when I was rereading the piece about Serrano. From the corner of my left eye I saw him, standing in the bay window, but as soon as I turned to look he slipped away. It's always like that. He—it, whatever it is, a figment of my brain, the creature of my guilt—he never shows himself to me directly but always in the corner of my eye, on the edge of my vision, or very distantly as it might be along the beach by a breakwater or across the High Street, reflected obliquely in a shop window.

This isn't to say that I believe something supernatural is going on. I don't believe in ghosts, I still don't. He is the product of my troubled mind. Remorse has made him out of memories and old photographs and mind imprints. Much of the time I see nothing at all, only sense him standing behind me or feel the chilly draft as he opens a door or hear his footstep in a creak of the stair. Strange, because he was never in this house. In my mother's time I was hardly ever here myself and all it ever knew of him was his voice on the phone, his clear resonant voice that sometimes carried from the earpiece into farther reaches of the room. His ghost shows itself to me wherever I am and I know he would come to me wherever I was, his evanescent appearances have to do with me and not with a place in which he and I were together.

He lives inside me and if I died would die with me. By writing about him, do I mean to kill him a second time?

2

This house on the seafront, facing the sea, is one of a Victorian row, each different in architecture and in height from the rest. Ours is narrow and tall, with a wide triple-paned window on each floor, the top story surmounted by a step gable. The outside was once painted the color of creamy custard, but the sun and the winds have worn it to a pale dirty sand. According to a council ruling, it should be repainted every third year, but my parents ignored this and I've ignored it too. I can't afford things like that. I'm saving up, not for a rainy day but because of one.

Ever since the year the spring tide drove the sea up over the shingle bank and the wall, over the road and in through our front door, we've lived on the second floor. I can just remember a paddling pool where rooms had been and carpets floating on muddy water. The ground floor now is the unused dining room, its floor uncarpeted, and at the back the huddle of kitchen, scullery, and pantry, nothing modernized or "converted" in the twenty years of my family's occupation or, come to that, for a decade or two before, all kept in the mode of 1959. Up beneath the gable and on the floor below it are five bedrooms, all small and poky, only one by this time really habitable and that one inhabited by me. The best room in the house is this one where I am now, where I always am when I'm at home, a big room overlooking the sea, and though as shabby as the rest of the place, at least containing books, chairs and a sofa to sit on, and pictures all over the walls.

Almost everything is worn-out. The chair springs are broken and the upholstery is threadbare. The worn patches on the red carpet will soon be holes. Wallpaper is gradually detaching itself, bubbling in places, in others gracefully describing a backward curl as it begins its descent toward the floor. And this hasn't happened during my sole occupancy. It was always like this, in my memory at any rate. The only occasion when anything in the house was painted or papered or made good was after the flood, and then only in the most basic way. Nothing new was ever bought and nothing was repaired. My parents didn't seem to notice and I didn't notice until I came back here a year ago. Now I notice but I don't care.

The pictures are all rubbish and the framed photographs have turned yellow so that all of them, not just those dating from pre-1920, look like sepia. These photographs are of family, school and college groups, and I've never been able to recognize a single face in any of them. Nor, for that matter, could my parents, though that was no reason as far as they were concerned for taking them down. They got a lot of pleasure from speculating if this or that face belonged to uncle so-and-so and if another was grandfather's friend who went out to India before the First World War.

I said that almost everything was worn-out. This isn't true of the books, though all of them are old, having belonged to grandparents and great-grandparents. They are in good shape through having been so little read. Probably the best among them is a set of Russian novelists, Tolstoy, Dostoyevsky, Gogol, Turgenev, all bound in dark blue leather, embossed in gold. They were presented to my great-grandfather, my father's father, on his retirement in 1910 from the bookshop and stationer where he was manager.

Did he ask for them? Was he offered a gold watch and did he ask for these books instead? Did he read them? The answers to these questions are not known. What he did do, or his son did, is commit a violation against one of them, enough to horrify any book lover. Using a sharp knife and a steady eye, he cut a square or, to put it more accurately, a cuboid, hole out of the middle pages, leaving the first fifty and the last fifty intact. When you open the book, as I did for the first time when I was eleven, all seems well for a while, and then, suddenly, the rectangular wound in the text is before your eyes, the box-shaped void exposed.

Not so much a great reader as an inquisitive one, I opened the book, turned over those first pages, and there, to my great surprise, came upon my mother's pearls, two five-pound notes and a half-hunter in rose gold, snug in the hidden repository.

My father had thought me too young to be let into the mystery. But now that I'd discovered it for myself I was initiated, as into some secret society. This was where you put your precious objects. I could put something of mine there too if I chose. My geode of amethyst quartz or my dried seahorse. The book that had been so brutally operated on was a collection of Tolstoy's stories and always known as "the safe" or Sergius, after "Father Sergius," the first story in the book and the only one to remain intact, for the last, "The Kreutzer Sonata," was too long to have escaped and had lost its first ten pages.

Such false "books" for hiding treasures are commonplace now, are specially made that way and on sale in gift shops. I've seen them in the High Street here. It's made me wonder if burglars make the bookcase their first call, on the lookout for a sumptuous leather spine, exquisitely gilded. But my parents knew nothing of that. They thought Sergius the result of the most thrilling and ingenious ruse ever to derive from the mind of an inventor. They even seemed pleased that I was old enough to be in the joke and exchanged meaning glances with me if any visitor remarked on the Russian books or even if books of any kind were discussed. I think now that they lived in a world of their own where time stood still or, rather, had stopped on their wedding day in 1965 when they were both already middle-aged.

But I did read some of the other books in the set, not allowing myself to be put off as my father had been by Tolstoy's gloom and Dostoyevsky's preoccupation with suffering. My father was fond of animals. He used to say Dostoyevsky couldn't write a book without having a horse flogged to death somewhere in it.

So, having glanced at the dark blue and gold set of the Russians, with Sergius among them, I shall follow their example and refer to this place where I live as the town of N. "To the door of an inn," writes Gogol, "in the provincial town of N. there drew up a smart *britchka,* a light spring carriage of the sort affected by bachelors . . ." And what's good enough for Gogol is good enough for me.

N. is situated on the Suffolk coast, that flat eroded coast where the cliffs are not much more than sandbanks and hills of shingle and the river estuaries cut sluggishly through the low-lying meadows to the sea. There is no coast road. The towns and villages are linked to one another and to the north–south highway, as much as ten miles distant, by lanes either uncompromisingly straight or twisted corkscrewlike. The wetlands and the heaths are the habitat of birds and I'm awakened every morning by the cries of geese, being rounded up by their leader, before flying inland. There are more geese now than in my childhood, or else, most likely, I slept more soundly then.

The town itself is quite small; bigger, of course, than when I was seven and came to live here with my parents. Estates of small houses have gone up all round its periphery. A new, and very ugly, visitors' center has been built opposite the thirteenth-century church and the Latchpool Hotel on the seafront has grown a huge barracklike extension reaching right back to the High Street. The mansion, once Thorpegate Hall, has been converted and extended and now houses the concert hall some journalist has called the finest in Western Europe.

But most people would call the heart of N. more attractive now than in former times. Conservationists and preservationists have been at work. Householders have been encouraged to restore their houses and paint them frequently. An annual "best front garden" competition has resulted in whoever decides these things calling N. the floral capital of East Anglia. The retailers that used to be thought of as indispensable even ten years ago, the butcher, the baker, the greengrocer, have closed—the citizens of N. do their shopping in the supermarkets of Ipswich—and been replaced by souvenir shops, antiques emporia, and boutiques selling "designer" clothes or the work of local craftsmen and painters.

Much of this has come about through the Festival. For N., if you haven't already guessed, is the home of Europe's most celebrated Festival of Song and Dance. Or perhaps I should say *center,* for in the years since I left and before I returned, the ambitions of the N. Consortium have grown to dizzy heights and now the town is not only given over to song and dance for two weeks in July but also sees the Sainsbury Marathon in October, the Nativity Revels at Christmastime, and the Paschal Gala at Easter.

No variant of vocal music lacks representation here: opera and operetta, concert arias, the "musical," madrigals, Ambrosian chant, choir singing, amorous ditties, ballads, *lieder,* folk songs, spirituals, the blues, jazz, rock and country. Everything known to what the N. Consortium's director, Julius Grindley, facetiously and too often calls the terpsichorean art can be seen: ballet, country dancing, flamenco, the sailor's hornpipe, the Gay Gordons, polonaises, mazurkas and czardas, the military two-step, the farandole, the hesitation waltz and the can-can. We are not elitist, we are not snobs. Country and Western is regarded as sympathetically by us as is *opera seria* and in our selections the bossa nova has as much chance of finding a place as *Swan Lake.*

Notice my use of the first person plural. I say "we" as of right, not only as a resident of N., but as the secretary to the Consortium. I was lucky, some would say, to get the job, though Julius persists in telling me, while apologizing for the minimal salary, that I'm too highly qualified for the post. Sexist that he is, he once said that a woman could do it, and a woman who'd left school at sixteen at that.

What, after all, have I to do but walk the two hundred yards to the Consortium's headquarters, answer letters and the phone, send out brochures and tickets, and field all significant inquiries in the direction of Julius? Someone else is responsible for fund-raising. I have no fares to pay, no stressful travel, no parking place to compete for, and my lunch is sent in every day from the fast-food counter of the Thalassa restaurant next door. From my office window I have much the same view of the sea as from the living room at home, even if at Consortium House the gardens of the Latchpool and the Esplanade tennis court intervene. At five o'clock every afternoon I exit from the computer, switch on the phone answering machine, and go home.

Looking back over what I've written, I feel disgusted by my cowardice and my escapism. For what have I been doing, after all, but postponing the true account of the thing I know I must give? I've even been writing in a cheerful brisk way, as if I were happy or satisfied.

I've been writing a travelogue. If that is what's wanted the Consortium's brochures or even the memoirs of Julius's predecessor, *Making a Song and Dance About It* by Carlton Kingswear, give a superior portrait of the town and a better description of our kind of music. For me N. has been a place of refuge, the Consortium and its activities so far removed from those events in my life, passionate, violent and—perhaps, yes—evil, as to seem their absolute antithesis. Ironically, it's at work that I've been able to find rest.

I read a lot and the books I read aren't usually light or even contemporary fiction. But I've had almost no contact, social contact that is, with anyone. I sometimes discuss the weather and the day's catch in the pub with the fishermen. Of course I've had to go to Consortium parties, I've made my small talk and drunk my Rioja with the rest of them. Luckily, my status has been too humble for me to be invited to the dinners that follow. When Julius or even Sir Brian have pushed me into it, I've shown myself at, say, Palestrina's *madrigali spirituali* or some ballet by Sauguet or Hindemith, performances unlikely to draw even moderate-sized audiences, still less fill the theater. Afterward I've hurried home.

On first coming back to N., I found myself recognized wherever I went. My mother, before admission to the hospital in Ipswich and then retirement to Sunnylands, had been a sociable woman and active on local committees, a hard worker for charities. I was stopped in the street with inquiries after her and, inevitably, to receive invitations. It isn't hard to rebuff people if you're indifferent to their reaction or the way they think about you. But I had to give a good many the brush-off before they understood—or believed they understood—and left me alone. I was set down as a recluse or a snob or emotionally disturbed. Only one or two persisted.

No one else has made a comparable attempt. The drinkers in the Mainmast talk about the climate, about fish, and sometimes about the extensions to the nuclear power station up the coast, but never of personal things. My mother, in Sunnylands, often doesn't recognize me. On my rare visits she takes me for one of the doctors or the nephew of the woman she sits next to in the circle of wheelchairs in front of the television. She can identify no one absolutely but her sister, my aunt Clarissa, who lives in Ipswich and is a frequent visitor. I've more or less given up going because my only reason for a visit would be sentimental or to impress the staff and neither of those things interests me.

Clarissa pulls no punches. She asked me straight out what was wrong with me and why I had become such a "misery." Another time I heard her say to my mother she'd always said there was "something wrong with me" and had suggested while I was small that this might be the result of having been the only child born to a woman nearly forty-seven years old. Since then I've always phoned before going to Sunnylands to make sure Clarissa won't be there.

But during our last encounter she did ask me how I was earning my living. Had I "written that book yet"? I said something brief about working for the N. Consortium.

"I thought you went to a college to learn how to write books," she said.

Enough sense of humor remains to me for me to find her description of the celebrated post-graduate creative-writing course at the University of P. very funny. I could imagine Penny Marvell's face if she heard it or Martin Zeindler's, and by association—as if I needed association—Ivo's. His was a face I had no need to imagine, for it was constantly before my eyes. And even as I thought of him then I sensed his shadow fall across my mother's wheelchair. Of course, when I turned he was gone.

"Learning how to write books," I said, "is only the first step—if writing can be taught. Books have to find a publisher and a readership."

None of that meant anything to her. I might have known it wouldn't. Narrowing her blackcurrant eyes, she said sharply that she supposed they had to be written first.

"Six years of higher education," she said, making it sound as if I'd done a Higher National Diploma in agricultural engineering. "I wonder if you'd have gone in for it if you'd had to pay for yourself?"

People like her would have every student in the country working for ten years after they'd graduated to pay back government loans, and with interest too, no doubt. But as I sit here, writing something at last, listening to the suck and withdrawal and rush of the sea, I understand that this will be as good a place to begin as anywhere, the point at which I "went to a college to learn to write books."

My childhood in N., my years at my public school on the other side of the county, my time as an undergraduate reading English literature, all this is unimportant. I shall gloss over it and if I need to revert at all to my school it will only be to say something about the nature of that place before girls began to go there a year after I left.

I shall begin when I was twenty-one and came into this room with its big windows and its view of the sea one summer afternoon to find my father dead in his chair. I've mentioned Sergius because when I found him he was holding the "safe" open in his hands, as he often did, and half-smiling at what it contained.

He died of a heart attack. In the sunshine, at three o'clock, something stopped his heart. Though he died here, in this room, his chair drawn up into the bay window, I've never seen his ghost or heard his footstep. The difference is, I suppose, that I did nothing to contribute to his death. He'd been by the window so that when he was tired of contemplating the treasures inside Sergius and the Sergius phenomenon itself, he could raise his eyes and see the sea.

There was plenty of money for my mother, but this didn't stop people telling me they supposed I'd now feel it my duty to give up any ideas of further education and get a job. It was lucky, someone said, that I'd got my degree before my father's death. Everyone expected me to live at home and "go in for" teaching. A surprising number of people think that so long as you have a degree, no matter what in, education committees and school governors are going to welcome you to their staffs with open arms.

I told no one about the one job I'd been offered. This came from a PR woman representing the sponsors of a flamenco program in that year's festival. She asked me if I'd ever thought of becoming a model and made me feel like the prey of a talent spotter in Hollywood's heyday, in line for a screen test.

"If you were a woman," she said, "you'd take it for granted that exploiting your looks while they last is as legitimate a way of earning your living as exploiting your brains."

"I'm not a woman. In any case a lot of women don't feel like that."

"Only those with no looks to exploit."

I didn't say I was going to try to be a writer before I considered anything else. I didn't say I'd like to avoid all kinds of exploitation. Imagining myself in designer jeans, and perhaps nothing else but a gold neck chain, lounging negligently on the bonnet of a sports car against an alpine backdrop, made me laugh and, eventually, her too. We had too many drinks in the theater bar and I went back with her to her room at the Latchpool.

She was drunker than I, not surprisingly since she was six inches shorter and ten years older. Most likely it was this and not my performance, a mediocre business, that made her fall on her knees in front of me and, embracing my legs, give herself up to worship. Fellatio, at that stage, wasn't acceptable, I'd made that plain. There was something repellent about her thick crimson lipstick. She praised everything about me, my appearance that is, in a paean of adoration. I was led to the mirror on the bathroom door and told to contemplate my image.

I hardly saw myself. What I was contemplating, or rather con-gratulating myself on, was that I had done it at all, for she was my first, or at any rate my first successful, consummation. If she guessed she didn't say. I put my clothes on and phoned room service for a bottle of champagne to be sent up. The Latchpool management had probably never before been asked for such a thing at midnight, but the champagne came. The dour waiter who brought it asked grimly what we had to celebrate. Only I knew that.

When my companion passed out I put her to bed with a bottle of mineral water from the fridge and a glass on the table beside her. I never saw her again. They say you always remember what your first was called, but I can't remember her name, only that it was one of those Irish names, Sinead or Siobhan.

Two days later a letter came from the University of P., accepting me for enrollment in the two-year creative writing course. I'd succeeded on the strength of my first degree and the sample of prose I'd sent them, a short story that had been shown to no one else. The signature to the letter was indecipherable but underneath it was typed: Dr. Martin Zeindler, M.A., Ph.D., Course Tutor and Tutor in Post-graduate Studies.

That was the first time I ever saw the name of the man who was to be my supervisor. You could call him the catalyst, I suppose, the unconscious director of events, who moved the pieces on the board as if in his sleep, unaffected himself by the changes in the game and unaware even that changes were taking place.

Penny Marvell or Piers Churchill might easily have been allotted that role instead of him. They usually arranged these things alphabetically. Penny or Piers took everyone whose name began A to M, Martin the N to Z people. Only this time there were more with surnames starting with the early letters of the alphabet, two Browns, for instance, and no Smiths or Wilsons. Martin told me this himself, he told me one day after saying I'd disappointed him.

"I picked you out," he said. "My choice was entirely governed by my having been on holiday in Cornwall. Cornish, I said to myself, why not? He'll do. God knows why I didn't pick Dunbar. I spent a delightful weekend there once."

Sophie Dunbar was the only one of us who has so far achieved any success. I sometimes see in the paper hype about her second novel, to be published this autumn. Why didn't he pick her? I wish he had.

3

Martin Zeindler knows all about how fiction should be written but he can't write it himself. His only novel was as abstruse and elusive as anything of the later Henry James and as tiresome as *Finnegans Wake*. After ten attempts it failed to find a publisher. So Martin is the living example of what Shaw said about those who can, doing, and those who can't, teaching. I expect he still gives those intense tutorials at home, tête-à-têtes with two or three students, while he sits there wearing his black cat round his neck like a stole. Probably his face still lights up and his eyes shine as he tries to awaken in the beginner a passion for perfect prose.

We were twenty-four beginners, fifteen women and nine men. Everybody was either twenty-one or twenty-two except the single mature student who was somewhere in her thirties. All of us wanted to be a Best of Young British Novelist and some of us said so out loud. Of the twenty-four, two dropped out at the end of the first year and three were given what Penny called the old heave-ho; one died mysteriously, probably of AIDS, one got pregnant and went to live in Germany, and Sophie Dunbar wrote a novel that was reviewed in the *Sunday Times* and short-listed for the Whitbread Prize. If the rest had any success I haven't heard of it beyond seeing Jeffrey Brown's name under a sonnet in the *Spectator*. Perhaps it's early days.

P. may have been a nice city once. If you have a lot of imagination you can get some idea of what it was once like from the remains of the old town with its narrow lanes, stone buildings and twelfth-century cathedral. This memorial to the past is surrounded by office blocks, shopping malls and mock-medieval multistory car parks with castellated ramparts. There's more traffic in P. on a Saturday and at the evening rush than in central London.

Built in the sixties of gray concrete and composition blocks the color of tarpaulin, the university stands in its bright green partially wooded campus out on the exit road for Birmingham and the Welsh Marches. The creative writing course had its being in a vast block called the Arts Center, approached from the other buildings by overhead walkways. By the time I arrived, these walkway were in a dilapidated state, safe enough to use, but with panes of glass cracked or broken and the concrete between covered inside and out with graffiti. The architect had designed them so that each one enjoyed a view of the distant spoiled city, interrupted by the six halls of residence, charcoal-colored towers with copper roofs, weathered to a dull green. Rumor had it that the inside of the towers was like an inner-city slum, the lifts not working and the plumbing hazardous.

None of us lived in them. They were for undergraduates in their second and third years. To accommodate us, in the suburbs of P., or on the housing estates that lay beyond them, the university owned houses, all small but each thought big enough for four of us. The house at 23 Dempster Road originally had three bedrooms, but flimsy dividing walls had made these into four. There was one bathroom, two lavatories, a very small kitchen in which we were each allotted a shelf of the fridge, and a common living room dominated by a large television set.

Of my fellow post-graduates in Dempster Road, only one was also in the creative writing course. This was Emily Hadfield, nearly two years younger than I and the only student at that time in the course to have had anything published. She'd won a short story contest run by a women's magazine, which had used her story in a later issue.

Emily was a small dark girl with a pretty monkey face and a mass of Afro hair. She had a car, which she had to park in the street, and after the first day she began giving me lifts to the campus as a matter of course. We sat next to each other at Penny Marvell's first lecture and found ourselves paired off to attend Martin Zeindler's tutorials. Emily became my girlfriend.

I write it easily, as if it were a natural step. The reality wasn't like that. For one thing, I wasn't specially attracted to her, although I liked her, and for another, "friend" was more the operative in that conjunction of words. At least, for some weeks. Emily seemed content, as her grandmother might have been, first with good-night kisses and then with the kind of lovemaking that stops short—far short—of the thing itself. Or I thought she was content until one evening, in her small cluttered room, she extricated herself from my arms and said flatly, "I'm not a virgin, you know."

I said nothing.

"And I shan't get pregnant."

If there are people now who add to these qualifications a line to the effect that they aren't HIV-positive either, it wasn't happening three years ago. I'd been feeling a certain excitement up till then, an inkling that all might be well yet, but Emily's words chilled me. I muttered something about her practical attitude being the "bane of romance" and walked away across the room, a progress of all of eight feet.

Emily said, "If you write the way you talk, don't be surprised if Penny sends you down."

Those words of hers had a strange effect on me. She'd meant to hurt, they would have hurt *her,* but they almost pleased me. They were a distraction, weren't they, from what was really bothering me, my feeble sexuality? And they served to show me, in the space of a few seconds, that I was never going to commit myself to writing. I didn't care enough. I cared far more about my sexual orientation. What was it? What was *I*?

We'd quarreled and I went away to bed. Emily did the only thing that could have worked. How she knew I don't know, perhaps she didn't, perhaps helping me in that particular way was far from her thoughts and she wanted nothing more than comfort and forgiveness. I'd been in bed half an hour and was lying in the dark on the verge of sleep. She came into the room very quietly and got into the narrow single bed beside me. Her hands were warm and she held my face in them.

"I'm sorry, I shouldn't have said that. I came to say I was sorry. I didn't mean it, I lashed out because I felt rejected."

For some reason, I couldn't say anything. My voice seemed to have deserted me. It was pitch dark, the streetlights went out at midnight, and my body was totally relaxed, ready to sink into sleep. I began to make love to her, to caress her, because this seemed to me what you did to someone in the same bed with you. She responded in a way I can only describe as passive but hopeful. And it was all right, *I* was all right. No doubt because I hadn't been drinking, it was much better than with the sponsorship woman, Sinead or Siobhan, at the Latchpool. I had the satisfaction of feeling Emily grip me tight and utter a cry I'm sure wasn't feigned. I'd heard that women do that when things have worked out, so I was proud of myself but not so proud as to stay awake. By the morning she was gone. The bed was just too narrow, she said.

After that we slept together a couple of times a week. It was pleasant and it was comforting. I'd read enough English literature to have known better, to have known that these thoughts of mine had a certain meaning that would make itself all too clear in an imminent future. I'd even read the same words as those in which I expressed my feelings to myself and a chapter or so on had seen Nemesis come stalking.

"I suppose I am just one of those people who aren't very highly sexed."

That was what I had the nerve to tell myself. Look at my past, I thought, forgetting or deliberately ignoring my schooldays. Only a man indifferent to sex is content to have slept with only two women by the time he reaches twenty-two. And one of those no more than once. I disregarded my failed attempts with several girls while an undergraduate. Surely this low libido was something on which to congratulate myself. What pangs and agonies I should be saved, what troubles attendant upon promiscuity, and, come to that, passion, I should be spared.

I really told myself all those things while making love to Emily twice a week, like an unthinking, dutiful, steadfast husband, married for twenty years.

During our first year, apart from a few essays, the principal piece of work required from us was either a novella or a screenplay. We could choose.

Emily and I were both planning to produce novellas. Hers was to be a Gothic tale set in the 1870s, mine a "sensitive" atmospheric piece about a boy growing up in a seaside town. Write about what you know, said Martin Zeindler, qualifying this with, "Of course, at your age you don't know much."

He insisted on watching over the progress of our work. In this he was like certain American publishers' editors, or so I've heard, who work on a novel with a writer chapter by chapter, suggesting, discarding, sternly dictating, and sometimes, I suppose, approving. On Martin's part, with us, there wasn't much of this last. Sophie Dunbar came in for his scathing criticism as much as the rest of us. Of course it may be that it was only on her that his technique worked. It may have been Sophie alone who really absorbed his advice because she was a natural writer. On the other hand, perhaps, as a natural writer, she'd have succeeded without him, thus going a long way to prove the spuriousness of creative-writing courses.

Martin concerned himself and us less with subject matter, character, liveliness, originality, or imaginative flights than with a point of style. Naturally enough, we were expected to read a lot, particularly certain masters who were favorites both of himself and Penny Marvell: Meredith, Virginia Woolf, Golding, and Malcolm Lowry are some I remember. We were expected to understand about postmodernism and structuralism and deconstruction and to have a firm grasp of why Elizabeth Bowen was "good" and Maugham and Walpole were not. But all this was of small account compared with Martin's hatred of colloquial contractions.

Along with most of the class, when we first heard the term, I had no idea what these were. Martin, expressing an astonishment that approached disgust, set us right. It seemed that all his life, or since he embarked on his own first degree, he'd been vexed by the problem of how to write elisions without making the prose sound either stilted or too colloquial to the interior ear. In other words, what do you do about "don't," "doesn't," and "didn't," contractions constantly used in English speech, and therefore in English prose? "Do not" is impossibly stiff, "don't" sounds common, careless, over-demotic. Martin got round it by elaborate systems of avoidance and expected us to do the same. It was his obsession.

No essays were required of us, only the first chapter or part or section of our novellas. Mine, when returned to me by Martin in his house on my first visit there, astonished me by the rings and underlinings in red ballpoint that made a pervasive design all over the typescript. Emily, my companion then and on future visits, had fewer on hers, largely due to the 1870s being popularly supposed as a time when "do not" and "does not" were used as a matter of course.

Just the same she was obliged to listen while Martin took my chapter apart.

"A serious writer can ill afford to be lazy," he began, demonstrating in his first sentence how to avoid another similar problem in English prose. "Laziness has made you write didn't here, Tim. But suppose you had determined not to be lazy, to concentrate instead all your intellectual powers, how might you have avoided the colloquial mess you have fallen into?"

I didn't know. Or, as Martin would have preferred, I had no notion. The sentence in question ran: "The boy on the beach, staring out to sea across the long wide expanse of shingle, then dune, then wet flat sand, didn't believe he had a chance of seeing the ship, didn't believe in the ship's continued existence, or that it hadn't long ago come to grief."

It seemed all right to me. It sounded all right when I repeated it inside my head. Emily's opinion was asked for and I could see that, if she had one, she didn't want to give it. After a moment or

two, during which Martin sat expectantly, slightly irritably, strok-
ing the big black cat on his lap, she offered the suggestion that I
might have said: "had no belief in a chance of seeing the ship."

That made Martin laugh rather angrily. By this time I had at any
rate some sort of clue as to what he was getting at and proposed:
"had no faith in seeing the ship." But Martin lifted his hand from
the cat's back and waved it in a dismissive gesture.

"What we are trying to avoid is not only vulgarity, Tim, but also
stiltedness. This is something I've noticed you people forget. If a
clumsy rigidity of style were our object, no inhibition would exist
in your sentence on 'did not' and 'had not.' Suppose, instead, we
try it this way: 'The boy on the beach, staring out to sea across the
long wide expanse of shingle, then dune, then wet flat sand, had lost
all hope of seeing the ship, no longer believed in the ship's continued existence nor in the possibility that it had failed long ago to
come to grief.' "

Whether or not this sounded better I really don't know, or as
Martin would have had it, I no longer know. But I don't think I
knew then either. The result of it has been to make me write
"don't" and "shouldn't" and "can't" in any prose I attempt. I only
mention it now because of the strangeness of the coincidence, of the
extreme oddness, that on that first visit to Martin Zeindler's house,
the passage he chose to analyze and recast in this way was about
the sea and abandonment and a lost ship.

It was almost as if he—or I—foresaw future events, I by my
writing the sentence at all, he by his insistence on its reconstruc-
tion, in the course of which it was repeated over and over. Of
course it's only now that I see it as predictive. Then it was merely
a sentence at the beginning of a piece of writing in which I had very
little confidence and which by the end of term I was to have
abandoned for a better idea. No more than two chapters of it were
ever written. That's why it came as such a shock to me to find them
still preserved intact among the work in the orange folder I brought
away with me from P. two years later.

The manuscript was in the chest of drawers in my old bedroom
here. This is the room I use as the store place for mementos of

that time. Or, rather, not mementos so much as artifacts I can't bring myself to throw away: Isabel's black and white scarf, the garnet I bought her from the children of Wrangell, Ivo's letters. The folder also contained the short novel I wrote as a dissertation under Martin's close guidance and which met with his much-qualified approval, and a short story about some people living in a Scottish castle. Those two chapters lay between them, with the sentence waiting to be found and reread and to reveal its uncanny appropriateness.

Those aspiring to a "good address" in P. lived either in the old town or in one of the two suburbs that were really expanded villages. The old town was marginally better. Its streets were narrow and picturesque and its stone houses had long, tree-filled, almost wooded, gardens that were invisible from the front doors, which opened directly on to the pavement. Martin Zeindler owned just such a house as this, in St. Mary's Gardens.

He had a system that unlocked the front door from upstairs when you announced yourself. Sometimes, when you pushed the front door open and came into the hall, other doors in the ground-floor passage and rooms at the rear had been left open, all the way through to a pair of French windows, and beyond these could be seen the varied greens of the garden.

It was like looking at a window painting by Bonnard or Dufy. At the same time it was more mysterious than either, for the hallways and intervening open rooms were always shadowy and dim, the green prospect so clear and expectant and inviting; the sun always seemed to be shining out there. The second time I saw it, again visiting Martin with Emily, it was still sunny though it was by then December, and, walking toward the stairs, I felt a tremendous urge to keep straight on down that passage, go out into the garden and see for myself.

Of course I didn't do this. The first of the open doors was the entrance to someone's flat, the tenant of the ground floor. Martin had to let part of his house in order to afford to live there himself.

Who this tenant was I then had no idea, man or woman, young or old. There might have been more than one, for all I knew.

As we reached the top of the stairs, Martin came out to meet us. He was wearing a fur hat and had wrapped himself in a plaid traveling rug. He said in an irritable peevish way, "I do wish Dr. Steadman would not leave all his doors open like this, it makes the whole house cold. I have never been able to understand this passion for fresh air, it's so old-fashioned."

This, on the face of it startling, statement he began to elaborate with particular reference to Emily's novella as we moved into the sitting room. The Victorians had a mania for fresh air, he said, except at night when it ceased to be therapeutic and became dangerous. He hoped she understood about these things, he hoped she hadn't embarked on writing historical fiction, generally a mistake anyway, without previously immersing herself in the speech, social usage, and behavior patterns of her chosen period. Frankly, there wasn't much evidence in the work he'd recently seen that she was doing this.

Emily was defending herself when he got up again and went to open the door, jumping back from it as if met by an icy blast. It wasn't a cold day and the upstairs felt very warm to me. But Martin, muttering about drafts coming from every direction, picked up the phone and was soon pleading for the French windows and the front door to the downstairs flat to be closed.

"Yes, I know, Ivo, I know heat rises. I may not be a scientist but I do know that. Provided there is any heat to rise. What about that? Have you thought of that? Just close your front door, like a good chap, that's all I ask."

That was the first time I heard Ivo's name. It meant nothing. I just about made the connection that Ivo and Dr. Steadman were one and the same. Martin put the receiver back, shaking his head. His face, which had grown rather pink while he was asserting himself on the question of heat rising, resumed its normal pallor. In the hat and rug he had looked Russian, some unjustly condemned *moujik* beginning the march to Siberia, but now as he took off the hat and laid the rug across his knees he was himself again, reminding me as he always had—partly because of his dark hair, mustache and geometrically trimmed beard—of pictures I'd seen of Peter Sutcliffe, the Yorkshire Ripper. He even had the remains of a Harrogate accent, most apparent when he was irritable.

"Dr. Steadman is a paleontologist," he said by way of explanation. "These people spend a lot of their time poking about with rocks, mostly in very cold places. They get used to it. Arctic temperatures mean nothing to them. They even prefer them. That's no reason to try to reproduce them here."

Neither Emily nor I was particularly interested in the vagaries of paleontologists. I had only a hazy idea what paleontology was, something to do with old things, the science of old things. The only old things I cared much about were the furnishings of Martin's room, indeed of Martin's two floors, or as much as I'd seen of them. I'd never been anywhere like it before.

It wasn't that the decorations were smart or newly done or the furniture obviously valuable antiques, though some of them may have been. Everything was nearly as shabby as at home. Two of the chairs had badly worn seats and string hung out of the arms of the sofa. But there was something entirely harmonious about the room from the yellow silk (fraying) curtains that hung to the floor to the large circular table that was polished to a shine so deep that you fancied you could see several yards into it. All the wood was like that, and Ivo told me later Martin polished it himself. Instead of "wall-to-wall," the carpet was a big Persian or Indian square that lay in the middle of the polished oak floor. There was a very large mirror in a gilt frame, but quite plain and classical, not ornate, and pictures of Venice, canals and palazzos, a church on an island that I suppose was San Giorgio Maggiore. But the picture I liked best was monochrome, gray and white, the Parthenon by moonlight, shimmering in a thin shiny mist.

On our way back to the university I said something to Emily about that room, how I liked it, and how I thought that was the way a Venetian palazzo might look inside. When I got a home of

my own I wanted it to be like Martin Zeindler's. She immediately
fired up.

"I've never heard a man talk like that before. Well, not a straight
man. I've never heard a man who wasn't gay go on about furniture
and carpets and that stuff."

That was ridiculous, I said. The majority of collectors of paintings and furniture were men and they weren't necessarily, or even
often, gay. What did she expect me to be interested in? Football and
beer?

"Don't be silly. You're *not* interested in furniture, you don't
know anything about it, it would be different if you did, if you were
an expert, if it was your job, but it's not, you just talk about it like
gay men do. And clothes too and hair and things. I mean, noticing
Martin's hat and that rug thing, noticing it was some Scottish
tartan, that's all part of the gay scene, you know it is."

I didn't say anything. Defending myself suddenly seemed the
most enormous bore. I sat in the car beside her, wondering at first
if her idea of a "real man" would have asserted himself and insisted
on driving, although it was her car. I wondered that for a moment
and then my thoughts went back to our departure from Martin's
house. The front door to the ground-floor flat had still been open.
Crossing the hall, I'd looked back over my shoulder.

The French windows were also still open and the green garden
glimpsed beyond them still sunlit, but the dim shadowy spaces
between were no longer empty. I saw the figure of a man, straight,
thin, almost gaunt as far as I could tell, standing at a table in the
far room where the open windows were. He was leaning a little
forward, his hands resting on this table, his head lowered as if he
were reading something, a newspaper perhaps, that was spread out
on its surface. Against the light, greenish, wintry, pale, his figure
looked very dark, revealing nothing of himself except, by some
mysterious indefinable process, that he was young.

At the sound of Emily's voice, he looked up and in our direction.
She had begun, quite shrilly, on her diatribe, but only then with the
preamble: "There's something I want to ask you." I couldn't see his

face and he made no other movement. He looked, stared even, then turned back to his paper or whatever was on the table.

That was all, yet it made a lasting impression on me. I don't know why. Perhaps it had something to do with the fact that I'd taken it for granted Dr. Steadman was old. Martin had made him sound old, a paleontologist, "poking about" in rocks, an eccentric, a fresh-air fanatic. But this man had been young, not as young as I, maybe ten years older, but still young.

It wasn't surprising, perhaps, that I dreamed about him. Or about the man I'd created to fill the dark shell of the newspaper reader, standing against the dazzlement. In the dream, instead of going upstairs to Martin, I did what I'd been tempted to do on my last visit and walked on through the open doorways, a whole series of doorways, many more of them than in life, until I came to the French windows. Outside I could see the garden, more beautiful than I'd ever imagined it, an Italianate garden of low stone walls and stone vases of lilies and moss-grown paths overhung by trees with dark shiny leaves and trees with cypress fronds. A dark still pool was just outside the windows, on its rim an earthenware jug pouring a perpetual stream of water. The sky was the bright blue of summer and the green turf was full of small summer flowers.

I tried to open the French windows but they were locked and there was no key. The urge to get out there became very strong, much stronger I think than it would have been in reality. But in my dreams I was often a child with a child's whims and violent needs. I rattled the handles and began banging on the glass. Of course all this was no use. Something told me I must find the key, the key was somewhere in the rooms behind me, and I turned round and began going back the way I'd come.

A man came out of the shadows and walked toward me. The darkness had deepened and his face was hidden, only his lean, straight, and extremely graceful figure was visible as he moved closer and closer. When we were face to face, in silence and without warning, he put his arms round me and kissed me on the mouth.

I woke up at once, breathing rapidly and tossing this way and that. I thought I must have an erection, for I was excited and unhappy at the same time, but I hadn't. All of it had been in my mind and of course I knew how it had got there. It was the result of Emily's suggesting I might be gay or that I talked the way some gay men do.

When we didn't have a lecture, and we didn't have many, Emily was a late riser. But the next morning she knocked at my door very early and came in saying she'd had a sleepless night worrying about what she'd said to me. She wanted to apologize. She hadn't meant to accuse me of being gay, she knew I wasn't guilty of that, she had reason to know, if anyone had, and with that she got into bed with me.

"I don't know why you use words like 'accuse' and 'guilty,' " I said. "You're supposed to be liberal and open-minded, or you say you are, you ought to take homosexuality for granted, as just another way of being, not as some sort of crime. When you apologize for calling me gay you act as if you'd accused me of telling lies or doing something violent."

"I didn't mean it like that," she said, but she couldn't understand what I was talking about. "I only meant that if you talk like you're gay, Tim, people will think you are."

"And that would matter?" I said.

"It would matter to me." She mumbled something into my neck and I had to ask her what she'd said. "I'm sort of getting to love you a lot," she said.

I couldn't do anything about that except ignore it. I'd never defended being gay before but I found myself going into quite a spirited defense of the gay way of life. And all the time, with Emily's body curled up against mine and her hands on my chest—she was sweating slightly—I felt more and more how distasteful she was becoming, how I was losing even my liking for her. Her cheek was resting in the hollow of my shoulder and from time to time a drop of saliva slid from the corner of her mouth on to my skin. It wasn't exactly dribbling, but I was glad I could only feel and not see it.

When she realized I wasn't going to make love to her she fell asleep for a while and then got up. We were to have a talk that afternoon given by our new writer-in-residence, quite a well-known postmodernist, but before that Emily wanted us to have lunch together at some café/wine bar she had discovered on the river. She'd arranged to meet Sophie Dunbar and Karen Pryce for lunch in the university cafeteria but she would put them off. It was such a lovely day for December. I said I was going to work in the library, I meant to work there through lunchtime and have a sandwich half an hour before the lecture was due to start.

"I do love you, Tim," she said, as if I needed reassuring. There are only two possible replies, short of the brutal, to "I love you." One is "I love you too." It was the other I gave her.

"I know," I said.

Emily and I went together to Martin Zeindler's because it was a tradition he'd established that members of the creative writing class should pair off when they came to him for tutorials. Thus, Sophie paired with Karen, Jeffrey Brown with Selina Bridges, and so on. We were the only pair sexually, or in her eyes romantically, in-volved with each other. I made up my mind, at that time, two weeks before the end of term, that this must change. When we returned to P. in January we'd still be living in the same house, and that might be awkward though inevitable, but sharing a bed would be out and I'd pair off for Martin's tutorials with someone else, Ann Friel, perhaps, a quiet, studious girl, and leave her partner, Kate Rogers, available for Emily.

Had I only known it, I'd already paid my last visit to Martin's in Emily's company. We were due to go there again two days before the end of term, but Emily got the flu and stayed in bed. One of the other members of our household, a graduate student in chemis-try called Roberta Clifford, volunteered to look after her. She'd had the flu herself, was probably responsible for giving it to Emily, and wasn't afraid to be in and out of the sickroom. Emily was insistent that I keep clear.

Thus I went to Martin's alone in Emily's car. As I approached the house I wondered if I should see Dr. Steadman and rather hoped I wouldn't. It wasn't the first time I'd dreamed of someone in a sexual situation, as sexually involved with myself, and then felt diffident at the prospect of encountering them in the flesh.

The weather had become much colder. There was frost in the air at only four in the afternoon. It seemed unlikely that the tenant of the ground-floor flat would have left all his doors open today, and in fact he hadn't. The front door was shut and, I don't know why, for no reason, it looked implacably shut to me, as if the occupant had left and locked it up in as many ways and as tightly as possible.

Martin asked me to read my new chapter aloud to him. Sometimes he preferred it that way. He would sit with his eyes closed, his head resting against a cushion, looking more than ever like Sutcliffe, in a mask perhaps made for Madame Tussaud's. That afternoon, as usual, he wanted no lights on until it became too dark to see even with the utmost eyestrain. I'd seated myself by the window to get the maximum light from a sunset that was dyeing the sky orange and the roofs of the city below various shades of crimson.

Not for the first time, during a reading, I thought Martin had fallen asleep. It had been the occasion on past visits for exchanges of smirks and shrugs between Emily and myself. But there was no one to smile at today. I came to the end, stopped and look down into the street below. A man was getting out of a car in front of the house. He slammed the door and stood a moment, looking up. Although I'd never seen his face, not even in that dream, I knew who it was. My eyes met his and I immediately looked away, in fact pushed my chair away and stood up, my heart beating violently.

"Why have you stopped?" said Martin, who hadn't been asleep. "Have you finished? Is that it?"

"That's as far as I've got," I said.

"No critic will ever accuse you of prolificity," he said, "provided you get so far as to be of interest to critics. Why are you standing there as if you've seen a ghost? Have you? You've gone as white as one. Perhaps you've caught Emily's flu."

I was about to sit down again when there came a loud knocking at Martin's door.

"Would you mind going to see who that is? Of course I know

who it is, no one else bangs like that. I mean, would you go and let him in, please. Since you're on your feet, as they say."

I also knew who it was. Who else could get into the house without ringing the bell? I could see his face before opening the door, it was imprinted on my mind's eye from that brief glimpse at the window, a lean dark face with hooded eyes, the lips full, the cheeks hollow, almost cadaverous, a weary look, worn and tired, the look of one who suffers sleepless nights. Black hair, a lock falling across a lined forehead.

We all have a type. I used to think we didn't. Now I know better, oh, how much better! That is my type, male or female, the face that is oval yet thin, the sensuous mouth, the large eyes black as night, life-weariness overspreading it, a kind of latter-day decadence, youth worn out by dissipation but still youth, the kind that pays no heed to health or care or prudence. This was Ivo's face that I opened Martin's door to and stood looking up at, for he was a little taller than I.

For all Emily's admonition, I've no idea what he was wearing. If I noticed, I don't remember. Something informal, I suppose, jeans I expect, I never saw him in a suit. He looked at me as if he remembered the dream. It was as if he had willed me the dream and acted in it.

"I'm Martin's student," I said, and then, "Won't you come in?" as if he'd already demurred.

His voice was accentless, beautiful, simple, rather deep. "I've lost my key again. I suppose I should say 'mislaid.' No doubt it's downstairs in there on the table."

By then we were inside the room with Martin. As soon as he realized who his visitor was he adopted the scolding tone I had heard him use to Ivo on the phone. I later learned this was habitual. The only way he felt he could handle Ivo was by a kind of irritable bossiness that was at the same time quite friendly, even paternal.

"You are always losing that key. Or, as I should say, leaving it behind. What would you do if I were out, I wonder? Why don't you put it on the same ring as the outside door key and hang them both round your neck on a string? That would be the best way. You really are very tiresome."

"Yes, I know. I know all that. You've told me before. You'll just have to accept it as one of my faults, Martin, like leaving doors open. Now will you please introduce me to your student?"

"I should have thought you could do that yourself. Ivo Steadman, Timothy Cornish; Timothy Cornish, Ivo Steadman. Dr. Steadman to you. He is known as 'Tim,' Ivo. What a pity we aren't brought up like the Americans; advance, stick out a hand and say, Hi, I'm so-and-so."

We didn't shake hands. I felt, though I was wrong, that he'd lost interest in me. He began walking round the room, looking at things. This was Ivo, typical of him, very much the way he always was, a restless man, a man of a devouring curiosity who noticed every new thing and had to examine it, read it, or speculate about it. In fact it was a week since he'd been in this room and during that time the *Economist* and the *Spectator* had found their way to the table along with two new novels and an old paperback of Empson's *Seven Types of Ambiguity;* some bulbs in a pot were poking shoots through the very black earth; Martin had changed one of the Venice pictures for a painting of a Victorian girl, a copy of a Millais, perhaps; a letter lay by its torn envelope on the desk beside a small china cat Martin said one of his students had given him, perhaps as a Christmas present. Ivo wandered about looking at all this, scrutinizing the picture, picking up the pottery cat and looking under its base to see what kind of porcelain it was, even reading the letter. He put a cigarette in his mouth and gazed about him for the means to light it.

"I don't allow smoking here," Martin said. "You know that, I've told you—"

"Umpteen times. I wonder what the origin of that strange expression is? Umpteen? I hope you know, you *ought* to know, oughtn't he, Mr. Cornish? Anyway, I'm not smoking. I can't find a light in this museum."

"Of course I know its origin," Martin said. "First World War army slang. 'Umpty' was signalers' slang for a dash in Morse. It signifies an indefinitely large number."

His temper much improved by the chance to answer a fairly obscure question—as it always was—he began expounding on the word "teen" and its many meanings. It might, for instance, mean "hurt" from Old English *teona* or "to grieve" or "to distress." Trust Martin to come up with a simple definition: it might have just meant ten.

Ivo stood there in silence, listening perhaps or perhaps not, the unlighted cigarette in his long brown fingers. I felt for the matches in my pocket, took them out, and, risking Martin's rage, struck one and held up the flame. I came close to Ivo. My hand wasn't quite steady. Somehow I knew he was aware of the reason for my hand's shaking. I thought he might take hold of my wrist and I held my breath, but he didn't. The flame met the end of the cigarette and the end glowed brightly as Ivo drew in a long inhalation.

We stood there, about a foot separating our faces. I stepped back a little. I heard Martin say, "I shall go and look for that key. It may take me a few minutes to lay my hand on it. When I come back I hope you'll have finished with that disgusting object that is smoking the place out. And then perhaps you'll leave us, Ivo, there's a good chap. I am, after all, supposed to be teaching 'Mr. Cornish' something, that is why he is here."

He started laughing, no doubt at the idea of himself or anyone calling me Mister. I heard him chuckling on his way to the door and the door close behind him. I had never supposed I would be thankful for Martin's obsession with shutting doors and keeping drafts out. It had always irritated me. Now the soft click the door made was music.

The strange thing is that I wasn't afraid. I wasn't shy or diffident, I had no diffidence. It was rather like the best stage of being drunk, when inhibition has lifted but before there's any loss of coordination or any muzziness, when a feeling of tremendous excitement comes, though the aim and object of that excitement is never defined. I wasn't drunk and my excitement had an aim. I was without rational thought, not to mention caution or any idea of being sensible. But at the same time I was hardly aware of my body, only of my mind or my *self.*

I say "at the same time" but time, too, had gone, had departed. The door was shut, Martin was never coming back, or rather, if it was four-thirty when he left it would be four-thirty when he returned, no matter how long he was absent. Ivo and I were in a pocket or vacuum left out of time.

Our eyes were on each other. Without looking at what he was doing, he ground out his cigarette in a stone vessel that might or might not have been an ashtray. I went close up to him and laid my hand on the side of his face, on his cheek, drawing my fingers very softly and slowly down. I was breathing as if I couldn't get my breath.

He let me touch him, his face and his neck, and breathe in the smoky smell of him. For a moment I thought he was going to smile, he'd made a little sound that might have been a gasp of amusement or pleasure. I don't know if he smiled then, he may have done, but I couldn't see. His face went out of focus as he brought it to mine and kissed me on the mouth.

Like the dream, yet not like the dream. He wasn't touching me except with his mouth and I felt faint, I was afraid I would fall. I held on to him with my hands, I held him in my arms. The blood was banging in my head, or perhaps it was the blood in his head, or both, I couldn't tell. I'd lost awareness of the separateness of our mouths too, which part was his, which mine, in the long warm exploration, the hot bitter-tasting darkness, as if we were two adventurers dependent on each other, traveling through an un-known world.

He took my hands down, stepped aside, tossed back his hair. Martin came in with a key and a piece of string to hang it on, whether meaning this seriously or as a joke I never knew.

4

The newspaper I buy in Orford Street on my way to Consortium House has been running articles on teenage sex. Parents, teachers, and the children themselves have contributed to these pieces, and yesterday an interview appeared with the headmaster of my own old school. It was the same man too. After all, it's only seven years since I left school.

They began letting girls in at sixth-form level a year after I left. Now they start as the boys do at Common Entrance. The headmaster of Leythe, Basil Warwick Eliot, told the journalist writing the piece that there'd been one or two "incidents" since the girls' advent (his word). One girl had actually been made pregnant, though not, he insisted, by a Leythe boy. The interviewer asked if his wasn't a sexist attitude and he defended himself at length. The one thing he did say that interested me, in the way that only such total ignorance and misunderstanding can be interesting, was that in all his time at the school and in that of his predecessors there had never been the least suspicion of homosexual "vice." I'm not much given to laughter these days but that made me laugh.

No one could have passed through Leythe without regularly taking part in sexual activity, and taking part in it as a matter of course. You did it, and that was all. Of course there were variations and gradations, there were differences of degree and of kind. Absolute buggery, uncompromising, gross perhaps, a matter of hygiene or relief like defecation, took place all the time. There was nothing remotely romantic about it, no kissing, for instance, or touching or even preliminary talking. You knew that you did it with this person or that and you got on with it, it was necessary, inevitable. A sign was made or a code word spoken without the least embarrassment, and that was that.

Love existed, of course, or rather a lustful or sentimental obsession. James Gilman, five years my senior, was in love with me and wrote bad poetry to me. Prefects were always in love with some first- or second-year, and in a few cases this idol was kept on his pedestal, the recipient of love letters or even sonnets, his photograph on a study desk. Mostly, though, he too was used in the way of all flesh.

I've no doubt it had always gone on. After I left school and had things in some sort of perspective, I'd look at photographs of an eminent politician or distinguished churchman, all old boys of Leythe, and reflect on their school days, or rather their school nights, sodomy in the dorm or in the bushes behind the prefects' garden. Had such pasts ever been used for blackmail in the cases of politicians or Secret Service people? Had blackmailers broken up marriages and ruined careers with this evidence? Somehow I doubted it. It was all so much a part of public-school existence as to be silently accepted and taken for granted that I could only imagine a (for example) heritage under-secretary or bishop of somewhere laughing incredulously if challenged.

And what of me? Leythe's Cities of the Plain hadn't made me think of myself as homosexual, any more I suppose than it had made that heritage minister and that bishop. This was what you did when you were a child, like eating sweets, smoking joints if you could get them, not washing much. But when I became a man I put away childish things.

Had I? Had Emily been right? Not in accusing me of being homosexual but in defining me as such by reason of my tastes and ways? Yet I'd never before found a man attractive, if "attractive," that overused word, goes any distance to express what in those first days, weeks, I felt for Ivo. I'd never before been sexually drawn to a man. At Leythe it wasn't a question of attraction, only of physical need on the most basic level. You didn't look at faces or eyes or body shape, still less have that indefinable sense of another's essence.

On the other hand, I hadn't been much attracted by women either. I sometimes needed sex, that was the same as at school, but who with—that was less important. In my case, it had been with those who indicated their willingness, even their eagerness. None of it had been very successful. I was low-sexed, some people were, I believed this until that moment at Martin's when I touched Ivo's face and he kissed me.

When Martin came in with the key and his fussy bit of string, Ivo started to laugh. It didn't seem to me the kind of laughter the key and string might provoke but the laughter of surprise and perhaps delight. He was laughing at himself and at me, at my audacity perhaps. Of course Martin took it as some kind of applause for what he'd done. He got Ivo to give him the outer door key, and then he put both on his piece of string, which he insisted on looping round Ivo's neck.

"You can give me your own key back tomorrow," he said. "Now you must go. As it is you've outstayed your welcome by ten minutes. We have work to do. We are in the serious business of English prose."

He began pushing Ivo toward the door, one hand in the middle of his long, flat, elegant, and suddenly enormously desirable back. I could see the knot in the string lying against the brown skin of his neck. I felt a bit sick.

Ivo said, "Are you teaching him to write a blockbuster, Martin? Something very sexy and bold?"

"Out you go," said Martin. "And wear that string whenever you go out."

"I'll never take it off. I'll wear it in the bath."

He said nothing to me, not good-bye, not that it had been nice meeting me, and I was glad he didn't. It meant more that he said nothing. I listened for his feet on the stairs, for the door downstairs to close, but there was silence. Martin came back, his black cat draped round his neck, and began talking about the aorist, as usual, and then, for some unstated reason, about Bunin's short stories, which he recommended me to read. My heart had begun to beat very heavily, making a thudding I thought he must hear.

In the manner of a psychiatrist, Martin always ended his tutorials on the dot. An hour was what we were to have and an hour was what we got. "Time's up," he would say, looking at the clock or his watch, or, "That's it for now." Scrupulously, this time, he had allowed me an extra ten minutes to make up for the time Ivo was there. They felt like ten hours.

At the top of the stairs I paused, trying to make myself breathe normally. Ivo's door would be ajar, I was sure of that, and he waiting for me on the other side of it. I felt on the brink of a tremendous adventure, but one that was almost too big for me, that I wasn't sure I could cope with. About halfway down, looking over the banister rail, I could see Ivo's door but not see if it was open or closed. I still couldn't see when I was outside it. I gave it a light push. The blood rushed into my face, I felt as if someone had shoved me backward when the door didn't give, when I realized it was shut and locked.

The house was quite silent. Outside it was starting to get dark and the hall was darkish. Suddenly the ceiling light came on. It worked on a time switch and always came on at five-fifteen in winter, but I didn't know that, I'd never been there so late before. I thought someone had turned it on, I thought Ivo had. But the door stayed closed and the place silent. I went out, got into the car and drove home.

The experience of enduring the time lag between a sexual approach and the next move had never been mine. Possibly others had experienced it on my account but if so I didn't know it. I didn't know what it was to wait, to speculate, to suffer hope deferred; to be afraid to go out in case the phone call comes while you are out and afraid to stay in lest others overhear it and hear what you say. He didn't know where I lived, he didn't know my phone number, he could hardly ask Martin. I told myself these things. And I told myself that he could find out if he really wanted to.

Besides, I was so ignorant. How did men behave in these circumstances? I didn't know. I assumed as men behaved to women. A
man would phone a woman and ask her out. Would a man phone
a man and ask him? Our pay phone was on the wall outside the
door of my room. I spent a lot of time lying on my bed, waiting
for the phone to ring. I asked myself if this was love. Was I "in
love"?

Almost recovered by now, Emily kept coming in to ask me if I
was all right, if she could get me anything. She'd become a stranger.
I could hardly believe that we'd been lovers. Whatever happened,
I knew I'd never sleep with her again. Of course I now believed
nothing was going to happen. He'd seen the way I looked at him,
felt my touch, had kissed me for fun or even to teach me a lesson,
to show me I'd no business gazing at paleontologist Ph.D.'s that
way. But a kiss like *that*? What a kiss it had been. I wanted more,
oh, how I wanted it. He must have meant it, he must have been
serious. Was the simple answer that he now regretted his rash
behavior?

I couldn't forget the things he'd said as Martin was propelling
him to the door, about writing a sexy blockbuster and about
wearing the key string in the bath. He must have meant that
provocatively. I could see his worn dark face all the time and that
mouth I'd kissed and those large eyes in the bluish hollows and his
hands that were very long with big finger joints and his flat back
with the shoulder blades like the buds of wings. I heard his voice,
deep and soft and with laughter shaking it as he said to no one, to
the room, to the air, that I might be taught to be sexy and bold.

The day before we were going down, Emily asked me if I'd go
home with her for a few days at Christmas. To meet her parents.
They were longing to meet me. I couldn't imagine why, I was that
far gone. She said I'd have to understand we wouldn't be able to
share a room at her parents', they wouldn't tolerate that, even if we
were engaged, but if I could bear it she'd like me to come.

"I'm not the sort of person that meets people's parents and
makes a thing of Christmas."

I remembered just too late that I might more reasonably have said I couldn't leave my mother alone her first Christmas as a widow. Emily thought of it and said it for me. I must stay with my mother but she could come to me, maybe for the New Year.

"Not this time," I said.

"Tim, is it because we haven't—well, been together for quite a while now? Is it? It's only because I've been ill. I really have been ill, you know."

Perhaps there is nothing so frustrating as being misunderstood quite in this way, as having these bizarre reasons put forward to account for one's conduct. I felt like telling her to go away, to leave me alone, that I never wanted to see her again. Outside the door the phone started ringing and she went to answer it before I could stop her. I had a little fantasy about its being Ivo at last and Emily not having the least suspicion but listening just the same when I spoke to him, the veiled way I would speak to him and make him, somehow make him, suggest we meet *now*. I'd borrow her car for the last time. I could be there, in the middle of town, in ten minutes.

It wasn't him. It was Roberta's mother. But that phone call did something for me, or Emily did it, with her talk of meeting parents and being engaged, pointers to a dismally conventional way of life into which I could so easily and irrevocably be drawn. I asked myself, as I jumped up, what I had to lose. I could be humiliated but at least I'd have tried. Perhaps it's ridiculous to say to yourself that if you don't take a certain step you'll regret it all your life, but that's what I did say.

"Can I borrow the car?"

I suppose she had a right to ask me where I was going. It was her car. She was always asking me where I was going, when I'd be back, and often if she could come. Well, it was her car. But people who do this make people like me into liars. I often told Emily lies and now I foresaw that if things worked out, if what I wanted but hardly dared think possible, if that happened, I should be telling her more and more lies, happy lies, blissful lies, to keep her quiet and keep her away.

"You can't be going to Martin. Martin's gone away. Didn't you know? He was going this morning."

So much the better. It seemed a good omen. I think I visibly shivered at the thought of Ivo alone in the house, but she didn't notice.

"He's left a book he's lending me with the man downstairs."

It was very improbable. It wasn't the kind of thing Martin would do. I didn't care. I went down the passage to the bathroom and had a shower, considered spraying myself with the male scent someone had left on the shelf, but thought better of it as meretricious. Emily was still in my room. I was suddenly afraid she'd say she was coming with me and I could think of nothing to say that would stop her. She looked listless and pale, she watched me dress in silence. I had a brilliant idea of calling into a wine shop on the way and buying champagne. I couldn't afford champagne, but I did have enough money in hand to pay for it. Then I decided that would be worse than arriving smelling of Dunhill cologne.

Emily took off her jeans and sweater and got into my bed, turning her face to the wall. I gave her a kiss on the cheek, just to be friendly, I suppose, or for old times' sake. It seemed best to say nothing, to leave her and deal with this when I got back. I might be capable of dealing with anything when I got back—or I might not.

At Martin's the hall light was on. It came on automatically, I knew that now, but it was another good sign. I was no longer afraid, no longer anxious, no longer feeling sick. I rang his bell. The time he took to answer was very long and I could feel my euphoria sinking, changing, cooling. A dark cloud began to replace it, a cloud with a voice coming out of it and saying, you're absurd, you can't do this, no one does. Then it was his voice, his only.

I said, "It's Tim Cornish."

He said nothing. An age passed, the door buzzed and opened as I touched it. In the meantime he had opened the inner door, the one to which he so often mislaid the key. I found him standing just inside, in the hall, and all the other doors were closed.

"You've surprised me," he said.

. . .

As a matter of fact, I've surprised myself. I wasn't sure I could write about him and me as we once were; I didn't think I'd be able to recapture the feelings of it and the tone, my breathless, permanently excited state, my recklessness, the headlong nothing-else-matters atmosphere in which I lived at that time. But I have. It would be less strange if I felt the same now or had felt it the following year, if it had lasted. The strangeness of being able to recall it so precisely lies in its transience. I remember it as clearly as I remember my love for Isabel. The difference is not in the intensity of recall but in the pain.

What is it in most people that requires, in order to maintain passionate desire, a reciprocal coolness, a mild indifference? I'm not talking about one loving and one letting himself be loved. That would be too crude. I'm only saying that a lover must be a little hard to get, to a degree capricious, holding back always something of himself, reserved, not invariably to be found at home waiting. Ivo was like that at first, for a while he was like that, my amused, light-hearted, curious, surprised lover. I was the one who needed and demanded, who was peremptory, stimulated by a "no" but unwilling to take it for an answer.

That first time I stayed with him until some time in the very early morning. I must have been there for at least ten hours. Now I can't remember whether or not we ate anything, but I know we drank a lot, the champagne that I didn't take but that he had in his fridge, brandy, and a bottle of claret. I was still drunk when I drove Emily's car home.

Naked with him, his hard lean body a raft for me to lie on, I asked him when I should see him again.

"January."

"It's too long," I said. "I can't wait that long."

"Three weeks will pass quickly. Suppose it were the long vacation? What would you do then?"

"Die," I said in the petulant tone of a boyfriend of Dorian Gray, someone's sweet catamite. I was already learning how easy it is in my situation to slip into this coquettish mode. "You could come to N. and stay."

"With Mother? That would hardly do."

"In a hotel or a bed and breakfast."

"Not a B and B. No boys in the rooms during the hours of darkness."

He laughed, but he came to N. If I'd known I'd meet him, as if by chance, strolling in Orford Street on New Year's Eve, I might not have drunk my half of that bottle of red wine, a panacea for despair, and dented Emily's car trying to park it between a truck and a van. I dented the van too, but the truck was unscathed. She was waiting up for me, tearful, pink-nosed, in a brown dressing gown and slippers with button-down collars round the instep. She'd watched it all from the downstairs front window. I promised to pay for everything, I made wild promises, my head starting to bang, the smell of Ivo on my fingers.

"You've been with another girl."

"I haven't." I swore I hadn't, I came up with the funniest thing I could think of. "I swear by all I hold sacred," I said. "I swear on my mother's head."

That struck me as so hilarious I started laughing, I couldn't stop, I was manic with it, laughing so much that I fell on the floor and rolled about laughing. I thought Emily was going to kick me, but still I couldn't stop. Then Sharif in the room above banged on the floor with a shoe. Emily started to cry. She ran upstairs, sobbing.

It's hard to imagine it now, the laughter. The drunkenness and cruelty as well, for now I can see that I was cruel to Emily. I was laughing at her, at everything, the way children do with happiness, for I was happy. I went home to N. the next day with a dry mouth and a headache, but happy.

Rain was falling and went on falling day after day onto the brown choppy sea. There was nothing to do but read. I tried to borrow five hundred pounds from my mother so that Emily wouldn't lose her no-claims bonus, but she said she hadn't got it. She'd just handed that sum to Aunt Clarissa for a package holiday they were going on together to Tenerife. In the afternoon of December 31, a day on which no rain had fallen, I came out of the newsagent where I'd

been to buy the *Times Literary Supplement* and saw Ivo coming up
the slope from the sea.

"Not a fossil to be seen on your beach," he said.

"Aren't there?" I was breathless already. "I've never looked."

"A very tame English beach, a pussycat of a beach."

It was the first hint I had that he was used to wilder beaches and
stranger shores. We went along to the Latchpool for tea: scones
with clotted cream, Madeira cake. The windows in the lounge give
on to the terrace and the terrace on to the road, the seawall, the hills
of shingle. He said he had just arrived, was staying two or three
miles up the coast in a hotel that hadn't long been converted from
a simple pub. His bedroom had a view of the nuclear power station.
Talking about it made him start laughing, but he said he liked that,
the grim gray bulk of it, it was an antidote to his euphoria, it kept
him from losing his head.

"Can we go there?" I said.

"If you're sure you don't want another cup of tea."

New Year's Eve. A great storm got up that night and we lay in
his bed at the Kestrel listening to the onslaught of the waves against
the wall below. Once or twice a wave came high enough to lash the
bedroom windows with spray. It wasn't quite true about the power
station. You could see it only if you leaned right out and craned
your neck.

He had brought a lot of champagne. I'd never been much of a
drinker but with Ivo I took to drinking, it became inseparable from
making love with him. It was quite a long time before I realized I
was drinking much more than he was. Harder to face was the fact
that I seemed to need a drink first. But not then, not on New Year's
Eve and the early days of the New Year, the honeymoon on the cliff
edge with the rain endlessly pouring outside and the sea swelling
and exploding on the shingle.

We went up to Orford to the Oysterage for dinner and to the
Swan at Southwold. The Consortium's Nativity Revels didn't end
till Twelfth Night and they were putting on two operas in January.
We went to hear *Rosenkavalier.* It was a change for me to be able
to offer Ivo a new experience. Ochs's aria he said was the best song

he'd ever heard, so I bought him a tape in the foyer. It was highlights from *Rosenkavalier* with the Great Waltz on it and "Ohne mich, ohne mich." Although it was raining, we walked back to the Kestrel along the dune path, singing "Ohne mich," or as much of it as I could remember. I made my own translation, into bad verse. The words made Ivo laugh, he said it would have to be our tune.

> *Without me, without me,*
> *Every day's misery,*
> *But with me—am I wrong?*
> *No night is too long!*

Ivo stayed until the last day before term started and he drove me back to P. with him. I've never been back to the Kestrel. When I go for a walk I go the other way. But this past week I haven't been able to write. A depression settled on me, no doubt the result of writing and rereading those last few pages, and I expect I made it worse by walking up the coast, partly on the beach, partly on the cliff path, to the place where Ivo and I passed those heady days and nights.

The Kestrel Hotel. Bed and Breakfast. All rooms with bath. Bar Food. Three course dinner: £12.50. Vacancies. Well, there would be vacancies in October.

I stood on the shingle and looked up at the slate-roofed, white-painted building, put up perhaps a hundred and fifty years ago, and I marveled that it still stood, that the sea that took everything along that coast had left it still beetling over its little fragile bit of cliff. Not a tree in sight; green turf, a huddle of cottages, a fish-and-chip place, a church spire and the power station. It looked enormous from where I was, bigger than it used to be. They're always building extensions to it. If you half-close your eyes it might be a castle that you're looking at or even a modern city of towers. You'd think it was beautiful if you didn't know what it was.

Ivo's bedroom had been the one at the top in the left-hand corner. I'd been writing about us in the past days and, in order to do so, summoned up some remains of that physical madness that gripped me then, feeling actual lust in my body for the first time for over a year. Writing about it used it up, leaving me drained and dry and sexless like an old man. Now I could barely believe I'd done those things, felt those things, been so swept up, spellbound, crazy. I could barely believe I'd been Ivo's ardent lover.

These feelings were soon swamped by guilt, as they always are. A woman with a hard suspicious face was watching me from the window that had been Ivo's. I turned away and began to walk back inland, along the muddy paths between the rushes, under the heavy cables that carry electricity away from the power station. Rain in the air sang in the wires, making a dull, sorrowful musical note. I thought of how we do things that a few years later we can't believe we'd have dreamed of doing. And Ivo, or his shade, his imagined ghost, the shadow I've conjured, who has been absent while I was writing, came silently back into the corner of my eye. I turned my head just in time to catch the toss of his black hair, the dark bloom on his skin, and to see a thin hand raised as if to ward me off.

It was like one of M. R. James's stories. He knew this coast, this sea, these flat fields. The pursuer that recedes and dwindles as you quickly turn to catch him is his kind of thing, the figure that's half-seen, the companion that's always with you. James himself was probably homosexual but firmly locked in the most respectable and scholarly of closets. Whatever his pursuers and pursued had in their pasts it wasn't love-battles on a sweaty bed, the room sweet-smelling of semen and champagne.

When I got home I was so cold I lit a fire up here and sat in the armchair in front of it reading Dante, the *Inferno,* in the Dorothy Sayers translation. There was a purpose behind this. I wanted to see in which circle of hell he puts murderers. The worst part, I expected, Circle Nine, and to reach it I had to read the whole poem. It took me hours but what else, after all, when not at work, do I have to do? And do you know, Dante has no murderers in hell at all!

There are plenty of people there for something else, people who happen to have committed murder in the course of their crimes.

But no one in hell specifically for killing someone. Heretics and traitors, panders and seducers, hypocrites and spendthrifts, blasphemers and suicides, but no murderers. It opens up all kinds of strangeness. For murder surely is the worst crime we can think of, the ultimate sin. Seducing, not to mention blasphemy and a spot of wrath, is nothing to it. Not then, though, not in the thirteenth century, if Dante is to be believed, and he must be. These things are hard to grasp, for we can't transmigrate back six centuries. But can it be that if I'd lived in Florence in 1292, I'd have considered myself far less of a sinner than Julius's brother who killed himself with Ecstasy and gin last year?

In front of the dying embers of that fire, before I went at last to bed, I also reread the latest efforts of my transatlantic correspondent on his legal-pad paper. The writer gives me no chance to forget what I did. By now he has sent me five. One of the two most recent came last Monday, the other yesterday. Both envelopes were handwritten, one postmarked Seattle, the other Sacramento, California.

The first letter was as follows:

> The islands called St Paul and Amsterdam lie in the Indian Ocean roughly halfway between South Africa and Australia. In 1790 a Frenchman Captain Peron was marooned there from the American vessel Emily. The four sailors abandoned with him quarrelled amongst themselves and all died as a result of their brawls, leaving the poor Frenchman to a hermit's existence.
>
> There he remained for three years, living on a diet of fish, the eggs of seabirds, and seal meat, the only vegetation consisting of no more than mosses and ferns. Chance alone brought an end to his misfortunes. Vessels en route to China did not generally put in at St Paul but one did in July 1793, by mere chance. This was HMS Lion, a British warship, carrying the diplomat Lord Macartney. This distinguished passenger was curious to take a closer look at St Paul, a boat was lowered, and as a result Captain Peron was rescued.

Yesterday's contribution to the canon varied somewhat from the old-fashioned, gloomy and vaguely moralistic tone of the previous ones. It was a lot more bloodthirsty and the protagonist was stranded on a boat, not an island.

> This is a story of the herring fleet which operated out of Southwest Harbor, Maine. The date was 1904. When the boat Cannon foundered in a storm the only survivors of a crew of ten were three men who managed to reach a lifeboat. They were Jeb Cannon of Southwest Harbor, James Thomas of Damariscotta, and Clem Mallory of Ellsworth. A widespread search failed to find any trace of them.
>
> Cannon was picked up a month later. The other men had disappeared but there were large pieces of meat in the boat. Cannon admitted this was human flesh. Thomas and Mallory had died, he said, and he had eaten their bodies to stay alive.
>
> Fourteen years later, dying of a fever, he confessed the truth to neighbours on his deathbed. Two weeks after the storm he had shot Mallory with a pistol he had salvaged from the wreck. Then he had cut him up and eaten pieces of the body. When Mallory's remains went bad and had to be discarded overboard, he had shot Thomas.
>
> The confession over, Cannon's neighbours crept away and left him to die alone. Refusing him burial in their village, they took his body out to sea and dropped it over the side.

Is this sequence of letters intended to lead somewhere? If there is any progression or development, I can't see what it is. Each seems to be the isolated story of a man saving himself by escaping from a shipwreck or being abandoned, alone or with companions, on an island. And now, cannibalism.

Does my correspondent make up these stories or are they true? The experience of Alexander Selcraig/Selkirk is of course fact, it's the most famous of all desert island adventures, but are the others? If they are true, where does he or she get them from? Is he a collector of castaway experiences and if so for what purpose?

It looks as if, by asking these questions, it's merely my curiosity that has been aroused by these letters. But I'm afraid that's not so. Their purpose must be to frighten me and they do frighten me.

That in itself is strange, for a month ago if anyone had asked me, I'd have said that I wasn't afraid any longer of anything much, certainly not of being found out and punished. Only of my own mind and the tricks it plays.

5

The room I sleep in was my parents' bedroom. It's too narrow for its high ceiling and the Victorian bay window is ill-proportioned. But it looks on Sole Bay, as the windows of the living room below it do. A dark green roller blind keeps out the glare when the sun rises out there beyond the edge of the sea.

An unaccustomed whiteness of light awoke me this morning before the geese started. Without looking, I knew it had snowed in the night. I didn't want to look, I'd no wish to confront it, for snow reminds me—as if I needed reminding—of the Inside Passage, and when it's fresh and untouched, of the glaciers that Ivo loved and took me to walk on in the blue air and the bitter cold.

Lying there in bed in the still dark room where all the light was round the edges of the blind and shimmering a little through it, I saw his figure in the deep shadows of the alcove the chest of drawers only half fills. I put it in these words, though of course I knew within seconds it was not he, wasn't even a dream of him, but that what I saw was my mother's cheval glass I'd pushed to an angle and over which, for some reason, I'd hung my hooded waterproof coat when I came in the night before. It had been raining and the rain had turned to snow. For a moment only it had been he, tall and thin, his hand holding the mirror and reflected in it, his head turned to the window as if his eyes could penetrate the blind.

It was that waterproof jacket that started it, not only because of its shape I'm sure but because it was the one I got specially to wear in Alaska. I'm tempted to throw it away, but I can't afford another.

The snow had come early, and for a freak November fall it was deep. For us, on this coast, it was deep. It always seems to me to lie uneasily at the seaside, appropriate for countryside, most suitable for mountains, but wrong here on the coast, almost ludicrous. What could be sillier than snow on the beach?

The gulls have turned yellow-gray against its whiteness. The blanket of snow from this house to the sea was covered with the cuneiform patterns their twiglike feet make. It began snowing again as I walked to Consortium House and the snow flew in fast-melting flakes against the windows of my room as I sat down to work. We're making arrangements for the Nativity Revels' carol concerts, the biggest and best, Julius claims, of all carol services held in England. They go on for four days and between them the choirs and soloists sing every Christmas carol ever written. It's been my task, among a good many others, to see to the arrangements for televising the final one, the big Christmas Eve service. It's to be transmitted live and nothing must go wrong.

I suppose it's because I've been writing about Ivo—not because I have been thinking about him, I always do that—that I kept seeing him throughout the day. He was at my elbow but was quickly dispelled by a sharp turn of my head. When the snow stopped and the sun came out, his shadow fell long and black across my desk and streaked along the floor. At lunchtime I went outside, only next door, to Thalassa, but I saw him. He was in the bookshop, his face clouded and distorted but not hidden by the bookseller's mock sixteenth-century glass, hunting down a paperback in the science section. I was halfway across the high road, unable to believe this wasn't Ivo, when he turned his head and instead of those rather stern features, those heavy-lidded eyes, the lick of black hair, I saw a pink face, a mustache above a smiling mouth, a cheerful tourist come for the weekend of All Saints.

· · ·

After work I went to the public library and asked if they had anything on castaways, marooned sailors, that sort of thing, and was offered, from the children's section, a very old copy of *The Swiss Family Robinson*. Eventually I came away with quite a scholarly looking book, an examination of eighteenth- and nineteenth-century seafarers' tales, and the journal kept by the wife of the captain of the *Maid of Athens* between 1869 and 1870.

It seemed to stay light longer this afternoon because of the snow. As I walked home I could see quite clearly where the white beach meets the gray sea and the creamy hulk of the lifeboat rears up behind the seawall. Darkness is as strange as its opposite when snow is on the ground. It becomes black light instead of an absence of light, translucent, shimmering, ghostly. The irony of the lifeboat station's having been moved to within fifty yards of my own house isn't lost on me. It's as if some power-that-is has said: You shall see the life-savers every day, you shall see the boat, you who made death by sea and did nothing to save him.

Until I get the electric fan and the oil stove and maybe a coal fire going, the damp chill of the house is all around me as I step into the hall. Usually it feels colder than outside, such a still, moist cold that even the air indoors is misty. The snow hushes everything. The noisy world grows silent, for people stay at home and car engines are muted, slowly and softly driven.

I moved in with Ivo. It sounds simple, put like that, but in fact my move was the result of an enormous row that broke out in the house in Dempster Road. The evening I got back to P., Ivo dropped me outside the front door. In the holidays I'd forgotten all about the people I'd been sharing a home with. They were just a man and two girls I'd been thrown in among, and as for Emily, she'd become my girlfriend more through propinquity and convenience than any great attraction on either side. Certainly not on mine. She'd faded from my mind and kept a significance there about on a level with Gilman's or, say, my mother's friend who I used to call Auntie Noreen. Roberta Clifford and Sharif Qasir I'd never liked. I thought her an opinionated bore, while he took offense at the least things and was absurdly belligerent besides.

I walked into the squalid little living room. It was only at that moment that I realized I might be called on to give some sort of explanation to Emily for not having been in touch. The three of them were sitting in there. They weren't reading or studying anything or watching television. They were waiting for me and three pairs of eyes turned on me as I came in.

I suppose Emily had asked Roberta and Sharif to stay there and give her support. Emily's face was blazing with anger and the other two wore those grim, self-righteous expressions that indicate enormous enjoyment is being derived from taking a moral stand.

Emily began by asking me if I'd been ill. Her voice was held under considerable control—then. Only illness, severe illness, she said, would excuse my neither phoning nor writing to her since she went home nearly a month before. We were practically engaged to be married, she said. "Informally engaged" was the term she used.

"It's the first I've heard of it," I said.

"In Scotland," said Roberta, "Emily would be your wife by now in the law. Living together like you've been and everyone knowing it, that's enough to make her your wife."

"What a load of crap," I said. I didn't believe it, it was rubbish, and I was going upstairs. Sharif jumped up and stood barring the door.

"Oh, please," I said. It was one of Ivo's expressions, uttered in exasperation. "Oh, please."

"In another era," said Roberta, who'd read nineteenth-century social history, "Emily would have sued you for breach of promise. Her dad would have put a notice in the paper, warning other girls to have nothing to do with you. If they did that sort of thing now I expect it would go out on TV."

"It's no fucking business of yours," I said. "You keep out of it."

"How dare you speak like that in front of ladies!" said Sharif.

I couldn't resist it. "That was no lady," I said, "that was my Scottish common law wife."

He punched me. I leaped aside and kicked out at him. We'd have been fighting in a minute if Roberta hadn't grabbed Sharif's arm and Emily jumped up and flung her arms round me. I threw her off and she fell on the floor. I made for the stairs. Luckily, my door had a lock on it, so once inside I slammed it and turned the key. But that was far from the end. Emily came banging on the door in the middle of the night and shouted abuse at me when I wouldn't open it. I could deal with that. It was much harder coping with her tears when she caught me as I came creeping out to the bathroom first thing in the morning, again flung her arms round me, and began crying and sobbing.

There must be another woman, she sobbed. She wanted to know who she was and how long it had been going on and also wanted to assure me that no one would love me as she did, no one would ever do as much for me as she would do. I said, for God's sake I'd only known her four months. I said I didn't want anything done for me and she cried the louder. She began screaming and stamping her feet. It was six in the morning and the students in the house next door started thumping on the wall with what sounded like a broom handle. In the end I slapped her because that's always recommended in cases of hysteria.

That day I spent in the library, returning home rather cautiously in the late afternoon to discover that the three of them had been to the office dealing with accommodation placements at P. They told the accommodation officer that they couldn't live under the same roof with me. I expect they invented a catalog of my iniquities.

"You've got a strange way of getting a man to marry you," I said to Emily. "What do you do when you want to put him off?"

That inflamed Sharif. He picked up a green glass vase off the nasty wood-chip table and was going to hit me over the head with it, but once again Roberta intervened and reminded him we had to pay for breakages. I asked her where I was supposed to go.

No one knew. All they had done was extract a half-hearted promise that some alternative would be found for me "in the next few weeks." In fact, it happened two days later and came to me through Martin Zeindler. He sent for me to his room in the Arts Wing.

"What on earth have you been doing, sending all these women mad?" he said. "I didn't think you had it in you. By a piece of exceptional good fortune, Dr. Steadman wants a lodger and since I have no objection to his subletting, it's yours. If," he added, "you can stand the cold."

I don't think he suspected anything. It was all said in innocence. I must have been wreathed in smiles, as they say, for Martin put his eyebrows up and said something about icy temperatures and snow being forecast.

"Of course he can't wait. He has much the same attitude to the approach of polar conditions as a malamute in a heat wave." I didn't know what a malamute was and had to look it up, though I can't say this Eskimo dog much resembled Ivo. "I'm relying on you," said Martin, "to be my fifth column and make sure he keeps his doors shut."

I've sometimes wondered if this was his sole motive in persuading Ivo to take me in. But perhaps Ivo needed no persuading. Perhaps it was true that by an exceptional piece of good fortune, Dr. Steadman wanted a lodger. I never found out, I never asked, and a week after coming back to P., I moved myself and my things into the house in St. Mary's Gardens.

In accordance with Martin's prediction, it started snowing that night. Next morning I had nothing to do until Penny's lecture at eleven-thirty, so I got up late and looked out of the window to see Ivo making a snowman on the lawn. The garden, which had always looked so inviting, was in fact quite different from the way I'd seen it in my dream, being no more than a minimally tended half-acre of grass and trees. But there was a lawn, a big one, and in the middle of it Ivo had made a snowman as tall as himself.

I put my clothes on quickly and on my way to the French windows met him coming in. Again I was aware of the disconcerting yet exciting way he had of speaking as if we had parted not twenty-four hours but two minutes before.

"I'm looking for a hat for him. I wish I'd got a pipe—do you think Martin might have one?"

I could only lift my shoulders, stare at him.

"Could you spare a scarf? You seem to have a different one every day."

The Leythe scarf—this was a legitimate reason for getting rid of it. James Gilman had given it to me, it had been his, of an infinitely superior Jermyn Street quality to the one I had from the school outfitters in Ipswich. With a doting look he'd said, like Touchstone, "Wear this for me," and had exchanged it for mine. I carried Gilman's expensive blue-and-yellow-striped scarf outside rather ceremoniously and tied it round the snowman's neck.

Ivo produced a bowler hat he'd once worn in a college rag. We stood admiring the tall snowman. He said he'd made one every winter except 1985 when there hadn't been enough snow, and each year they got bigger.

"Right, I must be off," he said. "I'm late. If I don't see you tonight I'll be around in the morning."

I was dismayed. What had happened? We'd made love in his bedroom when I first arrived, the champagne already waiting in an ice bucket, and then, to my surprise, he'd announced he had an engagement, he was going out to dinner, it was unbreakable, he must go. This was my room, he said, opening a door and heaving in two of my cases, he hoped it was okay, he'd leave me to settle in.

I waited for him to come. I heard the front door and the inner door and his footsteps and I waited. The light in the passage went out and his bedroom door closed and I knew he wasn't coming. We met, briefly, at breakfast. Or, rather, he'd finished breakfast, was off to the Institute, and delayed five minutes only to explain to me where everything was and how, since there were two fridges, I could have the smaller one for my exclusive use. Without touching me, without even a finger on my shoulder, he left in a hurry.

The answer might be, I decided, that he hadn't really wanted me here, that Martin had coerced him into it. He liked having sex with me, he was passionately attracted to me, fancied me if you like, but he didn't want me living here, it was done as a favor to Martin.

Nothing happened in the next few weeks to alter this feeling I had. The snow went, the snowman slowly melted; Ivo was in and out, but we seldom had a meal together. The day after I put the scarf on the snowman, or rather the evening after, he knocked on my door and asked me very lightly and casually, but with a half-smile and leaving me in no doubt as to what he meant, if I fancied a drink. So it was champagne in the kitchen and then my room. He stayed half the night but was gone long before morning.

We're such creatures of habit, nearly all of us want patterns. I thought a pattern had been established, this was how it was going to be, every other night or maybe three nights a week there'd come a knock at my door or else he'd call out, "I'm opening a bottle of the widow," and we would drink and be together and make love. And then the week came when there was nothing, he was merely the landlord, a note was left telling me he'd be away for the night; his fridge was stocked with food but mine was empty. I saw him come home, it was a fine sunny day in February, and he was opening all the doors and letting the air blow through the house. The next thing Martin had come down to complain and I could hear Ivo's teasing defense and Martin's pedantic querulousness, I could hear it from behind my closed door.

To provoke Ivo I waited till Martin had gone and came out dressed in spite of the fresh cold air the way I thought someone in my position should dress to entice and beguile. You must remember that I didn't *know,* I could only conjecture from what I'd read and seen in the cinema and half-remembered from Gilman days. So I came out in ragged-hem jeans, barefoot and bare-chested with a gold chain among my golden chest hair and a brown leather belt with medallions on it reminiscent of the Wild West. And Ivo looked at me and said, his mouth twitching, "Our Lady of the Flowers, I presume? All dressed up for the rent-boys' ball."

He had such a tongue on him in those days. But I liked it, I liked his scorn. It didn't hurt or humiliate me, or not much. It excited me. Providing his sarcasm would lead to lovemaking, I looked forward to it. I didn't care if he brought the champagne bottle into my bedroom, gave us each a glass, and without a word pulled me down onto the bed for violent silent usage. But I did very much mind when he had friends in for a drink and I wasn't invited, when I became apparently no more than the student who rented the small bedroom. I began to think I must have it out with him, the whole thing. Why was it happening this way when the New Year honeymoon was so recent, when he had followed me to N., no doubt giving up whatever other holiday plans he had had? Why had he turned away from me?

It's true to say too that I felt sorry for myself. Life wasn't easy in other respects. Penny Marvell hadn't delivered to me her famous warning, notorious as the lead-up to the old heave-ho, that it wasn't unusual for people embarking on the course to find after a few months that creative writing wasn't their *métier*. But Martin had made plain his disappointment with my boy-by-the-seaside story. And Sophie had relayed a rumor she'd heard to the effect that eight out of the twenty-four of us were to be told at the year's end that we wouldn't be welcome back next October.

Emily not only didn't speak to me but avoided speaking to me as ostentatiously as she could. She gathered around her a band of allies who had a ritualistic way of conducting themselves whenever I appeared, gathering up their things, getting up and leaving, if it happened to be in the cafeteria, turning their heads all sharply away as if at a word of command when I came into the library or lecture theater. Emily, whether entirely for the purpose of persecuting me or out of a fear of being alone, had taken to going about everywhere in this particular group of three other women. On the occasions I was unlucky enough to meet them outdoors on campus, they spread themselves out across my path, arms linked, apparently to bar my way, and broke up only when I walked relentlessly toward them. Their behavior was more like that of schoolgirls from some rough neighborhood than graduate students. But I felt as Orpheus must have when pursued by maenads.

So I was lonely and self-pitying. Ivo and I hardly ever talked, and when we did we spoke on the most superficial level. I remembered my heart-searching confidences to him, the outpourings of my feelings, when we were together at the Dolphin, and I was sore and resentful. I was frightened too, I couldn't think what I had done, unless it was accepting a perhaps reluctantly made offer to live there. What terrified me was the feeling I had that his indifference was making me fall in love with him, I felt the threat of it, as if his cold demeanor combined with violent sexual onslaught was leading me fast toward that particular abyss. Already I was longing for him daily, nightly, and no less so immediately after one of our consummations, those aggressive near-rape struggles on my bed or his.

It was late March and nearly the end of term when I asked him if we could have a talk. Easter was coming and when I saw ahead of me the weeks alone with my mother in N., the east wind blowing, the old people walking past with their tiny, skin-smooth terriers, when I imagined the brown sea and the Felixstowe ferry moving slowly across the horizon, I nearly panicked, I nearly threw myself on my knees in front of him.

"What is it you want, Tim?" he said to me.

I mumbled something about our relationship, I'd thought we were having a relationship. Was I going to see him in the holidays? Everything was so indefinite. I had to go home the next day and as it was I'd be going without knowing anything of his plans or our future. This was not at all what I meant to say and I hadn't meant to sound so miserable.

"My sister is coming from America for a week. After she's gone we could go somewhere. Would you like that?"

"Where could we go?"

Ivo said, smiling, "I don't suppose you'd much fancy taking a look at some ancient sedimentary rocks on the Isle of Man, would you?"

I couldn't tell if he was serious or not.

"A geologist called Herbert Bolton published a report on fossils he found in the Manx slates. They're called grapholites. That was nearly a hundred years ago. No one thought much of it at the time but people are now beginning to think he was right and that the

whole geological structure of the island should be reassessed. I
thought I might take a look. But, no, I can see the idea fills you with
dismay. Let's go to Paris."

"Can we?" I said.

"Oh, yes, I think we should. We will. Now tell me what you
really want."

It wasn't easy to put it into words, that I wanted us to be a
couple but in secret, in the closet. Publicly, we could only be taken
for inseparable friends. The way things were, I felt he was holding
back from me, putting me at a distance. I quoted something I knew
a scientist wouldn't be able to place.

"I feel I dwell in the suburbs of your pleasure."

He burst out laughing but didn't ask where it came from, so I
couldn't show off and tell him about Cato's daughter, Brutus'
Portia. "You're asking for a commitment. I make one and you make
one. Is that it?"

"I just want to be with you," I said, "and know what you're
doing and where you are. I want to talk to you."

"Is that all? Not a very tall order."

The irony of that made me say what I shouldn't have, what I was
soon bitterly to regret saying, what I couldn't have said if I hadn't
been pouring down champagne all the while we talked. "I only
want us to be lovers."

It stopped his laughter. "Ah," he said, and then, quietly as if he
was afraid, "we shall have to see."

I went home to N. and wrote him letters every day. I wonder
what became of those letters? He said he burned them and he
wasn't a liar. I counted the days until it was time to go back,
obliterating the dates on my mother's Beautiful Anglia calendar
with a felt-tip pen. She and Clarissa went off to Tenerife and I
returned early to P.

His sister had been. Signs of her still remained, a nearly used-up
bottle of nail varnish in the bathroom, the kind of Greek yogurt we
never ate in the fridge. "She wouldn't go to the Isle of Man either,"
Ivo said.

He was happy, enthusiastic, inquisitive, the way he'd been that first day we met upstairs at Martin's. The dry, sometimes scathing, manner was gone. He wanted to know what I'd been doing—had there been any opera in N.? He played the tape I thought he'd forgotten about or lost and we laughed at Ochs's song:

With me—am I wrong?
No night is too long!

The next day we went to Paris.

It's true of the Consortium's music and dance functions, as it's said of St. Mark's Square in Venice, that if you spend enough time there you'll eventually see the whole world pass by. Sooner or later everyone comes to one of the theaters or concert halls or walks past the Consortium's door. Since taking this job I have seen several members of the Royal Family, all the Cabinet, dozens of television actors, and one evening last autumn I saw Martin Zeindler. It was a *lieder* concert, Schubert and Wolf. Martin was with a woman. She was a little older than he, tall and elegant with elaborately done gray hair, and when I saw them he had his arm round her waist. He saw me and recognized me, I was aware of that, but I took care not to take it further and hid behind one of the doors marked Private until the interval was over.

Lieder concerts aren't very sought-after, which was why I was there. Julius likes me to go to the less popular events and, along with a couple of secretaries and his own wife and sons who are roped in, swell the audience. He says it has a good effect. He once told me I ought to "get a partner" so as to have an extra woman in the freebie contingent. Last night's event, one of the interfestival concerts, was Indian ragas. I tried to wriggle out of it but Julius was insistent, particularly as his own family was engaged elsewhere and the snow would deter even ticket-holders.

I was sitting in the balcony, in the front row. Looking down five minutes before the concert was due to begin, I saw James Gilman come in with a party of eight. You can always tell, with these parties, whether the people have come because they want to or for business reasons, that is the tickets are part of a block booked by some company. Gilman obviously belonged in this category. For one thing, he was wearing a dinner jacket. He looked tremendously bored and at the same time suave and sleek. Even from where I was, a hundred feet away, I could see the grooves the comb had made passing through his butter-colored hair.

Any of the four women with him might have been his wife. They were all young, all in skirts up around their thighs, all covered in jewelry and makeup and all with the sort of hair that looks as if it has been pulled through a thorn bush. I watched Gilman take his seat and whisper something in the ear of the woman next to him. His lips were almost touching her ear. I thought of a sonnet he'd written me, the last couplet of which ran: 'Though you may turn my dreams to dust and truth to lies/I'll drown my pain in your unfathomed eyes.'

That made me start laughing and fetched a "ssh" from the only other person in the row. Instead of listening to the ragas, I thought of the day on which we'd exchanged scarves and how I told Ivo about it when I found Gilman's in the garden shed bundled up with the snowman's bowler hat. I think I told Ivo to make him jealous, though God knows I never had any more feeling for Gilman than a sort of coquettish need to provoke him and make him want me.

In the interval, upstairs in the bar, Gilman looked at me and said, "Hello, Tim," as if, instead of having last seen each other ten years before, we'd been meeting every day. I said, "Hello, James," and then I remembered someone had told me he'd become a lawyer, a solicitor I think, with a practice in London. I felt no desire to approach him and he obviously didn't want to say any more to me. But, strangely, because I rarely allow myself to think of her in this kind of way, it came into my head how entirely different everything would have been if Isabel had been with me, if she had been holding my arm as the pretty redheaded woman was holding Gilman's, and how proudly I would have introduced her, braving any possible snubs. With a glass of wine in my hand, my eyes momentarily closed, I saw her for an instant on the darkness, her pale oval face, the full-lipped mouth like a red lily, the dark hair with the eyebrow-touching fringe.

It was too painful to keep, that image. I opened my eyes and, turning in the opposite direction from where I'd last seen Gilman, looked into the face of Ivo. Or, rather, into the profile of Ivo, a dark-haired bone-thin man who stood in a graceful slouch talking to an elderly couple. Except that, of course, as I soon saw, the nose was too long, the chin too small, the hair receded too far, and when the face turned three-quarters toward me, Ivo's ghost became what it always did, a shadow, a nothing, an illusion or, as in this case, a man of his age but with quite different looks.

I've said somewhere, I think, that Ivo was absent from P. for three months each summer. I knew it before I moved into St. Mary's Gardens, he must have told me or Martin had, but it had slipped my mind. It must have been in late April, soon after the beginning of term, that he asked me what I meant to do while he was "away."

"What do you mean, away?" I said. "Away where?"

"You know I always go to America."

The fact is that I wasn't much interested in what he did in America, so I hadn't listened particularly attentively when he explained to me. The only thing that stuck in my mind was that part of the time he spent as a lecturer on the Alaskan cruise ships. Apart from that there had been something about visiting various geological sites in Montana, I think it was, and in northern Canada, and ending up spending a week or two with someone or other who lived in Oregon.

I'd simply concluded that, this year, he wouldn't go.

"I have to go, Tim. At least, I have to do the cruises, that's four weeks on the ships. It's good money, I need that money."

"What exactly do you do?" I said.

"I go with the ship wherever it's going, Kodiak Island or Anchorage or the Inside Passage, and I give—well, say four lectures on a seven-day trip and I take people ashore and show them things of geological interest, particularly glaciers. There are other scientists, bird people and botanists, all sorts of natural historians. That's what passengers go for, to learn about wilderness ecology. These are serious cruises, they're not luxury trips with drinking and dancing, you know. People book up partly for the lectures. They'd feel cheated if one of the lecturers wasn't there."

I thought it sounded deadly but I didn't say so. "I suppose I could come with you."

This, it turned out, would be impossible. Reservations were made, mostly by middle-aged or elderly Americans, business people, and academics, nine months in advance. It would be useless putting my name down; they already had waiting lists of would-be passengers hoping for people with reservations to drop out.

"Surely you could get me in on it as your—friend."

"Tim," he said, "don't you think I would if I could? Don't you think I'd jump at the chance?"

Then he'd just have not to go, I said. He couldn't leave me alone for a month. What was I supposed to do? I sounded petulant and I was pouting like an affronted bimbo, I know I was, but I didn't know and don't know now how a man in my situation avoids that kind of behavior. The relationship between two such as we were, a young, not very strong-minded, penniless boy and a clever, comfortably-off, dominant older man, seems naturally to make for it. I who had never before been sulky, coquettish, a creature of moods and explosions of temper, was all these now. But perhaps, yes, I had been so once before, with James Gilman.

It frightened me and I hated it and that only made me angrier with myself. I felt my maleness being sapped. I shouted at Ivo that of course he couldn't go, he must give it up. I even asked him if he could bear being parted from me for four weeks. He said he was going and that was that, and as for me, I couldn't even stay in the house. Martin liked the place to himself in June and July.

I did it deliberately. Hating myself for it, I made my eyes big and round, I made my expression winsome, and said that if I meant anything to him (note that the word "love" had not at that time ever been used between us), if I really meant anything to him, he wouldn't go away like this and leave me alone.

He turned on me a look of the coldest contempt. "Oh, stop it," he said. "Look at you, making faces because Sugar Daddy won't take you on holiday. Have you any idea how ridiculous you are?"

I went over to him and hit him in the face. Of course he hit me back and we fought for a while, which led inevitably to love-making and making-up and champagne. He'd have to go, he said, but for the following year he'd book up well in advance so that I could go with him.

The following year . . . It was a long way off but it didn't seem like that then. It made me feel happy because Ivo had not only said we'd still be together the following year but had taken it for granted we would be.

Term ended, I went to N. and he to Vancouver and thence to Juneau and the Panhandle of Alaska.

This evening when I got home from Consortium House I made myself go into the bedroom that used to be mine. Behind that always-closed door were all the things I had brought home with me at the end of my last term at the university of P. I put them away in my bedroom and the next day I went with Ivo to Alaska. When I returned a month later I put the things I'd brought back with me in there too, Isabel's scarf, the garnet, my binoculars, the guide to Seattle I'd bought, Thierry Massin's address, written down on the inside of an airline ticket envelope. I couldn't bring myself to sleep there among it all, so I moved into the room my parents had used.

But I knew I had to go in there now. I was going to find the letters Ivo wrote to me from Juneau and the ship that first summer and reread them. If I could. If I could bear it.

It was very cold and very dusty. The two suitcases and the two canvas bags were still standing where I had put them, between the desk and the window, and a fine coating of white dust covered them like a sprinkling of snow. I'd taken my mother's suitcase to Alaska, and a big backpack.

The letters were in the outer pocket of the larger case, and at some point I had put the pages of the ultimately abandoned boy-by-the-sea novella in its orange folder in there too. I had total recall of exactly what was where, the disposing of the books and papers, the distribution of clothes. Or I thought I had. What I had forgotten was his photograph, for some reason stuck in the file with the novella pages.

I couldn't take my eyes from it. Sitting on the floor in that cold, dirty room, hearing the sea out there, the rush and pebbly withdrawal of the tide, I devoured his face, the features both grave and full of laughter, the deep eyes, the tired mouth, the lock of black hair falling.

And I was nearer being in love with Ivo then than I'd ever been in life. I was even breathing the shallow breaths of the lover as I gazed. Whatever it had cost me, if I could have done it, I'd have brought him back.

There's a story the ancient Greeks tell of the man who found a frozen serpent. He took pity on it and put it in his bosom, but when it was revived by the warmth it stung him. Before he died the man reproached the serpent for its ingratitude, but all it said as it wriggled away was, "I was still a serpent."

Ivo didn't save my life but he was good to me, he loved me, and when I woke up I stung him. His eyes gazed sadly at me. I looked at the hand that had killed him and laid it heavily across the photographed face.

6

Ivo wrote better letters than anyone in creative writing. I remember how this surprised me at the time. That was when I still believed in an absolute divide between scientists and those concerned with the arts and expected scientists to be more or less illiterate.

Ivo wrote to me that first summer when I was at home in N. and he wrote to me while I was with Isabel in Juneau, waiting for the cruise ship to come back. In those letters, especially the second set, he wrote about the beautiful places he visited and the ugly interesting ones, the gold rush towns and the disused mines. He wrote about the glaciers, about the animals and birds and unspoiled places. The people on board ship amused him and some excited his admiration, especially those academics whose learning was so enthusiastic. There were others that maddened him by their hugely comprehensive knowledge of their own subject and total ignorance of almost everything else. He wrote about them and the funny or clever or foolish things they said.

He told me how it rained day after day. For some reason people think rain forests are confined to the tropics, but because it was so wet, when a sunny day came it was the more gloriously appreciated. The lecturers, along with the ship's company and the staff, slept deep in the ship well below the waterline, so when Ivo got up in the morning he had no way of knowing what the weather was till he came up on deck. He wrote to me about the glory of a fine day at sunrise when the sky was blue, the mist gone and the majestic mountains revealed in the clear air.

Rereading the letters gradually became more and more painful. And this wasn't only because they were Ivo's letters but also because of their subject matter. They were, after all, about the rain forest on the northwest coast of America, where he was to die and I was to kill him, and they brought back everything, including some things I'd succeeded in forgetting.

I read three of them, constantly stopping to shut my eyes, to clench my hands, once to put my head in my hands. There was no one to see me, but if anybody had they'd have thought me ill, with some sort of palsy or chorea. But what do I mean, no one to see me? As I sat there in the bay window—for I'd brought the letters down into the living room—I was aware more strongly than ever that he was watching me. He was standing behind my chair, look-ing over my left shoulder. I even felt him, I felt his hand touch my shoulder as I dropped my head into my hands, I heard him say softly: "Tim . . ."

I jumped up with a cry. There were more lights in the room to put on and I put them on. I even fetched a lamp in from the bedroom next door, a lamp with a hundred-fifty-watt bulb, and switched it on, trembling. The room was bright, dazzling, and shadowless and it was quite empty. I tried to read on; I couldn't. At the end of the third letter he'd written: "I wish you were with me. Because you aren't I'm not enjoying this the way I usually do and I have a strong sense of my heart not being in it, no doubt because my heart is elsewhere. I miss you very much."

That was too much for me. I wanted the letters out of my sight and pushed them under the window seat, letting the flounce or whatever it's called fall down and hide them. Then I seated myself at the typewriter and wrote this, an attempt at exorcism more needed today than ever. Of course it doesn't work, but it helps. It's as if I'm saying, when I've got it all down I can't go through it all again, that isn't the way it happens, something at least will be over. I even have a feeling that I'll be cleaned, I'll be washed white.

When Ivo came back from Alaska we were longing for each

other. In spite of what he'd said about missing me he'd nevertheless taken an extra week to visit friends, and I was desperate for him. Martin might have wanted his house empty all summer, but Ivo was, after all, paying the full rent, not a retainer, and I hadn't any compunction about moving back in the middle of August. I was there waiting when the taxi brought him home.

At the end of *A Long Day's Journey into Night,* James Tyrone's wife says of him and her, when they first knew each other—it's the last line of the play—"We were so happy for a little while." Well, that was Ivo and me. We were so happy for a little while.

One thing I haven't mentioned in this chronicle, narrative, account, whatever you like to call it, is the money I stole from Ivo. Of course I know I can't right it. I can't give it back to him, the $700 I took from his cabin, all the booze and food I bought with the traveler's checks he gave me to sign and stood over me while I did it, the meals Isabel and I shared, my airfare to Seattle and the cost of the hotel there, the coat I bought Thierry. Ivo's dead so I can't give it back. So far as I know, he had no next-of-kin except that sister whose name and address I've no means of discovering. So I've calculated what I owe him and I'm going to give the money to something or someone, a worthy cause, a charity, I don't know yet.

It's something like $2,000. Call it £1,300. That's about an eighth of my annual earnings *before* tax and a considerable sum to me, but I've raised half of it. If it's in the bank it will just get lost in my account, so I keep it in Sergius. My mother's pearls are still in there but now they lie between two thin piles of notes.

Rereading what I just wrote, I can see it would look very self-righteous and sort of goody two-shoes to anyone else. Well, it's a change for me to be like that. And I can't help it. I'm setting it down for my own benefit, to remind me to keep at it, not to make excuses for finding another use for the money.

In our second year of creative writing we were expected to write a novel. It was the equivalent, I suppose, of a dissertation. The writer in residence had written three novels, one of which had been

something of a success and adapted for television, so was supposed
to be an expert. With Martin it was more a matter of theory than
practice. But he was as astute as ever at picking out colloquial
contractions. My novel was going to be about a love affair between
a young student and—guess what?—an older university teacher,
only I thought it safer and wiser to make the teacher a woman.

Whatever ours had started out as, Ivo's and mine, by the autumn
it had become a love affair. I think that happened a week or two
before Ivo made his momentous statement, because it wasn't much
more than a couple of months after the statement that things began
running downhill.

We weren't in bed or anything. We weren't in any sort of
romantic situation. I was very cagey about letting him take me out
to meals, I didn't want to be seen dining alone with him. It was one
thing people from the university knowing I had a room here,
everyone knew that, but quite another for them to see us out
together. Sometimes, though, we'd go for a drink to a pub in the
country outside P., and it was in one of these places that he said it.
We were sitting at a table in the corner. The pub was quite crowded
and we sat opposite each other, looking, I suppose, like just a
couple of guys who knew each other and sometimes went out for
a drink. I used to fantasize about this a bit, I used to think, this is
how it is: He's my brother-in-law, married to my sister, and I've
dropped in and while she's putting the kids to bed, I've said, How
about coming for a drink? And he's said, Why not? Better make it
a quick one, though. That's how people would see us, I thought,
that's how they'd *place* us, and I liked it, I felt it put me more
securely into my gender. I was turning it over in my mind, looking
at the angles, when he said, out of the blue: "I love you."

He spoke very softly, but casually too, and not in an intense way,
not in a whisper. I didn't say anything.

"I'm very much in love with you," he said. "I can't bear to be
separated from you."

I've already written down what I thought in relation to Emily,
about there being only two replies to "I love you": "I know" and
what I said to Ivo, "I love you too."

But even as I said it I had a feeling I was answering like this to be polite, to avoid hurting him, to be *kind*. Perhaps, too, to avoid trouble. Because even as I said it I was thinking, I don't know what I mean by "I love you," I don't know what love is. And I was wishing, even then, that he hadn't said it, that he'd controlled himself, kept it back. It frightened me, hearing him say it, as if it conferred on me a responsibility I didn't want and couldn't handle, a responsibility I wasn't equal to.

All this should have made me cautious and careful. It didn't. Fool that I was, I compounded it. For some reason, I had to, I had to reinforce what I'd said even though I didn't really feel it, to convince myself, maybe, or to strengthen what in my ears had sounded wretchedly feeble.

"I really do love you," I said.

I wanted to make him happy. The trouble with that is, as I now know, that it's no use making a person happy for five minutes or five days, you have to keep it up, you have to sustain it. It's got to be a life's work.

Is it something in me or are plenty of people like this? Am I alone or is it just part of the human condition? He diminished himself in my eyes by saying he loved me. Contempt is too strong a word, I didn't despise him for it, but I pitied him a little, and that's the next thing.

That night, in bed, the sex had lost something. He loved me, therefore he was less desirable. He had confessed this weakness in himself, his need of me, his inability to bear separation from me, and I wanted him strong and cool and scornful. He loved me, therefore I loved him no longer.

Of course it wasn't the sudden happening I've described. I was even a little elated at the time by being told what I'd been told. I was proud of myself for my conquest. If the sex was somewhat below par I blamed the drink, of which I'd taken, not unusually for me, rather too much. That was when I started drinking in a big way, when I was with Ivo and Ivo paid.

Even then, our relationship might have endured if we'd had

something in common. It was easier for him because he was a reader and had read quite a lot of what for want of a better term I'll call English literature. He didn't stare blankly if I talked about this or that novelist or poet. About most things in physics, chemistry, and biology, not to mention maths, I was totally ignorant. Ivo was in despair over me; he wanted to know what I'd been doing when the "rudiments of these disciplines" (his phrase) were taught me in school. I could only say I'd forgotten, they'd gone from my mind, entirely evaporated. To save my life I couldn't have done Pythagoras' Theorem or explained Boyle's Law.

He said if some people were illiterate and others innumerate I was inscientious. Of course I took him up on that, asked what sort of Latin roots he thought those were, didn't he know "scientia" meant knowledge, not science? Did he realize he was actually calling me ignorant?

"All right," he said, "if you want to put it that way, you are. In the nineteenth century they'd have thought it ridiculous to go to a university to study English literature. That was something a man picked up in the course of the intellectual life. What was it after all but reading a few plays and pieces of poetry?"

I was hurt and we quarreled. He gave me Stephen Jay Gould to read and Lewis Thomas and John Bleibtreu and took out a subscription for me to *New Scientist* magazine. After puzzling over the first few issues I stopped even opening them, and Ivo found a pile of them later still in their plastic wrapping.

Perhaps love, real love, would have triumphed over this. In Ivo's case it did. He loved me even though I believed in—or had never thought of believing or not believing in—the inheritance of acquired characteristics in natural selection. Perhaps he loved me more, because my ignorance meant that he could instruct me in the theories of Lyell and Darwin and the errors of Lamarck. It probably wasn't his fault that I didn't listen, that I was bored. These lessons reminded me of childhood sessions with my father when he insisted on reading Kipling aloud to me. Ivo often said he wasn't aiming to teach me as he taught his students, only a little to lighten the darkness in which I lived. I was as ignorant, he said, as those

Elizabethans whose drama I'd spent so much time studying, and I didn't even have their pseudosciences of astrology and divination and other mumbo-jumbo; I had nothing.

But he loved me. In spite of everything he loved me, he couldn't help himself. One day I made him happy by remembering that there was something called the Pleistocene period. Of course I couldn't remember anything about it or when it was and I only remembered the name because it reminded me of Plasticine, a pliable clay for children's use that came before Play-Doh and of which I was very fond when about eight.

Then I maddened him by questioning Darwin's theory of evolution. Ivo was a totally committed neo-Darwinist and he refused to allow any alternative belief. When I said that it was just as likely God had made Adam and Eve and put them in a garden as that everything had reached where it was by chance, he got really angry.

"There is no room for opinion here. Darwin is *true*."

"It's not true like two and two make four is true, though, is it? You needn't shout."

"The comparison you make is stupid and ignorant, but, yes, it is an irrefutable truth about man and the physical world. You'll be saying next that Archbishop Ussher was right and something called God put the fossils in the rocks in four thousand four B.C."

"You can't prove he didn't," I said, "any more than you can prove your origin of species and that we all came from chimps."

Ivo shouted that this was the blinkered layman's view, Darwin had never said we came from chimpanzees. What had he said then, I asked, and we went through the whole business again. Ivo had a framed cartoon of Darwin in his bedroom, the naturalist's bushy-bearded face attached to the hairy body of an ape. I always found it repulsive, not to say off-putting, and one night I turned its face to the wall. It was several days before Ivo noticed.

All this sounds like a small thing, but it wasn't. I may have argued with Ivo, but I was beginning to feel that his intellect towered over mine, that he was proud of this, and in spite of the instruction he was always trying to give me, wanted to keep it that way. When I was unfaithful to him it was partly to assert myself, to feel that I was a separate person with a separate life, and perhaps that there was a society out there that didn't give a shit about neutrons, Gray's yearly genesis parameter, sea gel solids, and DNA.

Ivo had to go to a conference in Glasgow. He wanted me to go with him and I wouldn't. I knew what it would be like, all those scientists talking incomprehensibly and when they found out—as they would in two minutes—that I wasn't Ivo's assistant, either ignoring me or treating me like some catamite he'd picked up on the highway. I said I needed three days to myself to get on with my novel.

Since moving in with him I'd lost what friends I'd made in creative writing. They'd never been much more than acquaintances. Emily and her coterie had given up their persecution of me; now they ignored me and, for some reason, the men in the course followed suit. What reason I didn't know, for I doubt if anyone ever guessed about Ivo and me, and if they had, surely my own contemporaries in the 1980s would have been more open-minded than to ostracize me for being gay? I didn't know then, but I think I know now, and it doesn't make for comfortable self-appraisal.

I wasn't lonely when Ivo was there but once he was gone the loneliness increased with every passing hour. On the second evening I did a daring thing. Ivo wasn't the sort of man who goes to places like that but he'd once in passing pointed out from the car P.'s only gay club. I repeated to myself the old courage-boosting formula, "They can't kill you," and went down there on the bus, Ivo having taken the car to Glasgow.

Strange really, isn't it, that I should quote that formula now? After all, I know if anyone does that it's not foolproof. Most people say it some time or other, but if Ivo had said it before we embarked on that flimsy little boat for Chechin Island, if he'd said to himself, "They can't kill you," how wrong he'd have been. They could. Or, rather, I could. I did. It was such a gray day, the fog hanging in curtains over the mountains, even the shoreline, the place made ugly by the stultifying heavy obscuring mists. The sea was gray with little dancing waves, no fin piercing its surface, no phocine creature showing itself. Only the small, darker gray shape of the island, a shallow triangle, and its rock chimney wrapped in cloud—but the time hasn't come for this. Not yet. It will come, it must, but not yet. Now I'm on the bus going across town to William Street and the Fedora Club to meet there and pick up, really to be picked up by, the pretty Indian boy called Mansoor.

There's no point in describing the place or him. I took him back to Ivo's. Martin saw us come in but I don't think he suspected anything. He was on the stairs, having come in late himself, his cat stalking up ahead of him, and when he'd said good evening, asked me please to keep the doors shut on the next day, the drafts had been terrible lately. He probably took Mansoor for a fellow student.

Back in N. for Christmas, separated from Ivo for two weeks while he visited some old Cambridge professor who'd once taught him, I made friends with a girl I met at the ballet. Suzanne wasn't a dancer but something like an assistant deputy stage manager. We went to bed three times and when she had to leave and go up north with the company I didn't make arrangements to meet her again. I said good-bye and it had been nice but there was someone else.

It sounds strange, perhaps it sounds crazy, but I confessed both these infidelities to Ivo for what seemed to me at the time perfectly cogent reasons. The gay philosophy or lifestyle or mystique, whatever you like to call it, I'd never really got the hang of. What I had were a lot of ideas about it that were somehow off-balance. For instance, I believed that gay men were *always* much more promiscuous and inconstant than heterosexual people. I thought it was something to be taken for granted even in couples who were couples, who were living together in what on the face of it was a one-to-one relationship. I thought Ivo might have had someone else while he was in Glasgow and someone else in Cambridge, and when I didn't much like that idea I put this down to my not being all gay, being at least bisexual and perhaps not gay at all really. I was very confused.

As to Suzanne, believe it or not, I thought it wouldn't matter to Ivo about her because she was a woman and therefore this infidelity wouldn't be "real" to him. He couldn't be in competition with her.

While my being with Mansoor he would see as just a diversion when he wasn't there, something all gay men did, part of a cottaging philosophy. There were even couples who did it together, Mansoor had told me, picking up two or perhaps just one boy to take home, in perfect mutual approval and harmony.

I felt injured and shocked because Ivo didn't take it that way. Why had I told him at all, he wanted to know. He'd rather have not known, he'd rather have remained in ignorance. His jealousy and his hurt were so great they even altered his appearance. They made his face go soft and lined with pain. I muttered something about his having once said we must be honest with each other.

"I didn't mean about things like that," he said, and he sounded young and confused. He sounded like me.

Of course he "forgave" me. If you love someone and want to be with them you haven't much choice but to do this. It was early spring, our second spring together, and he began talking about going to Alaska. I'd forgotten he'd booked up for me, I'd also forgotten he must have paid for me, but I calculated that it wouldn't be expensive—there I was wrong—as Ivo had said these cruises weren't luxurious.

By this time I didn't want to go. I'd started thinking about my future. By the time we were due to go away I'd have my M.A. What was I going to do? Not write fiction, of that I was becoming increasingly sure, and not stay in P. London beckoned. I needed a job, I should need money. Going away, perhaps even abroad some-where, would ensure a natural break with Ivo, for his job was here at the Institute of Ontogeny, and there was no prospect of his following me to wherever I went. The end for me and Ivo was in sight and it was a kind of relief to think about it in these terms. I could tell myself that come August we should have parted.

He'd changed in more ways than just appearance. That soft look had gone and in that respect he was back to normal. But he'd begun to watch me. Not begun, no. He watched me all the time, and although I could never prove this I know he set someone else to watch me too. Not a real private detective, nothing so professional and unscrupulous, but just someone he paid a small amount to hang about outside and see what I did, where I went.

When I wasn't at the university, at a lecture or a tutorial, and mostly at this stage I wasn't, I was at home writing my novel. It was strange, neurotic really, writing about a particular kind of disturbed, fraught love affair while I was in much the same kind of love affair myself. From the window, when I looked up from the typewriter, I could see this boy watching the house. The odd thing was that I'd seen him somewhere before, though I couldn't think where. Usually he was in a parked car but sometimes on foot, strolling along the opposite pavement. It took me two or three days to realize I was being spied on. Once I did, I started going out the back way. This meant climbing over the fence and dropping down into the lane behind, but it was worth it to fool the watcher.

Then I decided to do better and give the watcher something to report back. By this time I'd realized where I'd seen him before. It was at the Fedora, the one and only time I'd been there. Having escaped by the back fence, I had the good luck to run into Roberta of Dempster Road days. She seemed to bear me no malice, so I asked her back for a cup of tea. The watcher was there in his car, taking photographs for all I know. I'd kept Mansoor's phone number and, though I didn't want him for sex ever again, I rang him up, asked him over and said we could go out for a drink. When he came I took care to keep him there for an hour before we left for the pub. Without his car that day, the watcher dived into the phone box when he saw us emerge, but he saw us all right.

Ivo never said a word about any of this. He never reproached me, he never asked, and I think this made me worse. I, who'd been almost reclusive, invited home everyone I encountered: Sharif one afternoon, Jeremy another. And then, after he'd kept up his surveillance for a month, the boy disappeared, never to be seen again. Ivo had decided he could no longer afford his services or that my promiscuity was so excessive that it was pointless to record separate instances of it. Perhaps too he thought there was safety in numbers.

One day he said to me, out of the blue, "That first time, at Martin's, why did you come up to me and touch me?"

"I don't know," I said. "I'd never done it to anyone before."

"Were you lonely? Did you see me as a father figure?"

"I suppose I found you attractive," I said.

He looked thoughtful. "Yes," he said. "Yes. You would put it like that. 'Attractive' is nearly as debased a word as 'nice,' it means nothing more than provoking a sexual itch, if that. Do you know what I thought when you touched me that day?"

I didn't want to know. I found a courage I hadn't yet been able to summon up. "Don't start, Ivo, please, do you mind?"

"No," he said quietly, "I don't mind. It's better if I don't tell you. Better for me, and I can't say I care how you feel."

"Thanks very much."

"I should have gone on as I meant to when I began," he said. "I know that now. Stayed cool, kept you guessing, kept my feelings to myself. But I didn't because I loved you. Too bad, isn't it? I love you too much for your own good and far too much for mine."

He was right there. At the time I'm afraid I just felt embarrassed. If he'd been sentimental with me that evening I truly think that would have been the end. I told myself I could have taken it from a woman, not from a man. The term and the course had only a couple more weeks to run and I think I'd have got out if he'd tried to talk about love to me then, I'd have found someone whose floor I could have slept on for those twelve or fourteen nights. But he was soon cold and practical, phoning his sister, marking essays, making a list of what I'd need for Alaska. We'd had no sex for a week and at ten sharp he went into his bedroom and shut the door behind him.

The devil in me that makes me conduct myself like this became active again. Ivo didn't want me, or appeared not to want me, so once more I wanted him. I forgot about not really being gay, not being bisexual, about really being a woman's man. For me Ivo became again simply the most attractive *person* I'd ever known. Was gender all that important, after all? Surely the civilized man desired the nature, the essence, the personality, not something dependant on physical shape, an extraneous bit here, a channel there. So I argued with myself, growing hungry for Ivo, dry-mouthed, his shut door an affront to me. His voice began once more to tease me and his tired dark eyes ("your unfathomed eyes," in the immortal verse of Gilman) began as of old to draw me to him.

It's useless to say it now, but I can't help it. If I'd kept myself aloof till the end of term, if I'd said what I'd made up my mind I felt, that it wasn't going to work, that it would soon be over, and above all, that I was sorry but I couldn't come to Alaska, he could say what he liked, storm at me as much as he liked, but I couldn't go with him, if I'd done that I would never have met Isabel or seen those sinister little towns or Chechin Island and he'd be alive now.

I fell asleep over the typewriter this evening. It was because I'd decided the upright chair I usually sit in was too hard, so I'm in an armchair, one of my parents' aged Parker-Knolls that look so ugly but are very comfortable. Weariness overcame me as I laid back my head for a moment and with sleep came Ivo in a dream.

Of course I've been aware of him in the room with me all evening, looking over my shoulder. And in the dream, anyway, he didn't come to me; I went to him. I went to him as I did in life, five nights before term ended, knocking on a closed door and, when admitted, going to him as I had done that first time at Martin's, to lay my fingers on his face and draw them gently down his cheek. In reality we'd made love, a rapturous resumption of a sex relation lost for too long; in the dream he changed into Isabel as I touched him, and I saw something I had never seen before, that they were alike, that they looked alike. I awoke, crying out.

The next day, close to me again, he gave me a batch of traveler's checks and $100. He checked up on my clothes, to see that I had the right waterproof gear, sound boots. Whatever I might think now, I should need binoculars. I should *want* if not *need* a camera.

The arrangement was that after the trip was over I'd fly to Portland, Oregon, and stay with someone Ivo knew there. He'd be fulfilling his obligations as a cruise lecturer and would join me later. A Greyhound bus tour of northern California had been fixed up for me before I flew back to meet him in Seattle. San Francisco was an obvious place for any newcomer to the western United States to visit, a "must," but Ivo had noticeably left it out of my itinerary, and of course I knew why. I was not to be exposed to the temptations of the world's gayest city.

Thus appeared the first new cloud in our sky. Who wouldn't resent being treated like a tempted child? I should have said no at this point. I didn't. I kept telling myself that if I didn't take this opportunity it might be years before another chance came. In any case, if I was careful with my money I might manage to save enough to take me over the Golden Gate on my own initiative.

But suddenly, the day before we left, Ivo said to me that he supposed I'd like to see San Francisco, he couldn't think how he'd come to leave it out. Of course I wondered what had occasioned this change of heart and concluded it was intended as a sop to me for having to suffer something quite unexpected and unwelcome. For the first part of our trip I was to be left alone in Juneau.

"I'm sorry," he said. "I got the dates wrong. I thought I was starting my first lecture cruise on the seventeenth but I find it's the tenth and you're booked in for the twenty-fourth."

Ivo wasn't a liar, but I didn't see how this could be true. He had been talking about this for nine months, he'd gone on at least six of these cruises in previous years. Was it probable, was it even possible, that he had made all these arrangements for me, had carefully planned such tight itineraries, yet made such a glaring mistake in the starting date? He must have some other motive, I thought. There must be someone going on that first week's cruise he didn't want me to meet, he must have changed the dates for me to keep me out of mischief. When challenged he only said he'd got it wrong, even he sometimes got things wrong, and he smiled his tired, worn smile.

I remained convinced, however, and I'm still convinced. There can be no other explanation. Some member of the ship's crew, some other lecturer, even some passenger, expected to be on board during that week beginning the tenth, would have constituted a threat to him and a chance for me. He wangled things, he pulled strings to avoid it, and as a result I was to be left to twiddle my thumbs (as Clarissa puts it) for thirteen days in what was surely Hicksville at the ends of the earth.

Juneau.

Ivo wasn't to know that I'd meet Isabel there, at the Goncharof Hotel in Juneau. What temptation on board ship could have matched her? Who could have threatened him one half so much as she threatened him?

7

When people visit new countries they read up about them before-hand. Or so I've heard. I never have. But until then I hadn't been to many countries, only the usual holiday places in Spain and Italy and, of course, to Paris with Ivo.

We had a *Fodor's Guide to Alaska* lying around and a couple of books by John Muir. I meant to look at them but I couldn't get down to it. I just wasn't interested. I didn't even know what part of Alaska we were actually going to because I hadn't looked at the atlas. On the other hand, I knew what it would be like from Ivo's letters of the summer before, temperate rain forest that feels cold and wet, a natural-history excursion that wouldn't be so very different from camping out in the rain.

My feelings must have shown because it was then that Ivo began really reprimanding me and taking me up on everything I said. He'd always had his sarcastic spells, but now he was everlastingly telling me off. I didn't protest much, I put up with it, anything for a quiet life. But every day that brought our departure nearer reinforced my feeling that I simply didn't want to go. At the same time I knew I was going, I couldn't get out of it at that stage, I'd resigned myself to the inevitable. Besides that, I had the idea that if I went on this trip I'd somehow be set free to tell Ivo as soon as it was over that we'd come to the parting of the ways. It was quite irrational, I knew that, but it was what I felt and it was a kind of pact I made with myself. Go with him, I was saying, not to enjoy yourself, not to expect that, not for anything but because he wants you to, go on sufferance, grit your teeth and endure, and then somehow you can leave him, put it all behind you and everything will be all right.

Who do we think is listening when we make these bargains? Who or what is going to make things right because we've honored our part of the contract?

My M.A. was assured and I didn't much mind missing the degree congregation at the beginning of July. The day after the University of P. broke for the summer I borrowed Ivo's car, filled it with all my stuff, including the novel about the young man and the older woman, and drove it to N. The day after that we flew to Vancouver and thence to Juneau.

The way "Goncharof" was spelled and the fact that "hotel" was put after the name and not before it did more than anything in those first hours to show me I was in the United States. That was something else I'd forgotten or not thought about. But everything was astonishing. Everything was a surprise from the moment we landed.

The weather, for a start. It was eighty degrees and the sun blazing hot. The sky was bright blue and the air the cleanest and clearest I've ever known. The only snow was on top of the mountains. The sea was blue and the grass was green, only these were like platonic ideals of green and blue, the truest, the brightest, the most perfect. And you could stand, surrounded by all this, as we did at the airport, looking at the bright, clear, pristine beauty and yet feel the sun hot on your skin. I started to feel happy. Contemptible, really, to think that this is what good weather can do.

The airport is about eight miles out of Juneau. We went there in a taxi and on the way we saw a little black bear fishing on the wetlands. Ivo smiled and pointed. He was as proud as if it belonged to him, as if he'd trained it and put it there himself. Except that when I said this to him, hoping he'd be pleased, all he said was: "I wouldn't own, still less train, any animal."

He'd been morose ever since we left Vancouver. But nothing

could have lowered my spirits except perhaps if he'd said the arrangements had been changed and I'd be going with him the next day. There's something oppressive about being with a person that you know disapproves of you and loves you at the same time. I was suddenly very much looking forward to being left alone, even if it was going to be for nearly two weeks. And if I was a bit taken aback at first to find that he'd booked a double room for us at the Goncharof, I soon told myself I'd be sharing it for only one night.

On the way, remarking on the Russian names we saw up on billboards and signposts, I'd been treated to an acidulous lecture on the occupation of Alaska by the Russians. Apparently the United States bought the place from them in the 1860s. Looking out of the car window, I thought I could see why anyone would want to buy it and that it had come cheap at the price. Later on I was to revise this opinion. But on that glorious afternoon I was in love with everything I saw, the long blue fjord, the neat houses with waterfront gardens, the flowers everywhere that were the flowers of spring, over at home two months since. I don't know the names of flowers—well, tulips and daffodils I know and they were out in June, as well as trees with pink blossoms on them and yellow buttercups in the grass.

They call it a city, Juneau. They call every village a city in America. But Juneau looked more like a country town to me, not a bit English, Canadian perhaps, I wouldn't know, with little crooked streets and little touristy shops. The mountains covered in pine trees soared up behind, and among the trees were the scars of gold mining.

The taxi driver wanted to take us on a "city tour" that was to include the governor's mansion and the state capitol. I wouldn't have minded, but Ivo was adamant. Straight to the hotel. I've said I was in love with everything I saw, but it would have taken someone absolutely obsessed to love the Goncharof, or at least to love its appearance.

It occupied the whole area between the High Street or Main Street, whatever they called it, and the roads that turned out at right angles toward the harbor. "The entire block," the driver said. It was made of dark purplish-grayish-red brick. If you had to name the worst color in the world, I think most people would choose that one, a kind of dried-blood-mixed-with-ashes color or red rose petals ground into the mud or the scab on a dark-skinned person's wound.

(That was my creative writing getting the better of me. I must watch it.)

The main entrance was on one corner, no doubt to give the architect the chance to put in a curved flight of steps up to the door that filled a whole half-circle. These were of concrete with a bit of Astroturf up the middle. A sort of onion dome, a very Russian dome, painted a dull gray and red, soared above the steps and was held up by eight pillars in granite, or if not granite some ostentatiously veined gray marble.

"Hideous," I said. "Did the Russians build it?"

"The Russians had gone thirty years before it was built," said Ivo. "Don't you ever listen?"

"Then I can't see why they didn't make it more attractive."

"Ah, your favorite word. We haven't heard it much lately. I was beginning to miss it. This is the most expensive hotel in Juneau I've brought you to, so you must make the best of it."

He was doing his making-me-feel-like-a-bimbo bit again. The driver picked it up and smirked to himself. I said no more. We checked in and were treated to a long apology from the reception clerk for the lack of air conditioning. They never had this weather, this was freak weather, nothing like it had been seen for years, and so on. While Ivo was filling in forms and we waited for someone to carry our bags up, I had a look round. It was comfortable but gloomy, excessively, unexpectedly somber and drab. Large sofas stood about, upholstered in dark brown leather or rust-red velvet. The rest of the furniture was either of marble or polished wood with metal decoration. Is that called buhl, or is it ormolu?

I'd swear the houseplants were aspidistra. Oil paintings of snowy landscapes or hunting scenes covered great sections of wall. The sun didn't penetrate here and lamps were on, their bulbs glimmering under parchment shades.

Never having been in the United States before, I didn't know then that all American bars are either fairly dark or very dark. No doubt the drinkers like it that way. The bar at the Goncharof was a vast elongated chamber, in which free use had been made of pillars, this time in dull yellow marble. They gleamed faintly through the dimness like so many trunks of trees in a petrified forest. You could just make out the deep, curlicued ornate carvings on the ceiling, the unlit electroliers of steel-gray metal, as many-armed as some Indian goddess, the heavy folds of velvet curtains tightly drawn across the windows, velvet of a color undiscernible, slate-gray or chocolate or that dreadful blood-ash, it was impossible to tell.

If there hadn't been people sitting at tables, a very few at four in the afternoon but still people just visible in the gloom, I might have supposed it was closed until evening, when perhaps all would become a place of light and liveliness. But there was no doubt the bar was operating. A barman in a monkey jacket moved desultorily between the tables. Behind the bar, where ranks of bottles glittered, a single lamp was lit. Under an ocherish parchment shade painted with some ancient oceanic map, the lamplight shed a yellowness like the sodium vapor that gives such an unearthly look to motorways at home.

I remarked on it to Ivo in the lift. He said coldly that things were different abroad; if they weren't there would be no point in going away. The boy who was carrying our bags grinned to himself. I pictured myself sitting in that bar with Ivo in the dark for half the evening, neither of us speaking, me drinking too much, and I resolved that nothing would get me in there, tonight or ever. I had no way then of knowing how much I'd come to love the bar of the Goncharof, what sanctuary it would provide and its darkness what cover for an increasing passion.

The radio was on in our bedroom when the bellboy led us in. It was one of the best bedrooms and perhaps that was why, out of deference to whatever the Alaskans call a better class of guest, the radio was switched to a program that plays classical music all day long—and all night, for all I know.

What exactly it was playing when we arrived I don't know,

Mozart perhaps, I was walking about examining the bathroom, the way the windows opened and what was in the fridge. The grim Victorian decor extended only to the ground floor and our bedroom was bright and light with a normal carpet, light-colored armchairs, and a television.

Then the music changed and they started playing the great waltz from *Rosenkavalier.* Ivo smiled. He quoted my translation of Ochs's song, "With you—am I wrong?—No night is too long," and then he said he was sorry, he was bitterly sorry for the way he'd spoken to me, he would never speak like that to me again, and he came over to me and took me in his arms.

I wrote all that yesterday, quite late at night. I expected to dream as a result and I did, but not about the Goncharof Hotel or Isabel, not about the dark bar or the bright weather, not about the champagne we drank that evening or the dinner we ate in the restaurant on Front Street.

I dreamed about drowned Ivo coming up out of the sea.

I was leaning over the seawall. It was night but moonlight and there was no one about except that I could see a fishing boat a long way out. The sea was flat calm, a thin skin of it crawling over the stones and slipping back with a sigh as the tide slowly came in. Everything was gray and silvery and as quiet as death.

The waters parted and Ivo reared up out of them like a dog surfacing, and like a dog he shook himself. He shook his wet hair, which was long, which came down to his waist. And then he began to pull it off and I saw that it wasn't hair, it was seaweed. His clothes were pale and greenish from long immersion. They clung to his skeletal thinness. He left the sea and stood for a moment at the point the encroaching tide had reached. Then he came on, up across the stone-filled sand, over the ridge where there is nothing but stones, and toward me, toward me, between where the lifeboat stands and the hut where the fishermen sell their catch.

I would have liked to turn and run. Is there any feeling of paralysis comparable to being weighted to the ground in dreams? I couldn't move. My feet were planted in the stones. Ivo came to me and I saw that he was blind. Sea creatures had eaten his eyes. He took me in his arms, in his wet stinking embrace, and held me tighter as I struggled with such terrible revulsion, such sick horror.

And all the way through I never knew it was a dream. I wasn't granted even that consolation. When I woke out of what seemed hours of wrestling with a corpse I was wet, soaked in sweat, streaming with it.

It took me a while to get over the dream. I had to get up, open the window and put my head out into the cold. I'd only experienced that floundering in a sweat bath once before and that was our first night in Juneau. But there it was from the heat. The windows in our bedroom wouldn't open very far, I suppose there were seldom occasions when guests wanted to open them at all, and the thick air smelled of sex and Ivo's cigarettes and the champagne he'd had sent up after dinner. He hadn't drunk much but I had, I'd got through a bottle and a half. It was the only way for me to make lovemaking possible. I could only do it when I was stupefied and sledgehammered with drink. The sweat streamed off me in the night and the sheet under me grew cold and clammy.

Ivo was awake, but he didn't speak to me. I could see a gleam of light on his open eyes. He was on his back, staring at the ceiling. It shows what a state I'd reached when I say I was so guilty already by that time and so apprehensive of the future that, though the bed was a king size, I made myself lie on the cold damp patch to cover it up. I didn't want him to reach out and touch it. I felt as I had long ago, when I was six or seven, and for the last time in my life I wet the bed, guilty and horrified and wanting to do anything to keep it hidden.

My head was bad in the morning, but I knew better than to mention that to Ivo. He wanted to take me up in a helicopter to the Mendenhall Glacier and I'd said I'd go, so I went. All the way in the taxi taking us to the helicopter pad he talked about glaciers, what they were and how they had formed, using expressions like "resistant strata" and "bedrock jointing." I suppose I must have learned something about glaciers when I was at school, but if I did I can't remember. It was new to me and something I didn't particularly want to learn about. I knew the glacier would be beautiful and perhaps awe-inspiring in the brilliant sunshine and that was enough for me.

It wasn't enough for Ivo. The thing was I had the impression he was getting a sort of grim pleasure out of boring me. He was tormenting himself, of course, because it actually pained him that I was so uninterested in what amounted to a passion for him. But he couldn't help going on with it. He wanted to see how far he could go, how long before my eyes closed with the boredom of it or I screamed out at him to stop. His lips twitched once in an effort to stop an outbreak of bitter laughter. Perhaps too he saw it as a test of my love, that I'd endure this tedium for his sake.

All the people at the helicopter pad knew him. They seemed overjoyed to see him again. The youngest, a girl of about twenty, called him Dr. Steadman in a very respectful way. I'd never been up in a helicopter before but I didn't let on. We walked on the ice and looked down into the bottomless pools of blue water ("your unfathomed eyes") and Ivo gave me another lecture on how cold the water was and how deep, so that anyone falling in wouldn't survive for more than a few moments.

The ship he'd be embarking on that afternoon was in dock. We walked down to have a look at it. Its name was the *Favonia,* one of a line in which all the vessels were named after Roman women, *Fimbria, Flaminia, Fulvia,* and so on. It looked smallish and shabby to me but I said nothing. The registration was Liberian, out of Monrovia, but the officers were German, Ivo said, and the crew, as I could see for myself, Korean. Food was going on board, crates of cauliflowers and bananas. Someone behind a porthole waved to Ivo and he waved back.

We were back there by four for him to go aboard. He hadn't much baggage, just a backpack and a case. A man and a woman can embrace when one of them goes away, they can hug each other in public, they can kiss, and onlookers don't mind, they think it's nice, it's touching. I didn't especially want to kiss Ivo then, but I resented the fact that I couldn't, that we'd had to have our good-bye kiss in a hotel bedroom. I even said something about it to him.

"I wonder if it'll take twenty years or fifty years before it's possible for someone like me to kiss someone like you in public."

"Oh, I'll be dead before it comes to that," he said.

He did something unexpected. He took off his jacket, a leather one that had been very good once and whose shabbiness I liked, and handed it to me.

"Wear that while I'm gone. If it doesn't remind you at least you'll know you look better in it than I do." ("Wear this for me," Gilman had said, giving me a scarf for a snowman.)

Ivo patted my shoulder and went off up the gangway. I watched him for a while, walking along the deck toward what I now know was the staircase down. Once he turned and waved to me. Then, quite suddenly, a door opened and someone he knew came out, a man in uniform who shook hands with him and slapped him on the back. They were immediately talking animatedly.

I'd been feeling guilty and miserable up to that point, but seeing Ivo meet someone he knew had a strange effect on me. I felt like a parent must when he takes his son back to school at the beginning of term. He's guilty about leaving the boy but when he sees his son is all right, he's found a friend, in minutes he'll have forgotten his family and his home—when he sees that he knows the boy's fine and he can leave him, certain he'll be happy. That's how it was for me. My father had become my son, just as he'd be my father again one day. I was learning how endlessly interchangeable such relationships are.

My relief, or the euphoria it brought, didn't last long. I'd decided to go for a walk round the town once Ivo had gone and I set off up Main Street toward the Capitol. Ever since we arrived in Juneau I'd been looking forward to this freedom, this being alone, and now I told myself to begin enjoying it.

Without a guidebook, I'd no idea what the buildings were apart from the Capitol—more marble pillars—and the little Russian Orthodox church. But I pressed on, walking the grid-plan streets and those that weren't in the grid, up to the governor's mansion and Gold Creek. There weren't many people about and hardly any cars. The sky was still without a cloud and the sun still hot and bright.

Back to the waterfront at last and all the way along Egon Drive once more. The *Favonia* was gone. She must have left while I was exploring the town, gone out on the tide, or whatever the expression is. I hadn't told Ivo I'd watch her go out, but somehow I knew he'd have expected me to do that, come back at five-thirty for that purpose. Now I remembered he'd told me they expected to leave Juneau at five-thirty, and I felt a pang of guilt. Or not guilt perhaps, but something else. I realized I felt Ivo would be *cross* with me for not being there to see him off. I wasn't even acting like a bimbo but like a child. Father was back. I was afraid Daddy would be cross with me for not obeying him.

This told me more than anything could have that being with Ivo was bad for me. Continuing with him would just make things worse and worse. He would grow more hectoring and didactic and superior, I more petulant and coy and sulky. It would sap my will and ultimately destroy me. The whole of this trip was misconceived, I should have known better than to have come on it and now I wished I hadn't. I realized something else as well as I began walking back to the Goncharof, something on a far more mundane level. What on earth was I going to do with myself for thirteen days till Ivo came back?

It panicked me. I suppose I hadn't thought of it before, only of being free. But free to do what? Walk round the cemetery? Visit the museum? And then what? Knowing myself as I thought I did, I imagined picking up someone, boy or girl, in the Red Dog Saloon. Finding some bad company and getting drunk evening after evening. If I avoided that, maybe I could have a lot of big meals and spin out the time spent eating them—but on my own?

And what, come to that, had Ivo thought I'd do? Or hadn't he cared? He knew I was about as uninterested in plants and trees and climate, rocks and terrain and birds, as anyone could be. Like most people I get a kick out of seeing a bear or a wolf in the wild, but that's about it. I couldn't help feeling he was punishing me, this was all punishment and reproof, and for some reason it brought to mind an old saw or jingle my aunt Clarissa used to repeat to me when I was small. When I said I didn't care about something, she used to wag her finger at me and say: *Don't care was made to care/Don't care was hung./Don't care was put in the pot/And boiled till he was done.* I'd said I didn't care a good many times to Ivo. Goaded, I'd told him I didn't care about Darwin and his theory, whether he was right or wrong; I didn't care whether igneous rocks came before plutonic rocks or the other way about; and I didn't care about fossils, the whole idea of fossils made me want to curl up and die. So he was punishing me. Don't care was to be made to care.

I went into the great foyer of the Goncharof. Stacks of suitcases stood about. There'd been a new influx of tourists off the aircraft from Vancouver we'd come on and which got to Juneau in the late afternoon. I went up to our room, *my* room. I'd suddenly had a rather wonderful idea. Why shouldn't I just go home? Ivo had left me money and traveler's checks. I had plenty for a car to the airport, meals in Vancouver, even a sightseeing tour of Vancouver or a day or two in that city. There seemed no reason why I shouldn't get on tomorrow's flight out.

He'd asked for it, there was no doubt about that. And I was going to leave him anyway. I told myself it would be kinder to leave him now than raise his hopes and give him a false security by going on this cruise with him. He'd come back and find me gone and that would be the best thing for both of us. I wouldn't see the American West Coast, of course, the Golden Gate Bridge and the bay; Seattle, supposedly the most desirable place in the United States in which to live; Oregon and Washington State; and California, which has such a glamorous ring to it. But I was young, I'd plenty of time to come back.

I've often thought, since then, how different things would have been if I'd gone then as I meant to. Whatever had happened to me, my life must have been happier. Ivo would be still alive. I would never have met Isabel, and that means, like someone says in Shakespeare, that I'd have left unseen a very wonderful piece of work. But I'd have averted a lot of misery, for her as well as for me, I expect.

But I can't have any real regrets, still less reproach myself, over not leaving next day. My failure to go wasn't due to anything I did but to what you'd call a technical matter. I was so ignorant of travel arrangements, I'd only been in an aircraft twice before, and it never occurred to me a return ticket wouldn't necessarily take me back when I wanted to go. I even thought myself quite clever and *grown-up*, picking up the phone and asking reception to get me the number of Juneau airport so that I could make—and I even got the correct American term—a reservation.

I got through to them and they soon put me right. Mine was a Apex ticket, didn't I realize that? I didn't even know what they meant. Experience is the best teacher, as Martin Zeindler once said, quoting probably, but she takes very high wages. I felt I was paying some of those wages when the twangy voice, barely concealing its scorn, told me that on this ticket I could only return on August 4 (or whatever it was) and not before or after. Unless I paid a return fare, of course. I didn't have to add up the sums on those traveler's checks to know I hadn't even half the sum the flight would cost.

So I was doomed to stay, I was trapped, I couldn't escape. Something Ivo had said earlier in the day came back to me. You can get to places in southeast Alaska by ship or plane, but forget the roads. What roads exist run a few dozen miles out from the towns and then come to a dead end. The famous Alaska Highway was a long way inland.

All this time I hadn't put Ivo's jacket on. I'd been carrying it around, holding it slung over my shoulder, and then, I'd laid it on the bed. I put it on to go downstairs and, naturally I suppose, put my hand into the pocket. The notes crackled in my fingers. I pulled them out and saw they amounted to nearly a hundred dollars. He had given me his purse, that was what it amounted to, only purses these days have become jackets. It wasn't enough to get away, though.

After a while I went down in the lift. The front window of the Goncharof faced due west but the sun wasn't setting yet, it was hours off sunset. The summer nights are long in Alaska. A funny thought came to me then, that I liked night better than day, dim places or artificially lit places better than natural light and sunshine. Ivo liked daylight and fresh air, cool winds, and the drafts that so annoyed Martin Zeindler, and that was another of our incompatibilities.

I went into the bar. Where else?

Isn't it in one of the *Just So Stories* that Kipling says some creature in the darkness of the jungle was like a mustard plaster on a sack of coals? Yet she wasn't a bit like that, the simile is all wrong. She was a bright thing in the darkness, but as a star is bright in the night sky, as the Parthenon radiant by moonlight.

She was waiting for me at the end of the world.

8

I can see Isabel now. The impression I have is so vivid that I have only to shut my eyes to get a picture of her on that dark screen, under my closed eyelids. And I don't mean some vague image, half created in words and half from memory, I mean a real picture, like a colored photograph. There she sits on her high stool, her very slim, very lithe body turned sideways so that I can see how small her waist is. Her head has turned right round and she is looking at me appraisingly. Her hair is very dark brown, shiny and long, with a fringe just touching eyebrows that look as if drawn with a soft brush. She lifts a lock of that fringe back and combs it into her hair with two fingers. Then she stops looking at me and returns rather suddenly to her book.

So Isabel was . . . what? It's an odd thing to write but I don't know if she was good looking or not. I know she wasn't pretty and I know she couldn't have been described by that word Ivo said I was so fond of: attractive. She had a beautiful body and beautiful hands and feet. Her mouth was large, the lips with a swollen look and of equal size. In fact, strangely, her upper lip and her lower lip were exactly the same. I don't think I've ever seen this before or since in anyone. Her mouth was red but naturally that way. She never wore makeup.

Her skin was eggshell white with a faint sheen on its utter smoothness. But the most remarkable things about her were her eyes, a clear depthless hazel, large and tremendously shadowed, the eyelids domelike, a smooth grape color. I think it was the only time I've ever noticed the color of someone's eyes on first seeing them. The dark hair, the feathery fringe, framed her strange, rather long, hollow-cheeked face. In the moment her eyes met mine I thought how sleepy she looked, yet she sat on up there, uncomfortably perched, reading a book she had to hold up with both hands.

Her eyes were on me only for a second. I couldn't take mine from her. I found myself studying her, everything about her, the simple clothes she wore, a short black skirt, a white shirt, a jacket of tweed I suppose, a fine black and white tweed. A thin gold chain bracelet was around one wrist. Her shoes were black, with heels but not high heels. I watched her take a cigarette, light it, put the packet and matchbook back in the pocket of her jacket.

A distance of no more than ten feet separated us and we two were apart from the other people in the bar. In fact, we were isolated here because this was the nonsmoking area. I hoped the barman would come up to her and ask her to stop smoking because then I would hear her voice. But the barman seemed to have disappeared. It was hard to see in that dimly lit place. For all I could make out of what went on in the smoky depths beyond the mottled yellow pillars, we might have been quite alone, she and I.

This was one reason why it seemed almost wrong not to speak to her. I knew Americans were very sociable people. I might never have been in the United States before but I'd encountered enough American tourists. You could never sit in a train with one of them without being asked where you came from, what you did, and where you'd been to "school." Probably she *expected* me to speak to her, it wouldn't be an attempt at a pick-up in her eyes, it would just be a normal friendly gesture. At this moment, because I hadn't spoken, she was no doubt setting me down as a typical cold, reserved Brit.

I was longing to talk to her. I was curious to hear her voice, her laugh, to find out what kind of an accent she had, to see her beautiful well-tended American teeth. But of course I *was* a re-served Brit, I'd been brought up that way, as all middle-class

English people are. Oh, I could pick someone up, if we were in that sort of place, if that was what you went there for. But a woman in a foreign country absorbed in a book? She might be waiting for someone, possibly one of those Americans who are the size and height of a center forward in a Norwegian rugby team. Besides, picking up wasn't what I wanted. I was lonely, I wanted a companion, and for that companion, without knowing anything about her except what I could see, I wanted *her*.

Then something happened. One of the hotel staff came into the bar, looked around, spotted her and said something to her, almost into her ear, in a very low voice. I heard the word "call." She got down from her stool without a word and followed the man out, taking her cigarette with her. But not her book. The book she left lying open on the bar.

At least that meant she was coming back. The barman appeared from somewhere and I asked for another Coors. I started wondering who had phoned her. The six-foot-four rugby player to say he couldn't keep their date? As she left the bar I'd looked at my watch and seen it was twenty past six. The barman picked up the ahstray she'd acquired from somewhere, made a face at the ash and the dead match, and took it away. I looked at my watch again at six twenty-five and again at six thirty-two. It was a long phone call.

When it got to six forty-five I knew she wasn't coming back. She'd forgotten about the book. All he'd phoned for was to change their venue, and she'd gone off to the new place, wherever that was. There was no one about. The barman had disappeared again. I'd already told him my room number, I had no bill to pay. I got up, crossed to the bar and picked up the book. It was Saltykov-Shchedrin's *The Golovlyov Family*. Not exactly the big blockbuster of the year, but surely an intellectual challenge. The kind of book no one would read for pleasure, I thought, but only as part of some course. I'd never read it myself, though it was among the blue leather-bound "Russians" of which Sergius was another.

Instead of handing *The Golovlyov Family* in at reception, I took it upstairs with me. She might have written her name inside it, some people do that, but she hadn't. A label stuck on the back showed it had been bought from a bookshop in Los Angeles. Did that mean she lived in Los Angeles?

It occurred to me after about an hour that I'd have to eat somewhere. I'd have to have dinner and I'd have it alone. It wasn't much of a prospect. As soon as she saw me coming, the woman sitting at a desk at the entrance to the dining room asked me if I had a reservation and when I said I hadn't, it hadn't occurred to me, I was staying in the hotel, she shut her book triumphantly and said every table was taken. Driven outdoors, I found a small uninspired restaurant where they told me they would close at nine-thirty even before I'd asked for a table.

All through the meal I thought about her. Suppose she wasn't even staying at the Goncharof? Suppose she'd only come into the bar to await this escort of hers? It seemed likely. I didn't know her name, I couldn't ask at reception. All I could do was tote her book round all the hotels in Juneau. Inquiring for her? Inquiring for whom?

By then I was obsessed with her. Not sexually, if that isn't too hard to believe. At that time what I wanted was to talk to her and be talked to by her, to sit somewhere with her and have a drink. I imagined the two of us having coffee together in the morning, sitting on a terrace overlooking the water. Drinking champagne on a balcony in the long light evening. I'd got so used to champagne with Ivo that it was almost the only alcohol I ever thought of.

I thought of champagne but I finished the evening drinking brandy in the Red Dog Saloon. It looked authentic and frontierish but it was new and touristy, not really interesting, a fit place to find oblivion. Walking back to the Goncharof, I was seeing double, two sets of steps up to the entrance, two sets of six pillars, and in my room two copies of *The Golovlyov Family.* I lay on the bed with my clothes on and fell immediately asleep. Waking up three hours later with a raging thirst, I found myself still clutching the book, its cover dog-eared by now from where I'd bent it over and lain on it.

Strangely enough, I didn't feel too bad in the morning. Perhaps the brandy had been of very good quality. Of course I hadn't got around to filling in the card you hang on your door saying what you want for breakfast in your room, so I had to go down.

She was there, in the dining room, reading another book. I didn't wait to be seated, which is what you were supposed to do, but went straight back upstairs, got *The Golovlyov Family,* and put it in my pocket. Coming down in the lift, I had a momentary panic that she might have disappeared again, I hadn't noticed what stage she'd reached in her breakfast, but she was still there, concentrating on her book, pouring herself another cup of coffee with scarcely a glance at the pot in her hand.

I said boldly to the waitress that I wanted *that* table in the window. It was the one next to hers but still a good six feet away. She didn't so much as glance at me. The waitress took my order, came with coffee in the endearing way they do over there, without your having to ask for it. This time I'd decided to take no thought, not to be bogged down in thinking and putting the pros and cons to myself. I just got up, walked over to her and spoke.

"Excuse me. You left this in the bar last evening."

It seems strange to me now, sad perhaps, somehow regrettable, that those were the first words I ever spoke to her: "Excuse me, you left this in the bar last evening." I remember the last words too, uttered at the Juneau airport. "I'll die if I never see you again, I'll die." Death isn't so easily come by, of course. I know that now. You have to be braver than I am and more resolute.

I wasn't thinking of death then, I wasn't thinking of Ivo or of being bored and lonely. I held out *The Golovlyov Family* with its dog-eared cover.

"Excuse me. You left this in the bar last evening."

She was looking up at me. I couldn't conceal from myself the fact that she was looking at me apprehensively.

"I'm sorry about the cover," I said. "I must have done it, it wasn't like that."

She smiled, a slowly dawning smile. I had been right about her teeth. They were perfect. Not that I particularly noticed that then. I only noticed that she was smiling.

"I would have handed it in at the desk," I said, "only I don't know your name."

If ever there was a come-on, that was it. She didn't rise to it. She didn't tell me her name and ask mine. I began to think she would never speak, even that she *couldn't* speak. Was ever woman so consistently silent? She put out her hand for the book, looked at it, looked up at me again. Her voice was almost a shock because I'd waited so long for it. It was very low and very *English;* American, yes, but lightly so, the way we snobbish Brits want Americans to sound all the time.

"I thought I'd left it in the place where I had my dinner," she said, and then she said, "Thank you," in a very heartfelt way, as if it was her diamond bracelet I'd found and returned to her. "Thank you very much."

"You had another book with you, I see. That was lucky." This must count among the silliest and most banal remarks I've ever made, but I had to say something, I had to hold her attention, which I fancied was straying back to that other, luckily acquired book. "There's not much to do here but read," I said. "Not if you're on your own."

She closed her book, and put the two books, *The Golovlyov Family* and the other one, which I saw was Primo Levi's *The Periodic Table,* neatly lined up edge to edge, one on top of the other, between the basketful of jam jars and the coffee pot.

"Are you on your own?"

I fancied she'd asked as if she thought someone like me couldn't be, those brushstroke eyebrows raised and that snapdragon mouth turned up a little bit at the corners. I was saying yes, I was alone for two weeks, when the waitress appeared with some of my breakfast on a tray, and saved me. She saved me in a way I might have thought embarrassing but didn't. When she asked if I'd like her to serve me my breakfast there instead of at my own table, I could have kissed her. But I said nothing, I waited for the table's occupant to say I could stay and I held my breath.

"Of course," she said. "Do sit down."

I told her my name before she told me hers. I had the impression she didn't want to tell her name, that she hesitated very briefly, but when I'd given her mine she had to.

"Isabel Winwood."

It was then, I think, that I saw the wedding ring. But I told myself perhaps it wasn't a wedding ring, just a ring she happened to wear on the third finger of her left hand. The way her eyes were deeply set was what gave her a slightly tired look, I decided, for there was not a line on her face. Those soft swollen lips fascinated me, but I couldn't afford to waste time gazing raptly, I had to speak, I had to make conversation. My arrival two days before, the coming cruise—I wasn't going to mention Ivo—Juneau, the weather, all were possibilities. She listened, sometimes smiling. I wasn't to know then that she hardly ever spoke unless she had something to say.

I was allowed to go on like this, desperately seeking new topics, somehow allied to Alaska, I was running short, wondering why she didn't ask me where I was from, what I did, and where I'd gone to school, when she picked up *The Golovlyov Family,* opened it and seemed to be reading from where she left off the night before. Of course that silenced me.

She looked up and smiled. "Have you read it?"

"No," I said, I very nearly gasped. "No, I haven't." Inspiration came from somewhere. "But I've read the Levi."

And everything was suddenly all right. We talked about Primo Levi, the tragic books and the lighter short stories, the camp and the time he'd spent there, his suicide. I told her about the creative writing course, she wanted to know what I'd read and what I'd written, and by the time we'd got through three pots of coffee between us I felt it was all right to ask her what she was doing that morning and could we do it together.

So we explored Juneau, Isabel and I. The weather held, it was bright and sunny and by lunchtime up to eighty degrees once more. Most unusual, she said. She'd been to Juneau before, she'd been there several times. We went to see Dick Harris and Joe Juneau's graves and the cremation spot of Chief Kowee. We went to the Alaska State Museum and when I asked her if she'd have lunch with me she said she would, yes, of course she would, and she said it as if she'd taken it for granted, even that it was odd of me to have to ask.

In the afternoon she had an engagement, the nature of which she didn't specify. She was mysterious at that stage but it only made her more enticing. I let her go and I thought I'd lost her. Looking back, it seemed to me the best morning I'd ever had. In my life, I mean. There had been no tension, I suppose that was partly it, no stress, no threat, no need to be something I wasn't. For some reason, we'd been perfect companions, interested in things together, laughing or sighing at things together, seeing things in the same way. I couldn't help my mind going to Ivo and how terrible life had been with him for almost a year now, how he'd said he loved me but despised me too and shown it in his words and actions, and how, increasingly, he'd treated me as an illiterate because I knew so little about science.

Once, when I'd been at home with the flu in the Christmas vacation and had nothing to read, I'd had to fall back on some novels of Somerset Maugham that had been my grandmother's. Ivo had grown more and more like one of those characters in his books who are always groaning about their miserable fate in helplessly loving someone unworthy of their love. Maugham never says much about what that's like for the poor old unworthy object. I could have told him. It's not exactly uplifting for the self-image.

But with Isabel we'd been equals and we'd read the same books. I could tell already that it was life we were both interested in, life and people, history and anthropology, not sterile rocks and organisms too small for the human eye to see. I started thinking too of the other women I'd known, the PR girl and Suzanne and Emily and the rest of the girls on the creative writing course. Being with them had been nothing like being with Isabel, even from the first meeting there'd been sexual tension and possession, or a wish for it, there'd been no real conversation and no companionship. Of course Isabel was older. I thought she was probably five or six years older than me. I liked her silences that were not cold or standoffish and the odd, unexpected things she did.

From one of those I was later that day to benefit. But I didn't know it at three in the afternoon, a Sunday afternoon as quiet and dead in Juneau as in any English suburb. I walked down to the waterfront and looked at the latest cruise ship to come in, a monstrous thing with seven or eight decks. I looked up at the snow on the mountains and the scarcely believable blue of the sky. And then I went back to the Goncharof and lay on my bed, wondering what I could do about getting to see Isabel again.

Nothing had been said about meeting later or meeting next day or even meeting again. She hadn't told me how long she was staying or why she was there at all, come to that, and because she had asked me no personal questions, I'd asked none of her. I knew her room number because I'd heard her ask for her key. Her room was a floor above mine and I pictured her returning there from this mysterious engagement, sitting down and writing letters. Who would she be writing to? Her husband?

That reminded me that Ivo had promised to write to me from the *Favonia,* or rather, from the places they put in at along the route. I say "promised," though "threatened" might be better, for I'd told him not to bother. But I knew he would, just as he had the previous year. I'd loved his letters then, they had made me admire him, though not enough, I thought rather bitterly, to keep me faithful to him. And then suddenly I was tired of the whole thing, of Ivo, of the past, of the quarreling and the prevarications and I knew I wanted no more of it. I didn't want to be gay. I didn't want women either. I wanted to be with Isabel.

Could I phone her and ask her to have dinner with me? Suppose she said no. Suppose she intended to do whatever it was she'd come to Juneau to do. The time went on and I was wondering what I was waiting for and wondering then if I dared phone, when there came a knock at the door. My heart leaped up because I thought it must be Isabel. Who else would come to my room door at five in the afternoon?

It was the bellboy. He had a note for me, he said. Again I felt I'd been transported back a hundred years. A note, when there was a phone in the room with a message light! But it made me happy, I loved it. "Will you have dinner with me tonight?" it said on lined yellow paper. "If you send no answer to this I'll see you in the bar at 6:30. Isabel." I gave the bellboy five dollars and said there was no answer.

"It's a legal pad, isn't it?" she said when I held up the note and asked her about the paper.

"Is it? You tell me. I've never seen it before. I'm glad you spell your name like that. It's the best of all the ways to spell Isabel."

That reserve of hers came back. Was it because I'd come close to paying her a compliment? "Are you going on this cruise alone?"

She seldom questioned me. That was the first personal question she ever asked me and it wasn't all that personal, was it? It made me realize how much I'd been subjected to questioning by friends and lovers, in the past, and how I'd disliked it. Sitting in the restaurant with her that evening, I knew I disliked it because it made me tell lies. The truth wasn't for airing. I don't know why it was that then it never occurred to me that it would be better to change the *facts* than distort the truth.

I was going to lie to her now. "Yes."

The look she gave me was of disbelief, an almost cold look.

"Do you think I'm crazy?" I said.

The coldness vanished and she smiled. Her smiles were mysterious but very gentle, as if she harbored a nice secret.

"I don't think that at all," she said. "But maybe you don't know what you're letting yourself in for. The average age of passengers is fifty-five."

"That means some of them must be in their thirties."

"And some in their seventies. That might not matter if you were interested in natural history. But you're not, are you?"

"I like looking at beautiful things."

As soon as I'd said it I thought of the construction she might put on a remark like that. Her calm face showed not a sign that she had taken it personally, but a little color came up to stain the white skin. It might not have been what I'd said but only the wine or the warmth. She took a sip of her wine. I'd noticed she didn't drink much and I wondered if she'd noticed I drank a lot.

I had to ask, I'd been afraid to but now I did. "How long are you going to be here?"

She hesitated. Or I thought she did. It might have been only that she paused while the waiter cleared away our plates. In that moment I thought, suppose she says she's going tomorrow?

"About two weeks. I might go home on the Friday. I shall have to see."

The day Ivo returned. But I couldn't think further than that. I was glad I'd lied then. For a few moments I'd been wondering how I was going to justify what I'd said about going on the cruise alone when the time came for Ivo to walk into the Goncharof that Friday evening.

She'd asked me to dinner but I insisted on paying the bill. She put up a little argument, then gave way gracefully, but I fancied she was rather surprised not to see the almost inevitable credit card come out. At any rate, she watched with some amusement as I paid with one of the traveler's checks Ivo had given me.

The sun was setting as we left the restaurant, so we walked down to the harbor and watched it sizzle down behind the mountains. I took her hand and hooked it into my elbow, giving it a pat to keep it there. She was passive, leaving her hand resting there, but certainly resting, without pressure, without, it seemed to me, enthusiasm. And when she saw a seal out there in the water, a bristly head bobbing anthropomorphically, she pointed, then dropped to her knees to be nearer the animal, to be on a level with it, her hand separating itself naturally from my arm.

She didn't touch me again. We walked back slowly, side by side but apart, and because I asked for history, she told me about the Tlingit, the Indian tribes of these parts. She didn't correct me, I noticed that, I knew Ivo would have, but when she referred to the Tlingit again it was as "native Americans" with a little extra emphasis on the two words.

And then, suddenly, she said, "You need not come back with me. I shall be quite safe. I expect you want to go to the Red Dog."

"Of course not," I said, and then, "unless you do."

"Well—no. I mustn't keep you from doing things."

"I'll tell you what we'll do, we'll have champagne. At the Gon-charof, we'll have a bottle of champagne."

No one had ever made her response to me before except my mother or Clarissa, and I hadn't offered them champagne.

"It's very expensive."

I laughed out loud. "I shall charge it to the room." As soon as I'd said that I realized she'd think I was on some sort of expense account. So well and good.

"Wouldn't a half-bottle be enough?" Her smile had become tentative, inquiring.

"Not for me."

Of course we had a whole bottle. We had it in the bar. I hadn't quite the nerve to suggest my room. She had just one glass. I told her how I'd once wanted to be a writer but wasn't so sure now, how I'd need a job as soon as I got back to England, how my home was at N., which no one had ever heard of, on the Suffolk Coast.

"I've heard of it," she said. "That's where they have the famous song and dance festival."

I think it was the way she said "famous" with some special stress or emphasis, a small degree of reverence, I think it was that. Or else the way she lifted her eyes to mine when she spoke the word. Or the wrinkling of her nose as she raised her glass and the champagne bubbled. Whatever it was, in that moment I fell in love with her.

Up till then I'd been fascinated. I'd been desperate for her company because I was lonely, I'd admired her looks, liked her voice, been I suppose physically attracted to her, though that feeling was never dominant, not then, I'd been excited to find we had so much in common. All those things I'd been but it was as if they vanished or became trivial. This other new emotion swallowed them up. I was in love and I knew at the same time that I'd never been in love before.

It silenced me. In a way, it shocked me. Five minutes before, after the first taste of champagne, a little tickling finger of lust had made me think, well, why not? If she drinks a bit more and relaxes, why not? What's the point of a woman asking a man out with her, after all, if not that? Champagne was an aphrodisiac to me, I suppose, I had conditioned responses to it, set in motion by Ivo. But all of a sudden there was no lust and champagne didn't matter and Ivo was of no account and I was stricken dumb by love. Sexless too, in a curious sort of way. What I was feeling didn't seem to have anything to do with sex.

We were alone in that dark bar. All the rest of Juneau had either gone to bed or were in the Baranof Bubble Room or the Alaskan Hotel, listening to the player piano. For once there was no background music at the Goncharof and they had put out the light under the parchment shade. I was aware that she was very tired. Her eyelids had grown heavy, the pupils of her eyes large and dark. I'd been talking of music, of how I'd once meant to be a professional violinist, but had never been quite good enough. Along with the champagne she drank in everything I told her about myself. But then she fell silent, we were both silent, sitting there watching each other, as if each waited for some move from the other, as if something huge were about to happen.

She got up. She said, "Will you excuse me? I'm very tired."

"So am I," I said.

She seemed relieved that I was going up too. The idea came to me that she was glad I wasn't going out somewhere without her. My heart sang at the thought that she might mind. My heart sang. I'd thought that expression a stupid cliché but I understood it then. It was singing arias from the grandest opera the Consortium ever put on. I said good night quite briefly, abruptly even.

There are times when you don't want even the one you love to be with you. I wanted to be alone in my room with myself, with my love, to think about it, ask myself what would happen now, if there was a chance for me.

My correspondent isn't making these castaway tales up. They are true, or three of them are. The library anthology included versions of the Serrano story and the one of the Frenchman Peron. Of course I already knew Selkirk's marooning was fact and needed no verification, but I looked in vain for confirmation of the account of the cannibal in the herring boat. Perhaps he wasn't included because of not being put ashore anywhere but only set adrift.

As for Emily Wooldridge's journal of shipwreck and life on Staten Island (near the Falklands, not the one in New York), I was halfway through reading it when a curious coincidence happened. The post brought me a précis of part of that work. If my correspondent had forgotten his reproving tone on the last occasion, he remembered it now.

Staten Island is not to be confused with that which forms part of the City of New York. This one lies off the extreme tip of Tierra del Fuego, being in almost the same latitude as Cape Horn. Off her shore, in the spring of 1870, The Maid of Athens, *a brigantine of 230 tons, foundered in a storm and caught fire. She had been bound for the west coast of South America with a cargo of camphor and iron boilers.*

Among the survivors were the captain, Richard Wooldridge, and his wife, Emily. They found themselves on a rocky island, barren of almost any vegetation, the haunt of sea lions and flocks of penguins. It was largely due to Mrs Wooldridge's courage and resource that they maintained an existence on Staten. When her husband fell ill and came near to death she nursed him back to health. So much for the superstition that a woman on board will bring bad luck!

These castaways rescued themselves, setting off in a longboat for the mainland. Emily Wooldridge kept the men in good spirits by entertaining them with tales of her travels by her husband's side in Gibraltar, Lisbon and Tangier. Before leaving the island she had promised her husband she would never let the men know how she suffered, so she bore everything with patience and cheerfulness. With no food left but bread and cold tea, she rallied the men and tended the candle, lighting their pipes when they came to her. On the afternoon of the eighth day land was sighted and they were saved. They had reached the Falklands.

Mrs Wooldridge was a shining example of devotion to a life partner, a worthy wife of a distinguished husband. Unfortunately, her conduct is rare in this world, yours all too common.

9

Ivo's first letter came on Wednesday morning. He'd posted it from Haines, the *Favonia*'s first port of call, so he must have written it on Saturday night, just after he left me. Something jumped inside my chest when I saw the letter in the dark wood pigeonhole behind the reception desk at the Goncharof.

I said nothing. I didn't ask for it. It was Isabel who pointed to it and said, "Look, a letter for you."

I still have that letter, and all the others he wrote me during those two weeks. I reread them when I came in from work this evening, or I tried to, I made the attempt. That first one seems to me to be full of guilt when I look at it now, guilt and love, for he begins with an apology. "I have no business to expect from you more than you can give," he writes. "You have given me and still give me so much. I am only now beginning to see how bigoted and censorious I have been and I know I must love you without reproaches."

Did that give me hope when I first read it? Did it make me think he'd changed and would set me free? I can't remember. I was learning only what an exasperating thing it is to have someone in love with you while you are in love with someone else. At the time I reacted by skimming through the letter, reading one word in five, in case there were any hard facts there I ought to know about. The expressions he used embarrassed me and his declarations of love made me shrink. I wanted none of it, I didn't even want to see it again. I put it back in its envelope and into the outer zip pocket of my suitcase. When I think of that now, rereading the letter, I feel more guilt and shame than I do about almost anything. He had poured out his heart, his soul I suppose, and it had been nothing to me but a source of distaste. Even to look at the letters now makes me hot with shame.

I was dining with Isabel that night. She'd told me by then her reason for being in Juneau. A friend of hers was married to some-one who worked for the state government, and that friend, though only thirty-two, was dying of cancer. In the past she'd stayed with these people for holidays; now she was here to see her friend for perhaps the last time. She'd spent part of Monday with Lynette Case and all of Tuesday and Wednesday morning, but Wednesday afternoon she'd given to me. And she'd seen Ivo's letter. Of course she hadn't asked about it, that wasn't her way, and I loved her way, her gentle silence, asking almost no questions, her discretion and thoughtful care for another's feelings.

In telling me about Lynette she'd also told me things about herself. Not many, just a few vital things. She was married. How she put it was that she was "still married." She lived in Seattle and taught in a high school. These facts were given to me in such a way as to make it impossible for me to ask more and they weren't accompanied by any questions about myself. We had hardly any-thing to say to each other about personal details; we talked always of abstract things, of emotion (observed in others), of tastes and likes and dislikes, of peculiarities of behavior, of the other people in the Goncharof and in Juneau, of happiness and unhappiness and of the differences between our two cultures. One subject we never talked of was science. Another was sex.

She disliked telephones and loved letters, notes, anything writ-ten. She sent faxes to Lynette's husband at the State Office Building on the Goncharof's machine and she took me into the room where the machine was to show me how it was done.

"Wouldn't it be fine," she said, "if everyone had one?" She often used "fine" like that where someone else would say "nice" or "good." "Wouldn't it be fine? Then telephones could disappear."

"But people don't like writing letters," I objected.

"They had to when they couldn't pick up the phone."

I said I couldn't see a world without phones.

"But faxes are cheaper," she said, "and that always counts for a lot. Do you think people especially want to hear someone else's voice? Silence seems so much better, silence and contemplation. The spoken word departs—well, it's out there somewhere in the spheres, but it's inaccessible unless you record it. Can you imagine taping your own conversation and listening to it over and over? I can't."

"But you can read and reread a letter?" I said, and then, impulsively, "Shall I write to you? And would you write to me?"

"I expect so. Of course I would. Shall we start a correspondence? That would be fine. I love letters. I've kept all the letters I've ever had and I do hope other people keep mine."

I'll keep yours, I said, but to myself, not out loud. This conversation took place before the arrival of Ivo's first letter. When it was handed to me and she saw me read the handwriting of the address she didn't ask me anything about it. I couldn't have said it was from someone at home because she'd seen the United States stamp if not the postmark. But she didn't ask.

We had dinner at the Alaskan Hotel that evening. I said to her, "Why do you always wear black?"

She delighted me with her answer, the correct, the only, answer. "I'm in mourning for my life. I'm unhappy." And then she laughed to show me it wasn't true, that it might have been true for Chekhov's Marsha but not for her.

I wasn't entirely convinced. The laugh had seemed forced. Of course I didn't suppose she was actually in mourning for anything, that she wore black for that reason, because she wore white just as much, but mostly just those two colors, black and white. I thought, I'm in love with a woman who always wears black and white and wants to abolish the telephone, and this made me laugh out loud.

She asked me why I laughed and when I prevaricated, said, "I can't afford clothes, Tim, or not many. That's why I stick to black and white, it's easier. Did you think I was rich?"

"I'm glad you're not," I said.

"I'm not sure I am. Glad, I mean."

Her departure was casting its shadow before it, though I didn't know that then. I only knew that her being poorish, like me, brought her closer to me and made her more accessible. We were inseparable, except when she had to be with Lynette, and I was getting the impression by the next day that she was with Lynette more from duty than anything else. It was becoming a chore. She would rather have been with me. Back from Calhoun Avenue, where Lynette lived, she was always with me, yet we hadn't even kissed each other.

Alone, I strolled along the waterfront or drank Coors in the Red Dog Saloon, and wondered how I was going to cross that bridge, how was I going to get to make love to her. Was it to be through a speech or a touch? I nearly groaned aloud when I thought that perhaps I'd left it too long, there had been too much *friendship* for it ever to be bridged. Because, of course, by then I'd forgotten about my love transcending sexual desire. I wanted her. I had to have her.

The weather had held, but that morning huge clouds had appeared, like snowy outgrowths of the mountains. They covered the sun and sank onto the land in masses of vapor that hid the other side of the strait and hung in white curtains over the ranks of pine trees. It was going to rain. I'd been allowed to meet Isabel from Lynette's the day before and I went up there again just before one, carrying the umbrella I'd bought in a shop in Senate Building Mall. The house was up beyond the governor's mansion, what we'd call a bungalow, made of what we'd call weatherboard, with a garden full of spring flowers, waiting hopefully for the rain.

For some reason, I was sure it would embarrass Isabel if I rang the bell, so I waited at the gate, putting up the umbrella when the first drops of rain came. She was surprised to see me but not annoyed. The black shiny waterproof she wore reminded me that she knew Juneau, the vagaries of its climate weren't a mystery to her. But her hair was uncovered, so the umbrella wasn't entirely useless. This time when I took her hand and put it under my arm, she didn't take it away but held on, giving my elbow a squeeze.

Emboldened, I said something about the way the Victorians held arms. "I've always thought it odd. They were so prudish, they even made a fuss about certain kinds of dancing, but a woman would always hold a man's arm even if she hardly knew him."

Isabel gave me a sidelong glance. "Is that a hint at my forwardness?"

"Of course not!" I was rather horrified, but the hand remained and gave a second squeeze.

"I know what you mean," she said. " 'Lean on me,' someone says in Jane Austen to a woman he scarcely knows, and there's no question but that she will, that she takes it for granted."

I said something then that I immediately regretted, that I felt it was folly to say. "And men too," I said, "men taking each other's arms, you read about it everywhere."

She gave me another upward-tilted look, half-smiling, half-inquiring. I thought, she mustn't know. Whatever I have to do, she mustn't know. The act I was to perform I didn't think of then, I never thought of it in advance at all, I didn't *premeditate* it. That small thing can at least be said in my favor. But I thought of other ways of concealing what Ivo and I had been to each other, lying, prevarication, and cover-ups.

The first of these was due. We ran up the steps of the Goncharof out of the rain. Collecting our keys at reception, I saw what was waiting for me in the pigeonhole, not one letter but two. The clerk handed them to me before I could stop him. But what do I mean, stop him? How could I have stopped him? They were for me, they were mine, and as I saw from the handwriting on the envelope, as of course I knew without seeing, both from Ivo.

Isabel said, "Two more. You are lucky. I wish someone would write me letters."

She hadn't asked but the question hung there, unspoken. I'd have said they were from my mother except that she had already seen the United States stamps. I was obliged to say something but I said nothing, I stuffed the letters into my jacket pocket—or, rather, the pocket of Ivo's jacket, which she'd remarked on and admired—and we walked into the dining room for lunch.

Later on, while she was in her room writing letters, appropriately enough, I looked at mine. Strongly tempted to put them into the pocket of my suitcase unopened, I reflected that whatever happened meanwhile I was going to see Ivo in a week's time, there would be no avoiding that, I had to know what he'd written to me about.

What can I say about them now that won't increase my shame? They were love letters. They *are* love letters. I don't want to quote from them, I don't want that added pain. Or perhaps it wouldn't be pain so much as remorse, for I read what Ivo had to say with impatience and with only half my mind on the content. The other half was on Isabel upstairs and wondering if it was her husband she was writing to.

It took me two minutes to read what had probably taken Ivo two hours to write. When I'd finished I put the letters into the suitcase pocket with the first one and tried to think what I was going to say if she was with me when I got the next one. She very likely would be. The only way she certainly wouldn't be was if she found out I was getting love letters from a man who had been my lover. I'd have to think of something to tell her, I'd have to tell more lies, invent a friend, use my creative imagination . . .

Then I had an idea that was very unwelcome. Suppose she spent so much time with me and had all her meals with me and drinks with me and explored the place with me because she'd seen that I was gay and felt safe, as some women are said to do, going about with a gay man. It's an awful expression and I didn't like using it about Isabel, but suppose she was a fag hag? I looked at myself in the bathroom mirror, trying to see if there was anything—well, epicene about me. I didn't care about clothes, I just wore whatever was to hand and was clean. That business of dressing up for Ivo with the bare chest and the gold chain had strictly been a one-off. My hair was shorter than most men's without being anywhere near

shaved; I hadn't got a pierced ear, God forbid. I never used men's
scent, I'd never possessed any. To me I looked just like any other
man of twenty-four, any *heterosexual* man that is, and if I could tell
I was good looking, I swear I was pleased about it then because I
fancied my looks gave me more chance of attracting Isabel.

I turned away from the mirror in disgust. It was then that I
remembered the way Ivo had told me he loved me, in a pub, just
like that, out of the blue. I knew I couldn't do the same. I wasn't
going to be able to look up from dinner in the Summit restaurant
and say, "I love you."

I've read somewhere, probably in one of those newspaper articles
on teenage sex, that young people today take sex very casually,
they're never obsessed about it, they don't even think about it very
much. If they want to do it they do it, always, of course, cautioned
by the fear of AIDS. But there's no soul-searching and no sense of
right and wrong, no hesitation and nothing shameful. It's not
daring or a gesture any more, there is nothing rebellious about it.
Things have changed utterly from when the generation before them
were young in the sixties and seventies.

I can only say it hasn't been like that for me. It wouldn't be an
exaggeration to call it the most important, and the most fraught,
thing in my life at that time.

There was a desk in the room. Isabel was probably sitting at her
version of it upstairs now. I sat down at the desk, took a sheet of
paper from the blotter in the drawer and started to write a love
letter, the first one I'd ever written in my life.

It took me three hours. I told her—but it doesn't matter what
I told her. I suppose the first love letter one man writes is much the
same as the first love letter another writes, in content, at least. As
for delivering it, I thought of doing that immediately but lost my
nerve. We were due to meet at six. I could imagine waiting downstairs in the bar for her, all among the aspidistras and the yellow
pillars, waiting and waiting and her not coming, realizing she
wasn't going to come because she'd read the letter and was bitterly

offended or completely disillusioned. I'd give her the letter when we parted for the night, but if we didn't part for the night maybe I'd never give it to her, I wouldn't have to.

Amazing, wasn't it, the whole thing? I'd wondered how I was going to pass those two weeks. I was so bored I'd even tried to get myself on a flight home and here I was now, wishing it was twice as long, a year long, wanting it never to end.

The end was something I didn't want to think about but I had to when we met and she started talking about Lynette Case. Lynette was very ill. The remission she'd had was over and it looked as if she'd have to go back into the hospital in Anchorage. Perhaps as soon as the beginning of the following week, if it could be arranged. That would surely mean there would be nothing to keep Isabel in Juneau. My face must have shown my feelings, but if it did she said nothing. We talked about the cinema. There was a film on we both wanted to see and we thought of going on the Saturday afternoon. Then Isabel asked me if I'd been up the Mendenhall Glacier.

If I'd said yes I would have had to have told her I'd gone with someone. She knew me well enough by then to be aware I wasn't keen enough on nature to go on to a glacier by helicopter on my own. But if I said no she'd want to take me up there herself, which I would have liked, I'd have liked anything with her, but it was too much to hope that the people at the helicopter pad wouldn't remember seeing me before. They knew Ivo and would remember I'd been with him. That obsequious girl would probably ask how Dr. Steadman was.

I knew it was my imagination but she seemed to watch me as I hesitated. Guilt makes for strange fancies. But when I said, a bit sharply for me, that I didn't much like the idea, not in the rain anyway, you wouldn't be able to see anything through the mists, she made no attempt to persuade me.

She was wearing her white silk blouse again and the black skirt, the clothes she had had on the first time I'd seen her. I was suddenly filled with a longing to know everything about her, all the personal things she kept hidden from me just as I, to be fair, kept mine hidden from her; if she loved her husband, how long she'd been married, if she *lived* with her husband, where she'd been that first evening after her arrival, why she came all this distance to see a sick friend. I was afraid to ask any of it. I don't usually ask questions because I'm not usually much interested. But I thought, if I'd made love to her, if we were lovers, then I could ask.

So we went out to dinner. We went in a taxi for the first time because the rain was coming down in sheets. I didn't look up from my plate in the Summit restaurant and say, "I love you," of course I didn't. We talked about the gold rush and she said that quite by chance she and some man—she said "we" but I knew it must be a man—had stopped the night in a little town in northern California. They'd gone into a bar for a drink and found themselves in the oldest tavern in the West. Sawdust on the floor and animal heads all over the walls, everything seemingly unchanged since 1848 when it first opened. They asked for a beer and a glass of white wine and the beer came in a bottle, slid down the bar. Asking for a glass would be outrageous. "He" had drunk it out of the bottle like the other patrons. I laughed and wondered if "he" was her husband.

" 'My companion,' " I said, "as the restaurant journalists say."

I wouldn't have said it if I hadn't had quite a lot of champagne. She put up her eyebrows, but she didn't smile or say anything. She could quickly distance me with a look. My love letter to her was in my pocket, "burning a hole in it," as Clarissa used to say about money. We went on talking, we talked about travel and then about me and my future. She reminded me, apropos of what I don't recall, that she was seven years older than me. By the time we left the Summit, the rain had stopped and the clouds had cleared away. Arm-in-arm, we walked by a circuitous route back to the hotel, and she told me she went to a dance class at home in Seattle. One day she'd come to N., she said, and see the ballet. Please, I said, please come.

We were out later than usual and the moon was up. It was romantic down there on the waterfront, like the setting for a film when the first kiss is about to happen. We stood there, talking about the stars, trying to decide which constellation was which. I wanted her so much and I was scared to touch her. I'd even withdrawn my arm from hers because the pressure of her hand on my arm was too much for me. I was almost gasping. A line from Eliza's song in *My Fair Lady* kept going through my head, the one that goes, "Don't talk at all: show me." I realized I didn't dare show her.

And when the time came to part for the night I didn't dare give her the letter either. I knew I wouldn't sleep if I did. I'd got up my nerve to take her all the way to the door of her room instead of parting from her in the lift. The letter was burning away against my right side, I fancied I could actually feel the heat from it. The stupid thing was that she gave me the opportunity, to give her the letter or, better still, *show* her. She kissed me.

It was a quick, friendly kiss on the cheek. She said, "Dear Tim, good night."

"Good night," I said.

I may even have sounded cold. I fled to the lift and hit the button repeatedly with my fist, as if that sort of treatment would make it come sooner.

There was no morning kiss. She planned to spend all day with Lynette. On the Monday we had arranged to take the six-hour cruise to the twin glaciers at Tracy Arm, because my week-long trip didn't take that in and Isabel said it was something I shouldn't miss. It was raining, of course. We met in the hotel lobby, Isabel in jeans and T-shirt and carrying the all-enveloping black waterproof, and once again she didn't kiss me. By this time I was paralyzed by the idea of actually touching her and I marveled at the nerve and self-control I'd had the previous week when I was putting her arm in mine.

I suppose they were beautiful, those glaciers. The great sheets of rain and ground-level clouds hid everything but the gray water and the dazzling white, water-sculptured ice. Ivo must have seen them many times, and I thought of him and his enthusiasm as we gazed from the little ship that went in among the ice floes. I thought of him but not for long because Isabel was telling me about glaciers and the way they were formed and making it a lot more interesting than Ivo had that day we went to the Mendenhall.

It wasn't until we'd got off the ship at the dock in Juneau and were walking up Main Street, not touching, a couple of feet separating us, that I remembered another letter from Ivo was sure to be waiting for me. Isabel liked to see Lynette every day and had said she meant to do so before dinner. I thought I could see a way of avoiding her being with me when I received the next letter so I suggested her going straight up to Calhoun Avenue and said I'd walk up there with her.

"I couldn't take a stranger in with me," she said.

We had been through that before. I hadn't the least wish to meet Lynette Case or her husband but, absurdly perhaps, that word "stranger" hurt.

"I'd like to go back to the hotel first and have a shower and change my clothes. I'll take a cab up to Lynette's."

So there was no help for it. But I'd miscalculated. Four letters seemed excessive, as if my eyes or my sense of touch when they came into my hands, must be deceiving me. I must have looked extremely taken aback but I also knew that if I was not to lose Isabel, if I was ever to get anywhere with her, I now had to give some kind of explanation. And she was looking at me inquiringly, plainly waiting to be *told.*

I said, "Please come into the bar and have a drink before you go upstairs."

She hesitated, but after a moment she went ahead of me in among the marble columns and the aspidistras. Because it was so dark outside they had turned on one of those octopus-shaped steel electroliers. The barman came over, his face greenish in its cold misty light. Isabel lit one of her rare cigarettes. Of course I know now why she was nervous, why she was so apprehensive, but I didn't then. Just as I began on my explanation it occurred to me that I could have avoided all this. I could have asked the hotel management to place all letters that came for me in my room. I suppose I'm just not used to staying in hotels.

It was too late now. I said, "You must have wondered why I'm getting all these letters."

"It's not my business, Tim."

This was very off-putting. Or it would have been if the hand that held her cigarette hadn't trembled. Our drinks came and I thought that if I wasn't an alcoholic already I could easily become one. The first mouthful of brandy does so much.

"I want to tell you that someone I know has gone down to Prince Rupert on a cruise ship. Well, they're on their way back now." It sounded silly, that terminology. "She," I said, "she's on her way back. She's a lecturer, she gives lectures to the passengers. She's a botanist. We were lovers but that's over now."

Isabel actually disliked asking personal questions. It wasn't a self-imposed restraint on her part but alien to her nature. She said diffidently, for my sake I suppose, to help me through, "But she keeps writing to you?"

"Every day. I wish I could stop it. I wish I could make her understand that our relationship is over."

"She must be very much in love with you."

"That's not my fault, is it?"

Isabel made no reply to that. She had gone rather red, very unusual for her. "Will she be on the cruise you're going on?"

I nodded.

"I see," she said. "You came here with her and you're here to wait for her to come back."

That was so, I said miserably. I'd nearly gone home, I said, that same day as she had arrived, but I'd discovered I had an Apex ticket and I hadn't enough money to buy another. It all came out then, the entire truth, except that I'd changed the sex of my lover.

"I could have left," I said. "I could have gone to Vancouver."

"That wouldn't have helped you much," said Isabel, not looking at me, looking at the ice floating in her glass of sparkling water.

"I stayed because you came," I said.

She was very still. I waited. I couldn't imagine what she would say. She got up, said, "I'll stay and have something to eat with Lynette this evening. It may be the last time."

I pulled the letter I'd written her out of my pocket. It was bent and a bit creased and rather damp. I'd been carrying it about all day.

I held it out to her and said, "Read it. Please don't throw it away. I insist that you read it."

She took the letter without a word and walked out of the bar. The long empty evening stretched before me, an evening that I knew would mean an inner turmoil for me of speculations, fears, arguments with myself, shame at what I'd done, and awful apprehension. On top of all that I still had four letters from Ivo to read. I called the barman and asked for another brandy.

Sometimes, in the evenings, I go down to the beach and walk along the shingle or the stretch of sand the tide has left hard and firm. I walk a little way up beyond the edge of the town, in the opposite direction from the Dolphin and the overhang of the low brown cliffs, and when I come back I go into the Mainmast for a pint of Adnam's. I did that this evening. There was no wind and it was mild for the time of year. I wondered what someone like Isabel, an American used to that spectacular West Coast, would think of our East Anglian shore where there are no soaring mountains, scarcely even cliffs, where the coastline is not scooped by tides into little bays and where a river estuary looks simply as if the sea has decided at this point to put out an arm and reach inland.

As well as an absence of mountains is an absence of islands. An island couldn't survive in this sea. It has eroded the coast, eating up whole towns, so that here in N. our Corn Exchange, which was once in the center of the town, now stands the same distance from the seawall as this house. The churches of St. Barnabas and St. Matthew disappeared during a series of eighteenth-century gales. Excavations on the beach still throw up bones from the engulfed churchyards. So what chance would an island have? The sea would wash its soft sandiness, pummel and stretch it, finally wring it out like a sodden cloth and set rags of it floating off in the streaming currents. That brownness we always see is what the sea does, scooping up sand from the bottom and churning it through the waves.

Tonight the moon was out, making a shining white road from

beach to horizon across the calm flat sea. The sky was a pale bowl, no color, or rather, a color not in the spectrum, something no one has described, clear and deep and glowing. One or two night skies in the Inside Passage were that unnamed color and it was like going back to a long long time ago when the world was young.

In one of those letters, one of the four that prompted my confession to Isabel, Ivo wrote about Chechin Island and taking a boatload of cruise passengers ashore there. It wasn't the only place where fossilized trees could be seen, he wrote, but nowhere so far north in the world were such marvels left as the fossil webbed and clawed footprints of some dinosaurlike yet amphibious creature. They had gone to Chechin in two boats, he leading one group and the zoologist who was with them on the cruise, the other. But the passengers' response had been disappointing. They had been much more excited at the sight of a grizzly bear that padded out of the forest and stared at them before beginning its hunt for shellfish along the shore.

Like you, wrote Ivo to me. You would have been like that. He was sickened by the "oohs" and "ahs" of the tourists, their comparative indifference to these unique geological records, their picture postcard–cuddly toy attitude to an animal that would certainly have killed any one of them that went close to it. But I'd have been the same, he suggested. And, in spite of what he'd written three letters previously about asking my forgiveness, he launched into another attack on me, my frivolity, my laziness, what he called my medieval attitude to "serious subjects." It was better, I suppose, I thought so at the time, than outpourings of love.

The second half of the letter was mostly devoted to inquiring why I hadn't written to him. I could have written poste restante to Petersburg or Sitka. What else had I to do all day? I was supposed to be a writer, wasn't I? Then he withdrew all that. He mustn't jump to conclusions, he said. I probably had written and my letter was awaiting his arrival in Sitka on his way back. That made me curse. Of course I hadn't written and I'd never even heard of Sitka.

The next letter was all love. The one after that contained a bitter reproach at the lack of a letter from me. He'd gone to the post office in Sitka and the one letter addressed to him was from someone else. The last of the four letters was rapturous again. He longed to see me, he could hardly get through till Friday.

Letters, letters . . . Always at the back of my mind I ask myself who is sending me these desert-island letters on lined yellow paper. For instance, is it a mad person? Almost by definition, anyone who sends anonymous letters or even just anonymous information of this kind, must be mad. But what do I mean by mad? A lot of people would call me mad.

I'll confess something. Once or twice I've thought it might be Isabel. She knows this address, she knows *me,* writing letters is something she does, and on legal pads. And they all come from where she lives, or near where she lives. Of course hundreds of miles separate these cities on the postmarks but to the people who live in the Northwest they're near each other. She probably has friends in Banff and Vancouver who would post them for her.

Against that is the fact that she doesn't know what I did and I can't see how she could know. Even if by some extraordinary chance she did know, she'd found out, she wouldn't do this. It wouldn't be in her nature. I've talked about my correspondent being mad and Isabel is one of the *sanest* people I've ever known. Not hysterical, not neurotic, not even especially emotional, a cool, sensible, considerate woman.

So she has to be dismissed from the list of suspects, with the resultant guilt on my part that I ever thought of her in this connection. I should have trusted her, I should have had more faith in her. For one thing, I need to believe she still loves me. It's all I have.

That Tuesday morning was the first time Isabel didn't appear at breakfast. My letter had offended her, I thought. She must be having breakfast in her room. Worse than that, it might have driven her away, first to stay at Lynette's house, then to go back to Seattle. I drank a cup of coffee, I couldn't eat anything. Her room key was gone from the hook under her pigeonhole. I went back to my room and phoned her, but, too frightened to speak to her, put the receiver down when she answered.

It had been raining all night and it was still raining. I came the closest I'd ever done to feeling imprisoned, if it's possible to be shut up in *nowhere*. For that was what had happened to me. I couldn't be in my room because the chambermaid was there; I couldn't sit downstairs because if I did so it would be impossible to avoid a direct confrontation with Isabel when she emerged. To go out would be more like plunging into a river over which a waterfall is pouring than walking in the rain. But in the end I did go out. There was no other choice. I put on the waterproof gear, pants to cover my jeans and the hooded jacket, and struggled down to a bar I rather liked on Fourth Street.

That was an awful day. Or the first half of it was. It began with brandy and Coors chasers and by midday I was almost on my knees. I made myself walk and I must have walked miles as the rain eased off and became a sad gray drizzle. In the middle of the afternoon I had something to eat in the Goncharof, knowing that at that time Isabel would almost certainly be at Lynette's. I wasn't drunk any more, it had worn off and left me dehydrated. To the barman's surprise, I had a pint or so of fizzy water in the bar and then I thought I'd go to my room and have a bottle of something sent up—a bottle of wine to give me courage or send me to sleep, by that time I didn't much care which. It was almost five.

The lift came. She got out of it. Or, rather, she stepped out and stepped back into it, taking hold of both my hands and drawing me in. She said nothing but immediately she was in my arms. If it was she who embraced me first or I her I have no idea. We clung together, kissing each other, mouth over mouth, devouring each other, past the first floor, on up to the second and the third and fourth before we noticed. She whispered, "I've forgotten my key," so it was to my room we went.

She took my key from me. She was remarkable, the cool way she unlocked that door, her hands quite steady. Inside the room, it was darkish, the light swallowed up in rain. The roaring sound was a fresh burst of rain drumming on the windows. She put her mouth on mine and her hands behind my head, and like that, in the dim rushing warm noise, we kissed. We touched each other's bodies with anxious hands, we whispered each other's names and I said, "At last, at last." Her back arched and her body reached for me and she wasn't silent any more, her gasps—or mine, they were indistinguishable—as eloquent as the rushing water.

There was no battle, no savage roughhouse of struggle and violence and wounding. After that first time, necessarily quickly accomplished, it was a warm slow measure, a gentle long-drawn beat and an exalted flight.

10

I stayed there all night with Isabel. We went downstairs for dinner and then came back again. It was ridiculous, that dinner. I held her hands under the table, we pressed our knees together, I pushed my knee between hers, and then because we could no longer bear that table between us, I moved to sit beside her. Our bodies touched along their length. I'd just made love to her twice but the warm feel of her, ribs in silken flesh, the indentation of waist, the rounded curve of hip, the long muscular flank, knee, shapely calf, and cluster of fine bones that was her ankle, all this that was the physical Isabel was almost too much for me. I trembled as I held her hands.

It was new. I was twenty-four but I felt that before her I'd never made love, to woman or man, I was a virgin. Such beauty I'd never possessed before, nor had I known the depth of feeling her murmuring brought me, and her cry of delight. That these things could be I hadn't known. Such a degree of sweetness I'd never imagined or that passion could go hand in hand with licentiousness or desire be satisfied yet remain quite unsatisfied. I shouldn't have looked back to the others and made comparisons but I did, I couldn't help myself. To think of Emily and Suzanne not only made me shudder but wonder why I'd bothered, why I'd gone on and on, what had there been in it for me but an itch relieved. Now, more reflectively, I ask myself what can have been in it for them. As for Ivo, I thought of him and a great swell of nausea swung up through my body. Isabel put her cool hands on my face and said,

"You're hot, you're blushing. You've gone as red as fire."

"At my thoughts," I said.

She misunderstood me. "You needn't blush for your thoughts now, Tim. It's too late for that."

My love letter was never mentioned between us. There was no reason to mention it perhaps, for everything I had written in it I said to her again. And now I said it with a fiercer meaning, a greater reality, there was no longer need for fantasy. "I love you," "I want you," this was a litany I couldn't keep from speaking, punctuating all the things we said with these two expressions of longing. I had written to her, as all lovers write, that I couldn't live without her, and now I said it with my arms locked round her, skin to skin pressed close, and my lips against her hair.

"I love you. I can't live without you."

I said it because she'd told me she was leaving the next day. Not the Friday but the Thursday. They'd taken Lynette away to the hospital in Anchorage and now there was no reason for her to stay longer.

"Aren't I the reason?" I said.

It was Wednesday night and we'd been in bed all that rainy afternoon, had slept a little and then gone out to a restaurant, walking with our arms round each other's waists. There was a new ring on her finger, a ruby or some red stone with diamonds, and, seeing it across the table, I felt the sharpest pang I'd ever known of jealousy and fear.

"Who put that on your finger?" I said. It was the way Ivo talked.

"Lynette," she said. "It was her mother's. A parting gift."

Her tone was so serious, her eyes so grave, that I had to believe her. I woke up in the night, in the small hours when the early dawn had already come, and looked inside that ring for a love message, initials, a date. There was nothing. Her bag, that she called a purse, was on the desk. I checked that she was asleep and felt inside the bag for an address book. Instead I found a card with *Isabel Winwood* printed on it, an address in Seattle and a phone number.

She whimpered in her sleep and put out her arms to me. We slept with our arms round each other till morning. I kissed her white breasts. I took her long skeins of hair and wound them round my own neck to draw us together.

I told her I'd stolen the card. She laughed and asked me why.

"I was afraid you wouldn't give me your address."

"I would have. But wise people in our situation wouldn't meet again. I think we ought to be wise, don't you?"

"I think we ought never to be parted," I said, and then, "We're too young to be wise."

She turned her face away. "I'm going home today."

"No," I said, "no, no, you can't." I held her tight. "No, you can't go, you mustn't, no, no."

"Tim, I can't afford to stay a day longer than I absolutely must."

Money—everything comes back to it. It's what makes the world go round. I'm not sure what I think now but I used to think money was the primary requisite of life. You had it and all else could follow. After ten days at the Goncharof I had hardly any of Ivo's left, I'd spent it all on Isabel. To be honest, I'd spent it on myself and Isabel. She too had to be careful with money. She was only a high school teacher with a husband somewhere, a husband who had been mentioned but never discussed.

"I'll go with you," I said, "I'll follow you. I won't let you go."

She moved a little way from me. She unwound the stream of hair and shook it back over her shoulders. "You can't," she said. "Remember? You'd have gone last week but you couldn't afford to." She spoke very softly, very tenderly. Her white, ringless hand stroked my cheek, my hair.

"After what you've been spending, have you any money left?"

"Not much," I said. I'd told her a lot of lies but still I didn't want to tell her more than I could help. "Very little. About fifty dollars."

There wasn't any more to be said, not then. We hadn't much time left together. We had none to waste.

Her plane would leave at lunchtime. I kept saying over and over to myself that I couldn't go on without her. It was actually impossible for me to imagine anything at all happening after midday. It was as if midday was a physical barrier, a great precipice that I'd either stop dead at or fall over. The morning was the path leading up to it, a downhill path that got me to the cliff edge more and more quickly as I advanced along it. Beyond was a bottomless chasm.

All that morning we weren't apart for an instant. We got up together and took our shower together, mouth to mouth, hip to hip as the water streamed down our bodies. Once or twice she suggested I go back to my own room for just five minutes, she suggested we go downstairs separately, but I refused. We'd got beyond the forms. As far as I was concerned, the whole world might know of my love.

"I'm not sure I want the whole world to know of mine," she said, and the smile she gave me was half-dismayed.

The husband, I suppose. Kit, for Christopher, she'd told me his name, and that he'd left her. But he'd left her before and always come back. How could any man leave Isabel? How could he give up the scent of her and the feel and the sound? Relinquish the deep joy of just being in the same room with her? She held my hands and looked into my face.

"Discretion never does any harm, Tim. I'd like these days we've had together to be a secret."

"Who can I tell?" I said. "I've no one to tell." No one but Ivo, who couldn't be mentioned between us. I'd tell *him,* I thought, or rather, Isabel would be my trump card, brought out to clinch things when he tried to argue me out of leaving him.

"You must do as you think best," she said quietly, and I knew she thought it beneath her dignity to plead with me for silence. I loved her even more for that, for the grace of it and the restraint. But I also knew she was thinking of Kit, that for some reason, though she didn't love him, though she loved me, though he'd left her, she didn't want him to find out.

"I promise I won't tell," I said.

This was all in the morning, at breakfast time. We stayed together, mostly in each other's arms, tumbling together as we moved about her room, even a brief apartness making us feel empty and naked. Wrapped in the Goncharof's white terry-cloth robes, we tried to eat. I drank black coffee. She drank orange juice, glass after glass, and the acidity of it turned her face from pallor to whiteness.

"I can't let you go, I can't."

"You must."

"I'll be skinned. I'll be like a flayed person. I won't be able to stand the cold and the rain without you. I'll die. I'll drown."

Why did I say that then? That I would drown? Because the rain continued to pour down, I suppose. Or because the island and its surrounding seas cast their shadow before them? From the window I could see people coming and going, in and out of the foyer of the Goncharof, wrapped from head to foot in waterproof coats and capes and hoods, like the ghosts of drowned fishermen. Everywhere felt damp, and upstairs, in the warm, it was steamy. Condensation dripped down the windows. I paced the room while she packed, and when she looked up to speak to me I caught her in my arms.

"Tim, you must let me go. You must. This will be too much for me. Think of me."

"I'm coming to the airport," I said. "I'm coming as far as I can."

And then I remembered what I was supposed to do after that week's trip with Ivo. I was to go to Portland and stay at someone's house, then go on this Greyhound bus trip, then meet Ivo in Seattle. I wouldn't go to Portland at all, somehow I'd fix it so that I flew straight to Seattle and Isabel. It had to be possible, if I played things right, if I managed to buy the air ticket myself instead of letting Ivo buy it.

The midday precipice was still there and the pit was on the other side of it. I was still racing down headlong. But beyond the abyss it was as if I could see a green country lying spread out in the sun. I told her. "I can come to you in ten days," I said.

She gave me a look of great tenderness. "Write to me. You know I like letters best."

"I'll write every day," I said. The husband's name stuck in my throat. "He won't be there?"

She shook her head. "Not any more. Not for a year now."

"Thank God for that."

"You may feel differently in ten days," she said, her head turned away.

I said I'd never feel differently, not in ten days, not in ten years. And, of course, I don't. It hasn't been ten years, it hasn't yet been two, but I love her now as much as I loved her then, more than I loved her then, and without anything for my love to feed on, without hope.

We went to the airport in the rain. The sky was a uniform dark gray, not clouds but cloud itself. The taxi splashed its slow way through sparkling rivers and great flat pools drummed by rain.

Careless of what the driver heard, I said to her, "Only ten days. That's all it will be. I'll be with you in ten days."

She held my hand, crushing it till the bones hurt.

"Ten days," I said. "That's nothing, is it? It'll be gone before we know it."

We talked while we waited but I don't remember what we said except that I told her I'd die if I couldn't see her again. I went with her all the way to where they do the baggage scrutiny and I watched her go through and on and on until she was lost to sight. Ten days, I kept saying to myself, only ten days, but it didn't help me, I couldn't believe in it. I shut my eyes in the taxi going back and tried to conjure up her face in the darkness but Ivo's came instead, his expression angry and vengeful.

Just enough money remained for me to pay the taxi. I went up to my room, hunted through my clothes to see if I had any money at all and found a ten-pound note in a jacket pocket. One of the banks in Juneau would have changed it into dollars, twelve maybe, or fifteen if I was lucky. I put it back where it had come from and resigned myself to eating and drinking at the Goncharof until Ivo came in the morning.

Drinking was what I did, mostly in my room. I slept and dreamed—horribly—of a woman with a woman's body and Ivo's face. The rain hadn't stopped all day and it continued unabated through the long, pale gray evening. I tried the dark bar where I'd first seen her and where we'd drunk champagne, had gazed deep into each other's eyes, exchanged long, slow kisses when the barman was away and I'd clutched at her hand and pressed my mouth to the blue veins, blue as a Spanish Infanta's, and the white skin and the long shell-colored nails. I sat there and thought about her, conjured her up, but she wasn't there and it was too much for me, the loneliness.

I suppose it was the drink that did it, but I had this fantasy that if I shut my eyes, when I opened them those twelve days wouldn't have happened and she'd be sitting up there at the bar, reading *The Golovlyov Family.* Of course one part of my mind knew this wasn't possible but another part thought it might be, that we know so little about time and even less about the human spirit. So I kept closing my eyes and wishing, trying to work a sort of spell I suppose, and opening them and looking at the empty stool, the parchment-shaded lamp, and the bottles gleaming dully.

In the end, when I couldn't stand it any longer, I went into the dining room and had dinner, but I was almost too drunk to eat. I remember taking that card I'd stolen from her out of my pocket and reading her name over and over. It had belonged to her and it seemed to me full of magic. I kissed her name and the waiter saw me. After that I went upstairs again and drank some more and fell into a sort of stupor, sitting at the window, watching the rain, watching the clouds split open to show a blood-red streak where the sun was going down. I must have lapsed into unconsciousness after that, for when I woke up I had my arms spread on the windowsill and my head on my arms and it was dark.

I drank all the water in the room and then some out of the tap. Ivo would come in the morning, I couldn't remember when, but before lunch. My face was wet and I knew that I was crying. Somehow I managed to get out of my clothes and I fell naked into bed.

At some very early hour I heard the television in the next room come on, a harsh man's voice and a strident woman's voice talking. I said to myself that as soon as I could raise the energy I'd bang on the wall with my shoe like Sharif used to do in Dempster Road, but I was asleep again after a few seconds. The next time I woke it was broad, bright daylight and Ivo was in the room, standing over me, bending over me, his face six inches from mine.

Here in N. we're preparing for the Paschal Celebration. Easter is early this year and the festival always takes place during Passion Week and Easter Week. We're working overtime now, sometimes late into the evening. *Rosenkavalier* is the high spot, to be performed by the Wessex National Opera on the night of Maundy Thursday, but I shan't be there. Julius would much rather I wasn't there, for there will be no complimentary tickets and all seats will be sold out weeks in advance. A seat going to me would be a waste, he says, but to do him justice, he says the same for his own family.

"It's the price we pay, dear lad," he said to me this morning, "for our gorgeous jobs in this glorious setting, up to our necks in culture. If we have to forgo Richard Strauss at his most sublime for a Morales Mass or Ruuta's religious school songs, who are we to complain?"

I know I shall be roped in for a front-row seat at this latter performance, sung by four Finns accompanied by a string quartet from Vilnius. The dearth of bookings for it is becoming embarrassing. At this rate, Julius will have to change its venue from the smaller hall in the Concert Complex to the old Methodist chapel in the town. I took him there at lunchtime and pointed out a few hard facts.

"Not so hard as these benches," he said, sitting on one of them and rubbing his back. "It's one thing to sit here for free and save your soul but quite another to expect two hundred people to pay thirteen pounds fifty each for the privilege."

I told him we'd be lucky to get twenty at the present rate, and then, to soften the blow, that the Methodist chapel was very pretty in an austere kind of way and did date back to 1832.

"We can't put the minister for the arts on one of these," he said, banging the bench with his fist. "He won't think it's pretty, he's a Roman Catholic."

I said we wouldn't see the minister for the arts in there for dust. He would stick out for *Rosenkavalier* or nothing. Nothing was decided and I went back to ticket allocations and seating plans.

Am I writing all this to postpone what I must write? Perhaps. It certainly isn't relevant, unless the weather is, Alaskan weather, rain-forest weather; it's been pouring since first thing this morning. The winds don't come off the sea much here because the prevailing winds in this country come from the southwest. But today a northeasterly has been blowing, the waves noisy enough for me to hear them in my office. The wild sea was stripy, banded in blue and green and purple and brown.

At seven-thirty the tide was high, making it impossible for me to walk home along the shore road. I tried it and was stopped by a tall wave breaking against the sea wall and flooding the road with spray.

I made my way back into the High Street through one of the many alleys along there and came into the house by the back way. The bulb had failed in the hall light and I had to grope my way toward the front. Spray struck me as I came cautiously out of the front door to put the duck boards up at the gate and the sandbags behind them. But the tide was on the turn, the violent sea already being tugged back to roar powerlessly and thrash the shingle.

Nature isn't often wild in this country. It's only occasionally that it does savage things. But on the American continent it wounds and kills people all the time, they're burned by it or swept away, engulfed in lava or frozen to death. Or drowned. Wild animals can kill you and even plants cause you injury. I thought of that this evening, protecting my house from a sea that only threatened but did nothing. The rain had slowed and thinned to not much more than a windblown mist. I came back into the house and felt for the hall light switch and then I remembered about the bulb.

In the dark I felt Ivo very near me. I thought I could hear him breathing and I was frightened. Usually, I can stand his ghost. I don't believe in ghosts and I know his is a creation of my imaginings, a projection of my guilt that takes on light and shadows and creaking wood to give it substance. But then, in the narrow passage downstairs, it was different. I hardly know how it was, for I could see nothing, only darkness and a little gleam of light too high up to be of use, a spot of light from the tiny window at the top of the stairs.

There is no other light switch until you come to the kitchen or inside the dining room door. That door was shut and I was afraid to put out my hand to open it. I thought that if I put my hand out it might be taken by another hand in the dark. I thought that if I moved along the passage my body would encounter his. My raised hand would find his cheek and the fingers run down his icy flesh. Even if I kept my hands as they were, wrapped round myself, I would touch him and he me. The breathing continued softly, with absolute regularity.

I got down on my knees. I got down on all fours and started to crawl along the passage. All the time I thought my advancing hands would encounter a foot. It was better, a little better, when I understood that the breathing I could hear was my own breathing, and the thudding I took for the drumming of his fingers on the wall, the beating of my own heart. At the foot of the stairs I pulled myself up on the banisters and stumbled the last bit to the kitchen light. It came on and I knew I'd see him, his face, just for an instant before he vanished. But I saw nothing, of course I saw nothing.

What is it I think is happening? I *know* he's dead and I know the dead don't come back. Ghosts don't exist and there is no life beyond death. There's rest and a long unbroken sleep if we're lucky, but no other life and no other side. So what do I think I see and hear and why am I so cravenly, shudderingly, miserably afraid?

Once I'd have had a stiff drink after an experience like that. Or three or four stiff drinks. Not that there ever were experiences like that before Ivo died. I don't drink these days, beyond a beer in the Mainmast. For one thing, I can't afford it. But it gave me up really, not I it. One day I realized I hadn't had a drink for a week, I hadn't thought of it, my head was too full of other things.

The hangover I had that Friday when Ivo came back should have begun the giving-up process but it didn't, not then. He walked about the room, saying it stank, he opened the windows and let in that cold clean *wet* air that is fresher than any air I've ever breathed.

It hit my face like a dripping towel swung at me. A procession of bottles reared before my eyes like Macbeth's line of kings. I said that, about Macbeth, groaning to Ivo, who didn't know what I was talking about. He had lined the bottles up, champagne bottles and one that had held red wine, I don't know how many Coors cans and liqueur miniatures, for the chambermaid to take away. There was a sticky brandy glass too, with a dead fly in it.

"I didn't expect you for hours," I said.

"What a welcome!"

I made myself sit up, though it was as if an army with bayonets was driving me down again, marching over the plains of my brain. My mouth was almost too dry for speech to be possible. Thinking—if I was capable of thought—that he might construe what I said as a sign of missing him, I managed to mutter that I'd drunk too much the night before.

"So what's new?" he said.

Why did I want to please him? Why did I need to placate him? If I had a reason then, if I tried to justify the way I apologized to him and excused myself to him, it must have been that I had to be on terms with him, brutal as it sounds, because he had money and I had none. Without him I was destitute, broke and stranded. But that wasn't the reason, it never was, I know that. I'd been brought up never to speak my mind, to prevaricate, not to "hurt others' feelings," not to be rude. All that asserted itself, especially at times of distress—and, God knows, I was distressed. I'd been taught it was my duty to please people and make them like me. Especially seniors and those in authority.

I suppose the truth is that once Ivo started admonishing me, and that had been going on for a good year by then, once that began, he ceased to be my lover in anything but a straight physical sense and became my father. Or, rather, *the* father, the archetypal parent in whom authority is vested and the power of exacting obedience. The power of inspiring subservience and creating hatred. Oedipus, Eyedipus, what does it matter so long as you hate your father? My father had come into his feckless son's bedroom and found the evidences of dissipation, and disgust was all over his face.

But why didn't I just say then that it was over, that I was leaving, that I'd met a woman I loved? Why didn't I? That Oedipal-father explanation isn't adequate, it never is. The money excuse isn't either. Fellow students had told me the British consular people will always get you home. They won't like it, they'll be unpleasant and you'll have to repay the money, but they'll do it. And they can't kill you, can they? It always comes down to that in the end. Not that it really does much to change the way you behave.

I know what I ought to have done. I should have got up and gone into the bathroom, killed or cured myself under a cold shower, drunk water, sent for black coffee, and told Ivo I was leaving. I nearly did. As he began, in an icy way, to tell me how he had missed me, had longed for letters from me that never came, had nevertheless anticipated this moment—or the moment it might have been, coming off the ship, running up the steps of the Goncharof to find me waiting for him in the hall—as he began all that and pursued it relentlessly (he was an adept at contrasting the real with what might have been), I thought of chucking prudence and caution and walking out. But I thought also of Isabel. I needed to be on this side of the Atlantic, I needed to be *here,* so that I could find her again. And it was only eight days.

I really thought then that in eight days I'd be able to tell him everything and it would be all right.

In the Summit restaurant that evening, just as we were leaving, a waitress handed me something in a plastic bag and said the "young lady" had left it behind. Ivo and I were having one of our truces. By that I mean that I'd apologized abjectly enough even for him, I'd fought my hangover and won the battle by lunchtime, we'd taken a packed lunch down to the State Office Building and listened to the Friday organ music and he'd at last asked me to forgive him for being jealous and demanding and exigent. But now, at the words "young lady," that look I knew so well was back, disapproving, superior, and—yes, incredulous.

"Let me see," he said when we were out in the street.

I handed it to him without a word. The package smelled of

Isabel's scent, which made me feel dizzy. Ivo put his hand into the bag and pulled out Isabel's black and white scarf. The pattern was very distinctive, an abstract design, and the material something diaphanous. I thought, he'll ask and I'll tell him, I'll tell him the truth, and then, I thought, I won't have to sleep with him tonight.

Base, wasn't it? Anyway, it didn't work out that way. Ivo put the scarf back in the bag and handed it to me. "Someone you picked up?"

I said nothing.

"Her trade must be profitable if she can afford Laroche scarves. Or did you buy it for her with my money?"

"Of course I didn't, Ivo," I said. "I'm not as bad as that."

He began to laugh. People walking along Main Street turned and stared at him. "He's not as bad as that! How old are you? Ten? Eleven? What does that make me? A closet pederast?"

"I meant," I said, "I'm not so immoral I'd spend your money on presents for another lover."

"Oh, she was another lover?" You could never win with him until he broke down, and then you could. "Now he tells me. But you didn't spend my money on her. What happened, she bought her own dinner? You went Dutch?"

And so it went on. I refused to go in the bar of the Goncharof, so he said he'd have room service bring up champagne. That was during a mini-truce. In a mild, casual way he asked me if I'd spent all the traveler's checks and when I said I had, merely put up his eyebrows. The champagne came. Ivo found his leather jacket in the clothes cupboard, put it on and felt in the pocket where the hundred dollars had been. He actually pulled the lining out of the pocket and held it taut to show its emptiness.

"I'll have this in my own keeping now," he said and added very unfairly, "There are some who would have the very clothes off one's back."

But he wanted me, I knew that. The champagne wasn't enough to make me want him. I was suddenly extremely afraid of having my body penetrated and equally of penetrating a man's myself. But I remembered that once before, after Suzanne I think it was, I'd asked him if instead of what we usually did we could have intracrural sex. The word made him laugh, that cold bitter laughter of his. He wanted to know where I'd got it from, where I'd heard it, I hadn't been reading *scientific* books, had I? For quite a while after that he would suddenly come out with it: "Intracrural," and begin to laugh. "Intracrural!"

So I just said, "No." I said I'd sleep in the armchair if he liked.

"Don't be more of a fool than you can help," said Ivo.

I got into bed with him and he turned his back and was asleep before I was. The next morning we checked out of the Goncharof. They gave him the bill with all the lunches and dinners on it that I'd had with Isabel, all the drink I'd had and the miniatures out of the fridge. He sat down to it, with me sitting beside him, and he went through the bill item by item, very slowly, but not saying a word till he got to the sum total, which was much higher than I'd expected.

Then he looked at me quite dispassionately, almost as if he were amused. "How does it feel to be kept?" he said. "Fine, I suppose, once you've said good-bye to self-esteem. Know what that is, do you? They used to call it conscience."

I write this because I'm ashamed of it now. I wasn't at the time. It seemed to me quite justifiable. After all, he'd invited me, I hadn't wanted to come, I hadn't wanted to stay. The last thing I'd wanted was to be dumped at the ends of the earth to stay on my own for a fortnight. Once there, I had to live. I said to him, like that ten-year-old he had accused me of being, I suppose, "Oh, leave me alone."

That afternoon, still barely on speaking terms, we went aboard the *Favonia*.

11

Isabel's scent still lingers in the folds of her scarf. Some kinds of perfume seem to last for decades, changing only a little, sharpening or sweetening, as year gives way to year. The black and white pattern is of swirls that are like the sign for the bass clef. Ivo's knowing it came from Laroche had surprised me at the time. There was no label on the scarf or it had been cut off. Until then I'd always believed he wasn't "that sort" of gay man, he wasn't the kind Emily suggested I might be taken for, the sort that knows about designers and who makes what perfume. And realizing that he was that kind, that there was a side of him that was, helped along the repulsion I was starting to feel.

It brought me a big sense of relief to find that I'd got a cabin to myself on the *Favonia*. It didn't worry me that it was tiny and well below the waterline and that the adjoining shower room almost too small to turn round in. Ivo was on the deck below where all five lecturers were and the ship's officers, the crew being down in the bowels of the ship.

He shut the door and said he was sorry, he was sorry he'd been harsh to me, in future he would keep some control over his jealousy, he wouldn't carp. What did he care about money? I was welcome to everything he had. Then he took me in his arms and kissed me and said, laughing, that I wouldn't have much chance to be unfaithful to him on this ship. The average age of the passengers was around seventy. Once I'd probably have made some sort of joke about the crew, the handsome Korean crew whose average age was around twenty-two, but since Isabel I no longer said things like that.

The first thing we were supposed to do on board was all meet in the *Favonia* lounge for drinks and snacks at six o'clock, meet the cruise organizers and the lecturers and be told about the plans for the next day. That gave me my first sight of my fellow passengers. Some of them were very old indeed, but most were in late middle-age and the youngest in their mid-forties. Or so I suppose. I'm not very good on ages when people are over thirty-five. One old couple looked as if they ought to have been in wheelchairs and were only on their feet assisted by canes because no one was allowed to go on the cruise unless mobile.

"I'd rather you didn't introduce me to anyone," I'd said to Ivo on the way up there. I didn't mean these old people, I meant the other lecturers, two men and two women, who were all about his age.

"Why not? They know I'm gay."

"All the more reason," I said.

I anticipated an explosion, at least an argument. We'd been through all that many times but I'd never felt so determined before. I had no closet any more, I had nothing to come out of. There's no point in standing up and being counted when the cause is one you won't profit by. Or so I thought.

Ivo said, "Are you saying we are to seem not to know each other? We are to pretend we've just met on board?"

"I don't see why it all has to be gone into like this. We can just behave naturally."

"If I'm going to behave naturally," said Ivo, "I'd chuck you down on that bench and fuck your brains out." And then he said quickly, overcome by remorse, "I didn't mean that. I'm sorry. We'll do whatever you want."

Of course we didn't. No one ever does do what the other wants. At any rate, he stuck to what he'd said and didn't introduce me to Megan the anthropologist, Fergus the historian, Betsy the ornithologist, or Nathan the wilderness expert. But we sat at the same table as these last two for dinner and seemed perhaps all to get to know each other at the same time. Apart from a grandchild a couple had brought with them, we were the youngest people on board and it seemed natural for us to sit together. I still think that, though I couldn't have said it to Ivo without getting another stinging rejoinder.

The *Favonia* left Juneau harbor as we sat down to dinner. It was raining again, the sea gray beyond the window and rain and spray lashing the glass. Fergus was giving a talk on the history of Haines and Fort Seward with a video and when I said I thought I'd give that a miss, Ivo put up his eyebrows, said, "Nonsense," and hauled me up several flights of stairs to the lecture hall that was behind the bridge. He'd been to the ship's shop and bought me a pair of binoculars, having previously scolded me for not bringing any. Enjoyment of the Alaskan Panhandle was impossible without binoculars. I hadn't a camera either but I didn't tell him that.

Several of the old people fell asleep. I thought I'd attended my last lecture in the previous April when I'd listened to Piers Churchill on Ford Madox Ford's prose, and I rather resented having to sit through this one. The grandfather sitting next to me took notes all the time in a neat, highly legible hand. When it was over he introduced himself as Frederick Donizetti. His is the only name I'd remember if I didn't have the passenger list and the ship's log on the table here in front of me. His wife said gently, *"Professor Donizetti."*

Was I a student? Not any more, I said. Mrs. Donizetti said I looked so extremely young, not much older that Elianne, which reminded her that she must go and check on Elianne before they had a last drink in the bar. Would I join them for a nightcap? said the professor. Ivo's murmured rejoinder, that there was nothing I'd like better and he'd picked a right one here, went unheard by anyone but me.

Apart from Isabel, who was quite different, these were the first Americans I'd ever met socially and it amazed me the unselfconscious way they introduced themselves, and the ease with which they talked to a stranger. At first I thought they must be particularly extraverted, but when we were in the bar everyone behaved like that, coming up to me and shaking hands, saying their names as if it were the easiest thing in the world to do, asking me where I came from and what did I think of Alaska.

I spoke my thoughts aloud, perhaps because that was what they all seemed to do. "I shouldn't think anyone could ever be lonely in the United States."

This raised a good deal of dry laughter and a blonde woman who looked a bit like the aging Marlene Dietrich said I was kidding. According to the passenger list, she must have been a Ms. Connie Dorral. Most of the rest were academics or retired academics, there were two doctors of medicine apart from the ship's doctor—who was mostly absent, chain-smoking on deck—and a dozen or so members of a society called the American Avifauna Association.

"At home we'd call you twitchers," I said.

That raised a lot of interest. People wanted to know why and what twitchers did and how did I come to know what the word "avifauna" meant. I thought how you could never have a conversation like this in N. or P. or anywhere in England and I said so. Again they wanted to know why. I drank three dry martinis and started to enjoy myself. At any rate I felt happier and easier than I had done at any time since Isabel went away.

Ivo wasn't there and this had something to do with it. Our relationship had reached a stage where I could only be relaxed when I was away from him. After I'd met the Donizettis he'd abandoned me, and I hadn't seen him since. It was difficult to escape the conclusion that he was taking what I'd said seriously and behaving as if we'd only met when I came aboard. This didn't stop me being anxious that I might find him waiting for me in my cabin when the party broke up, and I went down there just before midnight.

He wasn't, but the discovery I made that there was no lock on the door rather disturbed me. Everything was very quiet but for the blowing noise the air-conditioning made. If you were inclined to claustrophobia it might have been very bad for you down there at night. Luckily, I wasn't. But I lay awake a long while, listening for footsteps coming toward my door.

The voice of the tour director wishing us good morning woke me. It came out of a public address system you could no more turn off than you could lock the door. The greeting was followed by announcements of various kinds, details of the temperature and precipitation level and a preview of what would be happening that day. It might have been the small hours or midday, there was no way of telling down there. I found my watch and saw that it was seven.

Instead of five lecturers already at our table, there was only Ivo. The others, Ivo said, had had theirs an hour before. The dining-room windows gave on to a calm gray sea and a sky of smooth gray unbroken cloud. I looked through my binoculars at it and saw the same thing, gray sea and gray cloud. Mrs. Donizetti waved to me from across the room and Connie Dorral called out "Hi" and "Good morning."

"I see you've been making friends," said Ivo.

An enormous breakfast was on offer, cereal and eggs and bacon and toast and fruit, so I asked for the lot. I fancied that one of the people I'd met the night before, a doctor from Boston called Thomas Ruffle, was staring at Ivo and me with more curiosity than our sitting at the same table warranted. It made me a bit uneasy about being there but I told myself not to judge by my former standards. The doctor was an American and Americans, I was learning, are interested in people, as against the English, who are interested in things.

Ivo, who when he read my thoughts always read the ones I didn't want him to know about, said, "If we have breakfast together now, run into each other by chance in Haines and accidentally have lunch in the same restaurant, happen to sit next to each other at the evening briefing and have a pre-dinner drink together, do you think we'll have done enough to make our fellow passengers accept our innocent friendship?"

"I hate your sarcasm," I said.

"It used to turn you on," he said. "It used to make you think I was cruel and violent and dangerous to know. I wonder why these unpleasant qualities are always so—what you would call—attractive?"

I ate my eggs and bacon. I waited a while and then I said, "Is it going to rain? Shall I need my waterproof gear?"

He looked at me and said very quietly, "Why do I love you so much? What would make me get over you?"

I didn't answer. Connie Dorral passed our table as she was leaving the dining room and said Dr. Someone had seen two seals bob out of the water on the starboard side. I made some sort of appropriate reply.

"So, how shall we contrive to meet by accident in Haines?" said Ivo in a lighter and more pleasant voice. "Let's say the Sheldon Museum at the foot of Main Street. I'll be coming out and you'll be coming in at eleven? How's that?"

"Are you serious?" I said. "Is that what you want?"

"No, what I want is for us to leave this ship together and explore Haines together, eat our meals together, and sleep together. It's not want I want but what I may have."

And so it went on. We did meet on the steps of the museum and we did have lunch together. The rain came down in torrents in the afternoon, so we stayed in the restaurant, talking to various members of the party who came in. Ivo, who never lied but was prepared this time to keep silent while I lied, listened while I told the Donizettis and Connie and a geophysicist from Milwaukee that he and I had no prior knowledge of each other. No cocks crew, it was raining too hard.

"It's nice for you to find a fellow countryman," said Mrs. Donizetti.

Megan gave the lecture that evening. It was about the Chilkat Indians and of no interest to me whatever. I sat between Ivo and Betsy and thought about how I was going to manage things, how I was going to tell Ivo about Isabel, or if it would be possible for me to avoid that and simply make it clear to him our affair was over and we had to part for good. The awful sordid truth was that I absolutely depended on him for money.

Writing about this now, nearly two years later and after all that happened, I'd like to leave out the money part. But I can't. If I'd been financially independent of Ivo I wouldn't have gone on the cruise at all, I'd have gone to Seattle with Isabel. Still, I suppose you could say that if I'd had money of my own I'd have left the Hotel Goncharof before Isabel arrived there. It's no use calculating things that way, assessing conditionals and might-have-beens. The lesson to be learned is never to put yourself in someone's else's financial power, and I've learned it, but much too late.

If I hadn't spent so prodigally while Isabel and I were together that past week I'd have had enough to live on, albeit frugally, for my travels to Portland and San Francisco and my return trip to Vancouver. But now I didn't intend to go to those places at all, only to Seattle. That would mean buying an air ticket to Seattle and staying somewhere while there. Could I stay with Isabel? And what of when the time came to use the Apex ticket home? How could I bear to leave her? But if I stayed how would I live?

It looks as if I am just making a list of excuses for what I did. Of course I know there are no excuses. There is barely an explanation.

Ivo came to my cabin that night. He knocked and, without waiting, came in. I couldn't think of a reason for saying no, making only a feeble protest that the cabin was so small, the bed so small.

"I'm not planning on spending the night," he said.

When he'd gone I did some more thinking. Not about money this time but about the most appalling thing that could happen, that Isabel might somehow learn of my relationship with Ivo.

We went up the mountain in the train to White Pass, gold rush country. A woman in the carriage with me took no notice of the scenery, the jagged peaks swathed in snow, the deep blue valleys, the sun that was hot and bright as the clouds sank below us, and looked only at the wildflowers growing on the right-hand embankment where there was no view. She was a botanist from Florida, made ecstatic by her discoveries, enthusiastically recording her own voice commenting on dogwood and hemlock and curious grasses.

A railway buff from Albuquerque told me this trip was classified as world-class among enthusiasts. He'd waited to make it until he retired from the academic post he held, and then, that same year of 1982, the line ceased operations. Imagine his disappointment! Six years later, to his joy, the White Pass and Yukon Route railway began to run once more, and here he was, making the trip as soon as he could.

These are the things that matter to you when you are old, I thought, wildflowers and mountain railways. The life of the emotions is all dead and gone, used up. But that life was all I could think of as a longing for Isabel took hold of me and at the same time the prospect of being with her again seemed to recede. Sex with Ivo the night before had done its damage. It was an experience I looked back on with horror, with a shrinking of my body into myself, my arms crossed on my chest, my legs pressed together. And yet I'd pretended enjoyment. Why? To avoid another confrontation? To hasten the end of it and his departure? It made her fade a little, our encounters become a falsely recalled memory, our future unreal.

At the top of the mountain we left the train for a few minutes to stand with icy feet in the snow and hot faces held up to the sun. Then the clouds welled up from beneath us, drowning us in thick wet whiteness, as cold as snow. I made the downward trip in the same carriage as Ivo, who had made it twice before. There was no one else with us. The others were all crowded at the front of the train. I was looking out of the window on the side the botanist had looked at when we were coming up. Thin streams of white waterfall threaded down the mountainside between the flowers and the green mosses. A downward smoke, as someone called it in some poem. Tennyson, maybe.

"If I can get hold of someone to take my place on the next trip I'll leave the ship at Prince Rupert and come to Oregon with you."

There's something terrible about being given a piece of news the speaker thinks will delight you but which is in fact the last thing you want to hear. In my case, I hadn't even imagined hearing it. You might say, I'd never thought of that.

"I've already spoken to Louise about it." Louise Conway was the cruise director. "She would be quite agreeable if I could get Oliver."

"Who's Oliver?" I said.

"Oliver Davies. He's a geologist at Berkeley, very young but he's already published quite successfully. A possible Stephen Jay Gould of the future. I know him, we've met a few times, and he once told me he'd like the cruise job if he could get it. Of course he doesn't know the Panhandle like I do but he's been here, he loves it here, and he'd learn while he was working. The money's good and he always needs money."

I didn't look at him, I was looking at the downward smoke through a veil of rain. I said Ivo could hardly get hold of this Oliver Davies before Friday. He shook his head. His smile was rueful.

"It may look remote here, Tim, but there are no inaccessible places in the world any longer. Not in America there aren't, and we're in America, we're in the United States. Things have changed since the gold rush and Soapy Sam and Frank Reid had their gun battle on Juneau dock. Alaskans have as highly sophisticated a telephone system now as the rest of the States."

There was nothing to say. I had never imagined this might happen. The doors of a complex trap seemed to be closing about me. I could almost feel the cold metal of the bars as I brought my face up against them and peered wildly out. Ivo said he'd phone Oliver Davies from the Golden North Hotel and leave a message if he couldn't get him.

With the rest of the party I explored Skagway, saw the Red Onion Saloon that used to have a brothel upstairs, and went to the curio shop where they have the biggest gold nugget in the world on a watch chain. I looked at everything without seeing. My thoughts were bent on escape, while I knew there was no escape. You can get away from Skagway by road, you aren't dependent on ships or helicopters. Inside my trap but looking out, I listened hungrily while Fergus told us the start of the Klondike Highway was here, traveling northwest into the Canadian Yukon. It's some measure of the state I was in that I speculated about how far I would get if I stole a car and tried to drive myself to Whitehorse.

But we don't stay in states; we change. Consciousness alters all the time, attitudes are in a condition of perpetual flux. I learned that in Alaska. The frightful intense, panicky fear that Ivo's announcement in the train had cast me into lasted only half an hour. He came back as we returned to the *Favonia* to say he hadn't been able to locate Oliver Davies. He'd left a message that he would call again from Sitka or Davies could call him or Louise Conway on the ship.

My heart lightened at once. Davies had probably gone away somewhere, he'd never be found in time. But Ivo's failure to find him and its effect on me made me feel much warmer toward him. This is an aspect of my character that I despise, the way a sudden relief, an influx of the pleasurable alleviating of anxiety, can make me feel something like love for whoever is with me; can make me feel what certainly passes for love in its effect on the other person. Or could once. There isn't much opportunity now and perhaps, anyway, I've changed. I came close to reviving my feelings for Ivo when he told me Oliver Davies couldn't be found. In his cabin, to which I followed him, I put my arms round him, I kissed him, I told him not to be too disappointed. What did two weeks of separation matter? We should soon be together again.

Why did I? Was I mad? Why did I pretend to want him and need him, to lust after him? When he pushed the chair against the door, jammed its back under the door handle and piled his backpack on it to add to the weight, when he pulled me down onto the floor and began his fierce lovemaking, why did I contrive an ecstatic response? Why did I?

To keep him sweet, for a quiet life, not to make trouble, not to be unkind, because it was easier. Because I was in a trap and I wasn't the kind of person who hurls himself against walls and bars until he is stunned and bleeding. I was the kind who sleeps with the enemy. I was the kind who joins them because he can't beat them. Perhaps I still am. I don't know.

· · ·

Ivo gave the lecture that evening. His subject was glaciers and the "calving" of icebergs. I don't remember what he said, I don't remember the slides that went with his talk, or if the lecture hall was full or half-empty. My memory is of the conversation that took place afterward, in the *Favonia* lounge, when seven of us sat round a table with our drinks: Ivo and I, Betsy and Megan, the Donizettis and Dr. Ruffle.

Mary Donizetti had been reading a murder mystery that she took from the ship's library, a couple of shelves of books that passengers had left behind them on previous trips. It had made her ask if anyone had set such a book in Alaska. There were so many opportunities, she said, for killing someone.

On the Mendenhall Glacier, for instance, when the guide told them about the coldness and profound depths of the blue water gullies that cut channels through the ice, she had looked down and thought how quickly it might be done. And who would know?

"I'd no notion you were cherishing these murderous thoughts, my dear," said Donizetti. "Who was to be your victim? Myself? Or Elianne? I seem to recall she'd been overly troublesome that morning."

"There was nothing personal in it. When someone tells you, the way the guide told us, that if you fall into a certain stretch of water no one could pull you out and you'll be dead in seconds, you can't help thinking that way. And then, up on the mountain today, with those sheer rock faces . . ."

"If there was no one by to see you," said Betsy, "you could just tip a person over and, like you say, who's to know?"

"Nature is so extreme here." This was Ruffle. "I think I'm right in saying that tomorrow we'll be in icy waters where no swimmer could survive for more than a minute or two."

"Or less than a minute or two," said Ivo. "It won't be much warmer than up on the Mendenhall. These are fjords, this is glacial water. Human beings don't have a seal's coat or a seal's blubber. But it's of no importance as no one is going to fall off this ship, still less be pushed."

I could tell he didn't care for this talk. To him it degraded the wonder and beauty of the place. He tried to change the subject by speaking of icebergs in Antarctica, where I knew he longed to go. He began on the Filchner Ice Shelf, from which three years before a huge piece had broken off and, splitting into three, floated off into the Weddell Sea, where it covered an area of I don't remember how many thousand square kilometers. Ivo loved talking about these huge icebergs, putting forward reasons for why they broke away when they did, but the others wouldn't have this, they were intent on easy ways of doing murder in a murder-favoring environment.

Did this conversation have any influence over me when the time came? I don't think so. The means I used, after all, was never mentioned, Megan putting forward the suggestion that you might present your victim to a grizzly bear. Betsy seemed to know all about grizzly bears, of whom the world's largest concentration were to be found on the island we were circumnavigating, and told one anecdote after another of friends who had been menaced or attacked by them. Professor Donizetti wanted to know if the hemlock that grew all over the mountains here was the same hemlock as Socrates used to make an end to himself. No one knew. The party broke up with various members of it promising to consult the classicists and botanists among the vast numbers of academics they knew.

Ivo kissed me gently and lay beside me for a while in the narrow bunk. After he'd gone I stayed awake for a long time, wondering how I was going to tell him, how I was going to stop him leaving the ship with me when I left it, how I was going to make him understand about Isabel. But when I fell asleep at last the dreams I had were of sheets of gray water in which icebergs floated, some as big as houses, some no larger than a piece of stone in a rock garden. Behind towered the mountains with their snowy summits and between them in the valleys hung the rivers of ice. The heads of seals rose above the water, shaggy and doglike, but as they drifted closer to the ship's side I saw that they had the faces of men.

This image kept returning in dream after dream. My mind confused dreams with icebergs, they followed close upon one an-other in the same sort of way, each a little different, but a seemingly endless progression. And the seals with men's faces came in procession too, changing at one point into the discarded bottles in my bedroom at the Goncharof, bottles floating in choppy gray water, each one containing a letter or message, the writing visible but too far away to read.

When I couldn't stand any more of it I got up. It was only a bit after five. I felt like the man who was drowned in a barrel of wine and who said of a night like mine that he wouldn't pass another such, not though it bought him a world of happy days. Going on to the observation deck, staircase after staircase and finally a spiral one, I fancied I should be alone up there to stare at the sea like Napoleon on St. Helena, but it was already quite crowded. The American Avifauna people were there with their field glasses and their cameras, getting very excited about a pair of tiny brown birds barely visible to the naked eye. And instead of the open sea, which I'd imagined must be out there, we were entering a fjord where the waters were like my dream, tumbling with clots of ice. But it wasn't gray, the sky was an unclouded blue and the sun had come up fierce and golden from behind the high mountains at the head of the bay.

After three people had asked me what had become of my binoculars I went back to fetch them and, coming up again, met Ivo, who made me go up on the bridge with him. He said the captain wouldn't mind so long as we didn't get in the way of instruments. I let Ivo take my hand for a moment at the foot of the spiral stairs. He did something he had never done before, brought my hand to his lips and kissed it. The effect of this was strange, it made me shiver, but not with disgust, certainly not that, and not with desire either. I think it was with fear.

I suppose it was a triumph of navigation, getting the *Favonia* in there. Ivo said it was, talking to me later when we were close up near the mouth of the glacier and the icebergs were all around us. On the bridge we had to keep silent and simply watch. She was a small ship, the bigger ones couldn't get in there, the passage was too shallow and treacherous. The sun turned the water to gold, it made a great gold pathway through the blue, and the boulders and spars and rocks of ice were silver stained with gold on their sunny side.

We came up that gleaming path and the glacier ahead of us was too bright to look at, a white dazzlement caverned and fissured with blue.

In those moments I began to understand why Ivo wanted to come, and come again and again. I even had ideas, rather stupid and sentimental I suppose, about being able to lose oneself here, to lose the self, and be made pure and new. I saw my seal heads in the bright sparkling water and they had the faces of seals, a cat crossed with a dog and much bewhiskered. A pair of eagles watched the progress of the ship from their perch in the high bushy crown of a spruce tree. In the unclouded sky the hot sun mounted.

I've even wondered if Emily Hadfield might be the sender of the castaway pieces. The *Maid of Athens* journal being by an Emily— Emily Wooldridge—and a ship called *Emily* in another story, made me suspect. But the next one that came disproved this theory, if the postmarks hadn't already done so.

Robert Jeffery was an eighteen-year-old boy from Cornwall, England, a seaman on board the naval sloop, HMS Recruit. *In 1807 the ship sailed for the Caribbean to join the Leeward Islands station.*

Her captain was Warwick Lake, the Honourable, youngest son of General Viscount Lake, a one-time harsh commander of British forces in Ireland. The son was not much better. His own brutality was reflected in the conduct of officers and crew. During the Recruit's *Atlantic crossing many men were flogged, mostly for drunkenness and disobedience. Young Robert Jeffrey was put in irons for two days and later received twenty-four lashes for no more serious offence than helping himself to a mouthful of the gunner's rum.*

Apparently undeterred by this punishment, a few days later he stole a cask of spruce beer. The matter was reported to Captain Lake. Jeffery might have expected even severer punishment but at first nothing happened. The Recruit *was at this time in the Anegada Passage, a wide sea lane east of the Virgin Islands, in the midst of which lies the barren rocky islet of Sombrero, so named for its resemblance in shape to a Spanish hat.*

That Sunday afternoon Captain Lake came on deck and asked the master: "Have we not some thieves on board?" On being told that there were two, one of them being Jeffery, he pronounced a punishment for the lad so astounding that few could at first believe what they heard.

Having first told Jeffery that he wanted none such as he on board, he said that he intended to set him ashore alone on Sombrero and that this was to be his "doom." One officer dared to protest but in fact there was no opportunity for dissent. Lake's word was law. The word "Thief" was painted on a piece of canvas and sewn on to the back of Jeffery's shirt. Then he was put ashore, on to a bare desolate rock almost forty miles from the nearest inhabited land.

The Honourable Warwick Lake was court-martialled for this offence, stripped of his rank and dismissed from the navy. Not then, not till much later, was it known that Jeffery had been rescued from Sombrero by an American schooner. He was taken to Marblehead on the coast of Massachusetts, where he ultimately settled, returning to his old trade of blacksmith.

There will be no court-martial for you. A suitable judicial process would be a trial for murder in the first degree.

That came yesterday in an envelope postmarked San Luis Obispo, California. Does the last sentence constitute a threat? The piece has told me more about the writer than any of the previous ones. Although the spelling is English English, he or she is American. I can see that in the way he has written "Cornwall, England," which no English person would do. Also I believe I'm right in thinking we don't have different degrees of murder under our system, only murder or manslaughter.

This afternoon, talking about *Peter Grimes,* I asked Julius if he'd ever heard the story of Robert Jeffery. I didn't have to say any more because he had, he knew all about the court-martial, and even about all the political uproar caused by the resulting efforts to improve conditions in the navy. So this one is true too. Julius said it would make a good opera and it could be called *The Island of Doom.*

The *Favonia* dropped her anchor and we went down to breakfast. The sun shone for half a day. We saw whales spout and their forked tails lash the surface of the water. Returning down the long inlet, the old lady who got about on canes but was eagle-eyed, spotted a black bear with its twin cubs standing on a little green lawn. Everyone rushed up on deck to look and the first rain of the day, a burst of it from the gathering clouds, struck our faces.

Glaciers, glaciers, glaciers, and Ivo was in his element, literally in it. He was indifferent to the rain, unaffected by the dense cold mist that formed the center of a fallen cloud. All the time we were moving, making our slow progress between the rocks and the floating ice, he was with one group or another, talking glaciers, how they came into being, how they declined, how their formation and their passing changed the landscape.

That was the day, the next day, when parties of us first embarked in the small boats, the Zodiacs that the ship carried. We had a lecture on how to conduct ourselves. It was Ivo who allotted to each of us, the lecturers and the cruise director as well as the passengers, a numbered tag on a ring, red on one side, black on the other, its number in white. These tags hung on hooks on a pegboard near the embarkation point. When we went out in the Zodiacs we were each to take a life jacket, then to turn our personal tag over so that the red face showed. When we came back we were to take off our life jackets and turn the tag to the black face. This was to ensure that no one was ever left behind. We were forbidden— insofar as paying adults on holiday can be forbidden anything— ever to turn someone else's tag. I still remember my number and I remember Ivo's.

Mine was 22 and his was 76. I can never see or hear those numbers with indifference. They are not so much magic numbers for me as fatal numbers, each invested with the power to stop me in whatever I am doing, to arrest me and take me back to that time, to run a cold thread down my spine, to ring in my ears and echo there: 22 and 76.

Ivo took charge of one Zodiac, Megan the other. We were not to land this time but to explore a certain long inlet, too narrow and too shallow for the *Favonia* to venture into. The glaciers were left behind, and the ice floes. Rain forest was all about us, dripping spruce and hemlock, water drops glittering on the red salmonberries that are food for bears, white flowers and yellow, and one that even I knew the name of, the columbine of English cottage gardens, though never orange-colored as it is in the Tongass National Forrest.

It was Lotos Eater country in there, the fjord like a still stream "between walls of shadowy granite in a gleaming pass," long-leaved flowers weeping from among the ivies and the deep mosses. The waterfalls, slender white threads, fell and paused and fell, the way Tennyson said they did. But he was writing about a warm place and it was cold in the Tongass, no dark blue sky vaulted above a dark blue sea. The mist descended in a white wall just as Ivo was telling us to look over there, to see the mountain goats up near the snowline.

But nothing disconcerted him, not rain or cold or apathy among people inadequately dressed for these hazards. As he brought the boat about and we turned in close under the overhang of green and sparkling gold, as the branches shook over us their gathered rain, he turned to me a face I'd never seen before, so enraptured was it, so caught up in the glories that he alone of us could truly see.

Coming aboard the *Favonia*, I turned tag 22 to black and asked Ivo if I should turn 76 over for him.

"You don't listen to what you're told, do you?" he said like a teacher.

"I'm sorry," I was meek, placatory.

"Remember next time."

But he came to my cabin later with a bottle of champagne and his own tooth glass. We sat on my bunk drinking champagne and he said he was sorry, he shouldn't have spoken to me like that, especially in the presence of others. No reply had come from Oliver Davies, but tomorrow we'd be in Sitka and he'd phone Davies at the time he had appointed.

I'd begun to feel as if swept along by uncontrollable events, a river of them, tumbled with ice, and for a while could only give myself to it. I yielded to Ivo in everything, I let him make love to me, hard and quick, all over in five minutes, I let him lead me to dinner, I preceded him upstairs, zombielike, to where Fergus gave the lecture on the Russians and the sea otter fur trade. That night I lay in his arms, thinking that I must tell him, I must tell him before he reached Oliver Davies and arranged to leave the ship.

I had to tell him before we came to Sitka.

12

Writing this, I've made a discovery. I'd thought that putting down my experiences on paper would be intolerably painful, I thought the pain of it might inhibit and finally stop me. But while the events themselves were deeply painful when experienced, and *thinking* about them equally excoriating, writing of them hasn't been like that. Writing hasn't been a relief or an exorcism but something quite other. It's been as if I described things that happened, not so much to someone else as to a part of me that has remained inviolate from them. I've found detachment without looking for it. I've found that living is one dimension, thinking another and writing a third.

Why did no one ever point this out during the creative writing course at P.? Perhaps they didn't know. Perhaps nothing had ever happened to them to give them a reason for discovering it or they were too much occupied by the aorist and deconstruction. What does it matter? We learn these things better if we discover them for ourselves. I'm learning now as I begin to write down what happened when I confessed to Ivo and asked for my release. And this time, so effective has the detachment process been that I'm not going to need any digressions to postpone the evil day.

Ashore in Sitka, while the avifaunists paid a visit to an eagle hospital, and the rest went to watch the Archangel Dancers, I wandered the town, looking for evidences of the Russians. There weren't many. Even the Orthodox cathedral had burned down and been rebuilt thirty years before. Ivo, keeping to his time to the minute, was in the Westmark Shee Atika Hotel, phoning San Francisco.

The nerve I needed to tell him had been paralyzed by a bad night, by dreams, by simple fear. If Oliver Davies agreed to take over from him, I'd have to arrange some kind of escape for myself in Prince Rupert or Vancouver. And I'd have to do it without money. I considered stealing money. From Ivo, of course, for I knew he'd never expose me. That was the state I'd reached. I had even made myself aware of how much money he had, far more in actual cash than I'd expected. He'd always disapproved of the overuse of credit cards and a checkbook was no use to him here.

It was base. I know that. Fear and anticipated panic will make one do almost anything. No, not "almost," anything. I tried to think of Isabel, but although her face and her voice, her whole appearance and her ways, are crystal clear to me now, they'd faded then. It was as if she'd stepped away from me into the mist. She was veiled and Ivo was starkly visible.

He came into the bar where we had arranged to meet and told me he'd spoken to Oliver Davies's wife. Davies was away until tomorrow. She'd no idea if he would consent to take over from Ivo. Sounding unhappy about the idea, she said she'd ask her husband and he would contact the ship. No, I'll phone him from Wrangell, Ivo said.

We each had a beer. Ivo wanted to show me the museum but I hadn't the heart for it. He asked me why I was depressed but I couldn't answer. We walked down to the waterfront, where eagles perched on hulls of boats and fishing tackle. It was raining a little but the clouds were high, smooth and white as snow. A little way out, on the calm silvery-white water, one of the big cruise ships lay at anchor, the *Northern Princess,* eight decks high. We stood on the wet stones and looked out to sea, real sea here, nothing on the other side until you got to Japan. The rain on my face was like fine, cold needles.

"I am going to leave you," I said. I spoke remotely. It was as if

I was reciting something I'd learned. "When we get off the ship on Friday I'm leaving you. It's over. I've had enough. It's all over."

He turned his head. *"What?"*

"I'm leaving you. I don't want to be with you any more. This is the end of it."

It was such an effort to say that it exhausted me. I felt physically enormously tired. Those few terrible sentences had used up a disproportionate amount of energy. He took hold of my arm, just above the elbow, in a hard, painful grip.

"Look at me," he said.

I did so, unwillingly. His face had grown dark—with rage, with pain, with simple disbelief? I couldn't tell.

"I'm not hearing this," he said. "You didn't say what I think you said."

His fingers dug into the muscle. I tried to shake him off. All I could think of saying was what Clarissa used to say to me when I was a child, "Don't. Not here. People can see us."

"Do you think I give a fuck what people see?"

He was holding both my arms. I struggled and he held on. We were on the dockside and in danger of falling over. I'd have liked to break free and hit him, strike him in the face and see him lose his balance and fall in the water. Of course I didn't. I said, "Let's go somewhere and talk."

What had I expected? That he'd accept it and let me go? Easily? Like that? I hadn't expected anything. I'd never climbed the great rampart of telling him, never imagined what was on the other side. We went back on board and up into the empty observation lounge. A crew member who had been going through it with a vacuum cleaner said good morning and then left us alone. The ship rocked gently, sitting at rest on the flat sea.

"Why did you say what you said out there?" said Ivo.

As if it had been just something to say, to provoke, to tease or to test, not a statement of intent. I tried to keep calm but I realized I was afraid of him. A flood of terror of Ivo seemed to flow through the vessels of my body, a petrifying fluid. I was afraid it would paralyze my voice, making it hoarse or squeaky. I think it did a bit. Ivo was looking at me with scorn.

"I am going to leave you. I meant it."

"What's brought this on?"

"I wasn't going to tell you until we were home again," I said, "but I'm doing it now because I can't stand any more. I can't be with you any more."

"I asked you why."

Because I no longer got anything out of the relationship, I said, because it was all irritation and annoyance and pain.

"You no longer love me."

It was spoken levelly, in an almost conversational tone. I'd moved far enough away from our connection to be touched with shock because a man had said this to me, a man. He saw it in my face, or he saw something, and gave a harsh laugh.

"You never loved me?"

I had that feeling one sometimes gets that the room is bugged or that invisible listeners, agog, are hearing what one says. "Do we have to dissect everything?" I said.

"No, we aren't dissecting. I asked you why you had ceased to love me and you've answered me whether you know it or not. Now I'd like to ask you why you ever made that approach to me in Martin's room that day. It was you that made it, if you remember. You came up to me and touched my face. Was it all nothing? Was it just for *fun?*"

The old couple coming into the lounge saved me from answering. On their canes, they proceeded slowly in our direction, stopped and spoke to us in their courteous way in their cultivated Boston voices. Had we enjoyed our visit to Sitka? Dr. Braden had been ashore but his wife had not quite been up to it. In better weather she might have managed, but when it was wet and slippery underfoot . . . However, remaining aboard, she had seen no fewer than three sea otters swimming in the neighborhood of the ship.

Ivo and I stared, nodded, achieved rictus smiles. We must have seemed ill to them. Out here, in the open sea, one or two passengers had been mildly seasick and Mrs. Braden evidently thought that was what was wrong with me, for she advised me to have a rest before dinner and be sure to try to eat something. Ivo and I went to my cabin. I sat on the bunk, he sat on the single metal-framed chair.

"I have to give the lecture tonight." He spoke in a dull monotone.

"I'm sorry," I said. "I'm sorry. Would it have been better if I hadn't told you?"

"Yes, of course."

"It could only have been a postponement."

"You still haven't told me why," he said.

And so it went on, I determined on not bringing Isabel into it, he wanting an explanation, as if there is ever a single clear-cut reason for breaking up the sort of thing we had. But he didn't ask if there was anyone else. At last he left me, he had to, for Louise's voice came over the system, calling us all on deck for a sighting of whales or otters or something, and I didn't see him again until I went up to his lecture. Maybe he had no dinner, I don't know. He talked about the formation of fjords and this wasn't a case of the professional rising above emotional pressures, doing a good job in spite of inner turmoil. He looked and sounded ill and several times his voice faltered.

I couldn't face prolonging our conversation and after the lecture I went off to do something I swore I wouldn't do once I was with Isabel and we were happy. I went to drown my sorrows. There were plenty of others anxious to do the same. There always are. I remember sitting with the ship's doctor, talking about loneliness and the means by which we'd found what it was. We drank brandy and he smoked all the time.

It was stupor rather than sleep that took hold of me around midnight. I made it to my cabin, but only just, the ship's doctor supporting me, the drunk leading the drunk, down the staircases and along the passages, as the *Favonia* made her way round the northern tip of Baranof Island and into Chatham Strait. A death-like sleep had hold of me when Ivo came to the door very early in the morning. I said something, "Who is it?" probably, and fell back into unconsciousness, to be wakened from it I don't know how much later by Louise's bright voice relayed. Ivo was sitting in the chair, watching me.

He looked as ill as I felt. His worn face had become cadaverous. I staggered into the shower room and drank from the tap, then I drank from a bottle of Perrier I didn't remember was in the cabin, up-ending it, draining the whole liter or whatever it was. He didn't say a word. Louise's voice was replaced by terrible music, hot metal and a woman's shrieking soprano. I grunted to Ivo something about why was he there. What was he doing in my room at this hour?

"It's a full day for me," he said. "I won't have another chance."

Thank God. I didn't say it. "I want to have a shower," I said.

"Have it."

"There isn't much room in here."

"Why did you drink so much last night?" he said. "Are you unhappy?"

In the shower, I started off with the water hot and let it run icy-cold. I don't know why it didn't kill me unless it was because I was twenty-four and you can play about a lot with your health at my age. Even if you'd never been particularly used to luxury, as I hadn't, it was horrible in that shower cabinet, everything wet, the wooden slats underfoot wet, all the surfaces you touched sprinkled with a kind of dew, the towels perpetually damp. I was shocked when I found out what Ivo was paying for it.

I came out with a damp towel tied round my waist. Ivo gave his harsh unpleasant laugh. "If it was all right for me to see you naked the day before yesterday, why isn't it now?"

Because, when a love affair is over, you begin behaving in the former lover's presence as you behave in the presence of those with whom you've never had a sexual relationship. A normal degree of modesty returns. If, for instance, I'd found myself for a night under the same roof as Emily, I'd have wrapped a towel round my waist when I came out of the bathroom. Well, with Emily I'd probably have put a dressing gown on and the more voluminous the better. Only with Isabel now would I have let myself be naked.

I didn't explain to Ivo. He knew why. I began putting on my

clothes. He said, "Will you have lunch with me in Wrangell today? We could have an hour together. To talk."

"There isn't any more to say."

"There's plenty more for *me* to say. Besides—" He was proud and this cost him an effort. I didn't want him to make it. "I have to know that you didn't mean what you said yesterday. If you were so unhappy last night that you had to drink that much, I have to think it was because you regretted what you said, because you found you needed me."

"No," I said, "no."

"Tim, I want us to be together permanently. I don't think you've understood that. I know I criticize you, I find fault and to some extent I admonish you, but that's only because I want you to be perfect. You're so young and you've a chance still of being someone remarkable. Isn't that permitted in someone older than you and who loves you, to try to set you right? You could say I'm trying to make a perfect partner for myself."

I said something about not wanting to be made into anything. But, in fact, I can't sort out any more what we said to each other in my cabin and what we said in the diner where we had lunch in Wrangell. The enormous hangover I had has left my memories confused. I only know that nothing was said in the cabin about a third party. At that point he still hadn't asked if there was anyone else.

He must have gone soon after that, but we left together to go up to breakfast. I had my hand on the door handle to open it when he stopped me. He took hold of my wrist.

"Have pity on me, Tim."

I said nothing. We went upstairs. Waves crashed inside my head but the sea was calm and the morning clear and blue. I drank black coffee, ate a piece of toast, watched over by Ivo who seemed to me once more censorious, condemnatory, paternalistic. I thought about how he'd been when we first met, how laid-back, with that tantalizing coolness, his wit, the faintly sexy innuendo. Megan came to the table to ask him something and he got up and left with her, giving me no backward glance and saying nothing to me.

A rather larger cruise ship than the *Favonia* waited outside Wrangell harbor but we went in and made fast at the city dock. Ivo and the other lecturers with a party of Tlingit enthusiasts had gone ahead and I saw that disc 76 was turned to red. I turned 22 over as I went ashore on my own. The children in Wrangell have some sort of franchise to be the sole purveyors of the garnets that are found there by the Sitkine River, and it seemed a good idea to buy a garnet for Isabel. They are only semiprecious stones, but I thought that Isabel had just the coloring that dark congealed blood-red would suit. Perhaps I could have one set for her as a pendant or a ring. That brought me up against the problem of money once again. Ivo had given me $300 as spending money on the previous Monday, the day he'd first phoned Oliver Davies and I'd been in that short-lived stage of yielding to the inevitable. There had been nothing to spend the money on.

I wandered the streets of Wrangell, searching for a fine garnet. A little Tlingit boy sold me the best one I saw for a dollar and refused to take more. Thinking of how I could have it set, in gold certainly, brought Isabel back to me and I felt her presence more than I had for days. I hadn't written to her. Once or twice I'd sat down to write but I hadn't known what to say because I couldn't write what I wanted to, that I'd see her soon and see her alone. Now I saw her again and her disappointment as she waited for the letter that never came. I imagined her sad eyes, the light shrug of her shoulders. Then I pictured her long white hand and my ring sitting there on the wedding finger, the plighted love finger. The garnet had been so cheap. I calculated that if I spent nothing more I'd have enough to get me from Vancouver to Seattle and perhaps enough for a night in a hotel.

It's a dismal feeling, that one of absolutely not wanting to see someone that not such a long time before one has wanted to see very much. My whole body seemed to grow heavy at the prospect of the meeting ahead. My footsteps dragged and my head ached. I got to the diner first and had a drink, hair of the dog. It was almost alarming the way it didn't work, it made me feel no better. He came in just as I was wondering whether to have another.

As if he were talking to Dr. and Mrs. Braden or Connie, he said, "The tide will be out this afternoon, so we can all make the trek to Petroglyph Beach. I hope you'll come, you'll find it very interesting."

"What is it?" I said.

"There are large stones on the beach, scattered among the other rocks, each bearing a device or logo that's been chiseled into the surface. No one knows why and it isn't known who the craftsmen were. The stones are very ancient."

I could think of nothing to say.

"Elianne Donizetti has been buying rice paper and crayons so that she can make a petroglyph rubbing as a souvenir. Perhaps you'd like to do the same."

"Are you serious?"

He smiled unpleasantly, the way he did when something he said got under my skin. Then his face altered and his voice.

"Though you think your feelings have changed, you could still stay with me for companionship. You'll be alone, otherwise, and I'll be alone, and is there anything profitable in that? Sex can be suspended for a while, if that suits you. I'll find it hard but some things are hard and that's all there is to it."

"Ivo," I said, "I just don't want to be with you."

It caused him pain, he couldn't hide that. A kind of spasm crossed his face. The truth is that we only care about someone's pain when we like him or when we don't know him personally and have no reason for liking or disliking. I observed Ivo's pain but I didn't care about it.

He made a strenuous effort, both to be calm and to be reasonable. "We shall inevitably be apart for the next two weeks, anyway. It's too late now for me to change with Oliver. While I go back to Juneau and come back again to Prince Rupert you'll be on your West Coast travels. We won't write. We won't do that this time." He flashed me a dark look. "Or, rather, I won't. You don't have any problems in that area. We'll have no contact until we meet in Seattle sixteen days from now."

He was giving me a way out. Or, handing me an opportunity if

I'd had the sense to see it. I had only to be a little nice to him, a little acquiescent, make a few promises, and I'd not only have been free but have had enough to be free on. For I've no doubt that if I'd said, yes, we'll have this separation, we'll be apart with no contact for two weeks, we'll meet in Seattle and see how we (I) feel, if I'd done that he would have ceased to nag me, begun to be pleasant to me, and, more important, given me more money.

It's hard now to say why I didn't agree. I'd like to think it was because I wasn't as bad as that but that's something that, if I'm honest, I'd be dubious about. Perhaps I reasoned that if I agreed it would all have to begin again in two weeks' time and Isabel would be there or would be nearby, would almost certainly have to be lied to, fobbed off, deceived, while I prevaricated and alibied myself. And would Ivo just go? Would he give me up more easily in a fortnight's time than he would now?

"I'd like to make a clean break now," I said.

He hated clichés. I was never allowed to get away with even such a semi-quasi-cliché as that one. "Any break you make is unlikely to be clean," he said. "Dirty dealing is part of your charm—or would appear so to those who find amorality appealing."

I said I didn't see how abusing me would help. Why did he always insult me when things weren't going his way? What was the point of insulting me, anyway? He'd been looking down at the table. He lifted his head and looked at me. There were dark shadows under his eyes and his eyelids looked heavy and swollen. Ivo's eyes were tragic, I sometimes thought, even when he was enjoying himself. They were very expressive eyes, not opaque like many people's are, but true mirrors of the soul.

The question was bound to come, though I'd genuinely hoped and believed it might be avoided. He was looking at me and I knew then that he was going to ask. But I was looking over his shoulder at the door and by the time he spoke I'd seen Betsy and Nathan come in with Dr. Ruffle. Our cruise was the enemy of intimacy. You could hardly ever be alone, a tête-à-tête was always interrupted.

Ivo would never use an expression like "someone else" or "another man." He said, "Have you found a new lover?"

What had he in mind? One of the jet-haired, ivory-skinned crew? The barman with the smiling brown eyes? I didn't answer because the others were already coming up to us. They'd had lunch, they said, they'd seen us through the window. I got up, smiling. They must have wondered why the welcome they got from me was so enthusiastic. But Ivo had gone very pale, he'd gone gray and he looked ill. Betsy had begun to talk about eagles, the bounty that the United States Government once had on eagles and their consequent endangerment, and Dr. Ruffle knew someone in Cambridge, Massachusetts, who had a pet eagle, imprinted when young, so that it fancied itself human. Ivo looked as if he was recovering from being struck in the face. Under the table he took hold of my knee and held on to it. He had never done that before, anywhere, ever. It was as if he held on for dear life, his nails digging into the skin under the kneecap. Just as I was thinking I'd cry out if it didn't stop, he took his hand away, got up, and said, "Let's go, let's find the others and go and see the petroglyphs."

It was a desolate place, that beach. We walked to it, up a long hill, where little houses in little suburban gardens looked out on to the sea. The sun had gone and we were not to see it again until the cruise was over and Alaska left behind. Of course I didn't know that then and as I trudged up the hill I kept hoping, the way a child does, for the clouds to part and recede. The grayness made it half-dark, though only two on a midsummer afternoon, and by the time we'd crossed a cliff-top field and started the descent to the beach, the Tongass drizzle had begun.

The sea was a paler, shinier gray than the sky, the beach itself a welter of gray stones, all of it flat, gloomy and cold, the mountains hidden in a mist like cold, wet smoke. It would have been rather like the beach here at N., very early on a wet morning, but for the great boulders that lay tumbled about. They may have been granite or limestone or something else, Ivo did tell me, but I've forgotten. Some of them were bare, sea-washed, natural, but others had carving on them, some kind of hieroglyph, a fish, a face, a hand, an abstract figure. I've never understood why people get so excited about this kind of thing, but they do. Ivo was even lifted temporarily out of his misery by the enthusiasm of the Donizettis and the touching simplicity of an avifaunist from Fort Worth who made a stone rubbing and then took a photograph of the only bird he found represented among the petroglyphs.

There was no atmosphere about the place, no sense of a distant past or of a mysterious lost culture. It had grown rather cold as the clouds sank and the white wetness became tangible. We were there a long time. I sat on a stone with something like the letter B carved on it and stared at the luminous sea. I tried to think about Isabel but I couldn't. When I tried to conjure her up and see her, which is one of the things we do when we "think about" someone, I could only summon an image of her walking away, her back toward me. I realized I was very frightened. I was frightened of Ivo. Ivo blocked out everything else and he came near to extinguishing Isabel.

On the return journey he ignored me. I was left alone. I walked alone while everyone else was part of a group. Behind me I could hear Ivo talking about the petroglyphs to some people called Blatt from Cincinnati, a keen couple who kept putting forward ideas as to who did the carving on the stones. Ivo was saying that the stones were there when the Tlingit first came, they were there before any known settlers, and Mrs. Blatt, who was a *Chariots of the Gods* fan and believer in flying saucers, suggested extraterrestrial agency. I looked over my shoulder, expecting to catch Ivo's eye, and I caught it, I held it, while he stared at me as if I were some worm crawled out from under a petroglyph. But no, he'd have given the worm a kinder look. He turned away and smiled at Mrs. Blatt, that gullible admirer of supernatural pyramid builders.

I was afraid of being alone with him. I was afraid of that question being asked again and of not knowing how to answer. But it's interesting how things are hardly ever as bad as you think they will be but often are very bad when you anticipate nothing much. Neither was true in this case. I was terrified of Ivo and I was right to be, for he was far worse about it than I'd expected.

He went on board ahead of me. I noticed that 76 was turned to the black side. I'd like to have gone to my cabin and slept but I was afraid he'd follow me there, so I went up to the observation deck with my binoculars and mingled with the twitchers who were watching a flock of tiny ducks. The *Favonia* weighed anchor and started on the southward journey for Ketchikan. Rain fell in straight shining rods, making a million punctures in the flat calm sea, "calm as a millpond," some woman said, as if she hadn't said it the day before only to have Ivo ask her, in a deceptively courteous way, if she'd ever seen a millpond. The rain made it very cold, only the little brown ducks, beloved of the American Avifaunists, seemed to enjoy it, bouncing and diving and plunging in the glassy gray water.

I went furtively into the dining room when the time for dinner came and, seeing a vacant place at the Donizettis' table, asked if I might join them. I could avoid sitting with Ivo that way. There's a lot to be said for Americans. They reacted as if I were their president or at least an Oscar winner and couldn't have been more welcoming, gracious, and apparently delighted. I didn't see Ivo at all. He may have eaten earlier. I made up my mind not to go to the lecture. The Donizettis were going, of course, they hadn't missed a single lecture, they hadn't missed anything. As far as I could gather, they had barely slept.

After two brandies in the bar, I went downstairs to my cabin. The ship felt empty, almost everyone being up in the lecture hall. I lay down in my bunk and thought, only one more day, one last day, and on Saturday I shall see Isabel. Again I considered writing to her but it seemed too late for that. Instead, I thought about money.

It's interesting that I hardly ever think about it these days, I've just enough and that's all right, I've enough to stow away a bit in Sergius, and that's all I want, but then it occupied half the capacity of my waking thoughts. Money, money—you're not supposed to work in the United States without a green card or whatever, I knew that, but I also knew that people do work, in restaurants for instance, and get away with it for months, for years. I could do that, I thought, and get some money together and persuade Isabel to come to England with me.

I really thought all that, lying there in the belly of the *Favonia,* as she moved through the narrow channels toward the open sea. It says something for my imagination that I could have those visions and see them as feasible, that I could see it as a cool practical concept, working as a waiter or barman, living with Isabel, planning a joint future for us. I left out Ivo. I tried to leave him out, though I didn't entirely, for all the time I was dreaming this way, I could feel my fear of him tensing up my shoulder muscles, moving nauseously inside me, drying my mouth.

And five minutes after the lecture began he walked into the cabin. He didn't knock this time but walked straight in and kicked the door shut behind him. I must have made a sound, some kind of exclamation of more than surprise, of actual fear, for he looked at me with scorn.

"Oh, please," he said.

"What is it?" I said. "What do you want?"

"Are you afraid of me?"

I didn't answer him but repeated what I'd said.

"I want to know who it is, of course. I want to know all about him."

I couldn't say I didn't know what he meant. I suppose people do say that, I've read that they do, "I don't know what you mean," though I've never heard it. We always know what the other one means in these situations, not that there had ever been a situation quite like this for me before. But Emily walked into my consciousness at that moment and stood there, looking at me accusingly.

A product of the creative writing course at P., I ought to have been able to invent a man, a male lover complete with name and appearance and occupation, I ought to have been able to describe some fictitious meeting and even have given a sample of our dialogue. The reason I didn't was that I wanted to leave all that behind, I wanted my homosexuality to have been a phase, prolonged in my case longer than such phases usually are, but over now. I didn't want to confirm it even if such confirmation was a lie. Superstition came into it somewhere, a feeling that if I boldly stated I was in a sex relationship with a new man I'd be holding out temptation to the fates and the result would be the loss of Isabel.

I was terrified but I said it. "It's a woman," I said.

He wasn't immediately upset. I suppose shock takes a while to strike home. "Another Suzanne? Another Emily?" It was like a blow in the guts the way he remembered their names. "Oh, please," he said again. "A little bit of pastime. Not the real thing, you know that."

"That's just what it is, Ivo," I said, "it is the real thing. I'm in love. I've never been in love before. You know I was never in love with you, I never said I was, I can't help it, I didn't know I was going to meet her and fall in love. It was a shock to me."

Cold as ice, he said, "Who is she?"

Why did I tell him? Why? "I met her in Juneau, in the hotel." He was silent.

"We were together all the time, for nearly two weeks. I saw her first in the bar." The sneer that curled his mouth I ignored. "She left her book behind and I kept it for her till we met next day. I was in love by then, it was love at first sight."

"You fell in love with a woman you met in Juneau?" He sounded as incredulous as if I'd said I was going to take over control of the ship from the captain. "A woman staying in the hotel? What happened—she picked you up?"

"I don't want her talked about like that, Ivo," I said. "I love her." I looked him in the eye. "And she loves me."

"I don't believe you. You're inventing this. I don't know what your motive is, I don't know what you hope to gain by it, but I know it isn't true."

"Ivo," I said, "you have to believe it. We're lovers, Isabel and I, we made love I don't know how many times, and we're going to go on, I'm going to her on Saturday and I'll be her lover again."

I hadn't finished, I was still talking, pressing all this home, making him believe, when he was up and attacking me, his knee on my chest and his hands round my throat.

13

It's growing light in the evenings now and there has been no repetition of my experience in the dark hall of my house. I haven't seen Ivo again, his ghost, his shade, I haven't even seen anyone in the town who resembles him. He no longer waits at my elbow while I'm at my desk and he no longer follows me home. It can't be that my writing has exorcised him, for I haven't been writing for weeks now. I got stuck. I got writer's block, though hardly for the usual reasons. When I reached the point where Ivo attacked me it brought on something like illness, I felt sick, I felt pressure on my head like the ceiling coming down on me, even felt for that night and the next day that I wouldn't be able to write any more.

And as if he or she sensed the predicament I was in, my North American correspondent sent me two more castaway accounts, one at the end of February, the second in the second week of March. Both were on yellow legal-pad paper and both were in envelopes with the address handwritten.

A Venetian merchant, Pietro Quirini, based at Heraklion in Crete, left port bound for Flanders in April 1431. It was an ill-fated voyage. Due to problems with his rudder he did not reach Lisbon until the end of August. The ship continued northward and in December another storm struck. It began to go down. Sixty-eight people were on board.

Forty-seven took to a longboat, twenty-one to a gig. The gig sank amid the wild waves. For the men in the longboat hell began. Their provisions and all their barrels of water were swept overboard in the heavy seas. The cold was typical of North Sea latitudes in the depths of winter. Deprived of fresh water they drank sea water, became dehydrated like victims of cholera, and thereby lost their strength to steer the boat. More than half of them were dead before they at last reached a snow-covered island in January 1432.

The starving, frozen men kept themselves alive by drinking snow and eating shellfish for three weeks until a fisherman landed on the island and told them they were in the Lofoten Archipelago off the northwest coast of Norway. Their rescue was arranged without delay.

Not everyone has been so lucky.

The second account outlined a less harrowing experience.

In the early 1700s, Philip Ashton, a seafaring man, was among a large number of sailors captured by pirates off Cape Sable in Central America. It was while the pirates were collecting drinking water in casks on Roatan Island, which lies in the Bay of Honduras, that he escaped from them and hid in the forest. Unable to find him when they were due to leave, one of them called out, "If you do not come away presently I shall go off and leave you alone."

Ashton chose to remain but wrote: "I was on an island which I had no means of leaving; I knew of no human being within many miles; my clothing was scanty, and it was impossible to procure a supply. I was altogether destitute of provision, nor could tell how my life was to be supported. This melancholy prospect drew a copious flood of tears from my eyes . . ."

He was nine months on Roatan before encountering any human being. Snakes inhabited the island. One of them "opened its mouth wide enough to have received a hat and breathed on me." Before companions, then rescuers, came, he almost drowned while swimming to a nearby, smaller island, one that was free of vermin. Another time a shovel-nosed shark struck him in the thigh. From going barefoot, his feet were severely wounded. Once he was attacked by a wild boar.

Ashton was lucky. He was rescued. Two years, ten months and fifteen days after he was first taken by pirates, he returned to his father's house in Salem, Massachusetts, and was received "as one risen from the dead."

What am I to make of these letters? There seems to be no pattern to them. For instance, if they had begun by recounting mild cases and progressed to the worst kind, the sort that ended in the death of the castaway, I could see some point to them. I'd expect a last one, of particular horror, and this followed by a threat of retribution or a demand for something. But Ashton's case is one of the least horrifying in the catalog of those sent to me and Quirini's one of the most dreadful.

One had a Seattle postmark, the other came from Banff in Canada. It's possible others may know what I did, but the only person I ever told was Thierry Massin. I can't imagine Thierry having the intellect and the resources to write these things. Besides, he could barely speak English, let alone write it. Whoever is sending me this stuff must have access to a reference library. Of course Thierry *may have told someone else* and it is this man who has taken it upon himself to torment me like this. A man—if Thierry has a hand in it, it won't be a woman.

I should stop opening these letters, I know that, but I can't.

One good result of them has been that these last two have stimulated me to start writing again. I don't know why. Perhaps it's because we only know about these people's experiences because someone, the victims or an observer, wrote accounts of them. Does this mean that I want my own account to be read, like a confession? That I *want* the punishment this would lead to? It's too confusing for me to sort out and all I can do now is go on writing.

I was rereading the piece about Quirini and his twenty-five companions when Clarissa rang to say my mother was very "poorly" (her word) and that I ought to "pull myself together" and go and see her. So I did.

What's the use of it? She doesn't know me. Clarissa was there, being extremely censorious, and saying I couldn't tell whether she knew me or not and sitting beside her, holding her hand, was the least I could do. My mother seems a very long way away from me and has done for years. She stopped understanding anything about me and the way I respond to things when I was about six. You might say, I suppose, that I stopped understanding her too, but it's not supposed to be that way, is it? It's supposed to be parents doing the understanding. My mother has become an empty, mindless shell, in a perpetual trance.

"You don't know what she dreams," Clarissa said.

I asked her what she thought I could do about that.

"You ought to be here every day to see her. You stop work at five, you could easily come every evening."

It's useless to argue with her and I no longer wanted to. Perhaps she's right. Those extracts I keep getting in the post are having a strange effect on me, quite different I'm sure from what my correspondent intends. I read about these miserable shipwrecked people, whose one wish seemed to have been to be restored to their families, and I wonder why I don't feel that way. I wonder if those dreams of my mother's that Clarissa spoke of feature me and a need for me. So, feeling this way, I've been taking the bus into Ipswich to visit her, and the journey hasn't been as bad as I expected. I sit there, holding her hand and thinking about Isabel.

In spite of what I've said about the detachment that's present when I'm writing of dreadful personal things, I *am* avoiding, I *have* shied away from continuing. I haven't kept to what I promised myself I'd do, allow no digressions or by-paths to hinder me. I've wandered and prevaricated, but through it all I've known one thing for certain: having come so far, I can't stop now. I can't just give up, I have to go on. My hope now is that I can recover that detachment, that it will come back, as the ability to write has come back, when I approach an account of what happened on the island. And not only when I approach it, but as I attempt to write it, to travel, struggling, through that Thursday night, through Friday, and come out into the clear terrible sunlight of Saturday morning.

I don't want to begin. That, at any rate, is plain. I'm doodling with words now, as others doodle round the margins of a sheet of paper, making configurations like the carvings on the petroglyph stones. Like the rubbing Elianne Donizetti made of some ancient, unidentifiable monster. It's that, remembering that, which must get me back into this history and on to the worst part.

That evening at dinner, Elianne showed us the sheet of rice paper with the smudgy shape on it like a grinning beast's mouth, full of teeth. Maybe it was one of Philip Ashton's serpents. Ugly and disturbing as it was, Mrs. Donizetti was going to have it mounted and framed. No one commented on the bruises on my neck, though once or twice I saw Dr. Ruffle staring at them.

Those few years I had over Ivo must have been enough to make me slightly the stronger. As we know from sportsmen's decline, that kind of real physical strength starts to fail by thirty. I fought him and I won. I tore his hands off my throat, I kicked him, I sent him flying across that tiny cabin, and he crashed into the door with a slamming sound that seemed to rock the ship. My windpipe felt as if it had been in a vice. I choked and grunted, trying to clear my throat. It must hurt a lot being strangled.

He got up and stood there, hanging his head, hanging his arms down and flexing his fingers. Then he threw back his head and tossed his black hair back. His face had a purplish flush. I'd never seen him look like that before.

"You might have killed me," I said.

"Yes. I wonder what they do to murderers in this state? Put them in the penitentiary or the gas chamber? In Utah it's still a firing squad. Did you know that?"

"I think you're mad," I said.

"No, you don't. You don't think I'm mad. That's just a manner of speaking. What did you think I'd do when I found you'd been unfaithful to me? Kiss you? Offer you a hundred bucks not to do it again?"

He went into the shower room and I heard him sluicing water over his face. When he came back his hair was dripping and his face was back to its normal color.

"Tell me," he said very calmly, "it isn't true. Tell me you never had her."

I braced myself. I got ready for him. "It is true. I did."

He didn't touch me again. He slammed out of the cabin. After he'd gone I drank a lot of water. It hurt going down. My throat felt like my bronchial tubes were sore inside. But I knew it wasn't over, I knew there was more to come. I went upstairs to where they were all, as usual, in the *Favonia* lounge, listening to the briefing for the following day, the last day. Ivo wasn't there. I asked the pretty Korean steward with the smiling brown eyes for a double brandy, no ice, and said, would it be big, would it be a sizeable drink? You have a triple brandy, sir, why not, no problem. It came and it was big, burning my sore esophagus as it trickled through.

I went to the lecture because I knew Ivo couldn't do anything to me there. He wouldn't even talk about it there. Nathan was to show a video, then give a talk. As soon as I came in I saw Ivo sitting in the front row. I sat at the back, next to the Bradens. The video, apparently made for children and in bright color, was of dinosaurs and kindred creatures roaming the earth. Nothing more about it remains in my memory. I was thinking about getting through the night and the day and the night, whether it was all over and he would just give up, whether there was more to come, if $300 was enough to get me from Vancouver to Seattle.

Nathan talked about the creature called Dacnospondyl and its footmarks, which we were to see the next day on Chechin Island. I may not remember the video, but I remember that. I remember every detail of that reptile and suppose I know as much about it as is known, just as I remember everything about the island, its precise latitudinal and longitudinal location, its appearance, its plant life, the great chimney of rock that spires out of its center, its loneliness. Yet I don't believe I listened very attentively to what Nathan said, and I'm sure I didn't attend to what Ivo had to say about it the next day. All the same, I could write a minutely detailed essay on Dacnospondyl and its habitat. This information must have filtered through to me subliminally, as things do perhaps in the vicinity of terrible events that can't be effaced from the memory.

Mrs. Braden asked me how I had come to hurt my neck and I said I fell over in my cabin. Her husband looked at me over the top of his half-glasses, but she believed me, innocent, sweet woman that she was, incapable of presupposing drunkenness but quite able to imagine me at my age stumbling and falling as she might stumble and fall herself. She had some arnica in her cabin that she wanted me to have for the bruises. I'd intended to make for the bar but I could hardly refuse. The Bradens had one of the two suites, much nicer than my damp, dark cabin. Set up on the *Favonia*'s battered furniture were photographs of children and grandchildren in silver frames. Mrs. Braden's pink dressing gown was laid out on one of the beds and her pink slippers under it. I mention this because it all seemed so far from my life, from what was being done to me and what I was doing, though I suppose I'm just being sentimental.

I did go to the bar and found Betsy there with Fergus, drinking Coke, so I had a Coke too, with two measures of vodka in it, a strange over-sweet mixture. The guarded way they spoke to me, a certain awkward unwelcoming manner they had, made me think they knew, that Ivo had told them all about it or they guessed. I got the barman to open a second can of Coke for me, pour away half, and fill the can up with vodka. This I meant to carry with me back to my cabin, indifferent to Betsy's stares and Fergus's remarks on the way alcohol speeded up brain-cell destruction.

Outside the door Ivo was waiting for me. I nearly dropped the can. He was standing in the passage, leaning against the wall, his arms folded. When he saw me he lit one of his rare cigarettes.

"Come out on deck," he said.

"I want to go to bed," I said. "I'm tired."

"No, you're not. You're not tired. You're halfway to being pissed and you'll be all the way when you've downed that. What have you put in it? Rum?"

"Vodka."

He laughed. There is something horrible about laughter when it isn't the natural consequence of amusement. Ivo had a way of laughing for all sorts of reasons. Because he was shocked or disgusted, or appalled, nauseated, enraged, and from a godlike eminence too, at the beastliness of human behavior.

We weren't just standing there while we talked and he laughed. He was propelling me up the staircases toward the observation deck. It was late by this time, after eleven, and that was late on the *Favonia.*

The night was clear and starry, the moon as thin as a curve of wire. We weren't yet in the open sea but coming to the southern-most end of the Inside Passage, and the islands we passed between were opaque humps of darkness against the shimmering bright darkness of the sky and the starlit calm darkness of the sea. I had never before seen starlight reflected in water, and when I'd read about it I'd thought it some writer's romantic fantasy.

Ivo began pointing out the constellations and naming them, Orion, Cassiopeia, Charles's Wain, and the Pleiades that are the seven daughters of Atlas, one of them so pale and faint that you can never be sure you see her. Isabel and I had done the same thing on the dock at Juneau, only we hadn't known the names. Ivo knew them all. It was strange, wasn't it, the two of us standing there, alone on deck at night, I half-drunk, sipping from a can of drink, he giving his astronomy lecture? The end of his cigarette glowed in the dark. He was consumed with jealousy and I with fear. He was sick to hear me say I hadn't meant it, I was his, and no one else mattered, yet he went on talking about the Milky Way and the Heavenly Twins and why Mars shines with a red light. And I listened and said Yes, and Really, and What's that one, then?

His cigarette end was as red as Mars, glowing in the bit of sky between us. There were lights on the shore in the distance on the port side. Ketchikan, he said, or it might be Metlakatla. And then he turned his back on the stars and the lights and said, "She knows about me, of course?"

"Isabel?"

"Yes, of course Isabel." He spoke the sibilant with a hiss and rolled the middle vowel. "Is-aa-bel!"

I'd told him so much there seemed no harm, no indiscretion, no danger, in telling him the rest. "She knows I had a relationship with a lecturer on one of the cruise ships."

"And she thinks it was a woman."

"How do you know?"

"Oh, please. You're so transparent. It's just what you would tell her, it's just what you would do. Did she believe you?"

"Of course she believed me."

"By that you mean that your mutual trust is so perfect that she takes everything you say for gospel? How very unfortunate for her. In some cases that would be—well, nice, touching, but with a consummate liar like you, she's simply in for disillusionment, isn't she?"

I said he must abuse me if he wanted to. I couldn't stop him, but I could go away, I could go to my cabin.

"No locks on the doors, though, are there? That's one of those disadvantages that have their happier side."

"I'm stronger than you, Ivo," I said.

"Only physically."

I don't know why that made me shiver. The implicit threat, I suppose. Of course I wasn't very clearheaded by that time, I'd drunk more than half the can, but I put my hand on the rail and looked over and thought how at this hour you could pitch someone over and who would know? Everything was so quiet and still, the sea so calm, nearly all the people on board asleep. But for the faint starlight, it was dark. Did he know what I was thinking? He often did, that was the frightening part.

Then he said something terrible. He stepped back and put one elbow on the rail. The shadows on his face were quite black.

"I shall come with you on Saturday. To Seattle. I shall come with you and meet her."

"You can't," I said. "How can you? You've another two weeks to do."

"Please. Do you think a mere job means anything to me compared with you? Do you?"

"Compared with revenge, you mean."

"Ah," he said, "I don't know." He pinched out his cigarette and put the end in his pocket. "Could I be wonderful, do you think, and give you up to her if I was convinced she loved you and you loved her? It makes me puke to talk like that, to use those words. But since I can't find other words, could I do that? No, no, it's all nonsense, I know that. You've known her ten days. She doesn't know you at all. She'll have forgotten you by now or you'll be a dirty little memory to put among a lot of other dirty little memories. Juneau where I screwed that British guy. That's what'll go through her mind when anyone says Alaska to her. If you turn up on her doorstep she'll be so embarrassed she won't know what to say."

"You couldn't be more wrong," I said.

"It may be a bit easier for her if I'm with you. I can imagine it, as a matter of fact. I can imagine us all having a drink and a good laugh."

"I'm going to bed," I said.

He didn't try to stop me. In some ways, with no cause, he had always treated me like a potential vandal or non-green, and as I went he said, "Don't throw the empty over the side, will you?"

I think I had no sleep that night. It's said that this is never quite true, that we doze without knowing it. But it seemed to me that I had no sleep. Most of the time I wasn't even lying down but sitting on the bunk with my head in my hands.

Of course, I knew Ivo couldn't come with me to Isabel unless I took him there. I had her address and he didn't. But this was no escape. I wanted her, I wanted to be with her, I wanted to go to her alone. It was almost certainly true that I could phone her in private. I could escape from Ivo for a few minutes at the airport in Vancouver and phone her, but to say what? That I couldn't see her yet because I had a friend with me? The ludicrousness of it made me wince. And what would "yet" mean? I would have to explain but explaining Ivo meant revealing who and what Ivo was.

At about six I went up on deck, my mouth dry and my head feeling the way it usually did in the morning. I had a pain too, not low down in my body, but in my side around where I thought my liver might be. Perhaps I was getting cirrhosis. It didn't worry me if I was. Death had begun to seem the only way out. It would be preferable to life with Ivo or life without Isabel.

Feeling too weak to stand for long, I sat down in a deckchair.

It was then that I noticed for the first time that we were in the open sea, that there was no land anywhere, for the first time since we left Juneau. The level gray shining sea stretched away on both sides. Up above my head that wiry moon still floated, a silver hook in the one piece of blue that wasn't obscured by dull masses of cloud.

Isabel had become clear and *present* to me again, for some reason, and imagining being with her again was curiously consoling. It was a dream, of course, almost a fantasy, because I wasn't going to be with her, if Ivo had his way I was never going to see her again, but while I thought of her and *saw* her, I was deluded into a kind of happiness. It sent me to sleep out there in the cold, fresh morning, and what woke me was Louise's voice brightly announcing that breakfast was now being served in the *Favonia*'s dining room.

Ivo was already there, sitting at an otherwise empty table. He saw me, he was waiting for me, and he patted the chair beside him in a peremptory way. Like a hypnotic subject, I made my way toward him. I heard myself say a formal "Good morning," and I saw his half-smile, his shrug. When the coffee had come and the stewardess had gone away again, he said, "We shall be in Prince Rupert by this time tomorrow. I shall have a lot to do today and we may not get another chance to talk."

"I've nothing to say," I said, "so that won't matter a lot."

"It will certainly make things simpler. I've taken no steps yet to alter our arrangements. That will have to wait till we get to Prince Rupert. Then I'll try to cancel your flight to Portland and get a flight for both of us to Seattle. I hope it'll be for the same day, that is tomorrow, but of course I don't know if that's possible."

"You're wasting your time. I won't let you meet her."

He didn't argue. He started to eat a piece of toast but I could see he had no appetite. Then he dropped his bomb. I wonder who first used that phrase about signing one's own death warrant? It's become too much of a cliché ever to be used again but it was a good metaphor, wasn't it? Imagine hearing it for the first time, the effect it would have.

He looked at me. "That money I gave you last Saturday," he said.

"You haven't been spending it, have you? I'll have it back to pay your bar bill. I'd rather use cash than a credit card."

"Why shouldn't I pay my own bar bill?"

"Oh, did you intend to? We may as well do it now, then. Any drinks you have tonight you can pay for over the bar."

There was no chance to say anything more because the Ruffles arrived and asked if they could share our table. Mrs. Ruffle said, did we know they had eleven *feet* of rain a year in Prince Rupert. They had so much they didn't measure it in inches. Someone had told her there was a storm warning out for later that day. Would we still be able to go ashore at Chechin and see the footprints of Dacnospondyl?

"It won't be much of a storm," Ivo said. "Rain and a bit of a squall. We won't let rain stop us, will we?"

"You betcha," said Mrs. Ruffle.

He was genial with them, even hearty, all pals together, the intrepid adventurers, undeterred by a menacing climate.

"What exactly does the name mean?" she said. "Dacnowhatever-itis. I meant to remember but I've forgotten."

"Roughly to be translated as 'biting-back' or 'backbite,' if you prefer."

"I like it," she said, but looking at Ivo as if it was he she liked. "I really like that old backbite. My kids are crazy about dinosaurs. They'll be wild that it was Mom who saw that big guy's footprints and not them. When was it he was around?"

"Between two hundred and fifty and three hundred million years ago."

"It doesn't seem possible," said Dr. Ruffle, who was a world-renowned cancer expert and ought to have known better than to mouth remarks like that. He helped himself to a banana from the fruit bowl. The bananas that were left had all gone black by this time but he went on eating his one a day. They were good for the cardiovascular system, he was in the habit of telling us all, being full of potassium.

Ivo was smoking again. When he was happy, when he and I were living together and happy together, he'd given it up. He lit a cigarette as if he was ashamed of his weakness, and perhaps he was. He and I went off in the direction of the purser's office. To stall him, I said I hadn't got the money on me.

"What a liar you are," said Ivo. "Of course you've got it on you. You never move without it."

My bar bill came to $260. I wasn't altogether surprised. My head felt as if £170 had been spent on getting it into the state it was in. The $40 I had left would pay for whatever I drank that evening, Ivo said. Perhaps I should sleep off my hangover before Chechin Island was sighted. Or at any rate I should rest. There was a book in the ship's library on the Cretaceous period and the culmination of the dinosaur revolution that I might find—he hesitated for a word—improving.

I sat on deck in the chair I'd slept in that morning. As far as the avifaunists were concerned, the cruise was over. There would be no more interesting birds. But the tailfins of humpback whales still broke the surface of the sea, someone saw a sea otter swimming on its back and from time to time seal faces appeared. I held the binoculars up to my closed eyes, trying to sleep behind them.

It was cold out there. For the first time since we left Juneau a real wind was blowing, chopping the sea into millions of wavelets, and the clouds were dark. They spat out bursts of rain that felt icy cold on the skin. The mist dropped and fell and rose again, the wind sweeping it aside. I asked Fergus, who came to stand at the rail by my chair, how deep the water was, but he didn't know, only that it was many fathoms deep, perhaps unfathomable. It was gray and sparkling, yet dull, stretching for ever, seemingly endless.

Chechin Island appeared on the horizon at about ten, coffee time. I wasn't sitting with Ivo but at a table I shared with Connie, Nathan, and the ship's doctor. Because I was seated by the window and facing the way the *Favonia* was going, because I wasn't taking part in the conversation, I spotted the island probably before anyone else did. I say "the horizon" but it isn't really like that when anything more than, say, half a mile away is hidden in mist. Chechin loomed out of the mist as if it, and not we, had moved. It grew upon me slowly, at first no more than a dark gray shape, but from the beginning it seemed to me one of the strangest, most sinister and ugly places I'd ever seen.

I said, "Look."

Nathan got up and stood behind me, peered and said, "That's Chechin."

"Is that where we're going?" Connie said.

"If you don't mind a rough sea and getting wet."

By the time the coffee was finished we were quite close to the island, had come under its lee, perhaps, only I don't know the right terms. I felt the anchor go down, that strange sound-sensation that is rather like feeling the descent of the wheels on an aircraft when it's about to land. The island lay before us, some two or three hundred yards away, perhaps more.

It was a longish island, humpbacked like a whale, but out of the hump grew a tall pillar of rock, pointing a gnarled finger into the sky. There's another island in these waters of a similar formation but looking even more like a lighthouse and named, by George Vancouver for all I know, the New Eddystone Rock. The rock column on Chechin looks more as if a temple had once stood there and all but a single pillar had been eroded away by the action of the sea. Trees grow there, spruce of course, and hemlock, and a green sward comes down to a white beach. Or, rather, you know the island is green when you land there. From the ship it looked gray, many tones of gray, like an etching on rough gray paper. A small cloud obscured the pinnacle of the column, wrapping it as a shred of cotton might wrap a distaff.

The sight of it brought back to me that picture that hung in Martin Zeindler's living room, the one of the Parthenon by moonlight. It must have been the grayness, the absence of color, and the sense of ancient things. But Chechin was the Parthenon in the dark, a troop of Goths having destroyed every column but one.

I nearly failed to go there. The rain had started again, dashing against the windows of the dining room, blown by the first of the squalls we had been warned of. I thought I knew what those lizard footprints would be like, indistinguishable from ice erosion or pits in the rock until Fergus or Ivo told us what they were. I imagined the trek through the woods, the dripping trees, the awful silence, the heady smell of a freshness, a pristine unpolluted *purity,* almost too unfamiliar to bear. But if I stayed behind? Boredom and fear are a terrible combination. Could I stand another three hours' solitary of boredom and fear?

I went down to my cabin and got into my waterproof gear, the pants, the jacket, the hood, the rubber boots. At the exit for the Zodiac embarkation I turned disc 22 to red and followed the others on to the gangplank, into the rain.

14

All yesterday I was thinking about how to write down what happened on the island. Perhaps I should say it's been at the back of my mind, though often pushing forward and emerging, for this is one of our busiest times at the Consortium. Apart from inquiries for seats, there have been the temperamental Harmonia-Balt Quintet from Vilnius and the loss of the cellist's instrument to deal with, the inability of the minister for the arts to decide which performance of all twenty-two he can bear to sit through and the prima donna–ish behavior of the world's greatest (so he says) flamenco dancer, who refuses to sleep anywhere in sight or sound of the sea. But I was thinking about the island and Ivo all the same, wondering how to set it all down, whether everything should be described in precise detail or some events should be given emphasis and others glossed over.

I expected to begin last evening, but at the last moment Julius more or less ordered me to go to the Pergolesi Mass at the Methodist chapel. It conflicted with the obviously much more popular Britten *Albert Herring* in the Great Hall of the Concert Complex and for the former we had sold a mere twenty-three seats. However, two of them had gone to a couple called Margie and Eric Krupka, last seen by me on board the *Favonia* in southeast Alaska.

If I haven't mentioned them before it's because I saw very little of them on the cruise. They never went into the bar and they ate all their meals at one of the four tables for two. Still, they were among the passengers in the Zodiac in which I came back from the island. That was the last time I remember seeing them. But here they were, looking just the same, sitting two rows behind me, a little to the left-hand side.

Of course it wasn't a particularly remarkable coincidence. It was hardly a coincidence at all. Sooner or later, just as they go to Glyndebourne and Munich and perhaps Verona, all the world and its mistress (as Scott Fitzgerald puts it somewhere) come to Song and Dance at N. I'd seen James Gilman there and I'd seen Martin Zeindler. Probably it will only be a matter of time before I encounter the entire passenger list of the *Favonia* as well as Penny Marvell, Piers Churchill, Emily, Suzanne, Mansoor, and Sharif Qasir.

Ivo I had seen there many times, but that was something else, that was another story. The Krupkas very likely had a visit to N. as part of their package deal, but on the other hand they might have been great church-music enthusiasts. And not much of their personal tastes or expertise emerged when, as we met afterward going down the aisle, they recognized me and spoke.

Sitting there, listening to Pergolesi, I'd wondered how to avoid them and resigned myself to the impossibility of doing so. In that small hall with its single door that was entrance and exit there could be no escape. I'd have to meet them. Pleasantries and reminiscences would be exchanged. I'd thought all that and been irritated at the prospect, bored by it, but I hadn't felt fear. Now, as Margie Krupka's eye lighted on me and immediately lit up, I was suddenly enormously afraid.

I was sure, of course, *am* sure, that there is much to know that has never reached me. When they found his body it must have been in the papers. At least in Alaska, at least on the West Coast. Before that there must have been a hue and cry. None of it reached me because I was gone and after that I *didn't want to know*. But the whole of the Panhandle area was alerted to it, probably it was the talking point of that summer, the disappearance of, the death of,

Dr. Ivo Steadman. So, when Margie Krupka called out, "Why, if it isn't Tim!" I would have liked to turn tail and run. As it was, I felt the blood go out of my face and goose pimples start.

"How've you been, Tim?" said Krupka.

It amazed me—Americans always amaze me in this way—that he remembered my Christian name. I knew his but I had the *Favonia*'s list on the desk beside me when I wrote, I was constantly referring to it. He hadn't seen me for a year and three-quarters, he'd known me for only seven days and that not well, hardly at all, yet he remembered my name. Could it be because . . . ?

But, no. "You keep in touch with that other British guy, the paleontologist—what was he called? What was the dark guy's name, Margie?"

"Dr. Steadman," I said, and then I said, "Ivo," finding I could actually speak his name aloud without fainting or bursting into tears or having a stroke. I said it again to make sure. "Ivo."

No comment on the lines of that-was-a-funny-thing-we-heard-happened, no exchanged glances, nothing. Politeness had been honored and they began to talk about themselves, life in the western United States on campus, where they both taught at a state university, this music-in-Europe trip they were treating themselves to in celebration of a twentieth wedding anniversary, the English weather. If they lived in Arizona, as it seemed they did, news of Ivo's fate would no more have reached them than it would me. Tomorrow they were off to Seville and Margie Krupka carolled some phrases from *Carmen* about her friend Lillas Pastia in a rich, tuneful soprano.

"Say hello to Dr. Steadman when you see him," said her husband.

I hadn't seen Ivo for a long time but it wasn't a parting shot I much liked going home with. The High Street was crowded, or rather, there was a crowd round the Methodist chapel, but the street that runs parallel to it, the alleys, the shore road, all were deserted. It was raining, it had been raining for hours, and the air was not misty but a clear dark blue, the colored lights making reflections on the wet stones like smears of paint, red, green, orange. The glassy sea looked black, a great spill of ink. I turned sharply as I came into Shore Road, for I could have sworn I heard the slap of a footstep behind me, the sole of a shoe sucked by the wet for an instant before it left the pavement. I turned and there was no one there, but he was back.

Suppose I turn round one day, I thought, and look into his face? Say hello to Dr. Steadman when you see him. Rain fell on my face like the sweet, unpolluted rain of Chechin Island and I wanted to scream out, save me, help me, don't leave me to spend tonight alone! I actually stood still in the rain out there, holding my arms wrapped round my body, my shoulders hunched, thinking, I can't go indoors, I can't, because if he isn't behind me he's in there waiting for me. And then I thought, not for the first time, of going quietly down the beach and walking into the sea, just walking on and on in all my clothes, waterlogged shoes keeping the stones off my tender feet, raincoat and jacket and trousers ballooning with water, and water coming up over my head while I walked in and in, deeper and deeper.

I wonder if he did that or if he tried to swim? The waste of waters, on either side, on every side, stretching for ever, and nothing in sight anywhere to swim to. If he drank salt water like Quirini's shipmates? Standing out there, looking at the sea, the tide far out, the silvery edge of it licking the sprawl of pebbles, I relived what had happened, I thought of what I must write down tonight. It brought me a kind of strength, of resolution, and it gave me the nerve to go into the house.

Liquid sunshine is what they call it in the towns up there, the faintly sunlit half-mist, half-drizzle that's classified as a fine day. This was the state of things when the Zodiacs pulled away from the ship and headed through a roughening sea for Chechin Island.

Eleven people were in Ivo's Zodiac and ten in Nathan's. I wish I could remember exactly who was in each but I can't and the ship's passenger list doesn't help. I do remember that Fergus was in our Zodiac along with Ivo, the Donizettis with Elianne, and the Krupkas, but there must have been two more and I don't know who. As for Nathan's, Betsy was with him and the Ruffles, and Connie Dorral may have been, but that's all I can recall. I do remember Mrs. Krupka wearing a black plastic rubbish bag over her clothes and her life jacket, with a hole cut out for her head. The ship's shop had weatherproof gear in stock but the Krupkas refused to spend money on that. That was what they said when Fergus commented on her strange garb, and they inquired rhetorically what they were to do with it afterward. It never rained where they lived and in any case they went everywhere by car.

So I remember them, for that reason. And I remember the little girl Elianne with her sheet of rice paper in a plastic bag, hoping to get as good a rubbing of Dacnospondyl's footprints as she had of the petroglyph. Ivo wasn't steering, Fergus was doing that. Ivo never looked back at the *Favonia* and he never looked at me, he kept his eyes on Chechin through his binoculars.

It took us about ten minutes to get there and during those minutes the sunny part of the liquid sunshine receded and the mist seemed to rise a little. The thin curtain rose and showed us the island clearly. Until then a shawl of white cloud had obscured the top of the pillar of rock, but now it unwrapped itself and a jagged pinnacle appeared. The rock now looked a dark blackish-gray but the green lawns had gained color. They sloped down to a fringe of beach, pale gray, not silvery, scattered with black moss-coated stones. (Fine writing, huh? Martin Zeindler would have made me cut it out. He'd have put his red ballpoint through "shawl" all right.) We came ashore, pulled the Zodiacs up out of the water and stripped off our life jackets. Everybody, for some reason, climbed the greensward and stood gazing up the length of the rock column.

I stood and gazed with them while Ivo told us why it was the way it was, what geological events had led to this island being here and retaining a single tall chimney, all that now remained of a once sizable mountain. Elianne asked him if anyone had ever climbed it, but he said not that he knew of, people hardly ever came here. Some of the cruise ships that had Zodiacs like ours put boats ashore, but it was a notorious bad-weather spot, the center of storms.

Did I take this in at the time? Did it influence me? I think it must have. I know that while Ivo was talking and the others gazing, I turned round and contemplated the sea from which we had come, gray, undulating, flecked with foam, a huge, wide, empty sea on which the *Favonia,* floating at anchor, looked very small. But nothing concrete formed in my mind, it was all dreams then, vague hopes, absurd fantasy ways of escape.

Ivo came down from the green hill where he'd been standing. He smiled at Elianne.

"We'll all go and see Dacnospondyl now," he said. "Or we'll see where he trod two hundred fifty million years ago. Unfortunately, we won't see him."

"Or her," said a woman from the other Zodiac. "You always say 'him.' They're just as likely to be the female Dacnospondyl's footprints."

"You're quite right. I'm sorry. We'll go and see *her* footprints and then you'll all be free to explore Chechin if you want to. It's eleven now, so I'll say we'll meet here by the Zodiacs at twelve-thirty. That should give you time enough."

So we set off, a straggling procession. The feminist's boyfriend asked Ivo if Dacnospondyl laid eggs and this started him on the definitions of a mammal, of a reptile. Someone said that anything with six legs must be an insect. There were none of those on Chechin, so far as I could see, and no mammals either, no birds but for the eagles, one of which had flown from the top of a spruce to perch on the rock pinnacle. It was very quiet—no, more than that, utterly silent. The only sound was our voices. And when no one spoke, as happened after the little discussion on animal taxonomy—Ivo taught me that word—a deep breathless silence fell.

Everyone had shoes with rubber soles or rubber boots. Underfoot it was moist, soft, almost virgin soil. No one ever walked here but visitors come to see where a lizard, extinct for an eternity, had once walked. The mist had risen and been absorbed in a gathering of clotted gray. You could taste the pure atmosphere now on your lips, salty, cold, and inhale a heady freshness. The temperature seemed to be falling. It was hard to believe this was midsummer, *after* midsummer, the year's warmest time.

We walked across grass, through a little grove of spruces, out the other side on to more grass. The verges along the fjords had abounded in flowers, the chocolate lily, the botanist from Florida told us, the aquilegia, the dwarf dogwood. Bushes were in fruit with the salmonberry, dream raspberries, twice the size they should be and the color of a tangerine. But there was none of that here, nothing but short, coarse grass, mosses, and tiny ferns. The place was quite barren, the soil no more than a skin over the rock. Nothing had ever been seen there but the ancient traces of Backbite, and here they were, this was what they were, this was what we had come for.

A plain of light gray rock, smooth yet faintly striated, with a look of running water petrified, the appearance of rock upon which the passage of ice had acted, as I was beginning to learn. It was as if the ice had stroked it, as a great hand might stroke and caress hair, but I knew the action must have been more severe, violent, savage, fiercely erosive. Down the center of this smooth sloping rock platform, Dacnospondyl had passed toward the sea, leaving behind five fossilized prints. They were plainly prints, no doubt about them, beautifully preserved footmarks, pads and claws outlined, bone pressure apparent, proof of a pre-dinosaur reptile's existence, legends made alive.

Ivo began to recount how they came to be there, what disasters, ecological and, to Backbite, fatal, had brought into being this record. Eric Krupka took notes, though I suppose he could easily have got the facts out of any encyclopedia. Elianne started complaining that the prints were too deep for her to make a rubbing.

"Take a photograph instead," Ivo said.

"It's not the same."

"You could draw them on your rice paper. You could make a drawing and frame that."

"Oh, wow!" she said, as if he had made a suggestion of startling originality.

"Is there any chance," asked the feminist's boyfriend, "of old Backbite here having survived? I mean, like that Loch Ness monster you have up in Scotland?"

"None at all," said Ivo. "There are positively no extant lizards of this type."

"Okay, but a hippo looks a hell of a lot like a kind of dinosaur, so how about that?"

Ivo only laughed. "Right, you've an hour to wander round in and take photographs. And if you do see *her,* mind you get a shot of Dacnospondyl. You'll make history." He often became facetious when he was unhappy. His irony, his *funniness* deserted him. His eyes were turned on me and they were full of pain. Not just pain, though, pain and determination, an intention of seeing it through, perhaps getting even, keeping me to himself at whatever cost.

As I've said, I hadn't brought a camera with me. I'm a rotten photographer, anyway. It suddenly seemed terrible to me that I had about fifty minutes to kill before we could get back in those Zodiacs. I was wasting time here, time that ought to be spent in finding a way to thwart Ivo and keep him from traveling with me to Seattle. I walked away from the others. They were all still occupied in photographing the footprints; in the case of Dr. Ruffle, making a film of everyone looking at the footprints and preserving their stares for posterity on his Camcorder.

Their voices were soon lost. There must be something about Chechin Island, some phenomenon of the acoustics, that deadens sound or absorbs it into the silence. As if it were a living thing, the deep quiet swallowed sound and rested. It rested and seemed to be waiting, the silence and the stillness lying there on the wide gray waters, no other land in sight. Winds rise and fall away there as fast as the clouds drop and lift. For the time being, the wind also rested and lay still.

I walked over the smooth rock, through the grass, through the groves of spruce and hemlock, to the other side of the island, the side from which the *Favonia* was not visible. There was no water on Chechin, fresh water that is, not a pool, not a spring. I don't know why I noticed this because it's not like me, perhaps my unconscious mind perceived it.

Mostly, at the edge of the sea, we'd seen marine life, shrimps and small crabs, clams and limpets. Nothing of that kind lived along the shores of Chechin. I peered through the water on to bare round stones, free even of seaweed. The sand was pale and glittering, the kind they call silver sand, and it was undisturbed by currents, it lay like a smooth floor under water as clear as that from a tap run into a glass. For a long way out I could see the sea floor, the water was so transparent and still.

And then, unaccountably, I was afraid to look at the sea any longer. I, who had lived by the sea for most of my life, was afraid of its extent, its mystery, and its potentiality for death. It occurred to me then, for the first time, though many times since I've thought of this, that this huge element is a lethal weapon. All that is necessary is to give yourself to it or be given, and it will do the rest.

So I turned my back on the sea and walked inland, across sheets of scree, over slippery moss of a green so bright that it hurt the eyes. I came up under the stony stem of the Chimney of Chechin and laid myself against it, holding it in my arms, my face against its cold, rough granite. And up there it was as if the sky was pulling back from the earth, all the mass of gray and white cloud drawn up very high, so that a vast space of fresh, icy air hung between me and it. I felt the stirrings of a breeze, the touch of it on my skin, and I saw the hemlock branches sway a little. An eagle flew, and so silent was the island that the sound of its wings was thunder.

If I'd stayed there I'd have been overtaken by the Donizettis and the Ruffles, whose voices I heard as they approached. The chattering sounds broke the silence like some violent act in a peaceful place. I climbed down the rocky platform and into the densest growth of shrubs on the island. After that I simply walked aimlessly, feeling the cold almost to the point of shivering, walking because I was too cold to stand still, sometimes clutching hold of a branch, sometimes touching a smooth shiny tree trunk. And all the time I was thinking of Isabel, of reaching her unsupervised, unattended by a vengeful man, I was thinking of Isabel and I was thinking of money.

It was with a shock that I came upon Ivo. He too was alone. The cold never much affected him, he who loved "drafts" and open doors and wide open spaces. He was sitting on a boulder, looking down, an aquilegia between his fingers. It must have been the only one on the island. I don't mean he had picked it, he was the last man to do that, but he was holding its stem and looking at the flower, its stamens and its rabbit-mouth shape, so rapt that I think I could have passed by and he not seen or heard me.

"Ivo," I said.

He lifted his head. "At a loose end?"

I knew that tone. He often used it, implying that I was such a slave to bright lights, drink, and entertainment, as to be impatient with the natural world after about five minutes.

"I want to talk to you," I said, though I hadn't thought I wanted to a moment before, I hadn't seen what purpose talking to him would serve.

"About what? Please don't say 'us' in that coy way you favor, putting your head on one side like Princess Diana. I don't think I could bear it."

I was used to taunts of that kind. You can get used to any verbal abuse. Coquettish behavior was always being attributed to me when he was angry, though I don't think I'm ever coy or effeminate. Ivo used to say, sneering at me, that if he wanted femininity he'd go after women.

He took his hand from the orange flower and got to his feet. "What is it then?"

"I want you to let me go," I said. "Go back with the ship to Juneau and leave me to go on alone."

"And then?"

"There won't be any 'then.' Not for us. It's over, Ivo. I have to make you see that it's over whether you let me go or come on with me. Coming with me would only be a postponement. It's over anyway. What difference does it make to you whether it's over tomorrow or over in three weeks' time? Inside my head it's over, it's been over for months. If you know I don't want to be with you, why do you want to be with me?"

"I'll tell you. Because I don't believe you know what you want. You're a frivolous lightweight, you're not a serious person, you live for the moment. At the moment, because you and she had a jolly time together, you think you want this woman. But you don't know her, and God knows, she doesn't know you. She doesn't know that after a few months of her you'd be off chasing boys or even coming to me."

"That's an absolute lie," I said.

He took no notice. "Do you think she'd want you if she knew what you were really like?"

The cold air touched me like a knife point. "Ivo, you wouldn't tell her?"

"About 'us,' as you put it. Of course. Why not? How do you know she doesn't know already?"

"How could she?"

He took a step back. He was standing with his back to a giant spruce and he laid his hands on its trunk. "What did you intend to use for money on this trip to visit your lady love? Taking it, for instance, that you made it alone?"

"Tell me, how she could know?" I said. I was trembling. He saw and it made his lip curl up. "Tell me what you meant."

"It's not a usual name. There can't be many Isabel Winwoods in America, still fewer in Seattle. Don't you think I could have found where she lived quite easily?"

I couldn't even remember telling him her name. "You're making it up," I said. "You *can't* have written to her."

He shrugged. "Very well. I can't have. Telling her is still to come then, is it? You haven't answered my question about money. Did you think I was going to give you enough money to get you to Seattle and live on when you were there, pat you on the head, say, 'Bless you, my child. Be happy with your sweetheart.' Did you?"

It was stupid, it was childish, I shouldn't have answered him, but I did and made things worse, made things terrible. "You said you'd pay for me before we started. That was the condition. You wanted me to come and you said you'd pay."

He stepped away from the tree and came closer to me. Suddenly he got hold of me by the front of my jacket and pulled me toward him. "Go on."

"Let me go, Ivo. What d'you mean, go on? That's all, I'm only stating the facts. You don't think I wanted to come on this cruise, do you? I knew I'd loathe it and I have. I've hated every bloody minute. I've never been so bored and miserable in my life. I came because you wanted me to and I couldn't have come if you hadn't paid."

He didn't let me go. He held me there in an iron grip so that I forgot about being younger and stronger. I shuddered. It made me lose caution. "I may as well tell you, I'd have gone home that first day in Juneau, I'd have gone home if the airline had let me use my ticket. I tried to go," I said, "and what stopped me was meeting Isabel."

Letting go of my jacket, he struck me in the face with both hands, a hard slap on each side of my face. I staggered back with a cry. I put one hand up to my face. He smiled.

"If you want money," he said, "I suggest you sell yourself in Vancouver. I can give you an address where they arrange these things. You're a bit long in the tooth for what they want, but after dark and if you keep the rates low . . ."

I hit him as I hard as I could with my fist to his jaw. It was the first and only time I've ever done that, hit someone. The noise bone on bone made was quite loud, a crack. The blow hurt my knuckles. He didn't cry out or even grunt. He looked surprised, utterly astonished, as he buckled up and fell, his head making another crack against the tree trunk. Ivo hardly ever showed surprise. I couldn't remember when I'd last seen an expression on his face so near amazement.

At first I was aghast at what I'd done. I hadn't meant to do that. There flashed through my mind film scenes in which men hit each other over and over, on and on, and keep coming back for more. Perhaps it was only like that on film. My own face still stung and throbbed where he'd slapped me.

I didn't touch him. I stood there for a moment, perhaps thirty seconds, looking at him. He was unconscious, lying on his back. A trickle of blood ran down through his black hair from where he'd hit his head on the tree. I said, "Ivo," but it was as if I hadn't spoken, he made no sign.

I turned and ran. As I came down toward the beach I saw a Zodiac pulling away. It was then, for the first time, that I was aware of how the wind had got up and how rough the sea was, not dangerously rough, but choppy, a mass of little energetic waves. The Donizettis and Betsy were putting on their life jackets but none of the others was anywhere to be seen. I walked down to where they were and where the second Zodiac was, drawn up on the beach, laden with life jackets.

Was I thinking? Was I planning? Or was it all reflex and reaction, self-preservation? I don't know. I only know that I wasn't reasoning. It came to me as a natural act to take the life jacket numbered 76 and, with it in my hand, climb up the greensward to look for the Krupkas and Fergus. In the lee of the Chimney of Chechin where no one could see me, I put the life jacket on under my waterproof and rezipped it. I went back to the Zodiac. Fergus had come. Eric and Margie Krupka came, running, breathless, they hadn't meant to be late, but it was all so fascinating, so overwhelming . . .

"Where's Ivo?" Fergus asked, wading in, pulling the Zodiac off the beach.

"He must have gone in the other boat," said Mrs. Donizetti.

My voice sounded hoarse and thin but no one noticed. "He went in the other boat," I said.

"Okay. Now are we all here?"

Fergus gave his arm to Mrs. Donizetti to lean on as she stepped over the heavy rubber flange that ringed the Zodiac. He gave his arm to Elianne. Eric Krupka, scorning aid, stumbled and nearly fell into the sea. Even on the edge of the shore, the Zodiac rocked and bobbed on the excited water, the waves lapping and sucking and making slapping noises. I expected Ivo to appear at any moment, at every moment. My own life jacket strapped round me, turning me into a fat man, I was the last to enter the Zodiac. I needed Fergus's arm, for I was shaking like someone with a high fever. He asked me if I was cold but I shook my head. I said nothing.

The sky was like no sky I'd ever seen, a huge sweep of gray cloud across which black cloud streaked as if a comb had been drawn through it. I kept my eyes fixed on the place I'd come from, where I'd left him, or rather, on the approach to that place, for the sandy ground, the mosses and the grass were hidden, only the top of the tall spruce visible above an undergrowth of hemlock. In there he was, he still was. I said those words to myself and I shook, but I didn't think. Fergus pushed the Zodiac out and jumped in, the engine spluttering, then roaring into life.

They go fast, those Zodiacs, when they have to. We described a great curve across the water, then headed for the *Favonia*. It was very rough. Margie Krupka said she was frightened. She held on tight to her husband's hand and with the other to the guide rope. We were all supposed to hold that guide rope but I couldn't, not with my shaking hands. Elianne Donizetti began singing some boating song she'd learned at school.

Chechin receded from us fast. All the mist was gone but the rain started before we reached the ship and the straight icy shafts of it hid the island behind a curtain of steely rods. I stared back at it. I stared at what I could see, a long gray humpbacked thing, without features but for the pillar sticking out of its middle, the Chimney of Chechin, a spire, a broken column, a gnarled pointing finger. It was just a shape now, an ugly and sinister shape, the color of the paler cloud, afloat on a rising sea. The rain streamed down my face and slid in rivulets over the waterproof clothes. I looked at the island and resolved not to look back any more, not to look at the sea again.

We went aboard the *Favonia*. No one saw me take off one life jacket, then another, and hang them both up. Everyone was too busy talking about the heavy sea, the storm that was coming. I turned disc 22 over to black and then I turned disc 76.

A great bolt of lightning split the sky into two halves, a tree of electric shocks. The thunderclap was immediate and the rain began in earnest then. Serious rain, Connie Dorral called it, meeting me on the stairs as I went down. She was one of those people who are excited by a storm, her eyes glittering, her breathing short. I could tell she wanted a companion to share her excitement, to watch the lightning and the heaving sea with her, but that companion wasn't going to be me. I ran from her, down the stairs. The rain beat against the windows so hard that you couldn't see out of them. I didn't want to see out, I was sticking to my resolve not to look at the sea again, ahead of us, behind us, around us, not to look. I was thinking again.

The *Favonia*'s anchor went up with a long shuddering clanking roar. It was as if the thunder were rumbling under the sea as well as above it. The whole ship juddered as the anchor was sucked into its bowels. In my cabin I sat on my bunk and shook and thought, he won't come, he can't come now.

15

If there had ever been a night in my life when I needed to get drunk it was that night. But I didn't. That night was the beginning of my drinking a lot less and of becoming just like anyone else who likes a drink sometimes. Not a drunk, not an alcoholic, not an endangerer of the only liver I've got.

I don't know why this was. It was as if I knew nothing would help, nothing would change things. Oblivion, which is the usual goal, wasn't even a wise thing to aim at. On a crude level, I had to keep my wits about me. This gives the impression, of course, that I was just a brute thinking of his own skin, of covering his tracks, of saving himself, and at that point I was. One part of me was and the other part was simply disbelieving. I hadn't done that, I couldn't have, I'd wake up soon.

At first, in that first hour after we got back, I was sure they would realize and go back for him. He'd be missed at lunch. Someone would ask me and I'd have to say I didn't know. It was the only thing I could say. The ship was rolling and I understood that this was a storm, we were in a storm at sea. It was raging round Chechin Island and it was here with us, as we made our twenty knots or whatever it was. I'd had no lunch, I hadn't been able to contemplate it, I stayed in my cabin, curled up fetally on the bunk while the little ship bounced and sank and bounced on the rough sea. The last thing I expected was that I'd sleep, but I did, I fell into a heavy sleep, and when I woke up it was nearly four.

There were no more than a dozen people in the *Favonia* lounge, having tea, while Louise briefed them on what would be happening the next day when we arrived in Prince Rupert. Megan was there and Nathan but no Fergus and no Betsy. No one who had been in the Zodiacs to Chechin was there. I felt a constriction in my throat and my mouth dried. But I sat down. I sat down by myself at a table near the dais where Louise was standing.

It seemed to me that her tone was grave. She seemed subdued. And where was everyone? It struck me that I wouldn't know if the ship had turned round and was going back the way it had come. I hadn't looked out—and what could I have seen if I had?

The New Eddystone Rock, apparently. Dr. Braden, at the window, announced its appearance on the starboard side. This time I did look, it would have seemed strange if I hadn't. The sea had calmed, heaving a little with no more than a soft swell, and the rain had become a thin, gentle spray. I joined the rest of them, a pitifully small number, at the windows and watched us pass the rock that looks like a lighthouse, smaller than Chechin, with no trees, its chimney broader, a natural tower. Through the drizzle its outlines were blurred. It was a castle seen through a curtain.

My imagination constructed a scenario. The passengers, the crew, everyone, were having a meeting about Ivo, to decide what must be done about Ivo, whether to go back or send a wireless message to whoever one does send such messages to, a helicopter station, a ranger's outpost. And they were also discussing me, what to do about me. I looked around me. I counted eight people where there were usually a hundred. Then Mrs. Braden, on her two canes, came up to me and asked me how I was feeling.

"I'm fine," I said, and "Why do you ask?"

"Not seasick?"

"No." Light dawned then. "Is that where they are? They're all seasick?"

"So it seems." She laughed her old woman's broken laugh that you'd have called a cackle in anyone less nice. "James and I are just too old for that nonsense and you, well, I guess you're too young."

They were all lying down in their cabins, that was all it was. That was why the ship's doctor wasn't there and probably why Dr. Ruffle wasn't there. We were out in the open sea now and in a storm and people were being seasick. *They would think Ivo was being seasick.* That's where he was, so far as they knew, in his cabin being seasick. I didn't have any tea but went into the observation lounge and stared out to sea through the bubble-shaped windows. The lighthouse rock had disappeared, everything had disappeared and it was just darkening, lowering gray sky out there and a calm gray sea meeting it at a horizon it took good eyesight to see.

On the way down I met Megan coming up.

"How's Ivo?" she asked.

I was afraid to lie and it was impossible to tell the truth. I said I didn't know. How did she know I *might* know? What had he told her?

"Fergus kept throwing up. They'll all get better now the storm's past. The last-night party's due to start after dinner."

But only ten sat down to dinner. Another storm blew up when dusk came. I sat at a table alone and knew I wasn't going to be able to eat anything. Dr. Ruffle came in, looking pale, without his wife, and finished up the last of the black bananas. Most of the soup and starters and roast chicken and apple pie à la mode went back to the kitchen. I asked for a glass of Chardonnay. Dr. Ruffle caught my eye and came over.

"How about we share a bottle?" he said.

I said yes, but not with the greed and the enthusiasm I'd have shown the night before. He sat down and began talking about seasickness, why some people have it and others don't, about migraine, about epilepsy and L-dopa. I don't know what he said, I didn't listen, but he talked away, apparently careless of my indifference. No doubt he thought that I was feeling queasy too. And I was, but it was a nausea of the mind or maybe the soul. I was starting to be sick with horror.

The party never took place. The bar was empty. Dr. Ruffle excused himself to go down and see how his wife was. I thought, suppose I dreamed it, it never happened, and Ivo really is down there, lying on his bunk, knowing his sickness won't go till we come into calmer waters. It was so unlike me, to hit anyone. And why had I? Because he suggested I'd prostitute myself? So what? I probably would have if I'd thought of it and knew how to go about it. For money. For the sake of getting to Isabel.

I wouldn't hit a man for accusing me of that. I'd had far worse insults from Ivo. Besides, I knew he insulted me when he was unhappy, and yes, when I'd made him unhappy. So perhaps I hadn't hit him and he hadn't struck his head on that tree, I hadn't run away and left him. I'd dreamed it when I got back and lay down and slept. During that sleep I'd dreamed of hitting Ivo, knocking him unconscious, running away and leaving him. It wasn't the kind of thing anyone would really do, so I'd dreamed it.

The lift was nearly always in use by old people who couldn't go up and down stairs, but not that night, it was free that night. I went down in it, got off at the boat deck and walked along to where the life jackets were hung up and where the discs were on their hooks. It was silent and empty and rather cold. It was as if there was no one on board but me. The life jacket numbered 76 was hanging up there and disc 76 was turned to black. I must have been a little bit mad, or else it was the effect of less than half a bottle of Chardonnay, but I felt a tremendous relief when I saw that life jacket and that disc, as though I hadn't put the life jacket there myself and turned the disc over myself. Ivo must be all right, he must be on board, because his life jacket was there and his disc was turned to black.

Others thought that way, of course, but why did I? I was a bit mad and that must be the only reason. In any case, it was a euphoria that didn't last long. I went down to his cabin and before I got to the door I knew I'd been deceiving myself. Of course I hadn't dreamed it, of course it had happened. I'd turned the disc myself. He was on that island, he'd regained consciousness and understood what had happened. It was cold and pouring with rain, the *Favonia* had gone without him, he had no adequate gear to withstand the coldness of the night, no means of crossing the water, fifty or sixty

miles of sea, before land could be reached. He had nothing to eat
and nothing to drink but rain, no shelter but the hemlocks and the
thin tall spruces. Or else he was still unconscious, losing blood from
a head wound, while his body grew colder, soaked by rain.

The passage down in the depths of the ship was deserted. A
superstitious fear came to me, not that I'd find his cabin empty but
that I'd find him in there. It was like that story, "The Monkey's
Paw," about the dead son coming back because his old parents have
wished for him to be alive. They have three wishes granted them.
The first one, I can't remember what they wish but it proves to
them that it works. With the second they wish for their dead son
to come back, but when he knocks at the door they know who it
is and they can't face him, for *they know he is dead,* so they use the
third wish to wish him dead again. I knew Ivo was, if not dead, at
any rate fifty miles behind us on an island in that waste of seas, but
I thought, suppose he's in there?

I opened the door and went in. The bunk was stored away in the
wall. Everything was tidy. I looked in the small hanging cupboard
that was all cabins of this size had for keeping clothes in. The jacket
he wore for going into the dining room was there and a denim
jacket, two or three pairs of jeans, a sweater, three shirts on
hangers, a pair of shoes, and a pair of trainers. My scarf, the Leythe
scarf that was Gilman's, hung over the hanger the good jacket was
on. I shut the door again and sat down on the single chair.

Half the point of doing what I'd done would be lost if I didn't
do this next thing. Having done what I'd done, this I was about to
do was nothing. Macbeth knew about that when he said he'd
stepped so far in blood that even if he went no farther, going back
was as tedious as going on. I don't think "tedious" meant the same
thing to them as it does to us. It wasn't boredom that bothered me.
What I'd done I'd done to get to Isabel, but if I didn't do this one
more thing I hadn't a hope of reaching her. Strange, wasn't it, I was
thinking of her then not so much as a woman but as a wonderful
country, a sort of paradise that I had to surmount all sorts of
obstacles to reach. Well, I'd surmounted one of them, or made a
start on surmounting it. Now it was as if I had to go through a

number of trials and tests, like Tamino, like Papageno. Only mine were the tests of vice, not virtue.

I wasn't sitting there deciding what to do. I'd already decided. Wasn't that why I went into the cabin? I was just putting off the evil day. I jumped up and flung that cupboard door open. It was then that I realized he must be wearing that leather jacket he'd left with me in Juneau and reclaimed when he came to fetch me. He wouldn't have carried money with him to Chechin, or credit cards. I went through his pockets. In the inside pocket of the good jacket I found his wallet with £30 sterling in it and something over $600. My hands shook when I counted the notes.

He only had two credit cards. I took the Visa and left the American Express. I left the traveler's checks, all of them in his name and no use to me. I took all the money. It's no good being sentimental, being so-called scrupulous, in these circumstances. That was what I told myself. He wouldn't need it where he was and I needed it very much. If left there it would only go to relatives, whoever they might be. I went through the pockets of the denim jacket and found a further $29 in five-dollar bills and ones. I took it all.

Then I packed his things. If they don't know he's missing, I thought, they may not find out if I pack for him. That way a steward will just come and carry his baggage up on to the dock at Prince Rupert. So I packed everything into his suitcase and backpack and left them in the cabin behind the unlockable door.

It had a bad effect on me, stealing that money. I had to call it stealing. It wasn't mine. I closed the door of Ivo's cabin and went up one deck to mine, where I was sick. I threw up on and on, voiding all that wine. My neighbors probably heard, but people were throwing up all over the ship that night. Afterward I drank a lot of water and lay down in all my clothes. I lay down and closed my eyes and thought about him on that island. The sickness had left me with shooting pains running up through my legs and in my stomach, it doubled me up. But I fell asleep at last and I'd like to be able to say, it would be appropriate to say, that I dreamed of Ivo and his fate, but I didn't. I dreamed of N. and being a little boy again. I was on the beach looking for enough sand among all that shingle to make a sandcastle. As is the way with dreams, the castle was made the moment I thought of it, and it looked like the New Eddystone Rock, but clear and sharp with turrets and castellations, the sun shining on it and the sky clear and blue.

Louise's voice, bidding us all get up, woke me. I had a few seconds of not knowing, of thinking things were the same, and then it came back, all of it in precise detail. At first it seemed unbelievable, *I could not have done that,* not me, not to Ivo, not to anyone. But I had and that was inescapable. I did something I hadn't done since I was the age to make sandcastles. I began to weep, sobbing and crying, my whole body shaking with tears.

While I write, even at this moment, they are listening to *Rosenkavalier.* If Julius had told me to attend it I'd have to have played sick, I couldn't have gone, I couldn't have sat there in that auditorium listening to Ochs's song and the Great Waltz. "Without me, without me, every day is dreadful, but with me no night is too long." It sounds a whole lot better in German.

The minister for the arts arrived late. Of course he was offered a drink but he didn't want that, he wanted a shower before the performance, so he had to be rushed down to the Latchpool and have a bathroom put at his disposal. The curtain went up fifteen minutes late and by that time the soprano singing the Marschallin had had a tantrum in her dressing room over the conductor calling her an old Slovenian whore. Not surprising when you know she's a happily married thirty-five-year-old from Cracow.

I saw the minister and his wife into their box and stood for a moment in the darkness of the inner foyer, surveying the audience through the oval glass in the door. And there, in the sea of faces, I saw Ivo's face. The strong light fell on it and showed me that worn look, those dark, deeply shadowed eyes, the sunken cheeks, the black hair that falls across a lined forehead. He was watching the stage, the heavy velvet curtain, waiting for it to rise up into the proscenium arch and *Rosenkavalier* to begin. But I was not to be fooled, not any more. I knew my mind was creating this image. My mind had taken a photograph and was projecting it inside my head, on the back of my eyes, superimposing this face over whatever face was really there between the woman with the curly ginger hair and the old man with the white mustache. I even told myself I wouldn't be frightened any more.

Finding I could make the face change, I shut my eyes, opened them again and turned him into a child with pigtails, then into a bald man with a big hairless forehead. I shut my eyes again. I opened them and Ivo was back, looking down at his program now, lifting his head and looking straight at me, or into the dark corner that concealed me. My eyes met his unseeing, light-blinded eyes. The lights began to dim and even outside the door I could hear the rustle audiences make as they settle and prepare themselves for the first bars of the overture. I turned away as the curtain slowly rose.

Of course I knew that seeing him in there wouldn't prevent my seeing him on the way home or inside my own front door. He could be in two places at once and often was. It's misty tonight and you can't see the sea at all. The seawall is there and the beach, but beyond that only a great white void. I had that frequent fantasy that I might see drowned Ivo coming up out of this mist, out of the fog-bound sea. After all, the sea is the sea is the sea—isn't it? Every bit or drop of it communicates with all the rest, none is cut off, and a drowned man might drift ten thousand miles from the far west to these European waters.

But I've no reason to think he drowned. There are a good many other ways in which he may have met his end. As for me, I came home. He didn't come out of the sea, he wasn't waiting inside the door, and if I can sense him behind me now as I write, that's normal, I'm used to that. It was only for a little while that he went away.

That morning, before I left the *Favonia*, several people asked me where Ivo was and how Ivo was. But none of them did so suspiciously. I'd no reason to believe anyone knew that Ivo and I had been lovers or suspected that he'd disappeared in strange circumstances. Some thought he was ill, others that they'd missed him because he was in another part of the ship. Once we'd docked at Prince Rupert, everyone assumed, or so I suppose, that he'd gone ashore. Our baggage, as I'd expected it would be, was stacked on the dock, waiting for us to claim it. His was there, I spotted it, I could have picked it out from a thousand bags, it had an iridescence for my eyes all its own.

Only Fergus, it seemed to me, had an idea that things weren't as they should be. But I don't know, it's only a fancy I had. A brilliant sun was shining, the kind that's too bright to last. The four lecturers stood on the dockside, waiting to say good-bye to us, with the captain, Louise, the chief steward, and various other important people. There should have been five lecturers but no one remarked on this. No one mentioned Ivo. We passed in front of them, shaking hands. It was like the line-up at a reception or a wedding. I shook hands with Megan and Nathan and Betsy but when I came to Fergus he turned away at the precise moment and seemed to be saying something over his shoulder to Louise. My hand was stuck out in front of me. I withdrew it and felt the color come into my face. But I don't know, it was such a small thing, and perhaps he really did have something he needed to say to Louise at that moment.

I wonder if it could be Fergus who's sending those letters? You think of naturalists as somehow being good people, *pure* people. But that's nonsense. Education doesn't teach integrity—as I should know—or reverence for the wilderness give you any sort of superiority of character. It's as likely to be Fergus as anyone else. He was Canadian and his home was in Vancouver, I can remember his telling us that at lunch one day.

But if he knew, wouldn't he have given the alarm? Wouldn't the *Favonia* have gone back for Ivo? Fergus can't have known. His contempt for me must have been brought about by my drinking. He can't have known, so the sender of the letters isn't him.

I hadn't gone home before looking in at *Rosenkavalier.* The post had come after I left in the morning, and there it was, on the mat, another of them. The handwriting is becoming as familiar to me as my own. This time the postmark was Seattle. One other thing I've noticed, it's more often Seattle than anywhere else.

Like Selkirk's adventure, the wreck of the Essex *has become famous through being incorporated in a book. In this case,* Moby Dick. *You are a literary kind of guy, maybe you've read it.*

She was a whaling vessel. Dear, oh dear, not politically correct these days, not to be mentioned. Some would say her crew deserved all they got. But this was 1820, before ecology was invented. The interesting thing was that a whale wrecked the ship. In revenge, no doubt, for the murder some hours previously of its three companions.

Pollard, the captain, and the crew abandoned the wreck and set off in three whaleboats. They drank sea water, they drank their own urine, they ate flying fish raw. A month later they came ashore on Henderson Island, one of the Pitcairn group. There they subsisted for a little longer on birds' eggs and peppergrass until seventeen survivors set off once more in an attempt to find Easter Island, leaving three men on Henderson.

A shark attacked one of the boats. There were storms, rough seas. One man died, then another, then a third. The survivors ate his body. Two months after the whaler went down they were rescued by the brig Indian.

Of the men in the other two boats, six died of want. Their bodies were cannibalized. Because this food was insufficient, a lottery was held and the cabin boy, aged sixteen, was chosen to be sacrificed. Captain Pollard said to him, "My lad, if you don't like your lot, I'll shoot the first man who touches you." But the poor starved boy laid his head down on the gunnel of the boat, saying, "I like it as well as any other."

Only two men on the boat survived. The three men who had chosen to remain on Henderson Island were rescued.

Ivo, at any rate, can't have resorted to cannibalism. There were no people there to eat, any more than there were animals or fish. I asked myself if it was possible that Mrs. Braden had guessed the truth. Or if she'd guessed when she saw in the newspaper of the discovery of Ivo's body, and if she'd told someone. I'd never have suspected Lillian Braden of sending anyone anonymous letters designed to threaten, I knew she was incapable of it, but she might have passed on what she knew and it's he or she that is doing it.

And then, suddenly, I thought of something. Of all those people in the accounts who'd been marooned on islands, either by chance or intent, not one had died there. They had endured terrible privations but all had been saved. Yet in the nature of things there must have been far more castaways who hadn't survived. Was it that the dead had no literature commemorating them? Or was there some other purpose behind my correspondent's choice of stories?

I've kept all the envelopes. While the typeface in which these accounts have been put on paper looks as if made by a word processor, the name and address on each envelope is always handwritten. I wonder if this is because the sender has a laser printer linked to the PC that won't print on envelopes. Ours won't at the Consortium and we have to use a typewriter for the envelopes.

The writing is forward-sloping and big with bold loops, rather old-fashioned by our standards, but a typical American hand. A man, I think, I have that feeling, but how can I really tell? Someone who was on the cruise and who later read of Ivo's death in a newspaper.

The letters have ceased to frighten me. I've stopped being frightened of them. I've almost ceased to be curious. The next one that comes I shan't open. If anything frightens me now it is the speed with which I seem to be growing older.

The plane to Vancouver wasn't due to leave till the afternoon. A guided tour of Prince Rupert by bus had been arranged for the *Favonia* passengers, this to be followed by lunch in a hotel and a walk round the shops for those who wanted it, finally the bus would take us to the airport.

A lot of ships were in Prince Rupert harbor, including two huge cruise ships, one of them the *Northern Princess* that we'd last seen at Sitka. At some point her more powerful engines must have helped her overtake the little *Favonia*. Everyone who had come off her seemed to be touring Prince Rupert. I went with the bus as far as the hotel, where I said good-bye to the Donizettis and the Ruffles, receiving from them pressing invitations to visit with them whenever I happened to be passing through Moscow, Idaho, or Athens, Georgia. But Mrs. Braden only wished me a good journey, her sad smile telling me—unaccountably and without any sort of foundation—that she knew everything, had read between the lines of my *curriculum vitae* and, weighing me in her balance, forgiven me.

The bus took them all away. By then the sun had gone and the sky turned a familiar dark gray. I asked Reception to call me a taxi. I phoned the airport and was told that a flight left for Seattle in the late morning. The taxi driver told me about Prince Rupert's annual rainfall. An inch of it was falling all around us as we drove through the town, a modest, pretty, deeply suburban sort of place, where bald eagles were as common as starlings. The driver said he liked rain. When he went away, as he sometimes did, he missed the rain and felt happy when he got back. I need not think I was going to avoid rain by going to Seattle. Everyone knew the rainfall in Seattle was among the highest in the United States. I said I hadn't given the rainfall a thought. He showed me the memorial to some poor fisherman from Japan who had been swept off course and whose body had been found in his boat when it was washed up on this coast. That was something I could have done without.

I bought myself a seat on the Seattle flight with Ivo's Visa card. There's no point in dressing up what I did or using gentler terms. That morning, after I'd cried, I got myself together and practiced his signature. It didn't take much practice, for he signed his name as a sort of scrawl, and scrawls are much easier to copy than a legibly written name. While I was doing the scrawl on the slip at the airport I felt a momentary terror, but the woman looked at it indifferently and made out my ticket.

I was on the plane before I started planning what to do when I got to Seattle. The first thing would be to find a hotel. I'd already got the idea that the United States is more efficient about these things than we are at home, things run more smoothly, people are more ready to help. Not that I'd ever tried this sort of thing at home. There would be something at Seattle airport geared to helping people find hotels, I was sure of it. I'd find a hotel and get into my room and phone Isabel.

All this planning kept me from thinking about Ivo. I was concentrating on it, purposely to keep Ivo away. But he came back as he always has done since. I started wondering how long he would survive, if he was already dead, and then by what means he had met his end. It was, I calculated, by then twenty-one hours since we'd left him there, since *I'd* left him there.

I've never made many excuses for myself. I'm not as bad as that. But in those early hours I did make some. I did tell myself that he struck me first, that he'd provoked my attack by saying a monstrous thing to me. Recalling how his head had struck the tree, I even decided he might have been already dead before I left him. I told myself over and over that it was done, it was past, it was too late to do anything about it, I'd known what I was doing and I'd done it, that was all. I slept a bit on that plane, I was very tired.

It has a beautiful bay, Seattle, a deep complex islanded inlet, just as pretty as Alaska only without the high mountains. In the airport lounges, the luggage reclaim area, I kept seeing telephones. I'm sure there weren't more phones than anywhere else but there seemed to be more. I collected my suitcase and my backpack and decided to phone Isabel as soon as I was through customs. As I was getting off the aircraft the idea had come to me that once I saw her again, once I was with her, Ivo and what I'd done would begin to fade away. When we'd been together in Juneau I'd have forgotten all about Ivo's existence if it hadn't been for those letters that kept coming. There would be no letters this time.

I'd phone her before I found a hotel. After all, maybe I wouldn't have to find a hotel. Perhaps I could stay with her. And I ought to phone her as soon as I could. She expected me today, she would know what time the plane arrived from Prince Rupert.

I felt in the outer pocket of the suitcase for her address and phone number. There was nothing in it but Ivo's letters. I shivered a bit at the sight of his handwriting. Then I remembered that I'd put the card with her address on it in my jacket pocket. I went through my pockets. I opened the suitcase, there in the baggage reclaim hall, and started going through my clothes. There weren't very many, and only one other jacket among the jeans and sweaters. The card wasn't in any pocket of that one. I tried the rainproof jacket and trousers. They felt damp and rather sticky under my hands. The card wasn't there.

It's an odd thing in these circumstances, what you do, how you react. I knew I'd put the card into the left-hand inside pocket of my jacket and I knew I'd never taken it out. Why would I have? We'd arranged I wasn't to get in touch until I got to Seattle. I knew where I'd put it but I still searched through everything, through my jeans pockets, inside sweater sleeves, in all the other pockets of the case and the backpack, among the pages of the two paperbacks I had with me, even between the pages of Ivo's letters. It wasn't anywhere.

The panic you feel when this happens is one of life's awful things. Well, it hadn't happened to me before. But I recognized it for one of those things. My heart had begun to beat hard and painfully. It hurts when your heart thuds away like that, as if it's an engine trying to drive itself out of your chest. I put the stuff back into the case and fastened the case up and sat there with my head in my hands. When my heart returned to normal I kept saying over and over, try to remember, try to remember. I couldn't remember because I'd never done a thing to commit that address and that number to memory, I hadn't even been curious about it, it was just a house number where the houses were numbered in thousands in a street that was also just a number and a meaningless zip code. If there'd been a 76 or a 22 in the numbers I'd no doubt have recalled them, but there wasn't, I did know that.

Then I remembered where that card was. It was in the left-hand inside pocket of Ivo's leather jacket. I'd been wearing it when I said good-bye to Isabel, and Ivo had taken it back the next day.

Ivo had been wearing that jacket the day before. When we started for Chechin he had been wearing it under his waterproof gear and his life jacket. It was on him now or on his body.

16

I knew then what he'd meant when he said I couldn't stop him from meeting Isabel. He had her address, he had it even then. I imagined him finding it in the pocket of that jacket, his anger, his misery, and his need to be avenged.

It was a beautiful day, clear blue sky, hot sunshine. They say it's always raining in Seattle, but the people who say that haven't been to the Tongass. A taxi took me to the hotel I'd found south of Yesler Way. It was one of the cheapest. I sat on the bed in my orange-colored bedroom (orange carpet, poker-worked with cigarette burns, orange curtains, Peruvian-crafts orange bedspread) and tried to think how I could find her.

I searched my memory. Finding the card in her bag I could remember, and the way she'd looked at me and the words she'd spoken when she saw it in my hand. I remembered being drunk in the Goncharof dining room and kissing the card in front of the waiter. But of what was on the card, apart from her name, I had no memory. Just one of those American addresses that may mean a lot to Americans but don't mean much to Europeans, all numbers, numbers that make us ask until we realize how the system works and how logical it is: how can a short suburban street contain three thousand houses?

There was a phonebook in the room. I looked up Winwood and

found just one: Michael Winwood, in a suburb or district called Kirkland. Isabel's husband was called Kit and I'd taken it that this was short for Christopher, but perhaps not, perhaps he was Michael, called for some reason Kit. I called the number and held my breath but the woman who answered at last said she'd never heard of Isabel Winwood, but she didn't say that the way an English-woman would, repressively and in an affronted way, determined to keep the conversation as short as possible. She was expansive, she wished she could help me. When her husband came home she would ask him, he had a big family, many cousins, and it was possible one of them had married an Isabel. But no, they didn't live round here, her husband had come from the East Coast. Still, I was to be sure to call her again if I was in need of more information.

How do you begin? I went out and walked about the city. I could see that it was a nice place, I could see why some poll had shown it to be the most desirable place in the United States in which to live. While I was out, that first day, I bought a map and saw how spread out Seattle was, and I read, I can't remember where, that at some point in its short history it had taken in twelve townships to be part of greater Seattle. She might live in Renton or Bellevue, Monroe or Snohomish.

I thought about her all the time. I have to make that plain, that I never stopped thinking about her those first few days. Reliving everything we'd done together and revisiting all the places we'd visited, I remembered waiting for her in that street near the governor's mansion and that made me remember Lynette Case. Lynette would know Isabel's address.

That brought me a huge excitement. It was so simple. I was there, I had done it. In my room I got hold of what they call directory information and they were very efficient, they gave me the number in an instant: D. M. Case, Calhoun Avenue, Juneau, Alaska. I don't remember the number any more, except that the four-digit bit started 22—I would remember that. It would be a long-distance call, but I wasn't worried about money.

There was no reply. I tried every hour till it was too late to try any more. Then it came to me. Of course. Lynette would still be in hospital, the hospital in Anchorage. I couldn't remember the name of it but it was in *Fodor's Guide to Alaska.*

The people there were just as obstructive and difficult as people in English hospitals are. At last I got someone, not a nurse, some administrator, who told me Mrs. Case wasn't available to speak to me and wouldn't be tomorrow or the next day. The voice sounded diffident, almost embarrassed, and its owner obviously didn't want me to press her. But I had to know. It was the most important thing in my life.

"Is she still in the hospital?" I said. "You can surely tell me that."

"She is not in the hospital."

"Is she at home?" I didn't know if they had hospices in Alaska for the terminally ill, I knew nothing of what arrangements they made.

The voice said repressively, "She's no longer with us."

"You said." I was getting annoyed, it was so important. "If she's not with you, where is she?"

"Mrs. Case passed away on Friday."

So that was that. I felt furious because she had taken so long to tell me and had been determined to embarrass me before she came out with it. Well, she hadn't succeeded. I reflected that the husband was still alive. I would get him at home on the following day.

But he wasn't. I'd tried his number five more times before I remembered he worked for the government, possibly even in that public office Ivo and I had visited and where we had listened to the brass band. They were nearly as difficult as the hospital. I was passed on from one bureaucrat to another and at last was told Mr. Case had gone off on "vacation." He had taken his annual leave immediately after his wife's funeral.

At the hotel I'd given them an imprint of Ivo's Visa card. I used the card again to buy myself dinner. Once I'd started it was easy and there seemed no limit to it. A shop in the old part of Seattle in Pioneer Place sold craft jewelry and the sort of ethnic clothes Isabel wouldn't have worn. But she'd have worn the gold and pearl earrings, the silver pendant. I'd chosen a pair and got the Visa card out—but what was the use when I couldn't find her?

In the United States you need a car. Public transport isn't very good, except for air transport and that's wonderful. Everyone drives. I could see it wouldn't be hard driving round Seattle, and I could imagine how much easier things might be if I had a car. My chances of finding Isabel would be greater, I thought, though I couldn't exactly say how.

I could have used Ivo's Visa card but I hadn't got Ivo's driver's license. I hadn't got a driver's license with me. Anyway, I think I'd have been afraid to fill in a form and make insurance declarations in someone else's name. On the second day I bought newspapers and I found out something else I'd never previously thought of, that the United States doesn't really have national papers; each city has its own paper or papers. What had happened up in Alaska might not be recorded down here. Unless it was a big story. Something like the Jeffrey Dahmer case might be in every newspaper across the country, but a man's body washed up on, say, Vancouver Island, wouldn't be.

There was nothing about Alaska or islands in the paper I bought. But what had I expected? His body might not be found for years, might never be found. I thought often of his being drowned, of his attempting to swim to the mainland from Chechin, but I'd no reason to think he would, I didn't even know if he was a good swimmer.

Isabel had expected me on the Saturday. I wondered what she would do. Perhaps only decide that I'd changed my mind, that our time together had meant less to me than I'd thought at first. After all, she'd made a half-hearted effort to say we shouldn't see each other again. She'd think I'd come to agree with her. I groaned aloud when I thought of that. I hadn't written, though I'd promised to write. All the time I'd thought that wouldn't matter because I'd be with her, in nine, eight, seven, six days I'd be with her.

I walked along the waterfront and sat in a little park looking at the harbor. There was a big farmers' market down there in Pike

Place and I thought, suppose she comes here to shop, I would if I lived in Seattle, I could sit here day after day and wait for her to come.

She didn't come but the Bradens did.

At the foot of the series of hills that rise in steps from the waterfront to the streets where the art museum is and the public buildings, a hired car disgorged them. The driver helped Mrs. Braden. Her husband, who needed only one cane, brought her own two and gently supported her while she grasped them. I'd liked them, but for all that I'd have avoided them if I could. Mrs. Braden stood and looked about her, her expression lively, curious, enthusiastic. She saw me and she waved. In order to wave she had to give her canes back to her husband and hang on to his arm, but she waved. She showed indications of coming over to me, so I went to her.

"Mr. Cornish," she said. "How very good to see you."

"Tim," I said. "Please call me Tim."

"How do you like Seattle? Will you walk round this very charming market with us? Maybe we shall have the good luck to see the young men juggle with the fish. I should like to see the fish throwers, wouldn't you?"

What was it about her? One day Isabel would be like this woman. She might have been Isabel's grandmother. They had the same graciousness, the same good manners and sweetness and dignity. A nonmalicious sharpness of tongue, they had that in common too. The thought came to me that when the twenty-first century was middle-aged Isabel and I might be like these two, I handing her the two canes she used, the ivory-headed and the ebony, if such materials were still in use then, if they weren't utterly outlawed.

We did see the two men playing catch with great slippery codfish. We saw the embroidery done by the people from some Far Eastern country, Vietnam or Laos maybe. Mrs. Braden bought a shawl, very fine pink and gray weave, for her daughter. She said to me, "They call this the Emerald City, you know."

I asked her why. Was it because the rain made it green?

"That, yes, but in the Wizard of Oz, when Dorothy and the Tin Man and the Scarecrow and the Cowardly Lion look for the Wizard, they have to go to the Emerald City to find him."

The Bradens asked me to have dinner with them that night. They were staying at the Four Seasons, very grand, perhaps the best hotel in Seattle. I told her I was here to look for someone but I'd lost the address.

"Not the Wizard of Oz?"

I managed a smile and said it was a woman I'd met in Juneau. Pleased with her joke, she suggested this must be the Wicked Witch of the West but apologized immediately and said she had connections in Seattle—was it possibly someone she knew or had heard of? I had this mad idea that she might turn out really to be Isabel's grandmother, but of course she didn't.

"Isabel Winwood? No, the name means nothing. But we'll ask my husband, he always has good ideas. He is a most resourceful man."

That evening I went to Four Seasons Olympic Hotel and dined with them, but I think that was the beginning of my losing heart or perhaps of my losing the *will* to find Isabel. It was bringing it out into the open that began this process. Telling Mrs. Braden, or Lillian as she asked me to call her, lifted my objective into the light of day and made it—ridiculous. And something else happened. That was the evening when guilt over Ivo began.

The Bradens were full of ideas. Registers of electors existed. I should try the Seattle Public Library. George Braden would himself find out where and how accessible these registers were. He was, it appeared, a former judge of the state supreme court. It's not hard to imagine the effect hearing this had on me. I stared like an idiot or a person pole-axed by drugs. Here were this old gentleman and this old lady, courteous and sweet and deeply *innocent,* upholders of the law in a significant sense, giving dinner to someone who had murdered his lover; someone who was living on stolen money and a stolen credit card. I stared. I started to feel sick.

George Braden took it for unhappiness, I suppose, and God knows I was unhappy. He made more offers. Winwoods could be looked up, traced, in the same way as we could trace people by studying birth and marriage records at St. Catherine's House. I was to leave it with him. He would do what he could. How long would I be in Seattle? Where was I staying?

Before I could answer, she astonished me. She took my hand that rested on the table and said, "I speak my mind a mite too much and George will be mad at me, but a week ago if anyone had asked me, I'd have said that you and Dr. Steadman, the—er, geologist, is he?—I'd have said that you were more than friends."

"Now, Lillian," said her husband. "That's putting it a bit strong."

"What did I tell you? It would only matter, as I see it, if what I said was spoken with prejudice or in an arch fashion, but since it wasn't, why should I not air my quite reasonable assumption? You were fond of each other, I think?"

I was silenced. I was stricken with horror. I think I went white. My face seemed to shrink as if it was growing old.

"I'm sorry if I've shocked you. Obviously, since you are looking for a lady, a lady that I think you love, I was wrong. So it doesn't matter. Shall I ask the waiter to give you more wine?"

I made up a name for a hotel. I made up a phone number: the code for Seattle, my age and a zero, then 22 and 76. When they couldn't find me they'd assume Lillian Braden's opinions had frightened me. As they had, as they had, though not in the way she would think. She wrote down the fictitious name, the made-up number. They would be leaving in two days' time but their assistance in my search need not end because they were elsewhere. They'd write, they'd phone. A daughter in San Diego was mentioned, a son in Los Angeles. In spite of their disabilities, they spent their life traveling. It was only in the early spring that you could be sure of finding them at home in Cambridge, Massachusetts.

Mrs. Braden's assumption of a sexual relationship between me and Ivo made knowing them any better an impossibility. I said good night, I thanked them, I walked home to my hotel, passing on the way the drunks and junkies that congregate, live, eat, sleep, in a park down there. For a while I sat among them, half-comatose people, truculent, paranoid. Near me on the bench where I sat down was a man wrapped in rags, nursing a bottle of something that would have been methylated spirits at home, was God knows what there, a dark red viscous-looking liquid. Ivo had been on that island for four days by then. I'd read somewhere that if you drink sea water you go mad and somewhere else that marooned people, people adrift in boats, drink their own urine. That was before whoever-it-is started instructing me in desert-island lore.

My guilt began down there among the street people. It paralyzed me and took from me the will to find Isabel. I suppose I knew that if I found her then I'd have to tell her what I'd done. I longed to tell someone, to *ask* someone for a verdict, a judgment. If I'd met the Bradens again, especially if I'd found myself alone with Lillian Braden, I'd have told her. The need to unburden myself was almost overwhelming. If he'd woken up and turned his eyes on me, I'd have told it all to that poor bastard with the bottle on the other end of the bench.

It was I who woke. In the middle of the night, to sit up in the darkness and feel the scream rising up inside me and hear myself whimper instead, I can't have done that, I can't have. It was like delayed shock. First the days of acceptance, of a queasy hope that I'd got away with it, then the fruitless search, then the shock. I can't have done that, I can't have. Things like that don't happen to me, people like me, I can't have done that. But I had.

In the morning I went back to the Pike Place market, mainly because I knew that was one place the Bradens wouldn't go. I went to the little park and sat on the green lawn, I lay there because lying down was the best posture for me. I walked like a zombie, I could hardly see straight. My mind had contrived a veil to hang between me and the external world, a gauzy barrier that was both blinding and deafening. I perceived things at a distant remove, I heard voices as from far away. It was a wonder nothing ran me over, for I hadn't got used to traffic coming from the right and the noise cars made was dulled to a murmur.

I couldn't eat and I'd forgotten about drinking. Drinking alcoholic things, I mean. It was as if I knew there could be no escape.

I had done this terrible thing and I was doomed to think about it and nothing but it for ever. The day passed in a haze. I wandered from park to park in the city and from green space to green lawn, sitting on benches, lying on grass, even sleeping occasionally, to wake up to the horror of it once more. It was that evening or the next that I began to think of going back to the island to find him.

Get a flight to Juneau, go to the helicopter pad and hire a helicopter to fly to Chechin. Or a seaplane. A seaplane might be better. I had the money. I had Ivo's Visa card. For a few minutes, more than that, perhaps an hour, I thought I'd do this. It buoyed me up, it took away all the pain and guilt. I felt energy returning. I went into a fast-food place and ate a burger with fries, a salad. I even had a glass of milk because I saw that other grown-up people were doing this. While I was eating I planned my strategy, how I'd tell them I just wanted to go back there, the island fascinated me, I wanted to explore it properly.

He would still be alive. It wasn't yet a week. I'd been a fool to tell myself he'd have had to drink sea water or his own urine. Only think how it rained. There would be rain water to drink, collected in pools, on large upturned leaves, in his hands; edible leaves, perhaps edible fungi.

Ivo knew about these things, he knew the wilderness and how to survive in it.

He might kill me. I felt brave and strong and reckless. Let him kill me—so what? Anything was preferable to this fear, this guilt, this continuing horror. Death was better.

In my constant walking I'd passed the Alaskan Airways offices. I started heading for it but when I was halfway up one of those streets that rise in a gradient of about one in three, I knew I couldn't do it. I was afraid. I was too frightened of what I'd find when I got there. A dead man or a dying man. The rain, the cold, an injured man wouldn't have survived that. Besides, how badly had I injured him when I struck him and he fell against that tree? I remembered the trickle of blood on his hair. I couldn't go back and face that, I hadn't the nerve.

It was later that same day, evening but not yet nightfall, that Thierry Massin found me. I was in the old part of the city, not where the drunks and the junkies were, near the entrance to the underground Seattle of the 1890s, but in a remoter more desolate square, empty after the shops had closed. There was a piece of statuary, an animal, maybe a bull, with stone coping round it, and I was sitting on this coping, staring up at the purplish sky and the stars. The evenings are hardly ever warm in England, not even after a hot day, but the warmth doesn't go away at night in Seattle. The air was so soft and so mild that you felt it wasn't such a bad life for those street people, lying out in the open, maybe with a bottle and a joint, with no cares and no guilt.

I saw this boy of perhaps twenty come into the square. He had a peculiarly graceful walk, he was very relaxed and at ease, a black-haired, delicately made boy, that I thought might be Hispanic. I thought those things and forgot him, all in an instant, returning to a notion I had of going down to where the dossers were—I don't know what Americans call them—buying myself a bottle of that dark red rotgut and joining them.

The next time I was aware of him was when he sat down beside me on the stone coping. He smelled of cloves. In an accent that wasn't Hispanic, that was French, he said, "What is wrong?"

"A lot of things," I said.

"Money."

It was the way he said it, in a matter-of-fact tone but one that allowed no room for argument, that taught me something. This is what trouble means to most people. Most people, when asked, would come up with that. Not love or loss or bereavement or being misunderstood or ill-treated, but money, basically the lack of money. It had meant trouble for me but no longer. I had quite a lot of money.

"No," I said, "I'm all right as far as that goes."

"You are lonely?"

In the lamplit half-dark I looked into his sharp-featured, dark face that would be a hatchet face one day. His hair was as black as Ivo's. A gold tooth, replacing an incisor, glinted when he smiled.

His smile was contrived with the lips alone, while the eyes remained still and staring.

"Lonely?" I said. "I hadn't thought about it."

"Come for a walk."

It was to his house that our walk took us—his room, rather. The house was in a silent, deserted street and it was a sinister-looking place, very old for Seattle, probably newly built after the fire of 1889. Its front was covered in dark brown shingles that made it look like a slice of decaying worm-eaten Christmas pudding. There was a low wall, made of gray breeze blocks, that divided the house and its narrow front yard from the street. For some reason, this was my night for sitting on walls, and we sat on this one.

"I'm Thierry," he said. "I am Terry here. It is more easy. You can too." He lit a cigarette and I smelled marijuana. "I am from Toulouse. I am a waiter. I am illegal immigrant."

If your rendition of a language consists almost entirely of statements made in the first person it must be quite easy to master. He didn't say these things diffidently or as if he thought there was room for improvement in his command of English, but with a kind of tough confidence. He passed me the joint and I drew deeply on it.

"I am going round the world," said Thierry. "This is old-fashioned, it is what my father do, he do it in sixties when he is young, but only for one year. Already I have been five year. Maybe I do it till I'm old, eh?"

I said I was on holiday. In a week's time I was going home.

"Home is for old people. I do not want home while I have money. But I don't have it, not much, money is always the problem. I have wine in my room. I take you up and we drink."

The joint had burned down to a half-inch. I was about to drop it and grind it out on the pavement but he stopped me. He produced a pin on which to impale this fragment and sucked it until it burned his lips. We went upstairs. I expected Indian cushions and joss sticks, drip-hung candles in beaten brass candlesticks, gays-into-black-magic posters, but his room was stark. A single mattress lay in the middle of the floor with two battered stereo speakers for bedside cabinets. There were no curtains, and a three-quarters-full moon filled the upper part of the sash window. On a kind of bench made from a plank supported at each end on two bricks were the materials for making Thierry's joints, papers, tin of tobacco, an unlabeled tin of cannabis, and a white powder laid out in parallel lines. He must have thought me very naive for not knowing at first what this was.

Something had been put in to fortify the wine. I don't know what but it was fiery and a moment after I'd drunk it my muscles started jumping. Thierry gave me the wine in a pottery mug, stained dark brown inside. He sat on the mattress and took off his clothes.

I did the same. It was a strange thing but I hadn't noticed the heat when I had my clothes on, yet when I'd stripped off I streamed with sweat. Naked, he was as thin as an anorexic girl I'd seen in pictures, with bones showing where you hardly knew bones were. But he was strong too and as fierce as a starving tiger.

The next day I took him to a Mexican restaurant on the Pike Street Hillclimb and bought him a good lunch. At the diner where he had a job there was never time to eat, he said, and the proprietor kept an eagle eye on leftovers, which he claimed to need for the pigs he kept on his land at Tacoma. Thierry wolfed down a chile relleno and tamales and tacos. In spite of being so thin and no more than five feet eight, he had a huge capacity for drink. The California wine on offer was good but he insisted on French, and he drank French brandy too. I paid for it all on Ivo's credit card.

I bought him a denim coat with a sheepskin lining because he meant to go up to Edmonton or Calgary where the winters were cold. Why did I? Because he asked me and because it was a new feeling for me to be admired for my wealth. I told him that at home in England I was a commodity broker. If he'd known anything about it he'd have understood that being in the commodity market wasn't the most prosperous venture in a recession.

"One day I come and we share, huh?" he said.

He was like a greedy, vicious child, and I was talking to him like a child at that point. "I keep it all locked up in a safe, Thierry."

The word was new to him. It was Sergius I'd had in mind but I gave a more straightforward explanation. A world of money and the handling of money was unknown to him—come to that, it was unknown to me. "You get me one of those," he said, his eyes on Ivo's credit card.

I gave him back one of his favorite expressions, the absolute negation. "No way."

All day long, except in the restaurant, he sniffed his coke. He smoked his joints and chewed cloves, one or the other to get rid of the smell of the other, I suppose. Most of the money he earned went on his cocaine habit and his marijuana. The cloves cost practically nothing. I was careful not to let him see me sign Ivo's name to the credit card slip, but he was too busy preening himself in front of the mirror to look.

Being with him was a way of escape. While he was at work that evening I sat in the cinema and watched *A Room with a View* twice round. By that time the Bradens would be gone and I came out of the cinema with a sense of relief. I treated Thierry to supper and took him back to my hotel, not being able to face another night in his room. There was no room service, so we took a bottle of champagne with us. It was like me and Ivo, only this time I was Ivo.

He added more brown dots to the burn pattern on the carpet. There was a cigarette of some kind in his mouth all the time he wasn't actually sleeping. The smell that was like being in one of those Indian spice shops woke me in the small hours. I woke Thierry and told him what I'd done. I told him everything, the weight of guilt was so huge. In the night, when remembering what I'd done was so bad to bear that I couldn't keep from whimpering and crying, I turned to him and held him, his slippery corded body of stringy muscles and sharp bones. I sobbed into his knotty spine and I told him everything except about the money and the credit card. I told him about Isabel.

Women meant nothing to him. You could go so far as to say that for him they weren't there. He reminded me of those men in Genet's novels who inhabit a womenless world, who never mention women, who seem not to know another sex exists. When I talked about her his face changed. He became as white as wax and he closed his eyes. As soon as I'd finished he said, "I don't know women. I am virgin." He laughed and reached for the remains of his joint on its pin.

Once he had gone, by lunchtime, I checked out and asked for my bill. I didn't want Thierry knowing where to find me. The cash I had with me was a lot less than I'd thought, but in my experience it usually is. I had to pay the bill with the Visa card, of which the hotel already had an imprint. There were still five days to go before my flight home. I found another hotel, the cheapest after the Seattle YMCA, and sat in my room there (frozen bean-green curtains coming adrift from their rails, green and yellow Peruvian weave bedcover, black and bean-green vinyl floor covering) asking myself what I was doing in Seattle, what was the point of being there.

Another thing I thought was that when I got home I ought to get myself tested for AIDS, that is, to see if I was HIV-positive. I didn't much care then whether I was, whether AIDS would finish me off. Later on I went out. I was back to drinking again and I walked down those steeply sloping streets, looking for a dark bar where I could be anonymous and relatively alone. And there, ahead of me, I saw Isabel. A taxi stopped and she got out of it, slammed the door behind her and went up the steps to the front entrance of an office block.

It was like some worshiper granted a vision of the Blessed Virgin. I could have fallen on my knees.

17

It was what I'd dreamed of and hadn't dared believe could happen. I didn't kneel, I hadn't quite lost my mind, but I stopped and stood on the corner of an intersection, watching her. She was no more than fifty yards away. If I'd called her name she would easily have heard. Or I could have run down the hill and been with her in a few seconds.

She hadn't gone into the building. It was taking her a while to get the intercom system to work for her. I could see her repeat the punching out movements she had already made on the device beside the door. I saw her speak into a grille, and though I couldn't see the door open I saw her vanish into the aperture that opening door created. She'd been dressed in a white and black shirt, but with blue jeans, with her long black hair scooped up into a knot on the back of her head.

I went down there. To the doorway. I read the names under the series of bells and hers wasn't there, but I'd known it wouldn't be. This was an office block and the names were of companies and practitioners, a chiropractor, a child psychologist, a dentist, a law firm. She was in there and I'd only to wait long enough and she'd come out again. Eventually she'd come out, even if not till the next day.

But I wasn't going to wait. In those moments I'd understood it was useless. That was why I hadn't called out or run down the

hillside. It was too late. What I'd done made it impossible and going
with Thierry somehow compounded that, though if this had happened the week before, if I'd seen her like this five days before, it
would still have been too late. I'd killed Ivo to be with her and the
act, paradoxically, made being with her ever again outside the
things I could do and still bear to be alive.

So I turned my back on that office block where some friend of
hers, or relation or lover, my successor perhaps, lived, and I found
a bar and got drunk for the last time. I used up most of the cash
I had left on a mix of unfamiliar drinks, no Coors and no champagne. Twelve hours later I was using Ivo's Visa card to buy myself
a flight home that day. To have stayed there a night longer would
have been unendurable.

The first time I saw him was at Heathrow. He was in the baggage
claim hall, waiting for his suitcases to come off the carousel. It was
Ivo to the life, his peculiarly graceful stance, standing so straight
and yet so relaxed, the angle at which he held his head, the loose-
ness of his limbs, the black hair that slicked over his forehead. I
should have been relieved. He was safe, somehow he'd been saved,
he was coming home. I wasn't relieved, I was terrified.

I couldn't look and I couldn't stop myself looking. I walked in
his direction, looking away. A quick glance showed me he was even
wearing that jacket, the one with Isabel's address in the pocket. I
looked away, I looked again and he'd turned someone else's face to
me, a face strangely not unlike Ivo's in that the eyes were dark, the
mouth sensual, the cheeks hollow, yet because of a subtle rearrange-
ment of features, a centimeter more here and a centimeter less
there, so entirely different as to make confusion impossible. My
mind had made Ivo out of a tall thin man, a bit of denim, a hank
of hair.

I saw him a lot more times on the way home to N. He was to
manifest himself to me in two versions: as the stranger who looked
like him, who belonged to the same physical type, and as the almost
unseeable presence, the shade that stands at my shoulder and
vanishes when I turn my head, that disappears no matter how fast

I turn in my attempts to catch him. I saw him in the tube and in the train, and he was waiting for the bus that goes to N. from Ipswich.

He came into the house with me. On the doorstep I had the superstitious fear that I mustn't let him in, that once I let him in he would be in for ever. But I felt him slip past me before I could close the door. There was no one else there. My mother wasn't there. I called out to her in a way I'd never done in my life before, I called for help to my mother the way dying men are said to do, but there was no answer.

She'd had a stroke while I was away and been taken to the hospital. It was all there in a series of letters from Clarissa that lay in a heap on the carpet inside the door. To make assurance doubly sure, she phoned an hour after I got home.

The other letters were just bills. I thought there might have been a letter from Isabel. There wasn't. But what, after all, would I have done about it if there had been? I'd had her, herself, within my sights, within call, within running distance, and I'd let her go. Would I have answered a letter?

I unpacked. I put everything but my clothes in that room that had been my bedroom: Ivo's letters, the garnet I'd bought for Isabel, her black and white scarf, the Alaska guidebook, the street plan of Seattle. Of the nearly $700 I'd had, under $20 remained. Ivo's Visa card I cut in quarters the way I'd seen him destroy an outdated card, but I didn't throw them away. I think I was afraid to put them out with the rubbish.

My mother would never come home again. When she was able to walk with a walker the hospital discharged her and she moved into Sunnylands. Fortunately, my father had left enough money to pay the £450 a week it costs to keep her there. Or let me say that he left enough to pay it for three or four years, after which I suppose this house will have to be sold.

Where will I go then? Most people who used to know me would think it odd that I'm living here at all. I always swore I'd never go back to N. after I got my creative writing M.A. It was to be London for me or Paris or, if I could fix it, New York. I'd always despised those people who had grown up here alongside me and whom I'd still see when I came home during the vacations, girls walking up the High Street with children in strollers, men driving to the station car park in Ipswich. That was before I understood that people don't live where they want to but where they have to, where they can afford to, where there's a job or a parent to babysit or a cheap house. Or where they know people and feel safe, or safer, because things are familiar, where the great threatening world is pushed outside. Living here and thinking, writing, remembering, I've learned and understood a lot that just used to pass me by.

Little people, I once called them. I'm a little person myself now. A recluse, a celibate, an old bachelor inside a young body, a quiet, keeping-himself-to-himself friendless man who sometimes goes into the pub and chats with the locals but mostly stays at home. A man with a poorly paid job that's walking distance away and a hobby to ensure a cheap and innocent way of passing the evenings. His mother is in a retirement home and he takes care to visit her two or three times a week, and to drop in afterward on his elderly aunt.

They all notice he has no girlfriends. (Well, he has no *friends.*) His neighbors, who are old, are rather pleased about this. The more daring among them, male and of military provenance, suggest he might be a "poofter," but since he's not a "practicing one," it doesn't matter, does it?

I was lucky to get this job, very lucky that "Auntie Noreen" happened to sit next to Sir Brian at a committee meeting and suggest my name when the question of who should be secretary to the Consortium came up. Luck didn't seem to come into it at the time and nor did permanence. I'd hold it for six months at the most, I thought. But I'm still here and unless I do walk into the sea one day and keep on walking toward Holland till the waters close over me, unless I do that I'll be here till I retire.

And Ivo with me, I suppose. It's strange to think that he'll stay young while I grow old, for that's what will happen. In dreams, when we encounter people we know, they aren't as they are now but as they once were. When I dream about my parents, my bent old father is tall and upright and my poor chair-bound mother is dark-haired and vigorous, the once hyperactive woman who boasted that she never sat down. So Ivo will stay young. Once he was seven years older than me but I've aged a bit since then. I shall be his age in six years' time and then I shall pass him, leaving him behind in his eternal youth.

I know that because when I saw him in the auditorium at *Rosenkavalier* he looked just the same. He was unchanged or, perhaps, he even looked rather younger. Before I wrote about what happened in Seattle I said that he didn't follow me home that night, he wasn't a few steps behind me, he didn't slip inside when I unlocked the front door. Nor did I see him rising out of the sea. I couldn't have done, for sea was invisible, whited-out by a mist that hung from the sky to the shingle bank. But the next morning, the day before yesterday, I saw him. He was walking on the beach, on the hard sand down by the waterline. The tide was as far out as it ever goes and the sea was striped green and gray and bluish-brown. It was no longer misty, and pale yellow cloud streaked the sky.

Am I going to see him in the mornings now? That was what I thought. Isn't it enough that he stands behind me as I write and follows me back from the pub and stands in the hall in the dark waiting for the lightbulb to fail? Sits in the concert hall at night, his face the only face I see in a sea of faces?

He stood at the water's edge and looked out to sea. There was a tanker on the horizon, a gray angular shape of an oblong joined to a trapezoid. It looked big enough from a distance but it would be unbelievably vast seen through a telescope. The ghostly Ivo watched it, or watched something, through binoculars. How refined my mind was at turning the screw, how subtle my imagination. It had given him binoculars now. What next, I wondered. A whale to replace the tanker? Bald eagles instead of cormorants?

I watched him and he watched the sea. Had he watched it like that from Chechin, searching the empty sea for a sail, as marooned sailors always do, as the castaways in all those anonymous tales sent to me had done? In a moment he'd turn and come up the beach, climb the shingle bank and come to the seawall. Only by that time he'd have turned into someone else. To put it more correctly, he'd have shed the aspect of Ivo my imagination had given him and become himself, whoever that might be. Some festival visitor, a guest of the Latchpool or the Dunes.

Sometimes great clouds appear on the horizon, dark masses and snowy peaks, so that if you half-close your eyes you see mountains beyond the sea. A wilderness of waters, gray waves, white-capped, pricked by rain, and bounding it all, the ranges of Alaska. It wasn't like that yesterday morning. A pale plain sky touched the brownish-bluish sea in a blurred line. There could be no fantasies and no illusions—except one, the one that's always left.

For when the man with the binoculars turned and began to walk up the beach he was still Ivo. My imagination wasn't quite yet to be conquered by my reason. His eyes were fixed on this house and I moved away from the window, knowing that when I looked again he'd have turned into the music-lover on holiday he'd always been. His wife would have come down the steps to meet him or his dog answered his whistle.

It was time to leave for work. The wind was blowing off the land, due west, so I put on a windbreaker for my short walk. This is what old bachelors always do. They take no risks with their health. I came out of the front door and he hadn't changed into someone else, he was gone. I felt like saying, "See you later," except that I don't make jokes with Ivo, not even grim ones.

That was two days ago. In the evening I went to see my mother, passing the Concert Complex on my way to get the bus. More Strauss, *Die Frau ohne Schatten,* and they were going in, hundreds of them. It would be another full house. I hadn't seen Ivo since the morning but there he was, going up the steps.

My mother fell asleep after I'd been there half an hour, so I took Clarissa into a café for a cup of tea. I'm only writing this part because of what she said. She looked at me across the table and said, "You've changed."

"Have I?" I said, waiting for her to tell me I needed to come out of myself, I ought to be less selfish, I ought to put my mother first, and so on.

What she said gave me quite a shock. "You've turned into a sad man but you're a lot more considerate. You're more caring about people."

"I expect that's because I don't see very many," I said, but I wondered if there's been some profit in all this guilt and all these recriminations. If it's true that my character has improved, that I don't lie so much and through Sergius I'm a prospective philanthropist, I suppose there must have been profit, there must have been good. Some people would see it as a matter for congratulation that for nearly two years now I've been celibate. But that's fashionable in these days of AIDS. Thierry, no doubt, would call it *chic*.

Something time hasn't altered is my feeling for Isabel. I shall never see her again, yet I can't imagine wanting anyone else. She is starting to take Ivo's place in my dreams and like a good succubus comes into my bed at night and creeps into my arms.

Ivo followed me home from the bus stop. I'm awfully tired of this pursuit, this shadowing. It's not as if I *need* to be reminded, it's not as if I don't already feel bitter remorse.

I turned round once and shouted, "Get away from me, Ivo! leave me alone!"

An old man putting milk bottles out on his step gave me a long, frightened stare. Mad, he was thinking, and perhaps he was right. The opera was over and the Great Hall in darkness. I walked along the seafront with Ivo's footsteps behind me, but disregarding them, knowing there was no one there, and thinking about the castaway letter that had come in the morning.

I'd promised myself I wouldn't open the next one. Of course I did and it was the one I've unconsciously been waiting for. If they are all true, and they are, this is the truest, the ultimate. This is what they have been leading up to. This is what underneath I knew all the time must be. This is the threat.

The extract that follows is from the Juneau Onlooker *of March 30, 1993.*

"*The body of a man, discovered three days ago by naturalists conducting a survey of the island of Chechin, has been identified as Dr. Ivo Frederick Steadman, 31, a British paleontologist.*

"*Dr. Steadman had been missing for nearly two years. He was last seen by passengers on the cruise ship* Favonia *on which he was a lecturer. Dr. Steadman, who was unmarried and appears to have had no relatives, was an academic on the faculty of the Institute of Ontogeny in Warwickshire, England.*

"*Although in an advanced state of decomposition, the body revealed at autopsy a head wound and cranial fracture. Juneau Police are treating the circumstances of the death as suspicious.*"

It shocked me when I first read it. Then I thought, how funny, his second name was Frederick and I never knew. What did they mean, no relatives? He had a sister. And why no mention of the University of P.? But newspapers do make mistakes like that. March 30 was two weeks ago, about the right length of time for the police to run me to earth.

Five minutes after I was inside the house, the doorbell rang. I was in the kitchen, spooning instant coffee into a cup and waiting for the kettle to boil. No one ever comes to the door except meter readers, and they don't come at eleven at night.

The Monkey's Paw. Wish for Ivo to be alive, I thought, then wish for it to be him, and on the way to the door use the last wish to wish it isn't. Don't answer it at all. It can't be Ivo because ghosts don't exist, the supernatural can't be, only the rational is true, so don't answer the door. The kettle started whistling. I turned it off. The bell rang again, the kind of ring that goes on and on.

I remembered the footsteps following me. I remembered the Krupkas, met two nights before. Perhaps I'd left something behind on the bus and this was some stranger calling to return it to me. Or Eric and Margie had had second thoughts and having been to *Die Frau ohne Schatten* and thence into the pub, decided to call on me. But they'd been going to Spain . . . Still, why was I shaking, the spoon knocking against the side of the mug when I lifted it up to pour the water in?

No longer frightened of anything? I set the mug down and went to the door. I took a deep breath and flung the door open. It wasn't the Krupkas or the only other person on the bus when it got to N., and of course it wasn't Ivo's ghost. Nor was it the police, come to question me about the discovery on Chechin Island. It was Thierry Massin.

I'd last seen him—I'd only ever seen him—in Seattle. He seemed smaller than I remembered, and slighter. The jacket he was wearing was the denim one with the sheepskin lining I'd bought him on Ivo's Visa card. It was filthy by now. It looked as if he'd been sleeping in it on a tarred surface. Probably he had.

"So," he said. "So, I find you."

His English hadn't improved. Nor had his appearance. There had been something sharply attractive about him the summer before last, a Latin darkness, knowing, astute, with a gutter sophistication. Now his face was skeletal and when he smiled, as he now did, a skull's grin, the gold tooth was obscene.

"I come in?"

It crossed my mind to say he couldn't, my mother was living here, but a lot of the point seems to have gone out of lying. I realize what a lot of lies I used to tell and how little they did for me, how small an improvement they ever made. When the police came to ask me about Ivo I wouldn't lie. That was a decision I came to before I gave Thierry his answer.

"Sure," I said, and, "Tell me what you've been doing. How've you been?"

He didn't look too pleased when I said there was no drink in the house. He used a French construction to ask for it: "Is there to drink?" and seemed amazed, seemed suspicious, when I said, "Only Nescafé." In fact, though I made him a cup, he didn't drink it, but did his French culinary superiority bit. No Frenchman would ever touch that stuff, he'd rather perish of thirst. While he talked he chewed cloves, so that I wondered if privation had forced him to give up his marijuana habit, but after a time a squashed brownish joint and a pin were produced from the sheepskin pocket.

Since Seattle he had been in Canada, in southern Greenland, and had worked on a whaling vessel in Icelandic waters. This last one I didn't believe, but it did remind me of the last castaway letter but one. He gave no details and shifted off the subject with a sidelong smile when I questioned him. In Ireland he'd washed dishes in a hotel in Galway and in England he'd been sleeping on the street.

"Everyone does," he said. "Is very chic, no?"

I said I hadn't seen it quite like that and then I thought I sounded like my own father or Clarissa. Thierry made me feel middle-aged. As my parents might have, I began to wonder what I was going to do with this unwanted guest. He said he was hungry so I took him into the kitchen, sliced up some sausage I had, cut a hunk of cheese, and made him a sandwich. He smoked another joint while he ate it. The house, its size, its position, he admired extravagantly. After he'd eaten he wandered about, praising my parents' shabby old furniture, eyeing the framed reproductions and the junk-shop oils as if they were the Armand Hammer collection.

It was then that it struck me why he'd come. In Seattle I'd told him everything. I'd told him what I'd done to Ivo. No doubt it was stupid, but I had to tell someone, I was desperate and afraid and lonely and I had to talk about it. To a stranger, of course, which is what Thierry practically was. Someone I'd never see again. He hadn't been sending me those letters, that wasn't his way and his English wasn't good enough. He had some quite other intent.

I've never actually known anyone who's been blackmailed, I don't think I've even read about blackmail in a newspaper, but I have in books. I've seen a lot of police serials on television with blackmail in them. Thierry, I thought, had come to blackmail me. This was how it always started (in books, on television), with the blackmailer strolling about, praising his victim's possessions, then saying how rich he must be, surely he could spare some of it without even noticing—and so on.

What I'd do when he asked for money I didn't know. Perhaps he'd ask to live here, be looked after, I couldn't tell. He was too late anyway. The facts were known, they were in the paper. But I waited in suspense while he said a certain late Victorian chair with a rickety seat was Louis Quinze and the Turkish carpet Aubusson.

I waited and nothing happened. It was as if he'd forgotten all about the confidences I'd made him in that room of his. Or he'd never taken them in, he didn't care. What was all that to him, murder, passion for a woman, some island at the end of the world? He was here for no more sinister reason than that he knew I had a roof over my head. And when it got to half-past midnight I said he could stay if he wanted. What else could I do? I couldn't turn him out to sleep on the beach or find his way back to his Ipswich shop doorway. But I made it plain he wasn't sleeping with me, even if he first had the bath he was threatening to take.

There are more than enough bedrooms in this house. I went from one to another while he was in the bath, locking doors where I didn't want him to go. In the end I showed him to the only other room apart from mine where there were sheets on the bed. It was gloomy and cold and the mattress was very likely damp, but he seemed happy with it. I left him examining an ugly old art nouveau lamp with two bulbs in glass lily shades that had never actually been made to light up in my lifetime.

I didn't sleep well. My door was locked. There was nothing in the place worth stealing except maybe my old violin and, of course, Sergius. There was £600 in Sergius's belly and the "safe" was there for the taking between *Resurrection* and, yes, *The Golovlyov Family*. But Thierry was the last person capable of finding it. In Seattle he'd boasted to me he hadn't looked inside a book since he'd left school in Toulouse five years before.

During the night, or during the small hours, I heard him moving about. I heard him on the stairs. He padded past my room and the sweetish smell of marijuana drifted under the door. He was looking for something, but so long as it wasn't me I wasn't much concerned. Eventually I went to sleep, waking again at about seven-thirty. All was silent but for the inevitable whisper of the sea, calm and glassy this morning, and the eternal crying of gulls.

Thierry had gone. I went up to his room to check. The smell was very powerful but he'd gone. He'd come for a chat, a bed for the night, a meal and a bath, and now he was gone once more on his way. He'd only come to see his friend. I'd already misjudged him once, as I'd found when I had that test and came out of it HIV-negative. I told myself I must be less suspicious, I must stop imputing awful motives to people without any reason but that they do drugs (Thierry's expression) and dress like the latest thing in grunge. I mustn't grow up too much.

One more thing is worth setting down. I went into the room where all the Alaska memorabilia is and found those four pieces I'd cut Ivo's credit card into. His name, printed on it in relief, was still quite legible, and the middle initial wasn't F for Frederick but C for something else. So I went back to the library and asked the librarian if she'd check up on something for me: was there a newspaper called the *Juneau Onlooker*?

It didn't take her long. There wasn't. There isn't and apparently never has been. I ought to have felt relief that my correspondent had made this last story up, but I didn't. I felt nothing but wonder that anyone could be so devious and so relentless. For what?

Today is Sunday and I'd meant to write all day, to finish this memoir. But I've already finished really and there isn't much more to write. Have I achieved my aim? I'll have to look back because I've forgotten what it was, something about stopping the dreams and laying his ghost to rest, I think. It's true that I don't dream of him so much, I dream of Isabel instead, but that makes the times I do all the sharper, all the more piercing, and, as for his ghost, I see it just as often and I'm just as convinced and just as skeptical.

I don't like these broad-daylight sightings. One of them occurred when I'd checked on Thierry's room and first walked in here an hour ago. I went to the window to look at the sea. It was flat and still, the brownish-blue of a bird's wing. The wind had dropped and a boat with white sails was becalmed about half a mile out. Fishermen were coming in with the morning's catch.

Ivo was leaning against the sea wall, looking up at this house.

I closed my eyes and counted to twenty. Then I counted another fifty to make sure. When I opened my eyes he—it—was gone. So I sat down at the typewriter and wrote some of this, these last lines, getting up once to take another look, knowing he'd have returned, so certain that I'd have been surprised if he wasn't there.

He was back where he'd been that first time. I felt like opening the window and shouting at him to go away, to leave me alone, to have pity on me. Wasn't I giving up my whole life to being better? Hadn't I suffered my share of remorse? Wasn't it all changing me in the way I ought to change? How long did he mean to persecute me? I didn't shout out because I knew how that would look, not just to the neighbors but to me, myself. It would look like madness. It would *be* madness.

But I think I may be mad. It was with fascination, it was almost with *pleasure,* that I watched him persevere. He saw me. He raised one hand in a kind of salute and then he began to cross the road toward this house.

I sat down again. That was thirty seconds ago. The doorbell is ringing. I shall go down and answer the door, but I shall make no more wishes. I used up all my wishes last night.

ISABEL

18

Writing to a dead man is a pointless exercise. But we were always great letter writers, you and I, we communicated more by letter than we ever did by phone, and when we had great things to tell each other we wrote them down and sent them by post. So this is my last letter to you, my memorial to you and my asking for forgiveness.

People often do write letters they don't intend to post and that they know will never be read by any eyes but their own. Anyway, Tim may read this. If he is allowed to. If they let him read this sort of thing where he is. Perhaps I mean where he ought to be, for I wonder if even now he knows what he did, what he set in motion rather, when he abandoned you on Chechin Island.

My dear, my darling. We were so close, though separated by mountains and seas. We had never quarreled, even as children. We loved each other. Until I spoiled it all.

If I'd been in your shoes, I'd have treated my sister just as you treated me, I'd have been as angry and as hurt. The truth is I can hardly imagine the magnitude of your hurt. Of course I believed he wouldn't tell you, and then one day, when you and he had broken up, as I could see you must do, I'd tell you myself. I'd tell you gently and cautiously, so as to hurt you as little as I could. But he told you, straight out, for once he forgot to lie, and you nearly killed him.

Let's go back a bit.

You were so much in love and you thought it was for ever. I'm not going to reproach you for that, I'm not going to ask you how you could worship someone like Tim. After all, I once felt much the same about Kit and had the same kind of illusions. Almost every sentence Tim utters begins with "I." Kit is cruel and deceitful but not as selfish as that. I suppose the point with Tim, the point *of* Tim, was his looks, he is so extraordinarily beautiful. One good thing is that he seems not to know it.

You sent me a photograph of him. Do you remember that? In this country there's a tendency to compare good-looking people to movie stars and he looked like the young Robert Redford. For a while I thought you were having me on and the picture was *of* Redford, taken when *Butch Cassidy* was made. That was why I did what I did, because of the way Tim looks. I think so, anyway.

Yet I'd so much wanted the course of true love to run smooth for you. In those early days. I was having a bad time, I was always jealous, always suffering the pain of rejection, but it would have comforted me to know that you were happy in that part of life where I was made most unhappy. That one of us was all right would have supported me. It was only a week after Kit went off with that woman that your letter came in which you told me Tim had been unfaithful to you. It broke me up. I cried all day. Then in the morning, when it was your evening in England, we talked on the phone and you said you were making a new start, the two of you, that all was well, that the poor fool (my words, not yours) had thought you would hardly mind and that infidelity was all right for gay people.

The big shock was when you wrote to me that you were having him watched. It was so unlike you. It would be so unlike me. Or so I thought at first. Then I remembered that though I'd never employed a private detective, I was in no position to afford a private detective, I'd watched Kit myself, I'd set traps to catch him, I'd even asked my friends to tell me when they saw him somewhere he wasn't supposed to be or with someone he wasn't supposed to know. While Lynette was living here I asked her. She had an apartment at the time opposite the newspaper and she could see him come and go. I hated doing it and I hated myself for doing it but I asked her.

It did me no good. It would have been better for me not to know about the girl who was admitted to the building ten minutes after the last employee had left for home, much better not to hear about her and Kit leaving together two hours later when he'd told me he was having dinner with a contact. But you know all this. It's because you know it that you felt able to tell me about your private detective and also to ask me to do what later on you did ask me.

I could only tell you that it would do you no good either. You went ahead with it. Of course you did. You never told me if Tim was guilty of any further unfaithfulness. I suppose you felt that in spite of having done a similar thing myself, I disapproved. Or perhaps there was nothing to tell. He was innocent or just never caught out.

In a way, if he'd shown an interest in anyone except himself, none of this could have happened and you'd be still alive. I wonder sometimes if you ever told him, if you ever said to him, look, you're young enough to take yourself in hand, take a look at yourself and see how utterly self-absorbed you are. Perhaps you did and perhaps he gave the classic answer, that selfish people project and are always the ones to ascribe selfishness to others. But you weren't selfish, though I expect he failed to notice.

The funny thing was that once we'd met, he and I, when we were together, he wasn't selfish then, he started putting me first. But a year before, if he'd been the least bit interested in me as your sister, things would have been quite different. I remember how chastened I was when you told me on the phone that he'd never asked anything about me. He'd never even asked my name.

"How do you refer to me, then?" I said.

"As 'my sister.' When I thought of suggesting he stay with you, I said that my sister lived on the West Coast, I may have said Seattle. He'd probably have preferred me to put him up in some flash hotel."

"And he's never asked my name or how old I am or what I do?"

"Darling," you said, "he's barely asked me those things about myself. He doesn't know to this day what part of the country I come from, he doesn't know where I took my first degree, he doesn't know I'm a twin. I might be married and have half a dozen children for all he knows or cares."

"Yet you love him?" I said.

"Oh, yes, I love him. I often wish I didn't."

So, as far as he was concerned, I was just your sister, nameless, jobless, married or single, it hardly mattered—no, less than that, it had never been thought about. I was nothing. All that I was good for was in that I might have a bedroom for the young traveling man to stay in and pay no rent. A whole apartment perhaps if I was going to be in Alaska while he was in Seattle. And maybe I would have been, only you begged me to go to Juneau two weeks earlier than I meant to so that I could be in Seattle while Tim was there. To look after him, to keep an eye on him, to see he kept out of mischief.

The way you felt about him must have addled your brains. You never made mistakes like that, my dear, mixing up dates and making the wrong arrangements. I can believe it, I can believe you were driven distracted by him. I can just about imagine how you would have felt when you understood what you'd done and that he was going to be left alone in that hotel in Juneau for a whole fortnight. But I know none of that is true. It wasn't like that at all. You didn't make a mistake.

You were testing him. You were putting temptation in his way to see how much resistance he had. And there was more to it even than that. You wanted to know the worst about him. To be cured of him? Or to know if the kind of love you had would withstand any infidelity, any cruelty? It's all part of the way it suits you to be in love with someone unworthy of your love, a talent you have for unhappiness. But it was sick too, you know, it was masochism. It wasn't far from old Sacher-Masoch himself, going off with his wife and her lover on holiday as their servant. Only in your case it wasn't you who were going to be there watching, but me, your sister, your twin, the other half of you.

A whole fortnight you sentenced him to in a strange place where he knew no one and no one knew him. Except me. Americans never say "fortnight." Have you noticed? To them it's a quaint old-fashioned British expression. I say "fortnight" for "two weeks" and "eighteen months" for "a year and a half" and "eight stone" for "120 pounds," "lift" for "elevator," "haven't got" for "don't have" and "bill" for "check," but he still took me for an American. He simply failed to think about it, I suppose, because I was myself and not him, I was someone else and whatever he may have said about loving me, I was still another person, somewhere out there.

You asked me to be your private detective. And quite half my motive in coming to Alaska at that time had been to see you. England was impossible for me that year and besides, Lynette was dying. Even *she* knew she was. She used to write to me about things that were going to happen after she was gone, about things going on the same but without her there to see them. She was brave. She'd been a good friend to me, the first friend I made when I first came to the States ten years ago, and the only one that lasted to the end. The only one too, I sometimes think, that Kit failed to get to go to bed with him.

But half my reason for arranging to be in Juneau at that particular time, in June, a week after school stopped for the summer, was to have a few days with you. And then you phoned to say you'd be starting on the *Favonia* the day before I got there. You had made a balls-up, your word. But Tim would be staying at the Goncharof and if I was there too . . .

"You're kidding," I said like an American, and then like an English person, "You must be joking."

You said, "Darling, you're going to *be* there. What are you going to do in the evenings, anyway? You can't be with Lynette all day and half the night. Wouldn't it be fun to have a charming good-looking young chap to go about with? He's very well-educated, you know. He can talk the hind leg off a donkey. Music, painting, books, all the things you like, he knows it all. When it comes to biology he's as ignorant as the babe unborn, but never mind that. And he likes women."

"What does that mean?"

You said your favorite thing then. "Oh, please." I miss that. I weep when I tell myself I shall never hear you say that again. If someone else were to say it it would make me love him. "Oh, please," you said, and, "he doesn't like them in that way. He's as queer as Dick's hatband, whatever that means. I suppose the hatband was twisted."

"Am I to keep my identity a secret?" I said.

"Please," you said and you meant you wanted no deceit and no subterfuge.

"Well," I said, "you never know with you, you've got so devious. You might want me to use a false name and wear a wig." It must have been then that you told me how uninterested in me he was, how I needed no alias when he'd never asked to know my name. "If he's really so indifferent, what makes you think he'll want to know me?"

"He'll be lonely. He'll be glad of company. If he doesn't get it he'll go looking for the other kind to pick up in bars. You just have to be nice to him. Say who you are and why you're there, show him the sights, take him out to dinner."

"If I'm going to do it," I said, "I'll play it my own way, thank you very much." I became sarcastic, the way you do, but you always laughed at my sarcasm. "Of course he's not going to suspect anything when your sister turns up by the merest chance for the identical fortnight he's there."

You did laugh. "Okay," you said. "Play it your way, play it by ear. Be someone else, say your name's Rosa Luxembourg. No, he'll have heard of her. Say you're Marie Curie."

I said no, it was no use, it was one thing to laugh about it, another thing to do it. And I wasn't going to do it. You phoned again a week later and you sounded so deeply wretched, you had had such a time with him, he was coming, he was not coming, at last he had agreed to come, that I softened and said I'd do it, I'd do anything. After you'd rung off I stood there and looked up at the ceiling and I just prayed that it would soon be over, that you'd get over him and leave him and be yourself again. But by then I'd committed myself to being Sacher-Masoch by proxy.

I've been playing the CD you sent me of that music. It's the most romantic music I ever heard. That's very strange when you consider that the words of the song Ochs sings are a piece of absolute self-deception on the part of an ugly, boring man who is unable to believe himself less than God's gift to all women. Another self-absorbed egotist. There's no sincerity in *Rosenkavalier*, is there? You know that the Marschallin will grow older and older and more desperate to find young lovers until she's a ridiculous laughing-stock. You know that Octavian and Sophie will be out of love as quickly as they were in it and Sophie will soon be a second Marschallin. But still the music is the most romantic that can be and so much the stuff of "our tune" that honeymoon hotels ought to play the Great Waltz every night in their cocktail lounges.

It was your tune, wasn't it, yours and Tim's? I guessed when he and I were together in Juneau. And now comes the hardest part as I try to explain to you why I became his lover and he became mine.

But we'll go back a little once again, if you'll let me.

Two weeks before I was due to fly to Alaska Lynette became terribly ill. She could scarcely move, you know, she was *scared* to move because her bones had become so brittle. One day she had reached out rather quickly to pick up the phone and snapped her collar bone. She was worse than very old women get when they have osteoporosis, and she was only thirty-two. They flew her up to the hospital in Anchorage and gave her treatment that was intended to make her "more comfortable." Another shot of poisons, I suppose. Everyone knew there was nothing to be done, that it was only a matter of waiting for the end. The great thing was to get her to the end with as little pain as possible.

In other years I'd stayed with her and Rob. Rob pressed me to stay this time but somehow I could tell he'd find it easier with no one else in the house. Lynette had written that she wanted to die at home and Rob was going to do his best to see it happened that way. I've never had a chance to tell you this and now I never shall, but as it turned out she died in Anchorage, in the hospital, though he was with her to the end and at the end. Anyway, I was very firm with Rob about not staying with them and, as you know, I made a reservation for two weeks at the Goncharof.

As soon as I got there I called Rob and asked him when I could see Lynette. He said she was asleep, she'd been asleep all afternoon, and this was a piece of luck because it meant that she'd be fresher and would want to stay awake in the evening, perhaps even until a normal bedtime. He'd call me back in a couple of hours and then drive down to the hotel and pick me up. I said not to bother, I could walk, it wasn't far, but Americans don't like you doing that, not even in a safe sort of city like Juneau, so I thanked him and said all right and I'd await his call.

The next bit sounds as if I did it on purpose. It sounds part of a deep-laid plot. But in fact I'd forgotten, for the moment, all about keeping an eye on Tim Cornish, I'd forgotten his existence. My thoughts were full of Lynette. I began waiting for Rob's call in my room but the people next door had their television on very loud and it was starting to irritate me. So I took this Russian novel I'd picked up in a secondhand bookstore and went downstairs. You can't really call it a lounge, the area that goes by that name at the Goncharof, can you? It's more like the waiting room in one of those vast American railroad stations, huge, high-ceilinged and with doors swinging open to blow in drafts. And not at all private. So I did something very unlike me. I told the reception clerk where I'd be and then I went into the bar and sat up at the counter with my book and a big glass of orange juice I got the barman to bring me.

I meant to read *The Golovlyov Family* but it was impossible. I'd suddenly realized I was afraid to see Lynette, not so much because I couldn't bear it myself, of course I could, but because of what my face and my eyes might show her of my feelings. She would be terribly changed. Rob had warned me of that. Was I going to be able to behave naturally when I walked into that room where she was? And by "naturally" did I mean the way I'd behaved last time we met when she was still fighting the cancer and with a fair hope of success, running up to put my arms round her and kiss her? Or would it be *better,* would that be more natural, to be honest and direct and to say as well as show how affected I was by what I saw?

I'd got to the point of regretting I'd come. Did they really want me there, either of them? Perhaps coming was just self-indulgence on my part, a selfish wish to see Lynette once more before she died. I felt very torn and indecisive and also, briefly, almost totally unaware of my surroundings. I'd gone into my own interior. But there was stress too and because of this I did something I hardly ever do these days, I lit a cigarette. Maybe, if I'd really stopped smoking for good, I wouldn't carry a pack with me and a book of matches.

Tim may have been in the bar a long time before I was aware of him. As I've said, I was aware of no one and nothing. My paperback was open in front of me but I'd scarcely read a line of it. When the reception clerk whispered very close to my ear I actually jumped. I had to ask him to repeat what he had said, guilt made me think he was asking me to put my cigarette out, but it was Rob's call he had come to tell me about. I got down off my stool and followed him to the phone and it was then, as I was leaving that strange dark bar with the yellow marble pillars, that I first set eyes on Tim.

I recognized him at once. Even so, his looks staggered me. The camera may not lie but it sometimes underestimates. It was only for a second that I glanced at him but still I took in quite a lot, his roving eye, his ready-for-anything expression, and for an instant I forgot Lynette and thought, oh, my poor brother. Yes, I did, darling, and that may be the height of short-sighted folly but I swear it's not hypocrisy.

There was no plotting or planning about it and my leaving *The Golovlyov Family* in the bar wasn't intentional. I was preoccupied and I simply forgot it. It was a wonder I remembered my purse.

When he gave the book back to me in the morning I was in a dilemma. I've sometimes wondered since what he thought of me in those moments, my utter silence, the way I stared at him like a madwoman. He just stood there, holding out the book to me and smiling, looking like a film star or an angel. And I was in a turmoil. Should I declare myself, say who I was, say I was your sister? How angry with you he'd be! I wanted not to have to think of this, be bothered with this, I was still hopelessly, bitterly distressed over Lynette, more than anything by the sight of these two people who loved each other knowing death would soon part them. I'd hardly slept. And now here was this Tim Cornish, this gloriously handsome vision, confronting me, forcing me to decide, to act.

For a ridiculously long while I said absolutely nothing. When I did speak I knew I'd lost my chance of telling him you were my brother. If I was going to tell him it would have had to be at once, the very first thing. I took the book from him. It was in a curious state, mangled and dog-eared, the cover bent in half. Secondhand it might have been, but it had never looked like this.

"Thank you," I said, "I thought I'd left it in the place where I had dinner."

The waitress brought his breakfast to my table. I asked him if he was alone. It sounds like a come-on but that wasn't the way I intended it. He still hadn't told me his name and a hope sprang up inside me that I was wrong, that in spite of the photograph, this wasn't your man but another, even more beautiful, that coincidence had brought to this far corner of the earth. But he was alone, he was Tim Cornish. We started talking about Primo Levi, God knows why, I don't remember why.

I told him my name and as I did so I thought, now he'll know, now the bewilderment starts, then the questioning, then the rage. But you'd been right. He didn't know me because he had never listened or asked. He heard me say Isabel Winwood as innocently as if I had said Mary Smith.

And now the time has come for the real explanation to be given, the real excuses, for it's one thing to share a table for breakfast with a man, another to spend the morning sight-seeing with him, to lunch with him and dine. When he asked me I could simply have said no. And now I honestly don't know why I didn't.

Except that I was lonely and unhappy and this was the only vacation I was going to have. And he was so extraordinarily good to look at and so charming and so easy to talk to. I don't know why I said that about him starting every sentence with "I." He may have done once but he didn't after the first few minutes. He was so nice. You'd said he would be. And I'd nothing else to do. Lynette stayed in bed till nearly lunchtime and I wasn't to go to her until the afternoon. For some reason, when I'd planned the trip, I'd thought I'd be spending all day from morning till night with Lynette, but that was because I hadn't understood. I'd thought I wouldn't have time to do your surveillance. Now that I'd seen her and talked to Rob I realized three hours would be the maximum stretch I could possibly spend with her at a time. For the rest I'd be quite alone—unless I was with Tim.

So I didn't say no to him. It was a glorious day, as hot as California. I showed him the sights, we lunched together and I went off to see Lynette. But I'd overestimated when I thought three hours. Perhaps the long evening spent with a friend from the past had overstimulated her, perhaps life itself was simply becoming too much, whatever it was she was exhausted and fell asleep while we talked. I crept away, went up to my room and wrote you a letter. It was the first one I wrote, the one that was waiting for you poste restante at Sitka, where you'd much rather have found a letter from Tim.

That was the letter in which I told you I'd met him, I'd taken him on a sight-seeing tour and to the cemetery, I'd had lunch with him, and I'd managed all that without revealing my relationship to you. But when I'd finished the letter I began to think very seriously about the consequences of this deception. If you and he were going to stay together, and it looked as if you were, no matter what pain it caused you, one day he was going to meet me and everything would come out. Any anger he might feel for you now would be nothing to the bitterness and resentment he'd feel if he discovered we'd banded together to deceive him in this way. I began thinking that the whole thing was a mess and I should never have agreed to

this surveillance game in the first place. I wondered why I had. But
I had and now all I could do was somehow or other clear things
up before I got further embroiled.

I decided to ask him out to dinner and over dinner to tell him
who I was. It would be awkward but the awkwardness not insur-
mountable. I might even put it to him that I'd said nothing earlier
because I realized how it would look: that I was spying on him for
your sake. Nothing, I'd say, could be further from the truth. I was
here to visit my friend who was ill and our presence at the same
hotel was the merest coincidence. I even toyed with the idea of
an outright lie, of telling him you thought I was staying in the
Case home.

The truth was that I wasn't at all clear what I would say to him.
I'd trust to the inspiration of the moment, to the effect of being
relaxed and drinking a glass or two of wine. The main thing,
I thought, was to make him understand that you knew nothing of
it, that you'd be as surprised as he to know I was also at the
Goncharof.

None of this sounds much like me, does it? This isn't the sister
you knew. Nevertheless, it is. He'd begun to have his effect on me.
I wrote him a note and had the bellboy take it to him. I suppose
I just didn't want to speak to him on the phone. It had to be a direct
confrontation or nothing.

We met in the bar and went out to a restaurant. I had that glass
of wine, psyching myself up to the approach to telling him, and I
began to by asking him if he was going on the cruise alone. Oh,
darling, he has such a way of looking at you that is all transparency,
all limpid honesty, those true-blue eyes, that steady earnestness of
expression. He looked me right in the eye and told his lie.

"Yes," he said. "Do you think I'm crazy?"

I know what I should have said. I should have said, I don't think
you're crazy, I think you're a liar. You're going with my twin
brother who loves you to distraction, who has in all likelihood paid
your hotel bill, bought the very clothes on your back, and financed
you to entertain women like me behind his back. But I didn't say

that. I was deflected from my purpose. Coward-like, I talked about Alaskan cruises and about anthropology.

The point is that I didn't tell him, not that evening or ever, and the reason was that sitting opposite him like that and later walking down to the waterfront in the dusk, I found myself so violently attracted that it was faintness and pain at the same time. It made me breathless, I almost gasped. In that marvelous air, the freshest there is anywhere, I felt deprived of oxygen, asthmatic, hyperventilating for him.

It was a hunger that took away my appetite for food and a thirst that made me afraid to drink any more. It was a need to touch that froze me into remoteness and a desire to kiss that made my mouth ache, but it wasn't love. I don't want there to be any confusion about that. I'm sure it wasn't love.

19

Pathetic though it sounds, I don't want you to think I gave in to it. Not then. I did fight against it. I really struggled. I nearly won.

Darling, you were an understanding man. Paradoxically, you, who didn't need to, really understood women. But still I believe you were a little bit like the man a friend of mine, a very old woman, told me about. They were very young at the time, engaged to each other, though they never married. He said to her, "I can feel like that, but oh, my sweetheart, you mustn't. Or if you feel it you must never never let on, you must never show it." A sexual revolution has happened since then and feminism has happened but men still doubt that women can "feel like that" to the extent they themselves do. They hang on to the belief that we have to have "love" as well.

I didn't love Tim. I wanted him the way you wouldn't have found it at all degrading to confess you wanted someone. It had been two whole years for me, darling. Kit hadn't touched me for months before he left. The one or two times he wanted to I wouldn't let him, not after those women who came to his office after five-thirty, a troupe of them, a succession, like call girls. And I'm not, you'd say and so would I, the sort of woman who has casual affairs. I've never, for instance, had a one-night stand. That won't cause surprise. What did surprise you—no, not that luke-warm word, but shock and horrify you—was that I went to bed with Tim at all.

I held out for a week and in that week I spent hours of every day with him. I spent most of the time I wasn't with Lynette with him. Just to make matters worse, I suppose, for it was a sort of torture, a torment mixed up with exquisite pleasure. At first I told myself nothing would ever come of it. You see, in spite of all the evidence, I couldn't believe he was really attracted to me. He was *gay*. If I say gay men can be very flirtatious with women, does that sound impossibly shallow? Perhaps it would be better to say gay men are often very easy with women, and very intimate, because they know it can lead to nothing, it's absolutely safe. I thought his attentiveness was due to that. I even thought, he loves Ivo, and I look like Ivo, I talk like Ivo, we have the same gestures, the same facial expressions. It's Ivo he sees in me and Ivo that attracts him.

I've been very stupid and very blind, to my own feelings and to yours and his.

The letters he received all came from you. He opened none of them in my presence and I thought they were too precious to him for that, too private and perhaps too sacred, to be read anywhere but in the seclusion of his own room. That their arrival obviously embarrassed him I attributed to the diffidence of the lover. We're ashamed of the weakness of love, of our vulnerability.

I spent all day Sunday with Lynette, watching what I guessed would be her final decline. There's nothing more killing to sexual desire than the prospect of death. While I was with her I forgot Tim and the state of excitement I was in all the time I was with him, that sensation of being suspended from a high wire. I sat with Lynette, subdued by that special gravity that belongs in the neighborhood of those who die young.

She said to me, "I'll never see you again after this week. That's why I have to be especially nice to you."

I said didn't she mean *I* had to be especially nice to *her*, but she only gave her thin wide smile. There was no pretense between us by that time that she was going to live. We talked about death that day and about reflecting on the things in our past life we felt we'd done wrong. Lynette was Rob's second wife. His first was not her friend but only someone she knew slightly, yet she felt she'd behaved badly to her and stolen her husband, even though the first wife and Rob had been getting on badly for years and were on the point of parting. Knowing she was about to die and having no religious faith, she'd given a lot of thought to these events and sorted out in her mind exactly how wrong she'd been and how much her behavior had been justified. I was taken aback by her courage and greatly admiring of the way she felt it necessary to come to terms with what she called her "serious misdemeanor," how much of her conduct she could justify and how much simply admit had been wrong.

Lynette was very weak and her voice had grown low and rather harsh. But the cancer never touched her brain. Her mind was clear and she was always lucid. Out of simple curiosity, she still had that, she asked me if there was any really bad thing I felt I'd ever done.

"You don't have to tell me," she said. "You can just say you'd rather not say."

But I couldn't think of anything. Of course there were plenty of small things, sins of omission, like not going to see Mother and Daddy as much as I should have after I left home, and forgetting to write to people and not remembering anniversaries and birthdays. There was plenty of that. And things which older people, our parents certainly, found morally wrong, like living for a while with Kit before we were married, and before him, living with Michael. And unkind thoughts and social lies and once, years ago, riding the train from San Francisco to Los Angeles without a ticket. That was worth mentioning because it made Lynette laugh.

It was strange though, wasn't it, that I who was about to commit a real crime, could think of nothing I'd done seriously wrong in all my thirty years? I was on the brink of committing a grave offense against the person who was the dearest in the world to me. Still, when I told Lynette, and meant it, that apart from all the petty things I'd never done anything I could assess as truly wrong, I believed most sincerely that I'd never make love with Tim, for, whatever I might feel or yearn for, he'd never want me.

Full of thoughts of Lynette and death and the parting of friends,

I met Tim in the morning and we went together to Tracy Arm. Did I tell you I'd already kissed him? On the Saturday night when we parted outside the door of my room, I had such an irrepressible longing for the touch of his skin, just to feel it against my lips, that I kissed his cheek. He drew back as if my mouth stung him.

"Good night," he said, the coldest I ever heard him.

I hadn't seen him since but I knew better than to repeat that kiss in the Goncharof foyer as we prepared to leave on our six-hour cruise. I thought I knew when my touch was unwelcome. I even thought how pleased you'd be with me for extending my friendship to him and at the same time keeping him under this strict surveillance.

It was raining, of course. It was pouring with rain and the sheets of rain and those huge clouds like icebergs in the sky hid everything. I understood that my arm was no longer to be tucked into his. Touching was at an end. I had ended it with my seemingly innocent but in fact calculating kiss. As the little ship went in among the ice floes I talked to him, as you might have done, of glaciers and how they formed, recalling everything that you had told me but not, I fear, making as good a job of it as you would have done.

When we got off the ship in the dock at Juneau he wanted to come straight to Lynette's with me but I stopped him. I couldn't have taken a stranger with me there, though when I uttered the word I could see I'd hurt him. Four letters from you were waiting for him at the Goncharof. He saw me looking at the handwriting on the envelopes. I was thinking, I must tell him, I shall tell him tonight, I shall tell him I'm your sister, and when he asked me to come into the bar and have a drink I said yes because I thought that that would be the time, then I could do it.

I had to have a cigarette. He took the book of matches from me and lit it for me.

"You must have wondered why I'm getting all these letters," he said.

I said it was no business of mine. It was my opportunity, wasn't it, to say, no, I haven't actually wondered, I've known why, they're from my brother. But I didn't. I said it was no business of mine and just stared at him. I waited. My hand that held the cigarette was shaking, though, and he looked at it, he could see. He was drinking brandy.

Then he said something that gave me an awful shock. It was a bomb he dropped. (Why do people say a bomb*shell*? They never do in any other context.) If you were alive, darling, I'd never tell you this. It's only because you're dead and can never read it that I'm writing it to you. Whatever he did to you afterward and however you may have come to feel about him, I still would never have told you this to your face or for you to read.

He was awkward about it. He stumbled over some of the words and very nearly stammered. For such a frequent liar, he isn't a good one. Or not when the lie is very important to him. The letters, he said, were from a woman, a lecturer on a cruise ship.

"She's on her way back," he said. "She's a lecturer, she gives lectures to the passengers. She's a botanist. We were lovers but that's over now."

For a moment I found it hard to speak. Then I managed to ask him why "she" kept on writing, if their affair was at an end.

"I wish I could make her understand that our relationship is over."

I said she must be very much in love with him, but as I said the word it sounded to me as if I was talking that awful language you used to call queers' cant in which men refer to each other as "she" and give each other feminine identities. I suppose I couldn't immediately grasp what he was really saying and why he was saying it. All I was sure of in those moments was how dreadfully this lying confession, these revelations, had turned me off him. I felt utterly repelled and much of it came from disillusionment.

Even when he said that he'd stayed because I had arrived, he hadn't left and gone home, even when he said that, it hardly affected me. I was frozen into silence by the enormity of it, by his denial of you.

After a little while I got up and said I'd be having dinner at Lynette's that evening. I would have done anyway, for I knew it might be the last time. She was going back into the Anchorage hospital on the next day or the day following that. He pulled a letter out of his pocket. At first I thought it was one of yours and I had a premonition he was going to show it to me and pretend that this fictitious woman had written it, that Ivo was a woman's name. But the envelope, though crumpled up and a bit damp, was blank.

"Read it," he said in a strange, breathless voice. "Please don't throw it away. I insist that you read it."

"What did I think would be in it? Further confessions about his love affair, I suppose. I thought I should read an account of your relationship over the couple of years you'd been together, but with the locations changed and some of the circumstances and, of course, your sex. I even wondered what name he'd give you. But, can you believe it, I didn't wonder then what his motive might be in transposing his affair into heterosexual terms, or if I did I thought it must be because he was still inside the closet and wanted to keep his sexual orientation a secret from me. And I wasn't sufficiently curious to open it before I left for Lynette's. The envelope looked as if he'd been carrying it about with him for days. There was a crease across the middle of it and it was damp.

The two or three hours I spent with Lynette that evening were very painful. They were taking her back to Anchorage on Wednesday and by this time I think she hardly believed she'd be granted her wish to die at home. We were to meet again the next day but she was having so much morphine that she could never be sure when she'd be conscious and when in a deep, drug-induced sleep, so she gave me what she wanted to give me that night. It was a ring I had always admired, a ruby set in small diamonds, that had been her mother's.

Tim's letter was there waiting for me when I got back. I didn't open it then, I went to bed, but I dreamed of the letter, in a curious dream in which I was reading it in a hotel room I was mysteriously sharing with you and Kit. You were both there, watching me, while I read it. Tim had become an oncologist in the dream, Lynette was his patient and he was writing to me that it had all been a matter of misdiagnosis. Lynette didn't have cancer, it was the drugs she had been given which were poisoning her. I believed the dream, I really thought it was true, and I was trying to reach Calhoun Avenue to tell her but, as is the way in these dreams, I couldn't find my way,

I kept coming back to the sea, and so I woke up, battling against a wind off the fjord.

It was only one in the morning. I put on the light, got up and read the letter. I've told you what I expected. The sort of thing it actually contained hadn't crossed my mind. It was a shock. I did rather an odd thing. There was still time to fill in the breakfast order card and hang it outside on the door. They gave you up until two A.M. I filled in the card in a numb sort of way. Whatever I decided to do I knew I wouldn't be able to face him at breakfast.

Again, darling, if there was ever any prospect of your reading this I wouldn't set it down. But you won't. Addressing you this way is just a conceit of mine, a format for confession. I read the letter again. It was an outpouring of passionate love. He loved me, he'd never loved anyone else, he couldn't live without me. If he had to do without me he'd die. No one else has ever written anything like that to me. It was the way I now believe you sometimes wrote to him.

And it has an effect, that sort of thing. It shakes you, in spite of yourself. While I was saying to myself, how could he, how dare he, he's Ivo's lover, how dare he write these things to me, while I was saying that, I was also thinking, can he really love me like that? Am I adored like that?

I was shivering. The Goncharof provides a refrigerator in its rooms but mine was empty but for a bottle of water. I don't drink much, as you know, but if there had been one of those miniatures of brandy in there I'd have drunk it at a gulp. All I could do was go back to bed and sit there with the light on, thinking about Tim's letter. I told myself it didn't matter, it was just adolescent outpouring from someone who should have left adolescence far behind, it was unimportant compared with Lynette. If I had to lie awake half the night, having a sort of crisis of nerves, I should have had it over her.

Eventually I did sleep and the arrival of my breakfast woke me. Immediately I remembered the letter. But that's the way we are, I suppose that's the difference between a saint and the rest of us. Altruism is fast forgotten when something momentous happens in one's personal life.

The phone began to ring while I was taking a shower. It's no good saying I knew it would be Tim, I didn't know, there was a chance it might have been Rob. So I lifted the receiver and said hello, heard Tim's indrawn breath for a second—oh, yes, by then I could distinguish his breath and his sighs from another's—before he put the phone down. The last thing I wanted was to meet him in the foyer, so instead of using the lift I went down the stairs and out the back way.

Of course it was raining but I walked to Calhoun Avenue. This was my last time, positively the last time, but instead of thinking of the ordeal before Lynette that could only end in death, instead of thinking of Rob left behind to mourn, my thoughts were all on Tim's letter. Much of it I'd involuntarily committed to memory and I kept repeating phrases from it over and over. I was flattered, you see, darling. I was flattered to be called beautiful, to be worshiped, to be told that if he was never once allowed to make love to me it would be a bitterness for the whole rest of his life.

Nonsense? Well, perhaps. It would be very wrong to indulge in self-pity now. I'll only say that with Kit I'd had a hard time, I'd lost nearly all my sexual confidence. Did I ever tell you that he used to refer to me to his friends as "the wife?" It's not an expression Canadians use, it's English working class, but he adopted it for his own use after he heard it in a TV sitcom. To him I'd been "the wife" and to Tim, apparently, I was a goddess.

Rob had taken the day off work. We sat and talked for a couple of hours while Lynette slept. The nurse told me it wasn't strictly a coma she was in but that's how it looked to me. Rob said he'd keep in touch and let me know of her progress, though "progress" was hardly the word. Overnight, while I had been fretting over whether or not to start a love affair, she'd aged another ten years. I kissed an old woman's yellow sunken cheek, I touched her hair with the hand that now wore the ruby ring, and I put my arms round Rob and kissed him good-bye.

The rain was coming down so hard I had to take a taxi back. It went along Fourth Street and about halfway along I saw Tim, smothered in waterproofs, going into a bar. My heart missed a beat and with it I felt that curious plucking sensation low down in the body that's the first sign in women of real physical desire—perhaps in men too, I don't know. You have to remember that I did want him, that I'd wanted him long before I read the letter. But there's no doubt the letter changed things. A good many men have used a woman's love for them to get her into bed and I was thinking by then along those lines, his love to gratify my lust.

And what of you? I wasn't thinking much about you by that time, darling. And after an hour or two in my room I could say I wasn't actually *thinking* at all. Wanting him was starting to consume me, I was fantasizing about it, telling myself that if I didn't take the chance now, like him the bitterness of regret would be with me for the rest of my life. I told myself a lot of other things, the way one does in these circumstances. Not that I've been in many of these circumstances, but it's a situation in which you learn a lot about yourself and about human behavior. I told myself that my best friend was dying, I'd miss her for ever, I *deserved* a bit of enjoyment, that Tim was the most beautiful man I'd ever seen, that it would be a swift affair, lasting at most two days, here today and gone tomorrow.

The next step was mine. I was the prime mover. By then he must have thought his letter had annoyed me and I'm sure he'd have accepted rejection. He'd have had no choice. But I wasn't going to reject him. I asked myself, where would he be now? I called his room and when there was no answer I guessed he'd be in the bar, so I went down in the lift.

I dressed up first. I brushed my hair and left it hanging loose. Humiliating, when you come to think of it, not to say degrading. The lift doors opened at the ground floor and he was standing there, waiting for it. I couldn't speak, I just stood there and held out both my hands. He took my hands and came into the lift and in a moment we were in each other's arms. I whispered that I'd left my key behind, so it was to his room that we went.

I can't write what happened there, even though you'll never read it. He was so sweet, he wasn't selfish then . . .

20

"You needn't blush for your thoughts, Tim," I said to him. "It's too late for that."

No doubt, he had plenty to blush for, as did I. For a moment his face on the pillow had gone fiery red. Neither of us ever mentioned his letter. He spoke aloud all the compliments and avowals of love he'd written down.

I won't say I didn't lie to him. My conduct was in itself a lie. But I never falsified my feelings and said I loved him. I spoke the truth whenever I could, excepting of course that one great truth.

He never said another word about the woman he was expecting to join him when the *Favonia* docked on Friday. How he'd have handled that I don't know but he had no need to worry about it as I intended to leave on Thursday morning, and leave I did.

Tim said he'd follow me, he'd come with me, but, you know, the absurd part was that neither of us had any money to speak of. He had about fifty dollars left and I had maybe a hundred and my return air ticket.

The friendship we'd had disappeared, all the comradeship and companionship, things in common weren't important any more. Maybe they'd have come back if we'd had more time. But as it was, sex took over. We hardly talked. That last night we did go out for dinner and I suppose it was there, in the restaurant, that I lost my Laroche scarf. Unless he took it and kept it for a memento. He wanted to know where the ruby ring came from—"Who put that on your finger?"—and I don't think he believed Lynette gave it me. We were about an hour and a half in the restaurant and then it was back to bed. For sex and for the oblivion sex brings. While I was making love with Tim I stopped thinking and I believe he did too.

I tried to stop him coming to the airport with me but I might as well have tried to stop the rain. It was a bit of a shock when I saw he had one of my cards with our address and telephone number on it. He told me quite frankly that he'd taken it out of my purse while I was asleep because he was afraid that if he asked for it I might say no.

"I do say no, Tim," I said. "I've tried to tell you there won't be any more meetings."

He just laughed. "I'm coming to Seattle. I'm coming in ten days' time. Ten days is nothing, it'll be gone in a flash."

"Call me first. Write to me first." I did have the presence of mind to say that.

"Oh, I'll write," he said. "I know you like letters better than the phone. I'll write tomorrow and keep on writing."

So I kissed him good-bye and he told me he loved me. He'd been telling me he loved me over and over from the time we got up. We parted and I was very near to falling in love with him then—only we'd parted and he wasn't there any more. I got on the plane and went back to reading that book I'd never finished, *The Golovlyov Family*. It wasn't until I was home, in my own house alone, that I started thinking about you.

After three days when no letter had come from him I began to breathe again, I began to think it might be all right, it might actually be all right and no harm done. But human beings are perverse and I was also a little bit piqued. Such is man's love, men were deceivers ever, so much for undying passion, I thought. But I didn't *mind*. I was relieved. You'd be back in Juneau by now, I thought, he'd have had second thoughts, second, third, and fourth thoughts. He'd be looking back on a mad interlude, a holiday adventure, a nice bit of pastime, rather pleased to discover himself to be bisexual.

And he'd never tell you. You'd never tell him. You knew from my own letter that he hadn't known me for your sister, so you'd keep quiet about that. He might say that he'd been befriended by a nice woman here to visit her sick friend, but he'd give no more away than that. And though you'd know who the woman was, you wouldn't suspect anything.

The distant future presented problems. What would happen if you and he stayed together and the occasion arose when meeting me or even hearing my name was inevitable? That, I thought, was a long way off. Besides, I didn't believe you'd stay together. What he'd told me about his relations with the woman lecturer was true in every respect except that he'd bent your gender. The chances were that by the end of the summer, at whatever cost to yourself in misery and recriminations, your relationship with Tim would be over.

So I reasoned. If I also say that so I hoped, I may be justified by the certainty that you could never, never be happy with someone like Tim. I'd no expectations that you'd phone me or write to me during those days, but it would have been a comfort if you had. I was alone and wondering and worrying and reassuring myself but still waking sometimes in the night in dread, remembering how you felt about Tim and what Tim and I had done. It served its purpose. Once I'd parted from him at the Juneau airport I thought I didn't want him any more, I thought that was gone, desire as well as friendship. I was even afraid to think about him.

But he must have been at the back of my mind. When the ten days were up, when it got to that Saturday, I had to think about him. I remembered how ardent he'd been, how he'd said nothing would stop him coming to Seattle. Yet he hadn't written and I couldn't really see how being with you might effectively have stopped him writing or phoning. You wouldn't have been together every minute. He'd promised. Still, he might just turn up. He'd promised to phone first, but what were his promises worth?

The phone didn't ring once that weekend. My life is a fairly solitary one, especially in the school vacations, and days often pass without the phone ringing. No letters came, from you or him. No

letters of any kind came. Then on the Monday Rob called to say
Lynette was dead. The next day I went into town for a dental
check-up, but apart from that I didn't leave the house and no calls
came. This time I had no feelings of pique, nothing but relief that
Tim had changed his mind and was no doubt having a fine time
touring the West Coast.

Two days after Rob had phoned, they brought Lynette's body
back to Seattle so that she might be buried beside her mother and
father. When I went home after the funeral, the house wasn't empty
any longer. As you know, Kit had come back.

New starts grow very stale when you've had as many as we have.
This one, which he proposed, must have been our fourth. After I'd
got over the shock of finding him in the house I said I was a fool
not to have had the lock changed.

"If you had," he said, "I'd just have sat on the porch and waited
for you. You'd have let me in."

"I expect I would," I said. "Anyway, you're a lot bigger than
I am."

"Come on, Izzy, when did I ever lay a violent hand on you?"

It's true. He never did. What used to be called mental cruelty is
his specialty. He's very good at that. At least, it was the spare room
where he'd put his things. He had nowhere else to go, he said, his
girlfriend having thrown him out, the one called Cathy. It's always
been hard keeping up with them and their names. We went out to
dinner together, to a pizza place, nothing at all grand, and he
proposed the fourth new start. I said I'd see, he could stay in the
spare room like any other friend.

"At least you said 'friend,' " he said.

I'd stopped worrying that Tim would come. Paradoxically, once
Kit was in the house I began to be anxious about it again, I was even
convinced that he'd suddenly turn up. Why did I care? If Kit were
to be made jealous for a change, why not? All the brunt of that had
so far been borne by me. It was his turn. Is there some rule that says
a woman has to stay faithful after her man has left her? But I
suppose that what I'd once felt for Kit, traces of it, still survived.

After all, he was still my husband, and in the past I'd done a lot to try and preserve the marriage. Neither of us had filed for divorce. We were as much married as ever.

Each time the phone rang and Kit answered I thought it might be Tim and hoped he'd have the presence of mind to put the receiver down. But it never was Tim. I'd hoped there would be no letters and I was relieved when there weren't, though I minded too. Anyway, there was no sign of Tim, and Kit, who used to be jealous of any man I spoke to while thinking me unreasonable to be jealous of his girlfriends, had no reason for suspicion.

Talking to me about him, other people used to forget Kit was still in Seattle. Because he'd left me, they used to take it for granted he'd left the city, perhaps even gone back to Canada, but of course he never had. He'd been here all the time, apart from his travels as investigative reporter for his magazine, still with an office on University Street, simply living in a different house in a different part of town. It was a Friday when I found him in the house and let him stay and on the Monday morning he went off to work, as in the old days.

I remember you used rather to like him and he to like you. Until in one of his crazed moments he accused you and me of incest. The fact that you were and always had been committed to a gay way of life made no difference to Kit. Nothing made any difference when he was in one of his states. You laughed when I told you and said you wouldn't hold it against him. More to the point was that he never held his suspicions against you. You were never the object of one of his revenges. As his ex-girlfriend was. I'll come to that in a moment.

So Kit went to work and I did the things I do in the school vacation, the marketing and the laundry, my dance class and a class I've signed up for in adolescent psychology. I caught up with my reading and painted the kitchen walls and cooked a meal for Kit and me in the evenings. All that was normal, the sort of thing we'd always done. But what began to happen afterward wasn't. We talked.

I don't mean that to talk was a conscious decision on his part or mine. Neither of us said, "We have to talk," or "Let's discuss this." It was rather a spontaneous outpouring of words that began when supper was nearly finished and which came at first from Kit—later, when I realized he would listen, from me too. Talker and listener, we gravitated from the table to armchairs, one of us fetching coffee or drinks after an hour or so of it, returning to talk some more. Nothing like it had ever happened before. He'd never wanted to hear my views on anything and he'd accused me of being uncaring if I protested at his confessions.

But something had happened to change him. Or so I thought. When I began to talk to him about what Lynette's departure for Alaska and then her illness and death had meant to me, he listened. He wasn't bored, he didn't close his eyes or mutter perfunctory nos and yesses, he actually asked questions and made comments. I talked to him about my loneliness in the past year and he seemed to listen sympathetically to that too. It was all very strange, as if we were two other people.

I talked to him but he talked to me far more and his talk was both a triumphant list of his conquests and a stream of confessions. While telling me what he had always told me, that those women "meant nothing," he was still able to say of one of them that he'd never felt such a powerful sexual attraction and of another that he'd been obsessed with her face, which he was always seeing in his mind's eye or, almost mystically, grafted on to the shoulders of other girls. I found I could listen to all this very nearly dispassionately and this may partly have been because he was still sleeping in the spare room, there'd been no contact at all between us, we hadn't so much as touched hands. After we'd talked for two or three hours, once for nearly four, we went our separate ways to bed.

Kit's is a vengeful nature and a lot of what he said was concentrated on the revenge he meant to take, and was taking, on Cathy. She had a fax in her office and another in her home and part of his punishing of her was to send her literature that used up all the paper on her fax roll. Apparently, Cathy had a tender heart where animals were concerned. She used to turn off the television if anything came on about hunters or endangered species. She hated the idea of the fur trade but was too sensitive to animals' suffering to be able to bear actually joining the anti-fur lobby, being aware of the kind of photographs she'd have to see and the descriptions she'd have to read.

It was this sort of thing, and far, far worse, that Kit was sending this poor woman by fax. Extracts from anti-cruelty societies' pamphlets about how bears were trained to dance and pit bulls to fight, about foxes in traps and deer wounded by crossbows. All these articles had big banner headlines that she couldn't fail to see even if she managed to avoid reading the text, and all of them incorporated dreadful photographs. They were far worse than anything that found its way into an ordinary newspaper. I was outraged when he told me, but by this time I was trying to act like a real therapist and not to show shock and horror.

"You must stop this," I said to him, as coolly as I could.

"I'll have to stop," he said, and he laughed. "I've run out of material and I won't get any more unless I send a massive donation to the homeless dogs or the starving donkeys."

Why did he hate her so much? "Oh, please," he said, and he must have caught that off you. "She broke up my marriage and tried to destroy me. Isn't that reason enough?"

"How did she try to destroy you, Kit?"

"I got her to put something of mine on the word processor and she altered—corrected, she said—the grammar."

You don't have to do much to incur Kit's wrath. But he did stop sending the catalog of cruelty to poor Cathy and one evening, in an outburst of self-abasement, confessed that he'd broken up his marriage himself. Was it too late to mend it?

I told him I didn't like the things he did. I'd overlooked them too many times. I thought these revenges of his were very nearly psychotic. His rages frightened me and his infidelities had been the cause of the worst pain of my life. He shouldn't be talking to me every evening but to a real therapist. He should be having counseling. That silenced him for a while. Then he said, if he did, would I have it too? I made the mistake then of saying I didn't need it.

"The people who say they don't need it are the ones that do, a therapist told me," he said.

"A therapist would," I said. "They have to live."

But perhaps he was right. If I was as adjusted as I thought I was, when he told me in detail of his life with Cathy and of his infidelity to her with *someone whose name he claimed to have forgotten*, wouldn't I then have told him about Tim? After all, during the course of our marriage Kit had been unfaithful to me with at least twenty women, while I to him only with Tim. He's hardly a man who subscribes to the sauce-for-the-gander-is-sauce-for-the-goose philosophy but he isn't a monster either, he'd surely have had some understanding. So I reasoned when I wasn't with him. When I was and we were talking, though sometimes tempted, I always resisted telling him about Tim.

And, seeing what happened later, I was right, wasn't I? For he is a monster, he is very nearly psychopathic, he doesn't know the meaning of rational behavior. It's only when things are going well for him that he pretends to know. He put up a good pretense as the time went on. I suppose things were going well for him, very well. He'd had his revenge on his ex-lover, he'd given her material for her mind to dwell on in misery and horror for years to come. He'd returned to his old home and found "the wife" apparently prepared to take him back. There was to be no expensive, messy divorce—and the world was full of women. No wonder he began to be so nice to me, even to the point of showing a very alien emotion, remorse.

When he'd been back in the house for three weeks, when we had talked to each other about every aspect of our lives more than we'd ever done in all the years of the past, he moved his things and himself into my bedroom.

By this time I thought that Tim must be back in England. That I could accept. It troubled me more that I'd heard nothing from you, but I told myself that in the past when you'd been on these cruises as much as two months had gone by without a letter or a phone call. Tim, after all, had promised me to tell no one of what had been between us. I hoped he was well on the way to forgetting. I wasn't, but it was early days.

Then one day Kit said, "Who's Tim Cornish?"

He had my address book in his hand. I wasn't particularly concerned. And, of course, I could give a truthful answer. "He's Ivo's partner."

"What a crazy term. Sounds like a couple of bank presidents. Don't you mean 'lover?' Why does he have a separate address?"

"It's his family home, I believe, his mother's house."

Kit said no more. He'd needed the phone number of an acquaintance of ours whose name began with C, so you couldn't say he had exactly been prying. I felt I'd got away with that rather well. And I kept on persevering in my efforts to forget Tim and what had happened. But try as I would I couldn't help wondering about him. I couldn't forget his—ardor, I suppose is the word.

I asked myself if anyone over the age of seventeen would protest passionate love with such sincerity, not once but a dozen times, would declare undying love, make such unasked-for fervent promises, and ten days later have forgotten all about them. Can a man be as shallow as that? As quixotic as that? Along comes a new person or, as in this case, an old love, and all is forgotten, lost, dismissed?

It wasn't that I wanted him. No, no, far from it. But people are strange and when we want to forget a love affair we don't want the other person to forget. We want them to remember and regret the loss for ever. No one had ever confessed such love for me as Tim had. I even wondered if he'd never meant it, if it was just a studied technique of his, including the writing of that letter he gave me in the bar at the Goncharof, which in the past had proved a good way of securing sexual partners.

I didn't want to think about you. It was better for me to keep you out of my mind and wait. Wait and see. One day the phone would ring and it would be you and from the first word I'd know that all was well, that you hadn't been told and you hadn't guessed. The paradox was that Kit often talked about you.

He'd like to see you, he said. It must have been two years. Why had there been no letters from you since what he called his "home-coming?" Did I think you'd ever work at an American university? Were you coming to stay when the cruises ended?

To most of this I had to say I didn't know. He said he hoped I wasn't "growing apart" from my brother and this led to one of his diatribes on the narrowness of my circle of friends, my disinclination to "go out and meet people," of whom there had been few since he came back.

The evening talks went on, necessarily rather repetitious by this time. But I suppose they were therapy for us, even though I wasn't as open as I might have been and he was back to presenting himself in the most attractive light possible. Another thing I'm going to tell you, or tell this piece of paper I'm writing to you on. Sex with Kit had always been good, that must have been what made me keep taking him back, but it wasn't good any more, and every time it happened I thought afterward, that has to be the last time and I have to tell him. Tim got in the way, you see. In Kit's arms, I saw Tim's face.

You know what time it was that the doorbell rang and what day it was. A Sunday evening at about seven-thirty. We'd eaten but all the supper things were still on the table. No one ever came to the house without warning. There was no one with whom we were on those sort of dropping-in terms. The doorbell rang and we looked at each other.

"Cathy," Kit said.

But that was his vanity. I knew better. I knew she'd never come near him again. Not after the starving donkeys with the crippled feet.

"That sort of ring at the door on a Sunday evening is probably the police," I said.

I thought of you. Something had happened to you and the police were coming to tell me because I was your next-of-kin. The bell rang a second time.

Kit said, "Why? What have you done?" And then he said, "I'll go."

That's a matter of course. Even in our neighborhood a woman wouldn't answer the door after dark if she didn't know who it was. Kit went out of the room and I thought, it's not the police, it's Tim. Or perhaps it's the police and Ivo is dead. Ivo has drowned among the ice floes. Or it's not the police but Tim, and Kit will kill him.

So I remember I got up from my chair and I put my hands up to my head. I got hold of my hair in two handfuls and stood there like a madwoman.

And I was standing like that when you came into the room with Kit behind you. For the first time since we were children you didn't come to me and take me in your arms and kiss me when we met. Your face was dark and sad and full of anger.

21

I'm in no position to resent punishment. You're the injured one and I injured you. If I thought at the time and afterward that you might have done it differently, that you might have tempered the blows, that you might at least have inflicted them on me in Kit's absence, that's only because we can always see some justification for our own actions. We always have self-pity. You were right in what you did. Only I loved you and I did mind dreadfully. You wanted to give me pain and you succeeded.

It's odd the things we notice. I noticed you had no baggage and you'd never come to me before without baggage. I even asked where it was. I asked Kit, my voice tangled up somewhere in my throat, and Kit said he'd asked the same thing himself, what have you done with your bags, he'd asked. Kit still wasn't aware of anything in the atmosphere. Your face hadn't seemed abnormal to him. It was nothing to him that you hadn't embraced me.

I had no more words. You said with a terrible grimness that you wouldn't be here for long. It was just that you had something to tell me, and since Kit was at home, to tell him too.

I wasn't prepared. I was prepared for something else. That came later. You sat down, saying it was hot, it was stuffy in the room and why didn't I have air-conditioning, or better still, open the windows. I was mesmerized by your eyes, your eyes were very bright and glittering, and I was like a creature on the highway, paralyzed in headlights.

Kit asked you if you wanted a drink.

You laughed. It was a harsh, bitter laugh that didn't even stretch your lips. "Only if you've got champagne," you said.

I knew what you meant and I trembled, but Kit didn't know. "There's Chardonnay."

Once you'd said to me that North Americans only know three kinds of wine, the three Ch's, Champagne, Chablis, and Chardonnay. Clever, if not exactly true. "Oh, give me anything," you said. "It doesn't matter. I haven't come for *drinks.*"

There was a bottle of white wine on the table. Meursault, not one of the Ch's. Kit had had two glasses of it during our meal. He poured a glass for you and said he'd fetch some ice.

"Oh, for God's sake," you said. And then you said, "I don't *need* a bloody drink. Two weeks ago I *needed* a drink and I had a drink, I had several, but that was two weeks ago and I've got over the shock by now. Not the pain," you said, "I haven't got over the pain, but I've got over the shock."

We didn't speak, Kit and I. He gave himself more wine. My eyes were fixed on yours until I could bear it no longer and I took my eyes away.

"My little friend Tim," you said and you were looking at Kit but you turned your gaze on me and said, "Isabel knows who I mean, my sister knows. She met him in Juneau. While she was visiting her sick friend, while she was Bunburying."

Kit didn't know what you meant but I knew. A lot of what you said was to be like that, Kit left out and only you and I having the esoteric knowledge. "By the way," you said, "how is Lynette?"

"She died."

For a moment you dropped the sarcasm, the awful dry, scathing tone. "I'm sorry," you said. "I liked her. She was a nice woman."

You only dropped it for an instant. "Yes, my little friend Tim and I. My lover. I'm not in general fond of these superlatives," you said, "but sometimes one must use them to give meaning to life.

One can't be always stuck in gray areas. I was going to say—I will say—that he was the great love of my life. I loved him, I'm afraid, to distraction. Yes, perhaps in a way neither of you—forgive me if I'm wrong—has ever loved anyone."

You paused, perhaps for one of us to deny it. I couldn't help myself. I said, "Please, Ivo, don't go on. I know what you're going to say and if it has to be said, let me say it."

Your eyebrows jerked up. They are my eyebrows too and they leap up into our high broad foreheads in the same way. "But you don't know. How could you? I hardly think he has told you."

"Where is he?" I said.

"God knows. Back in England, I expect. But surely *you* know where he is."

"Please, Ivo," I said.

"Please, Ivo, what? Please, Ivo, tell the rest of it? Of course I will. That's why I'm here. I'll tell you what he did. My little friend—or maybe I should call him *your* little friend—left me alone on an uninhabited island southwest of the Alaskan Panhandle, he left me to die. He took care to knock me out first and when the boat left went with it and told them I'd gone in the other boat."

"He did *what?*" said Kit, but he only said it in the way people do when they find something amazing, not because they haven't heard or can't believe.

I said nothing. Did you realize I was *relieved?* Could you tell from looking at my face that hearing Tim had tried to murder you was preferable to hearing what I dreaded? I'm ashamed of that, darling, but I can't change it. We can control what we do and to some extent what we think, but not what we feel.

At least I didn't put on an expression of shocked horror like Kit's, though to be fair to him, I'm sure he was shocked and horrified. Who wouldn't be? Well, me. Only I *was* shocked and horrified, by the act and the planning of the act, by who had done it and to whom it was done, but it was just another case of things never being quite so terrible when they aren't happening to oneself. A terrible thing happening to me had been averted. Or so I thought, in those moments.

You described it in detail, how you'd gone to Chechin Island in two boats, to see the dinosaur footprints, and how you and Tim had found yourselves apart from the others. You fought, you and Tim, and when he hit you you fell backward, knocking yourself out against a tree trunk.

"I don't know how long I was out," you said. "Probably only a few minutes. When I came to I didn't know where I was, but all that came back quite quickly. It was raining and I don't think it had been when we fought. There's a sort of beach where the boats put in. I had a bit of a headache and I had to sit down and reorientate myself. Then I walked down to the beach. The boats were gone. In the far distance I could see the *Favonia* at anchor, but she wasn't at anchor for long."

"He did that deliberately?" Kit said. "He left you there on a desert island?"

"I suppose you could call it a desert island," you said. "No one lives there, at any rate, not even bears. I suppose I should be thankful for that."

"He knew you were there and he just went?"

"Yes, Kit, I've said so. I don't know what he told the others. There was another naturalist with us called Fergus MacBride and one called Nathan Mills. I suppose he told Fergus that I'd gone in Nathan's boat, having previously told Nathan I'd leave in Fergus's boat. Something like that. It would have been quite easy. They have a system of tags on these boats to be turned to red when you go out and back to black when you return. One isn't supposed to turn other people's tags for them, for obvious reasons, but Tim Cornish is not a man to be much troubled by what one is supposed or supposed not to do.

"I stood on the beach, wondering whether I could see the *Favonia* moving. Of course it was hopeless. There was no possibility anyone on board could see me. I was alone on Chechin with old Backbite and a few eagles."

"Old who?" said Kit.

"Backbite, the three-hundred-million-year-old amphibian, Dacnospondyl. Never mind, he was dead and gone, and for a while I thought I soon would be too." You turned to look at me and the dry scornful tone came back. "Why don't you ask me questions, Isabel? Why doesn't my sister interrogate me?"

I was able to speak then. You see, I thought I'd got away with it. In spite of the way you spoke to me, in spite of the scorn and the contempt, I thought I'd escaped.

"How did you get away?" I said.

"He can be rather stupid, your friend Tim," you said. "Perhaps he doesn't understand how small the world has grown or he hasn't cottoned on to the fact we're not living in the days of Alexander Selkirk. Yet he'd seen it often enough. He'd seen the big cruise ships waiting at the dockside at Haines and Wrangell. He saw them waiting at the mouth of the fjord at Tracy Arm. Didn't he know they all followed practically the same course?

"I knew someone would put in at Chechin at least by the next day. Of course I didn't want to spend the night sheltering under the Chimney of Chechin, especially as a storm was coming. But it wouldn't have killed me. There was rain to drink if nothing to eat. However, I was lucky." You laughed again. I feared that laugh of yours when we were children—did I ever tell you that? I feared it even though it was never directed at me. "I was lucky," you said. "The storm came and that wasn't pleasant, I was afraid lightning might strike the Chimney and I got drenched with rain. When it let up I saw the *Northern Princess* on the horizon. She'd been following us. She was a massive vessel, eight decks, two thousand passengers, and her boats were vastly superior to the *Favonia*'s Zodiacs.

"Of course I knew there was a chance she'd avoid Chechin because of the storm. I just had to hope. I was like some poor marooned sailor and I when I saw a sail I hoped. It was late afternoon when the *Princess* put two boatloads of sightseers on to Chechin. I'd been there about five hours. The sea was a bit choppy and it was raining, of course it was raining, but the storm was over and the next one hadn't started. I can't say I'd ever been really anxious, I was never afraid for my life, I was racked by a lot of emotions in those hours but real fear wasn't among them. Pain was and anguish—yes, that's the word, anguish—and a sort of shocked incredulity, but not fear. Still, it was a relief to see the *Princess*'s boats coming."

"For Christ's sake," said Kit, "what did you tell them?"

"Nothing much," you said, and you cooled. You'd cooled to ice. "While I watched the boats coming I was thinking what I'd say. And I was also thinking that if I wanted, so to speak, to take it further, what I said immediately the boats arrived would be quite important."

Kit asked you what you meant. I knew.

"If I was going to tell the police, for instance. He'd tried to kill me, hadn't he? There aren't two ways about it. He knocked me out and abandoned me, he hoped I'd die there. My head was bleeding and I was unconscious. Was I going to tell the police? But first, of course, was I going to tell the people who were coming closer and closer to Chechin and would soon land, and then the captain of the *Princess*? I had about two minutes in which to decide and I decided, no, I wasn't."

"Why not, for God's sake?"

"Oh, please. You could say because I didn't want our relationship, Tim's and mine, aired in court. It would hardly do me much good in my profession. That's an obvious reason but it didn't occur to me till later. The reason that stopped me saying anything was that I loved him. Absurd, isn't it?"

"I don't understand you," Kit said.

"Too bad," you said. "I told you it was absurd. They took me back to the *Princess*. I said the mistake was mine for telling Fergus MacBride I'd be returning with Nathan and letting Nathan take it for granted I'd be going back in Fergus's boat in which I'd come. We radioed the *Favonia*. They were astonished, of course. They thought I was on board. Tim, who must have worn two life jackets to leave Chechin, had turned my tag to black. I spoke to Fergus. In the storm the *Favonia* tossed about like a cockleshell—that's the phrase he used and I can't think of another. He said three-quarters of the passengers had been in their cabins being seasick and because he hadn't seen me he'd thought I was.

"Fergus knew. He never said, he never gave a hint, but he knew.

Someone must have turned my tag and carried my life jacket. He was observant, he knew. Without my asking, he said he'd tell Louise and the captain and leave it at that. After all we'd all be in Prince Rupert next morning. I don't think anyone else suspected a thing. Another storm blew up and I spent the night on the *Northern Princess*. She put in at Prince Rupert a couple of hours before the *Favonia* arrived.

"I knew where Tim would go," you said, "but for some reason I'd no inclination to follow him. I felt sick with despair. I didn't need to go aboard the *Favonia*. He'd seen to it my bags with all my stuff in were waiting on the dockside. I went through them and found what else he'd done."

"What do you mean?" I said. "What do you mean, what else he'd done?"

"Going to an island in a Zodiac you don't need money or credit cards. I'd left mine in my cabin, a cabin with a door that didn't lock. Unwise, wasn't it? And not much use saying that I always do it. I could have used the ship's safe but I didn't, I never did. Our passengers were respectable citizens, not thieves. Tim left me the American Express but took the Visa. It's more versatile, the Visa. He left me my traveler's checks but took my cash, a bit less than seven hundred dollars.

"Then he packed my bags, all ready for the steward to take them up on deck next morning. I'd never have believed him so well-organized. I went down to my cabin and it was empty, stripped clean."

"Where have you been since all this happened?" Kit said.

You said very casually, "Doing my job. I had another fortnight's duty ahead of me. There didn't seem any reason not to do it."

"You mean you got back on that goddamned ship and gave your *lectures?*"

"Yes, Kit," you said. "As a matter of fact, in the circumstances, I needed the money. But it wasn't just that. I thought of going after him, I knew where he'd go." You looked at me. "But I couldn't face it. I couldn't face *him*. D'you know, I was actually embarrassed. I thought, I don't think I can go up to him and say, you tried to kill me. Why did you? I didn't think I could do that. It seemed sort of unlike me. I thought, I'll go with the boat when she goes tomorrow and I'll do my stuff and I'll think what to do. So I did and I thought, when we're back here in two weeks' time I'll get on a plane and go to Seattle to see Isabel."

The sarcasm was thick in your voice. It was almost a parody of sarcasm. But Kit didn't notice. I thought, what's coming now, what's coming, I can't bear it, and Kit said, "You said you thought of asking him why he tried to kill you. Why did he? Why do you think he did?"

The silence was engineered by you, contrived by you. You created this eloquent silence by maintaining it yourself and by catching and holding first Kit's eye, then mine. You looked from one to the other of us and then, somehow, at both of us, holding us as if your gaze were a net and we two birds swept together by it and held fluttering. The silence was enormous, thick, heavy, controlled by you. It was like the deep hush in a concert hall before the conductor raises his baton and the orchestra stirs into music.

But there was no music, only silence, and the silence was of your making and your keeping. You lifted your hands, as that conductor might have, though you had no baton. You brought up your hands and leaned back, casting up your eyes. It was disgracefully theatrical, I wouldn't have believed you capable of it. Tim, yes, but not you. At the time, though, I thought none of this. I felt only an increasing terror. For I knew that I hadn't escaped, I hadn't even yet begun to be ensnared, I was in the net, I wasn't yet in the cage, it was all still before me, all to come. You bowed your head and dropped your hands. It was so ridiculous. If it had been happening to someone else it would have been *funny*.

Kit said it again. "Why did he want to kill you?"

"To get me out of the way," you said in your coldest voice. "To get me out of the way to resume his love affair with my sister."

I'd known by that time it was coming. It was still a shock. I wanted to put up my hands and cover my face but I stopped myself doing that. I was beginning to feel unreal, not flesh and blood, a stone woman.

Kit made it worse. He honestly hadn't understood. "What d'you mean, your sister? You haven't got any sisters but Isabel, have you?"

"That's right, Kit," you said. "Think about it."

I don't know what Kit thought about it. I didn't look at him. I looked at you. "Did you set out to seduce him from the first?" you said. "I suppose you were bored," you said. "What happened? Did you try it on with that fellow—what's his name, Rob Case?—did you try it on with him first? But going with you while his wife was dying was too much for even a wimp like him to stomach, was it? There's just one thing I'd like to know—well, no, I wouldn't like to know it, I wouldn't like to know it at all, but I do have to know it, I really do. Did he read you the letters I wrote him? Come to that, did he let you read my letters?"

I forgot Kit was there. "Of course I didn't," I said. "How could you think I'd do that?"

"Please," you said. "Christ only knows what you'd do. I don't know you any more. I thought I did but I don't. I suppose I never did and I never will now, I shan't have the opportunity."

I think that frightened me more than anything you'd said. I cried out, "What do you mean? What do you mean?"

You didn't answer. Not directly. You got up and said it was time you went. You'd said everything, you'd made your position clear and nothing remained but for you to go. One thing, you'd appreciate it if we said nothing of this to anyone.

"And that includes Tim Cornish," you said.

"You don't suppose I'm in touch with him, do you?" I said. "I don't know where he is. I haven't set eyes on him since I left Juneau."

You smiled. I've never before seen such a smile of thinly covered disbelief. You had a rented car outside, you said. It seemed more convenient than bothering with cabs. You were staying at the Westin, but only till tomorrow. Your flight home was overnight tomorrow, at eight in the evening, you thought it was, that your plane left.

All the time our eyes were fixed burningly upon each other's. I had forgotten Kit and I think you had too. But I did remember something he'd said. I remember how in a jealous rage he'd accused us of incest. When you were standing there, killing me with your eyes, I thought, now I could, if you'd said to me, let's do it, why not, I'd have gone with you and loved you any way you'd wanted.

You said, "Good-bye. Good night. Whatever one is supposed to say," and then you said, "Well, good night" and you went out into the hallway and to the front door. We didn't move, we just sat there. I heard you open the door and close it, not with a slam, but quite softly.

I thought, I shall sit here for ever and nothing will ever happen to me as long as I live. I shall just sit here because there is nothing else. Of course I was wrong. I heard Kit move before I saw him. Then I saw him and I was aware what a big man he is. Not thin like you or slim like Tim and not fat either, but heavily built, muscular, strong. Burly is probably the word. I watched Kit come slowly across the room to me and I thought that word. Burly, I said to myself, burly, and I repeated it over and over until it meant nothing. And all the time I was looking at Kit. When he was standing over me he spoke.

"All that was true, was it?"

I said nothing. "I don't mean about putting him on that island, that's something else, that's his problem. This guy Tim, you and him, that's what I mean."

Of course it was true, I said. But he'd left *me*, he was living with Cathy, then he'd wanted to *marry* Cathy—but it doesn't matter what I said because in this situation what people say is always the same. It's as if there's a requisite scenario you have to learn at a certain stage in your life so that you've got it by heart when you need it. You don't even have to adapt it to the cues because they are always the same too. So I said those things and he said them and then he said, "You were still my wife," and he swung back his arm and struck me across the face.

I've said he'd never been physically violent to me. He never had. Yet I always knew the potential was there. I'd never given him cause before, you see. For men like Kit there's only one cause.

I was sitting on the settee and the blow threw me sprawling against the back of it. I gave a sort of cry and covered my face with my hands, all classic stuff, all things that women do. And he did what men like him do. He got hold of my hands and pulled them down from my face and pulled me up by them. For a moment he let me go to stand there unsteadily and then he began the onslaught.

Have you ever had a tooth knocked out? It's something you read about or see on TV (see someone acting it on TV) and it's quite funny, it's one of those joke happenings like falling off a ladder or slipping on a banana skin. Incredible, really, that the idea of a man beating up a woman used to be thought funny too, in certain contexts, in certain circles. And caning children. Well, I won't go on. I was crouched on the floor and Kit was kicking me, he'd knocked me to the floor with a punch in the mouth, and I felt something floating in my mouth which I spat out into the palm of my hand. It was an incisor with half the root still attached.

I screamed when I saw it and spewed blood all over my hands and the floor. That's what made him stop. He can't stand the sight of blood. I heard him go out of the room and when he came back I expected it to start again, I thought, he'll kill me, he could easily beat me to death, and I heard myself say, "Please, Kit, no, please don't, please stop," in a sort of mumbling lisp because losing a front tooth changes the way you talk. But he'd only come back to bring me a towel. He threw it at me, a wet towel that you'd put over a boxer's head in the ring.

"That's you seen to," he said. "Now it's his turn."

I heard him go upstairs but I'd nowhere to go. You know what a little house it is, nothing downstairs but the living room and the kitchen. By that time it was ten at night, after ten. My watch had got broken when he kicked me but I could see the clock on the wall and the face of it seemed to have got very big and shining, like a great round moon. I don't know the people next door very well. It's not a neighborhood where you know the neighbors. I should have called 911, I don't know why I didn't. Not because I wanted to protect Kit, that was the last thing, perhaps because—and it sounds absurd—I've still got some old-fashioned ideas left over from our upbringing. *It was only a man beating up his wife,* that was what I thought, I can't trouble them with that. Would you credit it?

But I was terribly frightened, I was too frightened to be in the same house with him. The moon-faced clock said ten-twenty. I wrapped that wet towel round my head and round my mouth and I went next door. Luckily, it was a very warm night.

They said they'd heard it through the wall. They'd heard me screaming. I hadn't even been aware of screaming that much but they'd heard it and Nicole wanted to intervene but Scott had stopped her, saying it wasn't their business. You see how familiarly I write about them. That's because we've become quite friendly since that night, since they put me in their car and drove me to the emergency room at the hospital. Is there anyone we can contact, they kept saying. Haven't you any family we can contact? No one, I said. There was only you. Only you, not very far away, downtown at the Westin, but I didn't say it. I was afraid you wouldn't come.

Two ribs were broken. My tooth—well, it could be capped. Lucky it wasn't worse, someone said. Someone always says that. I didn't want a hospital bed, I doubted if my medical insurance would cover it, so I went home with Nicole and Scott and I was going to bed in their guest room when Scott said he'd take a look next door. If Kit's car had still been there, parked on the street, I wouldn't have let him do that.

But Kit had gone too. The house was empty. Though I didn't have the nerve to go back there that night I did in the morning. I was all over bruises, especially on my sides and my thighs, and I had a great purple bruise on the left breast, which would have worried me until a year ago when I read that those horror stories are old wives' tales and a blow to the breasts doesn't cause cancer. My left eye was black and closed up but when I struggled to raise the eyelid I could see out of it, which was all that mattered. The injury to my mouth wasn't at all serious but it was the one that caused me most distress. The gaping hole was right in the front. Dentists probably have a name for the tooth that was gone, a primary or principal incisor or something, but to me it was just the one in the front on the left. I looked in the mirror and wondered, with considerable bitterness, what Tim would think of me now.

Then I went into my own house. That is, I hobbled in. Somehow, in the fracas, I'd sprained my ankle and it was bandaged up. Still, I managed the stairs, though it took me a long time. Kit had certainly gone. The clothes he'd brought with him were gone and so were a number of things he'd bought since his return, a raincoat, a sweater, a laptop computer, a clock radio and tape player and a few other electrical items, including a battery-operated toothbrush. And his gun, his Colt automatic. He'd taken my two new suitcases too to put it all in, the ones I'd bought to take to Alaska. That alerted me to what else he might have appropriated.

It was my fault for keeping money in the house. I don't usually, only this was in my purse, and I wasn't thinking about taking my purse with me when I sought refuge with Scott and Nicole. A bit over $200, I'd used the bank machine that day, not a very large sum but more than I could afford to lose. So what was done to you, darling, was also done to me.

Why do they do it? You could say for Tim, I suppose, that he needed the money, though for what it's hard to say, since he seems only to have gone back to England with it. But Kit didn't need it, Kit earns far more than I do, Kit didn't need to steal my suitcases and the cash I needed for two weeks' living. Revenge, I guess. Rob once told me that his first wife did much the same to him. They punish you, not because you've injured them, but *because you are their victims.* And what is a victim for but to take more and more punishment?

Once the dentist had put a temporary cap on my front tooth I filed for divorce. The strange thing was that on the same day I heard from Kit's lawyer that he'd already done so. That evening I got hold of my courage very firmly, I gripped it like you hold weights for a workout, and made myself dial your number.

The ringing stopped after three double rings and you said hello. I said what I've always said when I've called you since the day, the same day, we left our home and went out into the world, "Darling, it's me."

You put the phone down.

22

This long letter to you is nearly over. I wish now that I'd begun it sooner and sent it to you. But that's impossible. It was your death that made me write it.

You lived for nearly two years after you came to my house and told me what Tim had done. You went home and back to your job. "As if nothing had happened," as the phrase goes. But we have to live as if nothing had happened, we have to earn our livings, show a brave face to the world, continue our daily routines, behave to our friends and neighbors as we've always behaved. Acting as if something had happened, which is the alternative, is only another term for madness. If you'd done that, wouldn't you have torn that ship apart, told the world, pursued Tim, killed him, and wouldn't that be madness? If I'd behaved, not as if nothing but as if what had happened had happened, I'd have taken Kit's gun out of the drawer in the kitchen and shot myself.

But Kit is perhaps a little mad. Not for him the rapid return to normal life, the resumption of an equilibrium. Think of Cathy and the faxes. It came back to me how Kit had once told me he'd got the sack from some job on a newspaper and in revenge he'd stolen the editor's children's beloved dog. He didn't do anything to the dog, just kept it in his apartment for a week, and then, at night, left it tied up in these people's yard with a Coke can tied to its tail.

I didn't believe that story, I thought he was inventing it, he was a bit drunk at the time. I believe it now.

So what will he do or has he been doing to Tim? I've been asking myself that for months but I've done nothing. What can I do? I could phone Tim or I could write to him, but I'm afraid to do either. There was so much you didn't tell me that night. What, for instance, did you tell Tim about me when he confessed our affair, our very brief affair? And how did he come to confess to you? Did you suspect and tax him with it? I can't believe that. What I would half-like to believe is that he told you he was in love with me and intended therefore to end his relationship with you.

Half-like? I don't know why I said that. But, yes, I'd like to think Tim at any rate fancied he loved me. I'd like to believe he meant the things he said when he said them. Or that he thought he did. At the time and perhaps for a week or two afterward. I'd like it, darling, because no one else ever says those things, because I'm alone and really quite friendless. It's my own fault. I never meet anyone. I don't go to places where I might meet people. I go to school and I come home and sometimes I have a drink with Scott and Nicole and sometimes I spend the evening with Lynette's stepmother. Rob took me out to dinner when he came here on vacation in the spring. I go to my dance class, which is full of women, and to my psychology course, which is full of women and married men, so you see it is all my own fault.

The trouble is that I've been thinking of Tim quite a lot. I don't mean I'm in love with him or that I long for him or anything like that. I ought to hate him for what he did to you, but I don't hate him. Perhaps I would if he'd succeeded. It goes round and round in my mind, the question why. I'd like to know why. I'd like to ask him.

"Why did you say you were in love with me?" I'd like to ask him. "Why did you write me the love letter you gave me in the hotel? You didn't have to, you must know that. Surely you could tell I was mad for you. You only had to touch me. Look what happened when you did. So why write and tell me you were in love with me? Why did you have to keep on saying you loved me, you couldn't live without me, you couldn't wait till we met again?"

I can formulate the questions but I can't devise replies, not the kind that come anywhere near satisfying me. For instance, perhaps I was to be his cure for gayness. Do gay men still try to be "cured" by making love to a woman? Do they want to change? I don't know and the only person I can ask won't talk to me. Anyway, if that's what he wanted he didn't have to keep saying he loved me. He didn't have to keep saying he'd join me in ten days' time and nothing would prevent him. He didn't have to promise to write to me every day. If it wasn't because he loved me and wanted to be rid of the obstacle to his joining me, why did he try to murder you by leaving you on that island?

When he got off the boat in Prince Rupert he must have thought you were dead. Why didn't he come straight to Seattle? He had the money, he'd stolen it from your cabin. That, after all, was why he'd "killed" you. I've often wondered, and I've been cold and sick at the thought, if you told him unbearable things about me. You might even have told him that you and I set him up, you'd asked me to tempt him, to try and seduce him. That would be grounds for hating me and trying to kill you, wouldn't it?

But I don't really believe you'd do that. Tim isn't truthful but you are. You and I both make poor liars. Tim is a poor liar too but he hasn't realized it yet. Perhaps he'll stop lying when he comes to see how bad he is at it. You see how I harp on him, so much do I want to know. And I haven't had a great deal else to think about these past months, this past year and a half. There must be answers and you must have known them. Tim must know them. Sometimes I've thought a dreadful thing, that you and Tim met again and came together again and that you forgave him, though you could never forgive me.

This last part I'm writing in a plane above the Atlantic. When I started my letter I thought I'd never go to England again, I'd never go home. And I wouldn't have till I got your forgiveness or your death. Well, your death came first.

It was Martin Zeindler who called and told me. The police would do so, he said, but he thought it best for him to do it first. Poor

Martin. I never knew him very well but we'd talked a few times, we'd met socially in St. Mary's Gardens, and do you know, I'd never known him to be serious. Mock-serious, yes, pedantic, mock-severe, mock-everything, but not grave and *real* the way he was on the phone.

"I have some very bad news for you, Isabel."

"Ivo," I said.

"I want to tell you before the police do." The voice was the same man's voice but not the tone, not the words. "Ivo's dead, Isabel."

Without thinking, I said, "He drowned, did he? No, he died of exposure, they call it hypothermia."

I was living in the past, you see. I was altering the past to make it so that you really had died on Chechin or trying to swim to the mainland from Chechin. It was as if it were inconceivable for you to die from any other cause. You were a castaway and thus you died, as if it were all preordained and nothing else were possible. Martin thought I was distraught, the balance of my mind was disturbed.

"I hate having to break this to you on the phone, Isabel. I couldn't come eight thousand miles. It's better than a policeman coming to the door."

Wasn't that odd? That was exactly what I'd thought when you came to the door that night: a policeman come to tell me of your death in the water or among the ice floes. I said I was sorry, I was a fool. How did you die? When Martin said it would be a shock, I must brace myself, he was bitterly sorry, I thought he was going to say AIDS. That fear has been with me for years that one day you'd get and die of AIDS.

"He was—," Martin hesitated. It must have been hard to say because it was hard for him to grasp. The concept of killing someone as a part of life wasn't new to me. I was almost prepared for it. Martin tried again and succeeded. "He was killed, Isabel. He was murdered. Someone mugged him. On the beach at that seaside place where they have the Song and Dance Festival."

I didn't say anything.

"Isabel, are you still there?"

"Oh, yes, I'm still here."

"I'm so sorry to have to tell you like this."

"Martin," I said, "there isn't any other way."

"He'd gone there for the Easter festival. They call it by some pretentious name. There was a particular opera he wanted to hear."

I could feel dreadful hysterical laughter mounting. Only Martin Zeindler would talk about "hearing" opera at a time like this.

"He was staying at a hotel in Nunthorpe. Apparently, he'd gone for a walk on the beach before going to bed. He'd been along the seafront and he was walking back to his hotel along the beach. Or so I gather."

And then I realized. Martin didn't know Tim lived at Nunthorpe. Perhaps he'd never known or else he'd forgotten or thought he'd moved away.

"There's to be an inquest," he said. "They haven't fixed a date yet. I'll let you know. And then the funeral, Isabel—"

"I'll come," I said. "I'll come at once."

In the event I didn't do that. I waited till Martin called three days later to tell me the inquest would be on the following Thursday. And in the meantime I started writing this letter to you, from a full heart, to set it all down.

I think I know what happened. It wasn't opera you went to Nunthorpe to hear. When had you ever cared for opera? The only one you'd ever heard of was *Rosenkavalier* because the tune was in it, your tune. You were practically tone deaf and wouldn't have known *Tosca* from *West Side Story*. You went to Nunthorpe to see Tim. Why I don't know. Perhaps you'd never been in touch with him since you went home, perhaps you thought the time had come to confront him and talk the whole thing through. I'm sure you thought he presented no danger to you.

But he did.

Martin called just as I got to the part where Kit took my money and walked out. He told me the inquest date and said that someone had been arrested for your murder. I knew then. I didn't have to ask the name.

Martin told me without being asked. "I know him," he said. "He was one of my students. The extraordinary thing is that he used to live here, in this house."

It didn't seem extraordinary to me. Terrible, but not strange, not a cause for wonder. The word that came into my mind was—*disappointment,* bitter disappointment. I realized I'd been hoping for something, all this time I'd been hoping. For what? That Tim wasn't as bad as he seemed to be? That it was all somehow a mistake? Or that by a kind of miracle I could find him again, that he'd be changed into the person I wanted, that he'd be right for me and I for him?

All that is impossible now. It's really over.

The captain has just told us we're over the west coast of Ireland. It won't be long now. Good-bye, Ivo, my darling. I'm going to tell myself you forgave me before you died.

JAMES

23

I'm a conventional man. I lead a conventional life of order and routine and I don't do quixotic things. You know that. I suppose the only respect in which I differ from the received portrait of the city solicitor is in that I tell you everything. I can't imagine having a secret that I would keep from my wife or that my wife would keep a secret from me.

Having said that, I realize that I have kept my feeling for Tim Cornish a secret from you. You and I have been married for seven years and I've never told you. This is what men always say, that it wasn't important, and that was why. True, it isn't important now, but it was once. I don't think adolescent love is a trivial thing, that we look back on it with shame or as trivial, I think it's real and the memory of it may be everlasting.

When I was eighteen and Tim was thirteen I was in love with him. I was deeply in love and it consumed my whole existence. He wasn't in love with me, that goes without saying, but he was nice to me and compliant, he did what I wanted. You understand me, I'm sure, I don't want to use the words.

He was nice to me for the favors I could do him and at Leythe fourteen years ago, believe me, a first-year needed all the favors he could get. I believe it's different now, things have changed. For one thing, girls are among the intake and I expect that makes all the difference. The fagging system went at the same time. It had grown pretty benign in my day but still it amounted to little slaves scared to disobey their masters.

You remember that evening we saw Tim at the raga concert. I didn't introduce you but I told you afterward who it was, without further explanation. The truth is that I was very shaken by that encounter. I was cool with him, merely saying hello and nodding when he said hello back, but that was only a cover for an intensity of feeling. I had seen him several minutes before he saw me, I had had time to compose myself and prepare myself for a confrontation that turned out no more than a casual encounter.

I wrote just then of intensity of feeling. Intensity of memory would be to put it better. The mistake we make is in believing that when we are deeply emotionally affected by a chance meeting with an old lover, this means that love endures. Of course this isn't so. What remains is only nostalgia, the memory of our own profound emotion at the time. I expect you noticed how silent I was for the rest of the evening. My thoughts were a muddle of remembered things he once said to me, injuries he did me, his callousness and kindness, his opportunism and his gratitude. But the love was long gone.

Why then did I agree to go to Nunthorpe and represent him when he phoned me three days ago? Not for the nostalgia and certainly not for the love. I told you, while you were driving me to the station, that it was from interest and from curiosity. Both perfectly true. It's also true that what I was embarking on was to make a change from the daily routine of company law. And it was a first time. Before that, no one had ever phoned me from a police station and made me the object of the request: "I want a lawyer."

But it was more than that. It was also because I believe, and I know you do too, that we do ourselves and those we spend our lives with no good by forgetting, still less by falsifying, events long gone by. We diminish ourselves by denying the past.

I didn't know then why Tim picked me. There are at least two good law firms in Nunthorpe. Almost as soon as I saw him he told me that when they gave him the Code of Practice for the Detention, Treatment and Questioning of Persons by Police Officers, my name came into his head. My name simply became synonymous with the word "lawyer." He asked for a London phone directory and, miraculously, they fetched him one. I say "miraculously" because the Suffolk police I've encountered here are about as thoroughgoing and efficient, as unimaginative and obstructive, as the police anywhere else.

I'd been reading up the law in the train. They had cautioned him but they hadn't charged him with anything, so I told them what they knew already, the length of time they could keep him there without charging him, and then I talked to Tim again and at last got myself to this hotel, the Latchpool, where my room overlooks the North Sea with Dunwich to the north and Aldeburgh to the south.

In the morning I saw Tim again and sat in on the questioning. I gave them two hours and then I told them my client was entitled to a break. They brought us a cup each of brown stuff, coffee or tea, I'm not sure which. Tim said there was something back at his house he wanted me to read. If it was still there. If the police hadn't removed it. I asked him if they had had a warrant but he didn't know. I told them they couldn't remove anything without giving him a receipt. He asked me if he'd be allowed to give me the key and I said, yes, why not, he was under arrest but he hadn't been charged with anything.

He has changed out of all knowledge. I suppose he would in twelve years, especially when those twelve years are between fifteen and almost twenty-seven, but I have a feeling all the same that he has changed since that day I saw him at the raga concert and that's only a year or so ago. I wonder if I can explain what I mean. Once the first thing you noticed about Tim was the way he looked, and that was the second thing and the third. There wasn't much else there except charm and a certain gracefulness. I suppose egotism must be attractive in itself, there must have been something else, or why was I so wildly in love?

It's different now. The looks are what you first notice, of course. It's something of a liability, isn't it? The looks are always going to be what you notice first. Until he grows old and loses them. But a kind of melancholy is the next thing, a gravity that is the last thing one would have associated with Tim, and a certain self-effacement. I think it would once have been called humility.

I reminded the officers that they had another four hours. After that they would have to go before a magistrate to get an extension and a magistrate would only listen to them if they had some evidence. Alone with me for a moment, Tim said to go to his house and read what he had written, especially the last part. So I left them, the investigating officer beginning all over again on what Tim's relationship with Ivo Steadman had once been.

A lot of policemen still think that if a murdered man is homosexual, his sexuality must be the motive for murder. That's not really so different from asserting that if a murdered man is heterosexual the logical conclusion is that he was killed because at some time or other he loved some woman. Tim had told him repeatedly that he and Steadman had ended their relationship nearly two years before. The visit was solely to look up an old friend. He insisted that they had parted on good terms. Indeed, on parting, he had given Steadman a sum of money, or part of a sum, that he owed him. The chief inspector took it for granted that because this money wasn't found on Steadman's body Tim must be lying.

The piece Tim had written was where he said it would be, on the desk in the second-floor living room that faces the sea. I was taken aback when I saw the extent of it. There must have been three hundred sheets of manuscript. Then I remembered he had said it was only essential for me to read the last part, that which was most recently written. The final page was still in the typewriter, half-finished.

I took the whole manuscript back to the Latchpool. There I read not just the last part but the two chapters or sections that preceded it as well, and then of course I began to see what had happened after Steadman left the house and began his walk back here. That last part I would like you to see too but it's confidential and my conscience would trouble me if I let you read it. One's own secrets for one's wife but not other people's. That makes sense, doesn't it?

Tim denies most strenuously that he had anything to do with

this murder. Even if he had wanted to kill Steadman—though he didn't, he had come to love him again—he knows about remorse now, and the price he would pay for an act of violence. I'm not bound to believe him, only to act as if I do, but I do believe.

Whatever the outcome may be, I'll write again tomorrow. Now I'm going to reread Tim's memoir.

When I opened the door to Ivo I never had any doubt. I didn't have to touch him or pinch myself. I certainly didn't feel like running screaming down the street. He was real, he wasn't dead, and that was all.

For a moment I did wonder about all the hundreds of previous sightings, but I knew really when the phantoms and figments stopped and the real Ivo began. At Rosenkavalier on Saturday night. The men who followed me home and stood in the dark hall waiting for me and those who hovered on the corner of my glance, they weren't real. They were what I always told myself they must be, what I argued that they were even when I was most afraid. The man on the beach was really Ivo and so was the man who leaned against the sea wall, looking up at this house.

For all that, it was a strange feeling inviting him in, watching him go up the stairs in front of me, then sitting opposite him, just looking, adjusting to it. We didn't say much at first. We just looked at each other, not embarrassed, not even a bit awkward. I never felt he might have come here to be avenged, and afterward he told me he never felt that because he hadn't died that first time I might try to kill him.

Something odd had happened. The whole thing was more than odd but I don't mean that. I mean that it was as if the normal restraints and inhibitions that are present even when two friends or lovers are together, just weren't there. We could be silent, we could speak, it wouldn't matter. It wouldn't matter what we said either. We'd got beyond that. So I looked at him a bit longer and then I spoke. I asked him how he got off the island.

No retorts, no recriminations, no sarcasm, none of that how-can-you-ask-that-after-what-you-did stuff. He just told me. He told me in a cool practical way, as if he were giving an account of events to some board of inquiry. I shan't go into it here, it's enough to say another cruise ship called at Chechin between the storms. Ironically, it was the one I saw at the dock when the Favonia reached Prince Rupert.

"I never thought of that," I said. "Or rather I thought the big boats couldn't get up those narrow channels."

"Not that narrow there," he said, and for the first time he smiled. "That's the open sea, Tim."

He'd spoken my name for the first time. I asked him where he'd been since, for it seemed to me that he must have concealed himself somewhere out of the world or spent two years wandering those northern wastes.

He seemed surprised. "At home," he said. "Back at the Institute, living in the flat at Martin's."

It was so simple. It had never occurred to me.

"Let's go to the pub," he said.

We went into the Mainmast. It was early but you have to get there early on a Sunday if you want a seat. All the time I was saying to myself, this is me and Ivo, I'm walking in here with Ivo, this is Ivo who isn't dead. I'd even asked myself once if it was I that was dead and we'd met again in that afterlife I don't believe in.

The atmosphere of a seaside pub dispels heaven and hell fantasies. I was alive all right and so was he. He put his eyebrows up when I had a pint of Adnam's and wouldn't let him order a bottle of champagne. There'd have been some astonishment in there if he had, even supposing they had any.

I told him what I did in N. and he said he'd booked up months before to come and hear Rosenkavalier. *The reason for that was obvious, but he'd thought he might try* Die Frau ohne Schatten *as well, he thought he rather liked Richard Strauss, so he'd settled for one of our bargain festival four-day weekends. Of course there was the possibility I might be here but he hadn't thought there was much chance of it. You could generally count on people like me putting themselves as far as possible from the family home as soon as they could. But he couldn't resist a certain amount of nostalgic revisiting, going down what Clarissa calls "memory lane." He couldn't stop himself coming to look at the house, he came several times, it exerted an irresistible fascination. And then he saw me standing at the window . . .*

"Did you think I was real?" I said.

"Of course I did. What else?"

"I was always seeing your ghost. How d'you account for that?"

"Pure guilt."

"Or you projected part of yourself," I said. "Like a werewolf." He laughed. I didn't. "I tried to kill you."

"I know."

"I stole all your money and your credit card."

"That, I admit, was a nuisance."

"Don't you mind any more?" I said. "Did you ever mind?"

"Oh, yes, I minded. Rather a lot, as a matter of fact." He smiled.

"Have you still got my sister's scarf?" he said.

She looked like him. I'd noticed it. I have even remarked on it
somewhere in what I've written. The enormity of what I'd done
silenced me.

He said gently, "I stopped blaming you long ago."

"What about her?" Her name stuck on my tongue. I couldn't speak
it. "How d'you feel about her?"

"I'll go and see her in the summer," he said. "She's my twin. We
used to be very close and I miss her a lot. We can't go on like this."

We parted for the afternoon, Ivo and I. I felt I couldn't take any
more for the time being. I wanted to be alone to think about Isabel.
The thing was, I ought to have been cast down, realizing the extent
of what I'd done, understanding who she was and recalling the lies
I'd told her, but I wasn't. I was happy. I was full of hope. After all,
I hadn't killed Ivo, I hadn't killed anyone, and if I'd stolen a lot of
money I could make that right, I was seeing exactly how I could
make that right.

I could write to Isabel now. I could even phone her. Ivo wouldn't
care. I could tell after the first five minutes with him that he no
longer wanted me, he no longer loved me, all that was over. If
tolerance and forgiveness had survived the ordeals of my attempt to
murder him and my theft of his property, love hadn't, passion hadn't.
What did I expect? But, in fact, I was glad. I could imagine being
friends with him and how good that would be, will be.

It's wonderful to be forgiven, it's fizzy, heady, like champagne.

Soon after Ivo came back it started to rain. He'd left his car in P. and
come here by train. That made me put him off his idea of making
a sentimental journey to the Kestrel for dinner. It would be as wet
walking the beach or the dune path as it ever was on Chechin and
Ivo had nothing more waterproof with him than that famous leather
jacket he'd been wearing on the island. We decided to go up to the
Dunes instead and even for that short journey I had to lend him the
hooded rainproof jacket he'd bought me for Alaska. As he put it on
I thought of that morning when it had been hanging over the cheval
glass in my bedroom and in the shape of it I'd seen his ghost.

Over dinner I said I wanted to give him the money I'd stolen from him. So far I'd only managed to save up a bit more than half of it, but I wanted him to have that. Of course he put up a massive resistance, I'd known he would, he had more money than I had, he'd forgotten that credit card bill by now, it was all past and no longer painful. I believe he was thinking of me as the same person who once would have been relieved to have an offer like that refused. That man would have seized on the first murmur of refusal and said no more about it. And I didn't say any more about it—not then.

It was a dark night, starless, the moon like the reflection of a distant light in muddy water. The High Street was dressed with strings of flags as it always is at festival time. The little triangles, red, green, yellow, hung down dripping in the rain.

"I'm going home tomorrow," he said.

"Come in for a bit and I'll make us a cup of tea."

He burst out laughing. I loved him again then, the way I did when we walked here once before and he'd come up from the sea and told me the beach was tame, a pussycat of a beach. In the house, upstairs in the living room, I told him what it had been for me these past two years, the remorse, the haunting, the sense of being a pariah, isolated from other people. I told him about seeing Martin Zeindler at a concert and then James Gilman and the Krupkas, but how there seemed always to be a glass wall between me and others.

The one subject I didn't touch on was the most important to me: Isabel. And this wasn't only because it seemed a tactless thing to do. I didn't know what to ask him, I didn't know what to say. The first question would have had to be, "Does she hate me?" and I was afraid to ask that.

He said a bit more about how it had been, lecturing on the Favonia *as if nothing had happened, finding explanations for people who kept looking at the plaster on his head and asking him what he'd done to himself. After that, I went down to fetch the tea. It would be the first time Ivo and I had ever sat down to tea together.*

While I was away he'd been wandering round the room, looking at things, the way he does, the way he did that first time at Martin's. If he'd looked at the manuscript lying on the desk there was no sign of it, but he'd picked up the stack of envelopes the castaway letters had come in and was holding one of them in his hand.

"What's my brother-in-law been writing to you about?" he said.

So that also was explained. Kit Winwood had been both the jealous husband and avenging friend. He was, it appeared, inclined to these revenges. I didn't mind, it gave me more hope. If he knew who I was and where I lived, if she had told him, I could hope.

"None of the marooned people in his stories died on their islands," I said.

Ivo laughed. "No, well, I didn't. I expect that was part of what Kit was trying to say."

"How could she marry a man like that?" I said.

"You know better than to ask that sort of question about anyone."

I led him to the bookcase where the Russians were and showed him Sergius. He smiled when he saw the cavity inside with the money in it.

"There's something childlike about you still. I hope you'll never lose it."

"Take the money," I said. "Take the whole thing. I want you to."

He still said no, so I took my mother's pearls out of the cavity and put Sergius in the pocket of the waterproof jacket when he wasn't looking. Things tucked into pockets have been quite important for us in our strange history. And jackets lent to be worn for specific reasons or on certain occasions. ("Wear this for me . . .")

The rain had stopped. That made me afraid he wouldn't wear the jacket and I'd have to think of another means of giving him the money, but he said he'd walk back to the Latchpool along the beach. The sea was quite rough and there was a lot of spray. If the tide had been in, instead of about as far out as it goes, the waves would have come up over the shingle bank.

I'd been wondering how we'd part. With a handshake and a promise to keep in touch? At the foot of the stairs he took me in his arms and held me for a moment or two. Then he was gone.

I watched him go up the steps to the top of the sea wall. He didn't turn round to wave, he thought I'd gone in. His body, then his head, disappeared over the other side and I heard the crunch and rattle of his feet on the pebbles. The night was too dark and the sea too far away to see any more, but I stood upstairs at the window for a while, looking into the blackness until my eyes grew accustomed to it and I could make out distant lights at Thorpeness and a light on a fisherman's boat. Then I did something I hardly ever do. I drew the curtains.

Knowing I wouldn't sleep, I sat down and wrote this. It was my last chapter. Ivo wasn't there any longer, standing at my elbow, letting me catch sight of him out of the corner of my eye. Once I looked between the gap in the curtains but it was deep dark, the sea invisible, silent but for the crash and receding roar of the tide. Sometime around midnight I thought I heard a key tried in the front door lock. My imagination has to find something to act out, I expect, now it has lost the drama that was its mainstay.

This last paragraph I'm adding on in the morning. Although I nearly fell asleep over the typewriter, I couldn't sleep when I got to bed. Or else I did sleep and dreamed without knowing it, for I kept thinking I could hear someone trying, though trying in vain, to get into the house.

I was up at seven. The rain was past, the sun was shining and the sea was deep blue. I stood at the window, thinking that perhaps it was often blue, perhaps it was my grief and my misery that had turned it brown, and now I could hope and be happy it was transformed to the blue of a jewel. Sentimental slush? Maybe. Anyway, it didn't last, though the sea stayed blue, because at seven-thirty the phone started ringing. Of course I thought it was Ivo, phoning to tell me he'd found Sergius in the jacket pocket.

It wasn't. It was the nursing home to say my mother had died in the night. I shall go there now . . .

24

Tim was first questioned when he came back from the nursing home in the afternoon. They found an envelope addressed to him in Steadman's pocket. It was handwritten and the postmark was Seattle. The writer isn't important as far as this issue is concerned, but it led the police to Tim.

I don't think I've mentioned how Steadman was killed. It isn't very pleasant. He was stabbed a total of eight times in the chest and neck with a kitchen knife. Shown the knife, Tim admitted quite transparently that it was one of his. He hadn't seen it since the night before when it lay, as it always did, on a wooden board in his kitchen. He couldn't say how it came to be used to kill Ivo Steadman.

They arrested him two days later. He thought of me and asked for me. I've found my name several times in the manuscript I've been reading. He alludes to me flatteringly and unflatteringly, once in a way that touched me very much. While I was reading it, sitting in a corner of the hotel lounge, a striking-looking dark woman came in and sat in a chair on the other side of the room. After a while she came over, introduced herself as Isabel Winwood and asked me if I was Tim's lawyer. Not solicitor, but lawyer. She's not American, of course she isn't, she is the late unfortunate Steadman's sister, but she uses a few American expressions from having lived over there so long.

"Can I see Tim?" she said.

Probably not, I said, not at the moment, but I had reason to believe he wouldn't be held any longer, not now that I had new evidence for the police. I told her that with luck I'd be back by lunchtime and bring Tim with me.

From Tim's own account I was well aware of how he felt about Isabel Winwood. That made me curious to know more of her. For instance, I'd have liked to sit down with her for half an hour and tried to make some assessment of this woman Tim loved so deeply and enduringly. Of course I had no idea how she felt about him. It was possible she wanted to see him only to express her hatred of her brother's murderer. I couldn't tell, though I did know by this time, loyalty to my client and a natural bias apart, that Tim wasn't guilty of that act.

The police had to release him. They had been unable to get an extension. I indicated the way for them, gave them photocopies of the relevant pages of the manuscript, and pointed out a significant fact, that the knife had been missing from Tim's kitchen since the night before. One man, I said, looks very like another when covered up in a hooded waterproof, especially in the dark. The pocket yielded the only safe Tim had, whatever he might once have boasted to the contrary, one of those books with a hidden compartment. It's needless to say, probably, that the space inside was empty. The set of keys Steadman had on him was not capable of opening the front door of Tim's house.

Have you followed all this? Steadman's killer mistook him for Tim, perhaps never knew whom he had killed. He helped himself to the money inside the book and with the useless keys attempted to get inside Tim's house during the night in search of that elusive "safe." I suggested to the police that they search the streets of Ipswich and before I left I heard they had arrested the vagrant called Thierry Massin and charged him with Ivo Steadman's murder.

In the drama of it I forgot my promise to Isabel Winwood. I had said I would try to arrange a meeting between her and Tim, though I was somewhat nervous about bringing them together, but I am

afraid I forgot her existence. It was to Tim that I had to devote my
energies. He was relieved to be released, though not as euphoric as
I would have expected. Then I remembered his mother had died a
few days before.

I went back to his house with him. It's quite a remarkable house,
right on the seafront, with virtually nothing but the North Sea
between it and the Dutch coast. The interior is a horror, untouched
since the 1950s, and the furniture is the sort of stuff you see out on
the pavement in North End Road. But the house itself must be
worth a lot of money, even in these hard times. Still, as he said to
me, if he sells it where could he go?

There was nothing more I could do for him. I was getting up to
go when suddenly the front doorbell rang. It made poor Tim jump.

"I'll have to get used to it," he said. "I mean, to knowing it isn't
going to be Ivo." And he shut his eyes for a moment, he winced as
if in real pain. "And when the post comes it won't be bringing any
more Robinson Crusoe stories."

I have no idea what he meant and he didn't explain. He went
downstairs to answer the door and I waited and waited for him to
come back. I'd ordered a taxi to take me to Ipswich, the trains from
Saxmundham being few and far between, and standing in the bay
window, I saw it draw up outside.

There was nothing for it but to go down and find where he had
got to. I saw them when I was halfway downstairs, Tim and Isabel
Winwood. They were in a close embrace and they were kissing as
if the past two years had been nothing but a search for each other.
They had both loved him and each suffered deeply from his loss,
but whether they thought of it like that or not, Steadman's death
was the means that brought them together.

I came past them as self-effacingly as I could, but I need not have
bothered. They were lost to extraneous things, they didn't see me.
Can it possibly work for them? Can it last? I don't know and I
don't suppose they do. Stranger things happen all the time. I closed
the door behind me, got into the taxi and caught the 2:33 for
London.

I wrote this last bit in the train, coming home to you.